"This matter of an heir must be settled," he said.

"Of course," Sinshei said. "But who?"

Lucavi looked over his shoulder, to his two sons, and then back to Sinshei. Disappointments, all three of them. How to decide the proper course?

An eye for an eye, Ashraleon insisted. *Is there any other way?*

"The Vagrant took my cherished son's life," he said, agreeing with the founder. Perhaps he could solve two matters simultaneously. "So let his life be the key. Whichever child of mine slays the Vagrant shall be anointed Heir-Incarnate."

"A game," Kalath said. "I like it."

"A challenge, not a game," Petrus corrected. "Do not treat the prize of godhood so meagerly."

Sinshei said nothing, only remained low in her bow. Lucavi sighed.

"Stand," he said. "You have heard my decree, now take to your duties."

"By your will," she said, with a hunger in her eyes he did not trust. "Hold faith in me, beloved father, and prepare for me your love, for I will be the one to bring you the Vagrant's head."

Praise for
David Dalglish

Praise for The Bladed Faith

"Filled with intense action and complex characters who are easy to fall into, *The Bladed Faith* is what might happen if Final Fantasy crossed with *The Way of Shadows*! I loved it!"

—Rob J. Hayes, author of *Never Die*

"David Dalglish's beautiful, grandiose and expansive *The Bladed Faith* begins at the roots of a rebellion.... This is a rebellion with soul, and one that promises to reach even greater heights as the series continues. Given Dalglish's track record, don't be surprised if he somehow manages to top the triumphant standard he sets with *The Bladed Faith*."

—*BookPage* (starred review)

"This dark adventure will hook genre fans with its detailed world building, strong characters, and gory, action-packed scenes. Readers who enjoy Mark Lawrence and Erika Johansen will appreciate Thanet's masked, sword-carrying hero and rebel team of misfits, eagerly anticipating a continuation to Dalglish's new series."

—*Booklist*

"*The Bladed Faith* is an action-packed start to David Dalglish's new Vagrant Gods series. Full of sorcery, bloodshed, and a surprisingly charming found family, the story's twisty final chapters set up an ending that promises much more excitement to come."

—*Paste*

"In *The Bladed Faith*, Dalglish paints with epic, colorful action and poignant aftermath to illustrate the violent path of grief and the healing force of family found along the way."

—Essa Hansen, author of *Nophek Gloss*

"*The Bladed Faith* is gripping, violent and action-packed. It is also about colonialism, PTSD, fighting the good fight & what it truly means to put your life on the line for what's right. This is David Dalglish at his finest and the Vagrant Gods trilogy promises to be his best story that he's published so far."

—*Fantasy Book Critic*

Praise for The Keepers

"Dalglish manages to combine familiar elements in exciting ways... that's sure to keep readers turning pages."

—*Publishers Weekly* on *Soulkeeper*

"A dark and lush epic fantasy brimming with magical creatures and terrifying evil.... Dalglish's world building is subtle and fluid, and he weaves the history, magical workings, and governance of his world within the conversations and camaraderie of his characters. Readers of George R. R. Martin and Patrick Rothfuss will find much to enjoy here."

—*Booklist* on *Soulkeeper*

"*Soulkeeper* is a fast-paced, page-turning ride with a great, likeable main character in Devin Eveson. It's the definition of entertaining."

—John Gwynne, author of *The Shadow of the Gods*

"With strong world building, imaginative monsters, and a capable system of magic, this series will please readers who enjoy dark epic fantasy with engaging characters."

—*Booklist* on *Ravencaller*

"Fans will love the second installment of this dark fantasy about very human characters beset by inhuman dangers."

—*Kirkus* on *Ravencaller*

By David Dalglish

Vagrant Gods

The Bladed Faith

The Sapphire Altar

The Slain Divine

The Keepers

Soulkeeper

Ravencaller

Voidbreaker

Seraphim

Skyborn

Fireborn

Shadowborn

Shadowdance

A Dance of Cloaks

A Dance of Blades

A Dance of Mirrors

A Dance of Shadows

A Dance of Ghosts

A Dance of Chaos

Cloak and Spider (novella)

THE SLAIN DIVINE

VAGRANT GODS: BOOK THREE

DAVID DALGLISH

orbitbooks.net

Cover design by Lauren Panepinto
Cover illustration by Chase Stone

Map by Sámhlaoch Swords
Author photograph by North Myrtle Beach Photography

Orbit
Hachette Book Group
1290 Avenue of the Americas
New York, NY 10104
orbitbooks.net

First Edition: January 2024

Orbit is an imprint of Hachette Book Group.
The Orbit name and logo are trademarks of Little, Brown Book Group Limited.

Library of Congress Cataloging-in-Publication Data
Names: Dalglish, David, author.
Title: The slain divine / David Dalglish.
Description: First edition. | New York : Orbit, 2024. | Series: Vagrant gods ; book 3
Identifiers: LCCN 2023021890 | ISBN 9780759557161 (trade paperback) |
ISBN 9780759557154 (ebook)
Subjects: LCGFT: Fantasy fiction. | Novels.
Classification: LCC PS3604.A376 S63 2024 | DDC 813/.6—dc23/eng/20230508
LC record available at https://lccn.loc.gov/2023021890

ISBNs: 9780759557161 (trade paperback), 9780759557154 (ebook)

Printed in the United States of America

LSC-C

Printing 1, 2023

To Rob, who singlehandedly changed half the novel with but a few simple suggestions

N.
W.
E.
S.
The Crystal Sea
IALATH
PILION REALM
RAKLIA
SHIVERING RIVER
LYCAENA'S COCOON
THE MANE
RED GLADE
SAPPHIRE RIVER
SCYLLA REALM
GALLOS BAY
SCALE OF MILES
10
25
50

MAP BY SÁMHLAOCH SWORDS

A REMINDER, FOR THOSE WHO NEED ONE:

Cyrus Lythan was meant to be a figurehead for a resistance against the Everlorn Empire, which invaded his island of Thanet, slew his parents, and slaughtered his two gods, the Butterfly goddess, Lycaena, and the Lion god, Endarius. Instead, the leader of the resistance, Thorda Ahlai, organizes a sacrifice resulting in the death of forty men and women in the Vagrant's name. He becomes something more, a fledgling god against his will. Though he protests, and abandons Thorda's group for a month, he eventually returns upon hearing news that his friend the paladin Keles Lyon has disappeared while searching for the supposedly resurrected Lycaena.

Keles, meanwhile, has befriended a priest named Eshiel Dymling, a devoted follower of the Butterfly who, through daily ritual sacrifice, has returned a simulacrum of the goddess, only this time born of blood and fire and prepared for war. Cyrus, traveling with his mentor, the paladin Rayan, battles the reborn Lycaena but would have failed if not for the timely arrival of an unexpected ally: the Heir-Incarnate of Everlorn, Galvanis vin Lucavi. Together, they break the goddess, and Eshiel falls off the crumbling cliffside, believed by all to be dead.

A dejected Keles returns alone to the capital of Vallessau, only to be captured by Soma Ordiae, an enigmatic paragon working with the God-Incarnate's daughter, Sinshei vin Lucavi. Soma brings Keles to the capital, where she learns from Sinshei the truth of her island and her heritage. Cyrus's family, the Lythans, arrived with Endarius from across the sea, and came as conquerors to fight a war against the Sapphire Serpent, Dagon, and his chosen ruling family, the Orani. Keles is descended from that Orani blood, and if not for Cyrus, she might even be queen. She accepts the power of another paragon ceremony, only this time the sacrifices are followers of Dagon, declaring her the Returned Queen meant to restore her bloodline to the throne. As payment for this power, she hunts down Cyrus, supposedly to bring his head to Sinshei, though in truth she only hopes to convince him to lie low and fake his death. In doing so, she can accept Sinshei's offer: Once she is God-Incarnate, Sinshei will deliver Thanet back to Keles and order the imperial occupation to depart.

Keles twice attacks Cyrus in disguise, culminating in her reveal during a horrid failure to sneak soldiers into Vallessau through boats at the port. The plan was betrayed by one of their collaborators, Lord Jase Mosau, though Keles is initially blamed instead. Their lives are spared only by the timely arrival of Eshiel, who survived the fall from the cliff and has now returned, declaring himself thrice-born and still Lycaena's faithful servant.

The resistance is dejected in the aftermath, but not all is grim. One of Thorda's daughters, Stasia, marries her girlfriend of four years, Clarissa. The beautiful ceremony is tainted in the eyes of Thorda's other daughter, Mari, because she knows the truth Thorda hid: Her father was one of the last gods of their conquered homeland of Miquo. His power as God of the Forge was meant to pass on to Stasia, who still does not know of her divine heritage. Further darkening the event is the arrival of one of their friends and allies, the Heretic, Arn Bastell, who requests that Mari channel the spirit of the Fox, Velgyn, so he might offer his life up to her. Mari does so, but no sacrifice is demanded, only forgiveness offered.

Arn is overwhelmed by the offer, and also realizes just how much he cherishes his relationship with Mari. Once back in Vallessau, he decides to buy Mari a gift in thanks, only to be captured by his brother, Dario, who has arrived on the island alongside the Heir-Incarnate. Dario tries, unsuccessfully, to convince his brother to return his faith to the Uplifted

Church. And so, instead, Arn is used as bait for the rest of Thorda Ahlai's group. Betrayed again by Lord Jase, Cyrus leads his friends down into a recently unearthed gladiator pit used by Endarius in the earliest days of his reign. There Cyrus once more battles Keles to the amusement of the watching Galvanis. Instead of killing her upon winning, he kneels before her, declares her his queen, and vows to protect her. They break free the rest of their friends, and so begins the final battle.

Amid the chaos, Rayan chases down and kills Lord Jase, but in turn is cornered and defeated by the Heir-Incarnate. Keles finds his body, and amid her grief, Lycaena comforts her and grants her the power needed to defeat Galvanis. Together, she and the Vagrant battle the powerful Heir-Incarnate. Upon realizing his defeat is at hand, Galvanis tries to flee, only to be stopped by his sister, Sinshei. She cuts his head from his shoulders with her golden blades of faith, placing her as the now highest-ranking member of Everlorn upon the island.

Once more she offers her promise to Keles. If both she and the Vagrant lie low and pretend that Thanet is cowed, Sinshei will free the island once granted the power of the God-Incarnate. They begrudgingly accept, unaware that Sinshei's promise is a lie. The entire island will be sacrificed to facilitate the rebirth of a new God-Incarnate, only now it will be in her name instead of her slain brother's. She needs only the Vagrant to step aside and let her appear in control of the island.

At least, she hopes so.

For her loyal paragon, Soma, is the god Dagon in disguise, and most assuredly has his own plans for the island he has been exiled from for the past four hundred years...an exile that began at the final battle waged against the Lion in the War of Tides.

PROLOGUE

DAGON

"Trapped against the sea," Dagon said as he stood at the front of his pitiful army. Behind them were his several hundred faithful, hurriedly building rafts with what few logs they had cut and carried on their flight after their defeat at the battle of Illiam Crossing. The rafts would not be done in time, and even if they were, they could carry only a pittance of the gathered men and women.

Before them marched the army of the Lion.

"It is not too late," said one of Dagon's loyal priests. The bearded man stood at Dagon's right, his head barely reaching Dagon's shoulder. Seashells rattled on his necklace, which he clutched tightly in fearful hands. "Find safety in the Crystal Sea, I beg of you, my god."

Dagon glared at the thousands of approaching soldiers, most of them bearing foreign steel.

"If only I had sunk their boats before their hulls touched the sands of Thanet," he lamented. Ever since Dagon arose from the sea to look upon his beloved worshipers, he had believed he and Lycaena were the only two gods alive, meant to guide humanity on this little island they named Thanet. But to discover a third god? To learn of humans living across the Crystal Sea? It had been too much of a curiosity, and now he and his faithful suffered for it.

"My lord?" the priest asked.

"No, Aladine, I will not flee," Dagon said. "Here we make our stand. My blood will join yours upon the sand if that is the cost of our salvation."

He shifted his weight from foot to foot, never quite comfortable when bipedal. As he always did upon land, he had shed his scaled serpent tail for human legs. His movements across grass and rock were too slow when slithering, his tail too hard to defend when surrounded.

Aladine shook his head and kissed the shells of his necklace.

"There is no salvation here. The Lion is too cruel."

Dagon turned to the far cliff overlooking the shore, and in the distance he saw Lycaena watching with twelve of her priests and paladins at her side.

"The Lion," said Dagon. "And the Butterfly."

While his faithful numbered in the hundreds, Endarius's came in the thousands. They marched in neatly aligned rows, his bannermen carrying flags bearing the Lion's roaring face. The soldiers' steel glittered in the midday sun. Dagon faced the distant cliff, his divine eyes focused on the beautiful goddess draped with colors akin to flame.

"Come you to watch my execution?" he asked. His words traveled to the goddess's ears and hers alone. "Is this slaughter your idea of 'impartiality'?"

"You suffer for your pride," her voice responded on the wind. "If you cannot share the bounty of Thanet with Endarius, then you shall battle him for it. My faithful will not die for your stubbornness."

It was exactly as he expected. When Endarius's paws were still wet upon the shore, he had demanded land of his own. Dagon had foolishly given it. Land became titles. Titles became a crown, Thanet's third, as the island split into three kingdoms. Still, it was not enough. Endarius called for one king, not three, and against such insolence Dagon finally decreed, "Enough!"

Lycaena, however, fell for the Lion's words of unity and peace. She accepted the lie that three kingdoms upon Thanet meant too much conflict for the humans to bear. Yet she also pretended to honor Dagon's dissent, and so she ordered her faithful to remain neutral in the war that followed.

Neutral, impartial, as Dagon's faithful died beneath waves of foreign steel.

The Lion takes, as is his nature, he thought, his eyes narrowing. *But it is your cowardice I shall never forgive.*

Dagon readied his weapons. His sword was the height and weight of a man, its length gently curved and made not of metal but of hardened coral. The blade was a soft blue that shifted nearest the sharpened edge into the bright red color of blood. His shield was an oyster shell, the grandest from the entire ocean floor. His scales were his armor, and he trusted them more than any man-made chain.

"You must be strong," he told Adaline. "Have my priests pray for strength. Pray for courage. Call for the sea, and trust the sea to come. I do not fear the Lion's brutality. The ocean conquers all, even the hardest of stones. Thanet shall rejoice when Endarius bleeds out at my feet."

Except the Lion would not fight him. Dagon had learned that maddening fact during their first two battles. Endarius paced the outer edges of the conflict, watching. Hunting for weakness. Any progress Dagon made in the heart of the battle, Endarius would undo with a strategic attack on a flank. When Dagon would reinforce, he would find the other flank broken, or the center bending as the Lion charged anew. Slowly, steadily, Endarius stripped Dagon of his faithful. His instincts for war were greater than Dagon's, for Dagon had known only peace. It was a butcher's advantage, and it only solidified the need for Thanet to be saved from his twisted faith.

"To my side, paladins, warriors, and blessed priests," Dagon called, and he lifted his sword high. "We shall harden these sands with the foreigners' blood."

In the distance, the Lion roared, and his army charged. Dagon steeled himself for battle. Foreigners, he called his foes, but he could only wish that were true. Too many Thanese had shifted their loyalty from the Butterfly and the Serpent to the Lion, securing themselves a place in the newfound order. A desire for power defeated the call for peace and prosperity. Dagon tightened his grip on his sword. Damn the numbers before him. He would find victory. He must. And if he found victory, it would come from the sea.

He need not turn to know an enormous wave approached. He felt it in his mind, caressed by his divine hands, guided toward the shore as an ever-growing monsoon as wide as the beach they stood upon. His priests aided him, their prayers drawing forth the wave and granting Dagon strength to perform the miracle. Closer, closer, come to meet the charge of the Lion and his followers. Dagon lifted his sword and shield, and he dared believe victory could be his. The wave would pass like a gentle rain over his faithful, who closed their eyes and believed. They would be spared its wrath, but not the followers of Endarius. Not those who sought destruction.

Dagon opened his eyes, and he smiled beneath the shadow of the furious tide.

The Lion roared.

Tremors shook the sand. Wind howled, vicious and sharp. Hundreds of Dagon's followers collapsed, blown back as if struck by a physical force. Dagon dug his feet into the sand, grimacing, all his divine might pushing, pushing, but the wave could not abide. The land was not its place. It crumpled backward and then collapsed, carrying several of the rafts out with it. When the roar ended, the savage, jubilant cries of Endarius's charging army filled its silence.

They met no wave. They endured no wrath of the sea. Just Dagon's frightened, outnumbered, and broken few.

"Stand strong!" Dagon shouted at them. He met the charge with a swipe of his enormous sword, crushing soldiers with ease. He waded deep into them, aided by his paladins, adorned in blue plate and wielding long spears. They tried, these paladins, tearing into their foes with songs on their lips and bravery in their hearts, but with each passing moment, Dagon watched more die from the corners of his vision. He would weep for them later, if he could. Swords stabbed at his scales, most deflected, some not. Bruises built upon him, and his blood dripped blue across the sand. He batted away soldiers two at a time with his shield, swung wide with his sword, and cut two more in half. They did not attack, though, not truly. These soldiers surrounded him, keeping him penned in so the Lion could do his work elsewhere.

Endarius avoided the center fray to instead charge the northern flank.

Dagon pushed harder, enduring the barrage of strikes to his scales. Let his blood flow, so long as it mixed with the blood of his enemies. He had to match Endarius's savagery. He had to break his enemies at an even greater rate, for his people, they were so few.

Except he could not even advance. Endarius's paladins had come to form a wall before him, a dozen in number. They howled with primal glee, wielding metal claws and short swords to tear at his body. He twisted and shifted so his shield blocked the majority of their hits, but they were too many. Worse, a wall of spearmen came to give them support, so when Dagon tried to punish an aggressive maneuver, the paladins could always retreat behind the spears. Back and forth, Dagon swung his sword, and though he managed to kill two of the paladins, it wasn't enough, not when his people were dying, dying, so many, dying...

The northern flank was gone, utterly collapsed. The southern followed. His followers fled for the sea and the waiting rafts. Dagon crushed a third paladin beneath his coral sword, wishing he could take grim pleasure in the crunching bones. None would be found. He looked to the distance, where hundreds of soldiers were still fresh and eager to fight. Endarius walked among them, towering above his cruel human horde. Blood stained his lips and feathery mane.

"Fight me!" Dagon screamed at the distant Lion. "Fight me, you coward, you butcher, you wretch!"

Endarius said not a word. There was no mercy in his feline eyes. The Lion had taken, and taken, until victory was assured. Pride, for him, was found in victory alone.

And there was no denying that horrible reality. Dagon's people had lost, their morale broken, their numbers dwindled to nothing. Dagon sliced three men in half with a single swing and then turned to the shore. Only a third of the rafts were prepared, and the people upon them were hesitant to push out to sea. They didn't want to abandon their god, and wouldn't, not unless ordered. As much as it broke his heart, he knew what he must do.

"Flee, all of you!" he bellowed to his followers. "Hide, now, before—"

Dagon saw the spear punch out the front of his chest before he felt it enter his back. Pain followed, fierce and hot. Dagon turned and cut the wielder from shoulder to hip, disemboweling him upon the sands.

Screams of fear and panic reached his ears. What remained of the battle slowed around him. His knees wobbled as he walked toward the sea. Warm blood flowed down his spine and belly, and each step was agony. No one attacked. No one approached. Strange. Would they let him escape? Or did they think him already dead?

Through his fading vision, he saw his followers push the finished rafts into the sea. They were too few to carry everyone, though, much too few. Other faithful ran into the water, screaming for help. Some clutched at the sides of the rafts, pleading to be let on. Feet stamped their fingers. The sight of his faithful turning on one another filled Dagon's eyes with tears in a way the pain of the spear could not.

His knees buckled. The water. There was safety and life within the water. The Crystal Sea had birthed him, and in the Crystal Sea he would recover. He clawed at the sand with shaking hands. The spear's tip dragged a groove below him, filling it with his blood. The sea, it was so close, if only he could reach it. If he could...

"You were a mighty foe," the voice of the damned Lion boomed from above him. "But your stubbornness cost you your life."

The pain in his chest exploded, the shaft grinding against his ribs as it lifted him upward. Dagon hung, limp and struggling for breath, as Endarius clutched the spear between his teeth. Their eyes met for the briefest moment. There was no pity in them, no regret. This was everything the Lion wanted.

Dagon tried to whisper a curse, but his mouth would not open. He bled from a thousand wounds, but this spear through his breast, it would be his last.

Endarius padded to the water. His head tilted, and the world spun as the Lion jammed the spear into the center of an unfinished raft, pinning him like a beast. Endarius trotted away, stopping only to give an order to his paladins.

"Burn it."

Dagon closed his eyes. So it would be fire, then. This physical shell of his, already breaking, would suffer one more indignity. He did not watch when the torches came. He did not speak a word. The wood around him caught flame, and he felt its heat lick his scales and kiss the flesh underneath. From a great distance he heard sobbing and wailing. The heartbreak in those voices, tinged with faith, pierced the growing veil about his mind. Soldiers were murdering the last of his followers. What few who had not escaped to the sea pleaded for mercy, and none was given.

Damn the Lion.

Damn the Butterfly.

The fire burned. The spear held strong. All was smoke and suffering, yet through it shone a voice like blinding light. It was Lycaena, still watching from afar. Watching him die.

"Give his corpse to the sea."

Soldiers pushed the raft to the water, its logs groaning. Dagon, if he breathed, tasted only smoke. The rocking of the waves provided no comfort. His arms and legs charred to bone. His scales blackened. He burned, as did the raft, until the wood collapsed and the ropes and tar holding it together broke apart.

And then, blessedly, Dagon fell to the water below.

Within the dark and cold embrace of the sea, Dagon felt the call of eternity. He had no eyes to open, but a vision came to him nonetheless. It was of his faithful in the lands beyond. He saw only glimpses, like a blurred reflection on the surface of waves. The people stood upon a sandy beach, numbering in the tens of thousands. They sang his name and laughed in the joy of each other's company. It was the fate he promised his beloveds, an archipelago of paradisical islands, each and every one free from sorrow and pain.

They were waiting for him.

Farther and farther, falling into the deep. He no longer felt the spear piercing him, but he tasted his own blood spilling into the water. He felt the salt coating his wounds. To live, to hold on to this mortal vessel, required all his strength and more. He could surrender it. Give in. Go to his people in the eternal islands beyond.

But his rage.

His *rage.*

Dagon clutched the spear in his chest. Instead of the calls from his deceased faithful, the whispered prayers of the living comforted him. They were fearful and quiet, given to him in dark closets, in deep woods, and on moonlit shorelines.

Come back to us, these faithful prayed. *Come back to us. Save us from the Lion and the Butterfly.*

There, at the deep bottom of the sea that had birthed him, Dagon floated in perfect stillness.

Years passed.

His torn flesh was mended by the caress of sand. The salty touch of the sea rebuilt his sapphire scales one by one. With eyes closed, he listened to the prayers. The call of the eternal islands faded with each passing year. Broken bones became whole, and eyes that were dull white regained their brilliant glow.

When he was ready, when the eternal call was all but silenced, Dagon ripped the spear free from his body. He held it to his breast as blood flowed anew, until another year passed, and the vicious wound slowly healed. Only then did he swim to a little alcove along the southern tip of Thanet, where an elderly woman offered him a prayer beneath the watchful eye of the stars. Each word was a drop of oil falling upon a dwindled fire.

"My child," he said as he emerged from the waters and felt the biting-cold air upon his scales. "My beloved, tell me your name."

And this old woman did just that, and more. Forty years had passed since the Lion's attempt to murder him. Forty years, and so much had changed. He listened as she told him how the Lion's faith had spread throughout the island. He listened to the treatment of his beloved Orani family, and how they were forced into servitude of the Lythan bloodline. He listened, tears in his eyes, to the suffering of his faithful, persecuted and forced into hiding, the very name of Dagon now a curse spoken only in disgust.

The spear shook in his grip. He could not remain upon Thanet, not weak in body and few in followers. His old faith was slain. But this woman? She could be the start of something new.

"I will return," he told her. "I promise you, one day, I will return, and I shall reclaim all that was stolen from me."

Dagon kissed her forehead and returned to the sea.

He swam with the bloodied spear clutched to his chest, his tail fluttering as he plotted a new course. Ignorance had cost him dearly. When Endarius's ships appeared upon the horizon, he had known nothing of the land named Gadir. That there could be more gods stunned him. And if his name was a curse upon his home, then let him go to the land of the Lion and start anew.

He moved without urgency across the great sea he had always believed to be endless. Schools of fish were his guide, teaching him the deep currents. At night, he stared at the stars, etching their faint light into his eyes as he pondered the meaning of a world overflowing with gods.

Years passed.

Naked and clad in human flesh to hide his divine nature, Dagon washed ashore. He lay on strange sands, so much darker than the lovely white of Thanet. He clutched the killing spear to his breast, his lone possession in this new land, this new life. It was dark, the comforting stars shining brightly above, and the prayers of his beloved faithful on Thanet so distant they were but the faintest whispers.

An older man walked the beach, two dogs circling his legs in play. Upon seeing him they barked and howled, urging their master to come inspect. Neither beast dared approach too closely, though. Dagon suspected that they, unlike their master, could sense the presence of the divine.

"You all right?" the man asked. It was the same language that Endarius spoke, and which Dagon had learned in an attempt to bridge the divide between them.

"I do not know," Dagon said as he coughed and shivered. This mortal human flesh, it fit him poorly, but he must endure. "I suppose I have been worse."

The man knelt beside him and began removing his shirt.

"Bloody hells, where's your clothes? Here, put this on, before you freeze. Did your ship sink, or were you tossed overboard?"

Dagon shook his head. Any story he conceived could be poked apart with enough time, so best to tell none at all.

"I do not remember," he said. He accepted the shirt and put it on, a poor covering for his nakedness. The man helped Dagon to his feet and shared his weight. Together they took unsteady steps across the sand while the two dogs circled warily.

"The sea can be cruel, and take everything from a man lost to it for too long," his unlikely rescuer said. "Can you at least remember your name?"

Dagon hesitated. To keep his old name was a risk, so what moniker should he adopt during his exile? Cut off from his beloved faithful and hidden in new flesh, he decided there was but one name he was fit to carry. The body, separated from the spirit.

"Soma," he said. "My name is Soma."

CHAPTER 1

VAGRANT

Come nightfall, the old man led Cyrus toward the sea. His name was Jules, the village elder of the nearby town of Glinos. The two walked alone, the moon and stars their only witnesses. No conversation between them, just the sound of waves crashing against the rocks. There was no soft sand here, only sheer cliffs. The grass was patchy along the coastline and dotted with clusters of reeds. They halted before a rope ladder hammered into the clifftop. Down below, the receding tide left behind a stretch of craggy rocks and tightly packed sand. The old man tossed the ladder over the side and gestured toward the sea.

"Descend," he said. "Tonight we are blessed with a lunar tide. You have until dawn before the waters take you. Pray to Dagon. He will hear you; of that, I am certain."

"I will offer the Serpent no prayers."

Jules stared at the waves and then sighed.

"So be it. I shall pray in your stead. Do not disappoint me, Vagrant. We hear your stories in Glinos. The empire fears you. Blood of the God-Incarnate's children stains your blades. The hope you offer, I believe it true... but I cannot remove the dread I feel when I look upon your mask."

"I am Thanet's protector," Cyrus said. "You have nothing to fear."

Jules lowered himself onto the ladder's first rung.

"Endarius also claimed to be Thanet's protector, and we feared him greatly."

Cyrus followed him down to the sands below, and once there, he understood why the villagers had decreed this place sacred. The cliffs bent inward, and the steady shove of the waves had piled shells and sand so that when the tide receded one could walk about. It wasn't much, just a twenty-foot-wide stretch of ground. The drop-off was steep along all sides, and the water black in the night.

To stand in its center was to stand on a stage overlooking the sea, and he felt high up despite being below the cliffs. The reflection of the stars only added to the illusion. Cyrus breathed in the salty air and listened to the crash of waves to either side of him.

"It is here we leave our gifts for Dagon during lunar tides," Jules said beside him. "The sea swallows them come the morning. When we return the next night, we sift the sand."

"Does Dagon reward you in kind?"

Jules swiped the sand beneath him, ensuring nothing sharp lurked there, and then dropped to his knees.

"We seek no rewards. We seek reassurance. For so long, it would seem futile. Years would pass, but then..." He reached underneath his shirt and pulled out a beautiful pendant. It was a silver chain looped into a single scale so deeply blue it could have been carved from sapphire. "Our faith would be acknowledged. Our god, persecuted and hidden, would deliver unto us one of his scales. And we would know. He remembered us, and cherished our faith."

Jules clutched the scale in his wrinkled hands.

"My grandfather once told me how he proudly walked Vallessau's streets wearing such scales. That was before your father took the throne. The growth of our faithful was a sign of a sinful generation, and Cleon would tolerate none of it in his capital. Once more, we were banished. Once more, we bled and died for our god."

Though Jules described the actions of his father, Cyrus felt a sting of guilt all the same. Whenever Rayan spoke of banishing Dagon's people from Vallessau, it was with pride. Cyrus had never given it much thought, only accepting the paladin's words. Dagon's followers were cruel and twisted, and there was no place for them in a righteous society.

And so they were driven to the sea. They worshiped in secret, no different from those who now hid in their homes clutching the Lion's feathers or painting Lycaena's wings upon their wrists.

"I cannot undo the past," Cyrus said. "I can only walk the present with my eyes now opened. Pray to Dagon. Let me speak with the Serpent of the Sea, and with an open heart, hear the wisdom he offers."

Jules bent at the waist until his face pressed to the wet sand. His hands stretched out before him, fingers pointed to the sea. He whispered his prayer, a plea for the Serpent to come forth. Cyrus listened a moment, and as the prayer continued, he closed his eyes and bowed his head. At least he could show that measure of respect.

I offer you no worship, nor prayer, he whispered within his mind. *But if you hear this, Dagon, know I seek peace. I would not repeat the sins of my forefathers.*

It was not Dagon who answered, but the dark voice of the Vagrant.

Come to us, Serpent, and prove you are still worthy of being Thanet's god.

Jules suddenly ended his prayer and stood.

"The ocean stirs," he said as he wiped away the sand on his knees. He put a hand on Cyrus's shoulder. It was the hand that still clutched the sapphire scale, and its touch was ice. "Fare thee well."

Cyrus stood in the clearing's center, watching the approach of the waves as he waited. Their crashing was the only sound, and the dancing of the moonlight upon their surface, hypnotic.

"I'm here," he whispered as the minutes passed. "Will you not answer me? Will you not grant me your voice?"

His head grew light, and the world took on a glassy sheen. The ground beneath his feet fell away. The waves grew, and grew, above his head, above the cliffs, above the mountains, to swallow all of Thanet. Higher, higher, to sweep aside the very stars. Or perhaps it was Cyrus who fell lower, down into the depths as the sand gave way and he descended into the Heldeep the Serpent ruled as king.

As quickly as it began, the illusion passed.

Cyrus was not alone.

"This is quite a surprise, young prince."

Dagon rose from the sea with such steady grace it was as if the water itself lifted him. His beauty stole Cyrus's breath away. His entire body glistened with the sheen of sapphire scales. Even in the shallow moonlight they sparkled with depth and clarity. His neck and chest bore the only variation, the scales shifting toward a lighter aqua. His eyes were the blue of the midday ocean, and they glowed in the darkness. His hair was crystalline and white, curling around his neck like a mane. Though his face resembled that of a human, he lacked a nose, the closest resemblance being two thin slits slanted underneath his eyes. His feet and hands were webbed, and they ended in stubby black claws.

In one hand, he held a shield that resembled an enormous oyster shell. In the other, a gently curving sword shaped of coral, its upper half red, its lower a pale blue.

"The tales of my youth insisted you were slain," Cyrus said. He stood tall, refusing to cower before the ancient deity. Though he had learned of Dagon's survival through Mari's failed attempt to whisper the Serpent, he bent the truth a bit to disguise the Ahlai daughter's involvement. "So when your followers spread tales of your return, I thought it best I seek you out."

Dagon thrust his sword and shield into the sand and crossed his arms. "You have found me. For what reason, I wonder."

Cyrus lowered his head and dipped his shoulders in a brief bow. Surely he could offer the old god that much respect.

"I wish to learn of you," he said. "Who you are. What you believe. I was raised in ignorance but would escape it, if you are willing."

"Any of my followers could have told you the truth of my being. Either your arrogance demanded better, or it is not wisdom you seek of me, but something more. I suspect both."

"I seek an alliance," he admitted. "We struck a great victory in slaying the Heir-Incarnate, but Thanet is not yet free. The aid of you and your followers would be a great boon to the cause."

Dagon paced the sands. Little waves followed him, the water trailing like a cloak.

"You believe I should ally with you, son of Cleon, the great banisher of my people?"

"I am not my father. How could you view me as an enemy, when all I have done, I have done to save my island?"

Dagon approached, and as the distance between them shrank, Cyrus swore the god grew larger. His shadow loomed long, cast by the moon. His legs were no longer legs, and he did not walk, but weaved on a serpentine body. His voice deepened, and with every word, the surface of the ocean trembled.

"Listen to me, and listen well. You are a child of the Lythan conquerors. These four centuries have not erased your sins, for I have received not a drop of atonement from your bloodline. You cannot be Thanet's savior. Even the face you wear is foreign to my island. I have returned, and the descendants of those who cast me aside because of the Lion's barbarism and the Butterfly's cowardice shall open their hearts to me once more. Our people cry out, and *I* will save them."

For one long held breath, it felt like the Serpent would unhinge his jaw and swallow Cyrus whole. His power was absolute. His seething presence carried the strength of centuries. His rage could bury the world. Before that, Cyrus felt small and worthless. He was a child with swords, commanding thin, toothless shadows.

But the thought of kneeling flooded him with fury. The Vagrant, kneeling before a god who had abandoned his people and hid while the centuries passed? Who fled while his remaining followers were persecuted for their beliefs? No. Cyrus would never kneel to such a weak god. A pathetic god. He blinked, and Dagon's looming presence shrank. He looked like a man once more. Only his aura remained, an aura that shimmered blue in Cyrus's mind.

He must be shown his folly.

Cyrus reached into his pocket and pulled out the Vagrant's mask. Dagon spoke the truth. The mask came from Miquo. It first belonged to Thorda's husband, Rhodes, before it had been gifted to Cyrus.

"You are right," he said. "It is a foreign mask, and I have no need of it."

Cyrus tossed the crowned mask to the sand, an offering to the sea.

Dagon cocked his head in amusement. With a twitch of his fingers, a sudden wave washed across their ankles, dragging the mask out to the deep. Cyrus expected to feel regret at its loss but experienced none.

"You would cast aside the Vagrant?" Dagon asked. Cautious optimism dared reveal itself in his words.

"No," Cyrus said. He stood defiant before the Serpent and then grinned. "My mask may be foreign, *but my face is not.*"

The ridges of his crown pierced the skin of his forehead as if they grew from bone. His flesh peeled away. His toothy grin spread ear to ear. Neither lips nor jaw moved when he spoke.

"I am born of the cries of Thanet's suffering. I am the rage of widows and widowers. I am a promise of death, and it is a promise I shall keep. The people turned to me because they must. The Lion and Butterfly are slain, and you, long absent. I accepted our people's desperate faith when none were left to take it. If you would reclaim that faith for yourself, then end their desperation, and stand with me in battle."

Dagon's posture stiffened.

"Your family's crimes forced my absence, lest you forget."

"The blame changes not the absence. Damn the past, and all who live within it. I stand before you now, Dagon. Look upon me, and hear my words. Will you deny them still?"

Cyrus's anger was matched by Dagon's. It was not fiery and loud. When the Serpent answered, his words were slow, each one carrying weight. The greatest of rage, held back by the greatest of control.

"Speaks the god wearing a crown. Despite all your promises, I see the truth you cannot hide."

Cyrus was shocked by how deeply he desired to draw his swords. Whatever his family's crimes might be, Cyrus had fought to atone for them. He had given up everything, even his humanity, to become the Vagrant. By his deeds, the empire bled. And yet Dagon refused to acknowledge any of it. He cast blame and accepted no responsibility. So what if he had been gone for centuries? The Serpent was here now, so why was he not helping? Why did those loyal to Endarius and Lycaena risk their lives, yet those loyal to Dagon only lurk and watch?

His hands drifted toward the hilts of his swords. Perhaps animosity yet remained. Perhaps Dagon was merely biding his time, waiting to strike. The moment Cyrus reclaimed the throne, the Serpent would come to cast him down, to deny him what was rightfully his.

Have patience. We cannot win. He is born of faith so much older and deeper than you yet understand.

Cyrus relaxed his palms.

"So be it," he said. "We will reclaim Thanet without you, Serpent, if that is what must be done."

Dagon seemed almost disappointed.

"You intrigue me, Vagrant, but there is no kindness in what fate awaits you. Your origins are of blood sacrifice. Your purpose is forever bound to death and war. You are human flesh elevated into divinity, and the heavens will punish that sacrilege, even if it takes a thousand years."

"As they have punished the God-Incarnate?"

Dagon's blue eyes narrowed.

"You have a role to play in all this, that I will not deny, but death awaits you at its end. I will not walk that path with you. No, when we next meet, I suspect your blood will be on my blades."

The sapphire god marched into the sea. His final words bubbled up from the foam.

"Hurry home to Vallessau, where you are needed, Vagrant, for I sense the God-Incarnate's ships upon my waves."

CHAPTER 2

LUCAVI

Lucavi looked upon the island of Thanet from the prow of his flagship, the *Salvation*. It sailed at the head of an invasion fleet one hundred ships strong, a fine accomplishment built over the past centuries.

"What is the name of the city again?" he asked his divine bodyguard, Bassar. The paragon was a master of swords from Aethenwald, and armored in resplendent silver chainmail. His head was cleanly shaven, and much of it reddened by the sun. He wielded a thin blade of such length no proper scabbard would fit it, so he rested it across his shoulders as he stood at Lucavi's side.

"Vallessau," Bassar answered. His voice was soft, carrying a gentle sharpness that matched the edge of his sword. "The island's capital."

"Vallessau..."

Lucavi stared at the distant city nestled along the pale sands of the wide inlet, its structures winding higher and higher with homes forming rings carved into the edges of the surrounding mountains. There was little truly remarkable about the city. Gadir contained a thousand beaches and a hundred cities carved into hills, mountains, and caverns. Humans lived where they could and would break the world if they must.

And yet, the people of this city had done what none should ever do.

"How?" he wondered aloud. "How could such a small, insignificant place do such harm to me?"

Bassar took Lucavi's hand in his and dropped to one knee. His gaze lowered to the deck.

"We will find the one responsible for Galvanis's death, my lord. I promise it will be my utmost priority."

"Whoever is in charge shall hopefully have the killer ready in chains, awaiting my punishment," Lucavi said. His jaw hardened, and he fought back a wave of unwelcome emotion. No messages had reached their fleet from Thanet, but he had known the moment it happened. In the deep of night, he had felt the loss like a dagger to his spine.

Someone, somehow, had taken the life of his beloved son and heir.

Was Galvanis weaker than you believed? the voice of Ashraleon spoke within Lucavi's mind. *Or is this island and its gods far more monstrous than we presumed?*

"The people are blessed I need them alive for the six-hundred-year ceremony," Lucavi said, doing his best to ignore the voice of Everlorn's founder. He pulled his hand free of Bassar's soft grip. "I would obliterate most nations to ash and bone for such an unforgivable sin."

"They die for Everlorn's future," Bassar said. He gestured broadly to the entire island. "Is there not a more fitting fate for their transgression?"

"Perhaps."

An honorable sacrifice, no matter its purpose, still felt better than these people deserved. His mind drifted through memories, recalling the grace and power of his eldest son. Should he so desire, Lucavi could recall each and every second of his life with perfect clarity, but there was just...so much now. After Galvanis's loss, he had fallen into many of them to pass the weeks. Teaching his son how to wield a sword. Lecturing him on politics and the weakness of heathens. Little moments, passing words, casual utterances: They all gathered and impacted him like needles.

His glare hardened as he stared at the nearing port.

"This city, what was its name again?"

"Vallessau, my lord."

Vallessau, right. Lucavi clung to that fact in his mind, hardening it down among a million others he had learned over a long, long six hundred years. He would remember the name Vallessau, and he alone.

When the great sacrifice was over, no one else would ever utter its name except in the most fearful of whispers.

Boats split off from the main force. Lucavi watched them go with mild interest. His paragons had coordinated the event with the captains. They would arrive in full force at the capital, then split so the other large cities received additional garrisons. The entire island would soon know the true might of Everlorn, not just the sliver of it that had invaded under the command of Imperator Magus.

"There you are, Father."

Lucavi turned to see his two sons approaching. They both wore their fine armor, though in contrasting styles. Petrus, the older of the two, was a paragon of axes, and his musculature was like that of a bull: broad shouldered, enormous of chest, and possessing a skull thick enough to use as a battering ram. His hair was cut incredibly short, and the skin underneath red from the constant sun. His armor was as plain and dull as his personality, thick steel lacking in decoration.

Yes, his bullheaded son, more might than mind. Galvanis's equal in battle but inferior in all else. Memories floated to the surface. Petrus's impatience. His lack of imagination. That was why Lucavi had denied him the title of heir. Petrus would be too easily manipulated by the Uplifted Church.

"Are you ready for our arrival?" he asked them.

"We are dressed as fine as one can on this gods-forsaken boat," said Kalath, the youngest of his children. Though all his sons were handsome, Kalath seemed doubly so. His blond hair was long and loose. His pale blue eyes bore a wildness that Lucavi instinctively disliked. If not for the tragedy of Galvanis's death, Kalath would never be considered a potential heir. He was a spoiled man, comfortable in his wealth and privilege. His armor was thin, his sword thinner, and all of it encrusted with jewels from two dozen conquered nations.

"You seem to have done well enough," Lucavi said.

Kalath shrugged.

"I've learned to make do with what is available to me."

"As if you are ever in lack of anything," Petrus said, and snorted. "I have seen the chest you brought to keep your hair washed and shining.

If only you joined me on the battlefield sometime, Kalath. Then I could have taught you austerity."

"Heavens forbid. Some knowledge is unwelcome."

He has wit and charisma, the voice of Aristava, the second God-Incarnate, spoke within Lucavi's mind. *It could make him a fine ruler, if harnessed properly.*

Once joined with us, he will learn responsibility, Drasden, the third, insisted. *See not who he is, but his potential as God-Incarnate. That is the only measure that matters.*

Lucavi clenched his jaw. Too many were around. His sons were watching him. He had to focus on the here and now, not the phantoms of the past.

"Silence, both of you," he said. "This island is dangerous, and we are ignorant of the threats. Be on your guard. When the heathens look upon us, I want them to see strength and infallible will."

"As you wish, Father," Kalath said, bowing deeply. Petrus echoed the bow, but only managed a third of the way, for his armor would allow no better. Once they left, Lucavi sighed.

"When the age of life is at its end, and the Epochal War begins, I will treasure every minute I spend torturing the one responsible for Galvanis's death."

The city's docks could not hope to harbor all the boats that arrived, so the remainder hung back to form a blockade while Lucavi's flagship and ten escorts approached. Even then, they arrived with hundreds of soldiers and a dozen paragons. Lucavi walked at the head of them, his gold armor shining in the morning sunlight.

A crowd of thousands had come to greet them. Lucavi absently noticed their dress. It was simple: thin threads, no wool or cotton. Lots of color, though. It reminded him of Lahareed, just more garish. Did they know how outlandish they looked?

Of course not, insisted Aristava. *The candle in a cave thinks itself magnificent when ignorant of the sun.*

It was not their clothing that further fouled Lucavi's mood. It was the faith radiating off them, or more importantly, the lack thereof. He saw it like a golden mist rising from their bodies, weak and fleeting. A shallow faith. Fledgling. Unacceptable.

At the head of the crowd, flanked by a dozen of her priests, bowed the one responsible for nurturing that faith: Sinshei vin Lucavi, his ever-maddening young daughter. She looked beautiful in her deep red dress tied close to her waist with a black sash. Her long dark hair, capable of reaching down to her ankles when unbound, was carefully braided and decorated with local violet flowers and golden lace.

The dock rattled beneath Lucavi's weight. Kalath and Petrus followed directly behind him, and Bassar after. The rest of the army waited for his signal. When Lucavi stopped, so did they. Before him, Sinshei dropped to her knees and bowed.

"You brought my brothers," she said. "I thought them tied up with the rebellion in Noth-Wall?" Though she tried, he saw the way she shook at their approach. Did she fear them? Or was she angry? What reason had she for either, other than overwhelming shame for her incompetence?

"Noth-Wall will be subdued with or without my sons' involvement," Lucavi said, displeased with such a poor greeting. Where was her reverence? Her profession of love at the arrival of her father? "I would have them here, for the six-hundred-year ceremony. And given Galvanis's death, it seems prudent I did so."

Sinshei flinched at that.

"Yes, I already know of his passing," he continued. "I will hear the details elsewhere, in a better place, and a better time. All I ask is if you know the name of his murderer."

His daughter's bow deepened.

"They call him the Vagrant, my lord. He is the deposed prince, Cyrus Lythan, given power through faith and sacrifice."

"And have you captured and executed this... Vagrant?"

His daughter trembled.

"No, my lord."

His distaste grew, though why should he be surprised? How could Sinshei best a monster that could kill Galvanis? Still, it galled him.

He gave the signal, and the ten boats began their lengthy process of disembarking passengers and unloading cargo. Similar arrivals would be happening all across Thanet. Places and names floated through him like loose sheets of paper on the wind. Raklia. Ialath. Syros. Gallos Bay. Thousands of soldiers, sent to reinforce this tremendous failure that awaited his arrival. As for here in the capital, Sinshei's priests scrambled about, giving orders and trying to direct the chaos. It should be more orderly, he knew, for his daughter had known of his impending arrival for years.

Galvanis would have organized it better, the fifth God-Incarnate, Ululath, said.

"And Galvanis is dead," Lucavi snapped, only belatedly realizing he spoke aloud. His sons and his bodyguard were looking at him, uncertain what he meant. Everyone but Sinshei, who kept her obedient eyes to the docks. He frowned and crossed his arms as if he were only repeating his disgust.

"This matter of an heir must be settled," he said.

"Of course," Sinshei said. "But who?"

Lucavi looked over his shoulder, to his two sons, and then back to Sinshei. Disappointments, all three of them. How to decide the proper course?

An eye for an eye, Ashraleon insisted. *Is there any other way?*

"The Vagrant took my cherished son's life," he said, agreeing with the founder. Perhaps he could solve two matters simultaneously. "So let his life be the key. Whichever child of mine slays the Vagrant shall be anointed Heir-Incarnate."

"A game," Kalath said. "I like it."

"A challenge, not a game," Petrus corrected. "Do not treat the prize of godhood so meagerly."

Sinshei said nothing, only remained low in her bow. Lucavi sighed.

"Stand," he said. "You have heard my decree, now take to your duties."

"By your will," she said, with a hunger in her eyes he did not trust. "Hold faith in me, beloved father, and prepare for me your love, for I will be the one to bring you the Vagrant's head."

CHAPTER 3

SINSHEI

My, you all are a merry bunch," Sinshei said to the group. She stood in the center of the den with her arms crossed and her emotions hidden behind a frown. Members of the Vagrant's resistance gathered about her, their own faces disguised. The Vagrant slowly paced before her, wearing his grinning skull even though his true identity was no longer a secret. The Lioness curled up by the fire, sleeping like an incredibly huge and dangerous house cat. At least she seemed to be sleeping. The way her gray, bony tail twitched and her ears shifted showed her still on high alert. An older man stood beside the fire, tending the embers. A hooded robe covered his body, and the shadows of the fire hid all but his white beard.

Interestingly enough, Keles Lyon was among their number. She sat in a chair near the pacing Vagrant, her legs crossed and her hands steepled. She wore the black penitent armor Sinshei had gifted her, although instead of the closed helmet, her face was disguised with a crystalline half skull sparkling red and gold in the firelight. Hiding her identity was pointless, yet she persisted.

"We wait for one more," Keles had told her upon Sinshei's arrival.

"If I must, young queen," Sinshei had responded, attempting to drag out another response. She received only the slightest narrowing of the woman's eyes.

Keeping watch by the window in the crowded room was the one in the fox mask, Arn Bastell, otherwise known as the Heretic. He had found her when she walked the market holding a loose red ribbon, the sign they had agreed upon for her to convey a wish to meet. Heretic had brought her to a carriage, blindfolded her, and driven her here. The den's windows were heavily curtained, and she could only guess as to her location. No one had said a word to her since her arrival. The rudeness of it chafed.

The door creaked open behind her.

"Are we ready to begin at last?" she asked, turning.

The woman named Ax stepped inside, a small wrapped package held in her hands. Her brown hair was tied back into a ponytail, and her face covered by a large cloth decorated with the bared teeth of a panther. She kicked the door shut with her heel. Heretic reached out and tucked the package into his heavy coat. In the brief motion, she caught sight of the chainmail lining his coat's interior.

"Didn't have to wait on my account," Ax said.

"And yet we did," Vagrant said. He nodded at Sinshei. "If you're here, I assume it involves your father?"

"It does, as will all Thanese matters for the foreseeable future," she said. "Lucavi is a storm that will drown you all if unleashed. You would do well to understand that, Vagrant."

Cyrus, she thought, *he is Cyrus, not Vagrant. Why do you hesitate to name him so?*

"Lucavi was yours to handle," Keles said. "Our task was to lie low and allow you to take credit for cowing our island."

"A task you perform poorly," Sinshei snapped. She smirked at the guilt that immediately covered the young woman's face. "I've heard of your gatherings. It is a tall task facing me to convince my father the island is humbled when a potential queen gives speeches of her righteous claim to the throne. No matter how clandestine you believe these meetings to be, if word reached my ears, then it will also reach my father's. Stop them. Immediately."

"We'll take it into consideration," Ax said. She hopped over the back of a couch and sat atop a cushion with her legs crossed underneath her. "Is that why you wanted this rushed meeting, to berate Keles?"

The older, hooded man glanced the woman's way but said nothing. Sinshei felt the mood in the air shift.

"The Anointed One risks her life to meet with us," he said. His voice was harsh and cold, like rocks tumbling down the side of a snowy mountain. "Do not make light of her arrival, nor dismiss the risks we *all* endure."

Whoever that man was, he led this group; she sensed that without a doubt. Even the Vagrant paid him heed.

"Fair enough," he said. "So why are you here, Sinshei? Surely you have a servant or member of the church you trust enough to deliver a message."

Sinshei used her own coldness to hide the awkward hurt his question awakened. No, she did not have anyone she trusted to such a level. Soma, perhaps. He knew so much of her plans, but did she trust him? No. The paragon played his own games, despite how hard he pretended otherwise.

"If I am to risk my life, let it be done by my own hands," she said. "As for my reasons for being here . . . matters are more complicated than I first believed. My father did not come alone. Two of my brothers joined him on his voyage. With Galvanis slain, the choice for heir must be made anew. For the three of us, he has settled on a game of sorts to decide the matter. Whoever kills the Vagrant shall be named Heir-Incarnate."

The young prince tilted his head to one side. His face was a skull, and its grin, much wider than she remembered.

"So is that why you're here?" he asked. "To collect my head?"

"Far from it," Sinshei said. "I don't want your head. I want theirs."

"That's some ice in your veins to make such a request so easily," Ax said.

"There is no kindness or love to be found between us," she said. "We are related only by blood. Petrus is a brute, and Kalath cares only for his own entertainment. All the world will be better off in their absence." She turned to the Vagrant. "Once both are dead, bring me the head of someone who resembles you. We will spin a tale of your attempt on my life and your defeat by my blades. My father might seek to diminish my accomplishments, but with no other heirs, he will have no choice but to acknowledge my true place as heiress."

"And so we kill an innocent man to seal your deal," Lioness said. The words rumbled out of her throat, quickly translated by the word-lace around her neck.

"One life for an entire island seems a fine deal," Sinshei said, exasperated. "Make it a criminal, then, or find an Everlorn soldier who bears a passing resemblance. It matters not, so long as you keep hidden and do not prove my claims false."

"This is a lot of work on our part to put you on a throne," Vagrant said. "You're not offering much in return, either."

Sinshei approached him. She might need this group, but she would suffer these snide little comments no longer.

"Do you know what would happen to me if my father discovered my betrayal here?" she asked. "I would wish for death. Death would be a *kindness*. For a divine child, for a *daughter*, to betray him would be unforgivable. I would be made into an example, not just for Thanet, but for the entire empire. You cannot imagine the cruelty, and neither can I, but I know it lurks in waiting. My mother died upon a fire lit by the hair of our conquered people. My death would not be so swift, nor so plain. You may demean what I offer, *Cyrus*, but at the risk of my life, I offer freedom, and a throne for your chosen queen."

At last, Sinshei felt a measure of control over the situation. The faintest golden light shimmered around her fingertips, a reminder of the swords of faith she could summon at any moment. She was no fool, no easily swayed divine daughter. She was Thanet's Anointed, and these Thanese would acknowledge that privilege.

"So long as we ensure you become the next God-Incarnate," Vagrant said, refusing to cower before her rage.

"Forgive the boy's insults," the old man by the fire said. His head tilted slightly, and she caught the briefest glimpse of his eyes. They looked like smoldering coals. "Have you a plan, then? Killing Galvanis was no easy feat, and that involved the combined might of Keles, Vagrant, and yourself."

Sinshei had been pondering that same problem. Neither brother would trust her. Deception would have to be performed through other means.

"They are both new to Thanet and will have few resources to rely upon," she said. "I suspect they will trust members of the Legion who have been here since our arrival. Them, I can manipulate. Spread rumors of your location, false ones where an ambush would suit you greatly. Claim you left Vallessau to take refuge in North Cape, for example, in fear of the God-Incarnate. If I feed similar rumors through my priests, my brothers will walk into traps of your own devising. You do what you do best, eliminate my competition, and then my father will have no choice but to declare me heir."

"That's a whole lot of trust in Lucavi making that decision," Heretic said. He shook his head. "A trust I don't share."

"Neither do I," Ax said. The muscular woman glared at her with her red eyes. Miquoan eyes, Sinshei realized. "And to be honest, I don't quite understand this heir nonsense. Everything I've heard about Everlorn's God is that he is eternal. Why would he need an heir?"

Sinshei spun to face the entire room, ensuring that all their attention was upon her. This was a subject she was intimately familiar with, and had spent thousands of hours lecturing about throughout her life. She need only tell the truth... or at least the portions deemed acceptable for the public.

"Our beloved God-Incarnate is indeed eternal, but the physical incarnation undergoes a change every six hundred years," she explained. "The body that accepts the divine soul belongs to the Heir-Incarnate, who is always one of the God-Incarnate's children. This year is that six hundredth year, and there will be a grand ceremony to mark the occasion, during which Lucavi will sacrifice his own mortal vessel. I will accept his divine soul and draw all its power and memories into my own body."

"What then becomes of Sinshei vin Lucavi?" Vagrant asked.

"I will not be lost, nor erased. I will be one with the eternal, and I shall have my own will and my own desires."

The Lioness startled, and it bordered on comical the way her eyes widened and her ears tilted back.

"Something wrong?" Ax asked her. The bone-armored feline shook her head.

"An idea I had, that's all," she said, but Sinshei knew it was more than that. Just who, or what, was this creature? Sinshei had long assumed the Lioness was a particularly faithful member of Endarius's church and had been given the form as a way to fight back despite the god's death. Now, though, she wondered.

"So Lucavi needs an heir," the Vagrant said. His voice seemed to darken the very room. "What happens if we kill his heirs? *All* of his heirs?"

Sinshei stood defiant. She would not fear this path, no matter its dangers. She could not tell them another nation would suffer an invasion similar to Thanet's, but she could give them shades of the truth.

"It has happened once before," she said, meeting the Vagrant's gaze with her own iron will. "God-Incarnate Drasden deemed his only heir unworthy, and come the six-hundred-year ceremony, he used the prayers of Gadir to extend his life by another two decades. If forced, he will leave here, take multiple wives, and sire many children. You will accomplish little, while forfeiting the potential future I offer."

If only she could make them see her as she saw herself in the future. A proud Goddess-Incarnate, newly anointed and blessed with the worship of an entire continent. She slowly turned, looked to them all, these desperate, war-torn soldiers and criminals, and gave them her promise.

"I shall become Goddess-Incarnate, and for six hundred years enact reformation unlike anything Gadir has ever seen. The salvation I offer shall be made manifest, and the cruelties of Everlorn addressed at last. Give me your trust, and I will give you back your kingdom."

Again their attention turned to the older man by the fire. The leader of their resistance, perhaps? Maybe even the man known as the Coin that Magus had been so determined to locate?

"Go," he said after a pause. "But be wary. With your father's arrival, I fear even this meeting was too dangerous. Find yourself someone you trust to come in your place, someone who may go unnoticed, and have them deliver messages to my door, for my ears alone. You were naïve to attempt a meeting so recently after Lucavi's arrival. Do so again, and we will ignore your summons and leave you to your fate."

Sinshei bristled at the suggestion that she could be naïve. Had she not grown up in Eldrid's court packed with spies and intrigue? Had she not been careful to change her attire and sneak out of the castle unnoticed? Arguing felt pointless, especially after her grand speech about the dangers she faced, and so she let the matter drop.

"I will keep that in mind," she said. A quick dip of her head, and she exited through the door and took in her surroundings.

As she suspected, she was in the upper ring of homes built into the cliffs that formed a semicircle around the lower portions of Vallessau. Well-furnished homes and, until recently, crowded as well. Many owners had fled to supposedly quieter and safer cities on Thanet, leaving behind only a few servants for basic upkeep. Sinshei pulled her hood high up to hide her face and hurried toward the nearby crossroad that would lead her downward.

She managed only a few steps before she heard a man loudly clear his throat. She halted, panic flooding her veins in the instant it took for her to turn and find Soma casually leaning against the side of the neighboring home. His face was stoic, but his eyes gleamed with amusement.

"So how fared your meeting?" the sapphire-armored paragon asked.

"You followed me?"

"Of course I did. Have I not tossed my lot in with yours? I'd be a fool to let something happen to you."

"Your concern is touching."

He smirked.

"As is your cruelty. I heard much through the thin walls. To offer a throne to a queen who shall rule an empty island? Even I could not speak such a lie so easily."

The deception burned like fire in Sinshei's breast. If only there were another way. If only she could give Keles a better fate. The young woman deserved it. But then all of Gadir deserved a better fate. Exceptions for the few on this island could not be made at the expense of the many upon the mainland.

"I do what must be done," she said, and started for the castle. Soma bowed low, his smile ear to ear.

"As do we all."

CHAPTER 4

MARI

Mari could barely contain her excitement. The moment Sinshei was out the door, she bounded up the stairs to her room for privacy.

You treat with the invaders, Endarius grumbled in her mind as she reverted back to her human form. Her bones snapped, her claws shrank, and her fur faded away as if it had never been.

"This is the best way Thanet obtains peace," Mari said as she grabbed a dress she'd already laid out on the bed.

A coward's peace.

"Does it matter? We're saving the lives of your people."

You promised me their blood on my tongue. You promised me fury and revenge. Instead, they will sail away unbloodied with a new empress.

They had already claimed the lives of multiple paragons and the Heir-Incarnate, Galvanis. She wouldn't call that unbloodied, but neither did she wish to argue with the Lion god.

"We've a long way to go still," she said, as noncommittal an answer she could muster in an attempt to appease him. "Whatever it takes, Thanet will be free. Surely you can't begrudge us that?"

If he did, he did not bother to respond. That was good enough for Mari. Now dressed, she rushed down the steps, to where the rest of the gang were discussing Sinshei's proposal.

"Maybe your estimations are wrong," Stasia was arguing with her father.

"They would need to be wrong five times over for us to stand a chance in a fair fight," Thorda argued back. "Our best count puts their arrival at one hundred ships, and their soldiers numbering between eight and ten thousand. What forces Commander Pilus has mustered are a pittance compared to that."

Mari hopped from foot to foot at the bottom of the stairs. She didn't want to interrupt, for accepting Sinshei's offer had been contentious, to say the least. They needed to hammer this out…but did they really have to do it now?

"That's a lot of soldiers, no matter what the final count is," Arn said. She caught him glancing her way, and when their eyes met, he blushed and continued talking while firmly staring at his hands. "Which means a lot of mouths to feed. Whatever stores they brought with them have got to be running low. They'll force donations from all the villages, and when that isn't enough, they'll start pillaging to make up the rest."

"I am well aware of Everlorn's tactics," Thorda said.

"Then you know the results," Arn said. He snapped his gaze back up to her father. "More anger. More destitution. It also means more soldiers willing to join Pilus, assuming he can promise them revenge and keep them fed. Whatever coin and influence you have left, Thorda, you best spend it stockpiling food. Things are going to get grim, fast."

"All this sounds like more reason to refuse Sinshei outright," Stasia argued. "This is a fool's deal. How do we even know this supposed transfer of power will work?"

"But it will," Mari blurted out. "I know it will, because I know what the God-Incarnate is!"

All eyes turned her way.

"Do you, now?" Thorda asked. "Care to explain?"

Mari rushed to the center of the room. Her entire body vibrated with excitement.

"What Sinshei described, it seems strange at first, but not when you look at it in a new light. The God-Incarnate, and his chosen heir? *He's just like me.*"

Thorda looked visibly ill and was quick to respond.

"An Everlorn god-whisperer? Do not speak such blasphemy."

Mari shook her head and carried on.

"No, think on it longer. What am I but human flesh taking in the power of a god? The same is happening to these heirs. The previous god is slain, and then the power is placed into the Heir-Incarnate. Only instead of acknowledging the passing of the previous god, or that the inheritor is their own unique person, they claim to become a singular entity."

Curious looks all around, this time not quite so incredulous.

"I suppose it makes sense," Cyrus said. "But from what I understand, their transformation is permanent, and yours is not."

"But theirs isn't permanent! It may last longer, true, but why these rituals and secrecy? We're questioning the divine, and a process that began thousands of years ago. How much more do we not know? I take in gods who were slain, their physical shells broken. What if these rituals help supersede the damage? Or what if the God-Incarnate, being viewed as an aspect of humanity, makes him better suited to human vessels compared to, say, the Lion or the Butterfly goddess?"

"They do say the first God-Incarnate, Ashraleon, was once mortal and uplifted into perfect divinity," Arn said. "It's how they named the church, after all."

"Do they, now?" Cyrus asked. He'd shed his Vagrant visage once Sinshei left, but his face was still dark and haunted by the shadows cast from the window.

Mari bobbed up and down, still excited by her realization.

"So much has been lost to the past, but I do think the God-Incarnate might be like me. A god like all other gods, his essence plunged into a mortal vessel to give him form. And for whatever reason, that new vessel can only endure for six hundred years."

"Which means he needs a new vessel," Cyrus said, finishing the thought. "Just as Sinshei described. So if she is telling us the truth, aiding her in becoming Goddess-Incarnate gains us the most powerful ally in all of creation." He looked to the others. "I hate the idea, but how could we possibly say no to that?"

"We can by distrusting Sinshei," Keles offered.

"Do you distrust her?" Mari quickly asked.

The other woman shrugged.

"Overall? Yes. In this? I do not know. Your theory lines up rather neatly with what she's asked of us."

"And until we learn otherwise, we must do what seems best for Thanet," Thorda said. He rubbed at his beard. "As much as I would like Everlorn burned to the ground, there is the potential for incredible good in Sinshei's supposed reformation. This means our next step is obvious, though by no means less difficult. Lucavi's sons will be well-protected, and dangerous in their own right. With our fewer numbers and limited supplies, we must ensure our attempts are made with absolute perfection."

"I've a few ideas on that, if you're in need," Stasia said. She kissed Clarissa on the cheek and lowered her voice. "Go on home, all right? I suspect this will run late."

"Arn, Keles, and I are already heading out if you want an escort," Cyrus offered.

"To where?" Mari asked.

Keles smiled her way.

"To another meeting I suspect Sinshei would highly disapprove of."

Clarissa kissed her wife back, then stood and smoothed out her skirt.

"I would love an escort," she said. "The streets don't feel safe anymore with Lucavi's arrival, not that they've been all that safe before."

Stasia joined her father, the two discussing what they knew about Lucavi's sons as well as potential ambush points. The other three said their goodbyes and left, except for Arn. Mari lifted an eyebrow his way as he stood by the door, clutching whatever it was Stasia had purchased for him. Mari fought back a smile. The giant man looked so nervous, his shoulders hunched and his expression bordering on terror.

"Are you not going?" she asked.

"I am. I will. First, though, I can't go strolling about like your sister can, so I had her get these for you. From me, for you, of course."

"Of course," Mari said lightly. Arn coughed and then thrust the paper package her way.

Within were white orchids cut at the stem and wrapped in thin string. Mari withdrew them from the wrapping and beamed. They were beautiful, and when she lifted them to her nose, their aroma reminded her of the pale flowers that flooded the fields of Aethenwald.

Arn was staring at her, dying for a response. Her playfulness took hold, and so she widened her eyes in shock.

"Flowers?" she asked.

"Yeah, flowers," Arn said, now supremely self-conscious. "Everybody likes flowers, don't they? Even people from Miquo?"

Mari brushed her fingertips across the petals, using all her willpower to keep from laughing.

"In the forests of Miquo, the understory is most often bathed in shadow, and long-stemmed flowers are exceedingly rare. They are given as gifts, yes... betrothal gifts."

Every ounce of color drained from Arn's face. He stammered for several seconds before actual words could form.

"I didn't know, I'm sorry, I didn't mean... damn it, why didn't your sister say so?"

Mari held the flowers close to her chest and closed the distance between them. The big man stood paralyzed as she lifted up to her tiptoes and whispered in his ear.

"Because I'm joking."

She leaned back. His eyes bulged, and his face went from pale as winter to a fierce blush to rival the hottest summer sun.

"You... you..."

"What?" she asked, batting her eyelashes. "What am I?"

He pointed a finger, the digit hovering an inch from her nose. He still struggled for words, but before he could say something he might regret, she stepped right past, stood once more on her tiptoes, and kissed him. Just a quick one, the softest brush of their lips to shut him up.

"The flowers are beautiful," she said. "Thank you."

"You're welcome," he said, and then tugged at the collar of his shirt. "I better catch up with Cyrus and Keles. Make myself useful, you know?"

Arn hurried away like a rabbit with hounds at his heels. Mari breathed in the flowers, turned toward her room to put them away, and then froze.

Stasia lurked at the door to her father's study. Her arms were crossed and her face locked in a smile far too smug.

Oh gods, I kissed him, I kissed him right in front of her.

"So," Stasia said. "Arn. Can't say I saw that one coming."

This time, it was Mari's turn to fiercely blush and then flee.

CHAPTER 5

VAGRANT

There's nothing to be worried about," Cyrus told Keles later that night as the pair lurked at the door leading into the grand dining hall. Arn patrolled outside the mansion, ensuring the meeting of Thanese loyalists was not interrupted.

"I never said I was worried."

"You don't have to say it. I can tell."

Keles stood with her arms crossed over the chest of her immaculate black armor, which was polished to a fine shine. She peeked through the cracked-open door at the fifty or so people gathered inside. A few were dancing, while most talked quietly.

"Is that a god thing?" she asked, her eyes still on the group.

"Hm?"

A bit of a smile cracked through her perfectly neutral expression.

"Sensing my nervousness? Is that a new power of the Vagrant?"

Cyrus grinned back, careful to make sure it was his human face. He wore his full Vagrant getup, cloak, weapons, and all. Had to make a good impression on the crowd when he introduced Thanet's Returned Queen, after all.

"Does that mean I'm right?"

Keles slumped against the wall. The braids in her hair were tied into an intricate bun that had required the help of two of the mansion's servants. Keles moved to thud her head against the wall, then halted the moment the braids touched it.

"Lycaena help me, this is actually awful," she said, gingerly touching the bun. Little silver threads were woven throughout, and they rippled through her fingers. "It's like being the Light of Vallessau all over again, but worse."

Cyrus scanned the crowd. He recognized a few faces from his earlier visits, traders and builders who had been hit hardest by the empire's arrival. They looked nervous, but they also moved with excited energy. This was a room eager to meet with their promised guest...if only said promised guest could work up the nerve to leave the hallway.

"How is it worse?" he asked. "Surely leading an army against Everlorn is harder than a few minutes' talking with potential new followers."

Keles shot him a look, half amusement, half glare.

"That's some strong talk from a boy who didn't know how to dance, stammered and stuttered when pressed by any questions, and blushed so *very* red at a bit of cleavage."

Heat filtered up Cyrus's neck. Gods help him, it seemed Keles had noticed his wandering eye back when they first met...

"My own failings are well-known," he said with a cough. "Care to share why *you* are nervous?"

She wilted against the wall.

"What if the people do not accept me? At the forsaking ceremony, thousands of people watched me kneel before the Anointed One, deny my goddess, and profess my love of the God-Incarnate. I failed to find victory as the Light of Vallessau, and I failed to hold my faith as a paladin of Lycaena. Why should they hold faith in me?"

She closed her eyes and sighed.

"Why should *I* hold faith in me?"

A rare moment of vulnerability, one Cyrus would address carefully. Deep down, he trusted the island to accept her, but why? Why did he feel so certain it would happen? And how to put it into words that made some semblance of sense?

"The people will rally behind you because of everything you are," he said, breaking the silence. "Not just your successes, but your failures. You see the forsaking ceremony as a mark against you, but I don't. Neither will they. You were a hero, and then you were broken. The island, and its people? They're also broken. They're wounded, they're scared, and they're grieving."

Cyrus drew one of the swords Thorda Ahlai had crafted and stared at his reflection in the polished steel. For the briefest moment, he saw the grinning skull.

"To them, I am a killer," he said. "Brutal, deadly, and otherworldly. They cannot see themselves in me. But you?" He looked up and met the gaze of her lovely dark brown eyes. "When they see the woman who was once broken regain her faith? See her lift her sword and cry out there is still hope? Then they will believe they can do the same. That they can be just as strong. That Thanet can be made whole."

Keles reached out, her armored hands gently settling atop his gloved ones. Her gaze never broke.

"And it's because you never gave up on me," she said. "Even when I offered you my neck. Thank you, Cyrus. For that, and for this."

Cyrus had to swallow before speaking, he was so touched.

"I'm a blade, and you, an inspiration," he told her. "So let's go in there and be what we're best at."

He closed his eyes and summoned his other face. His flesh hardened, the sensation cold and decidedly unwelcome. The feeling passed, and he drew his other sword and focused on the opposite side of the room, visible from the door. He'd requested a shaded spot in the dining hall specifically for this reason. The magic of his Anyx ring flared black, and then he walked into the shadows behind the doorway.

Gasps met his entrance as he stepped out, little bits of darkness curling off his cloak like water. He immediately pointed his sword toward the original entrance and bellowed out with a deep, thunderous voice so unlike his own.

"Look not to me, but to your queen!"

Keles barged through the door, all movement and impatience, as if she were an army general. She held her head high, her red-and-orange cloak billowing behind her. Lantern light flickered off the splendid shield tucked against her left arm. Ever since Lycaena had blessed it after Rayan's death, it seemed to shimmer regardless of the surroundings. She crossed the dining hall to its center so she might address the crowd. She hesitated for the slightest moment, and only Cyrus could tell how nervous she actually was.

"I thank you all for coming," she said. "The trials our island has suffered are many, but hope yet remains. Their soldiers and paragons fall. Their regent, sent from afar, died by the blade of the Vagrant. So, too, did their Imperator. We cut the head from Lucavi's chosen heir, and loudly proclaimed to Everlorn... we shall not break."

Applause and cheers met the mention of Galvanis's death. Upon hearing it, Keles at last smiled.

"I am the Returned Queen, beloved of Lycaena and born of the blood anointed by the Sapphire Serpent. I shall not rest until the war is done and we are free. Free, my friends, my family. By my sword, my shield, and my prayers, I will lead us to that freedom."

By the reaction of the crowd, it was a fine enough little speech. More cheers, followed by a rush of people eager to speak with the Returned Queen and ask questions. No doubt more than a few would already be angling for positions of power come a return to the monarchy after Everlorn's defeat.

If only such victory were as assured as we pretend, Cyrus thought grimly.

He had planned to announce Keles and then immediately depart, but a familiar face in the crowd caught his eye. Instead, he sheathed his swords, crossed his arms, and then waited. Sure enough, the other man made his way over.

"I suppose I should not be surprised," Cyrus said.

"No, you should not," Eshiel Dymling replied. He sipped at his drink, a white wine of some sort. The priest wore the traditional robes of his order, red as a base with orange around the sleeves and neck, and gold to form the sash. "The link to Dagon to justify the Returned Queen's ascension is tenuous at best. Few hold love of the Sapphire Serpent. As such, I am doing my best to place Keles in Lycaena's beloved light as well. She is a paladin of the goddess, after all, and the people still look fondly back on her time as the Light of Vallessau."

"Two gods, and an overthrown bloodline." Cyrus stole a glance her way, and he felt a bit of undeserved pride at how well Keles gathered the room's attention. "It will be enough."

"So long as the Vagrant does not steal it away from her."

Cyrus glared at the priest. He might be dressed up in Lycaenean finery, but the hard look in the man's eye was a reminder of who he had once been, bare-chested, bathed in scars, and standing before a raging goddess of fire and blood.

"I seek no throne," he said.

"Perhaps," Eshiel said, unconvinced. "But there will always be those who would prefer to put a crown upon the head of the deposed prince."

Always, and forever.

Cyrus shrugged and pushed away the intrusive thought.

"I have knelt before our queen and offered my swords," he said. "She is the hope for Thanet, and the one who will guide us true when we banish the empire from our shores."

Eshiel finished his drink, twirled the cup in his hand, and then stepped closer. His movements were played casual, as if to offer a parting word, but there was nothing relaxed about his voice.

"I believe the same. And should any challenge her, be they man or god, I will be ready."

"Keles is lucky to have such a fierce protector," Cyrus said. "Though try not to reach above your own station, priest. Thanet has suffered enough from your mistakes."

If he thought the man would be upset at the challenge, he was wrong. Eshiel laughed and gestured for a servant to refresh his glass.

"I am no leech clinging to Keles's side," he said, once his glass was full and the servant retreated. "I am a protector and guide, nothing more. And forgive me if I speak harshly, Vagrant. My dreams have been troubled lately." Eshiel sipped from the glass and then dipped his head in respect. "May the rest of your night be pleasant, Vagrant."

Cyrus decided it was time for him to depart as well. He slipped out the door, returning to their waiting place. From there he watched Keles mingle, content to let her hold the spotlight. Lurking would only drag attention away from her. Of her nerves and doubts, none showed as she walked among the crowd. Her smile was brilliant, her laugh contagious.

"Thorda should have put me through paladin training instead," he muttered.

"You hardly look like a paladin, good sir."

Cyrus turned to address his surprise guest. By her simple dress and bare feet, he supposed her a servant of the household. Her face, though, was startling in its beauty. Her eyes and hair were both black as ink, in full contrast to the paleness of her skin. Her features were fine and slender, and he noted she bore the same red-and-orange splash of paint across her face that Keles wore when honoring the goddess.

"No, I suppose I don't," he said with a forced grin. He'd let the skull mask slip since exiting, and he wondered if he should summon it anew. His identity was no longer a secret, but without it, he felt... naked. "But surely looks do not decide one's potential?"

"A strange argument to make from one who wears a grinning skull for a face. You *want* people to judge you by your appearance, do you not? So by my judgment, that face does not belong to a man who heals the sick and prays over the dying. You are the one who creates the dying, aren't you, Vagrant?"

"You seem to know me well for a woman I have never met," he said, still trying to find his footing. It was her demeanor. She spoke with confidence and seemed almost playful with her questions. She couldn't be a servant, but if not, then... what?

"Before tonight, I knew you not at all," she said. She took a step closer, and her black eyes locked him in place. "And yet, a mere moment in your presence and I feel I know you all too well. Violence disguised as holiness. Fear and intimidation, justified and held sacred by the desperate and the furious. You kill, Vagrant. You kill, and you kill, and you pray that somehow the killing will be enough, because that is all you are. Anything else, and you will be lost."

Cyrus's hands drifted to the hilts of his swords.

"Who are you?" he asked.

This unknown woman smiled, her teeth sparkling white like stars.

"I am no one, my young prince."

The door behind him blasted open, and Arn Bastell barged through. He wore Thorda's chainmail layered underneath his heavy coat, and his face was hidden behind a fox-skull mask.

"Been looking for you, bud," Arn said, then skidded to a halt. "Oh, sorry. Didn't know you were busy."

"All is fine," the strange woman said, and she smiled at Arn. "I have many errands I must attend to this night. Farewell to you both."

Cyrus watched her calmly walk the hall. Her words burrowed into his skin like hungry worms. Who was she, to tear him down so thoroughly, diminishing his sacrifices and efforts? He wanted to shout for her to stop, to demand answers, but that felt weak somehow. Like it would acknowledge there was truth to her judgments.

"You still with me, Vagrant?" Arn said, snapping his fingers. "We're leaving, but Keles wants all of us together for the final goodbye."

"Yeah, sorry," he said lamely, and followed Arn to the door.

"Hey, don't worry about it," Arn said, and he smacked Cyrus hard on the back. "I get it. I have a thing for redheads, too."

Cyrus furrowed his brow in confusion.

Red?

He glanced over his shoulder, but the hallway was empty, and the servant gone.

CHAPTER 6

SINSHEI

As unpleasant, distrusting, unwelcoming, and overall dangerous a meeting with the Vagrant and his fellows might be, Sinshei would take that over time spent with her brothers any hour of any day.

"What was so urgent as to interrupt my prayers?" she asked Bassar, who guided her through the castle's stone halls. Like her, he was from Aethenwald. She tugged at her long hair and tried not to be offended by the paragon's perfectly shaved head. In their birth nation, hair was to be cut only when one was wedded, and then the pieces braided together into a symbol of unity. For Bassar, it symbolized his dedication to the God-Incarnate. To Sinshei, it was an insult, and an overreach of position.

"They ordered, and so I obeyed," the divine bodyguard answered. He glanced over his shoulder. The light of his torch flickered off his head, which she knew he polished with oils every morning. "If they request your presence, then it is your duty to come no matter its urgency."

Sinshei held back a shiver. Bassar had been her father's divine bodyguard since her early childhood, and his was a familiar face to her. Yet that familiarity never eased the crawling sensation she felt when he looked her way. Was it hidden contempt? Or a feeling of being judged? It seemed everyone deemed her a failure to live up to their lofty standards. Thankfully she could ignore most of those pompous and pampered nobles back in the heart of Eldrid who had never set foot in a conquered land.

Bassar halted before a door that was halfway ajar. The light of a roaring hearth shone through the crack. His smile was sickly and beautiful alike.

"We are here," he said. "Your brothers await."

Within was a humble library that paled in comparison to the archives of Eldrid, where one could spend a lifetime among mazelike rows and never finish reading the tomes of the first floor, let alone the six more stacked atop it. There were two hundred books within this room, maybe three. There definitely used to be more, for her younger brother, Kalath, was casually tossing book after book into the roaring fire while he reclined in a chair by the hearth, warming his bare feet with its heat.

"At last, she arrives," Kalath said, and a smile lit up his annoyingly handsome face. He lifted his glass of wine. "A toast to the ever-late daughter of our beloved Lucavi."

"I was in the middle of my prayers," she said, trying, and failing, to keep an edge out of her voice. "As Anointed One, I have many duties to fulfill. I sadly cannot pass away the late hours of the day drinking and… reading heathen literature."

"It's not much of a read, truth be told," Petrus said. The gigantic slab of muscle sat at a little round table in the center of the room, his ax resting atop it. His spine was as straight as a ruler, the only curve in his entire body seemingly the frown filling the lower half of his square head. He had a book in hand, leather bound and with pink flowers painted across its front. The lettering was done so fancifully that even Sinshei, who could read most Thanese, could not make out its title.

"Is it ever?" Kalath asked. He lifted another book from a giant stack at his side, ripped out a few pages, and flung them into the fire. "You expect much from this crude little island."

"There are always some surprises," Petrus insisted. "But here, it's the same. Their gods are wondrous, their royalty perfect, their homeland a precious jewel unmatched in all of creation. I almost wish for a bit of crudeness. Some drawings of native Thanese women would liven up the reading."

Kalath giggled into his wine mid-drink, spilling some of it onto his shirt.

"Father help me, you never saw those drawings I found in Aethenwald, did you? 'Holy scriptures,' the priests insisted, dedicated to their beloved night goddess." He pantomimed two gigantic circles with his hands. "Biggest damn tits I've ever seen, at least thrice the size of her head. I couldn't help it. I asked if it were holy to masturbate to their goddess's image. They were so offended, the perverted little heathens, I almost made them commit the deed right then and there."

"Surprised you didn't," Petrus said, looking displeased. "You've done more depraved acts than that."

"I figured if it *was* holy, then I'd be helping them commit a blasphemous act against Everlorn. Besides, they were all to be hung on the morrow. I'd like to think I'm better than a cat who toys with its prey. That was always Galvanis's thing, not mine."

Sinshei stood by the doorway with her hands crossed behind her back. Her fingers twisted little portions of her hair. It galled her that they would demand she arrive with such haste, then banter and chat without a care in the world. She dared not reveal her distaste, though. Her brothers would pounce on it like wolves. The best she could do was prod the conversation along.

"I suspect you did not want my opinion on Aethenwald drawings," she said dryly, hating how easily they mocked the art and history of her mother's country. "What did you need me for?"

"We've been discussing, that's all," Petrus said, and he shot a glance at his brother. "Thanet is in dire straits, and we must act accordingly."

A false smile hid Sinshei's utter disdain for the pair, especially Kalath. While Petrus would actively hunt the Vagrant, Kalath would do no such thing. He would feast, drink, and ensure a steady procession of Thanese women came to service his every whim. While all vin Lucavi wielded power and authority, Kalath was the only one who seemed to truly enjoy the benefits. Perhaps it was the blessing of being youngest and holding no expectations whatsoever of being heir.

"Preparing Thanet is all that matters and is a goal we share," she said, deciding maybe she could drag some useful information out of this miserable meeting. "What plans do you have?"

"Rumors posit the Vagrant is hiding outside of Vallessau in fear of our father's arrival," Petrus said. "Last word had him appearing in North Cape. I'll leave for there tomorrow and kill him if the rumors are true."

He spoke as if it were a dull, daily chore and not a battle against Thanet's fiercest defenders. Sinshei didn't know if it was an act or if Petrus truly believed himself capable of such an easy victory. Galvanis had long been judged the perfect heir, but Petrus had fought in more wars and even laid claim to slaying Lorka of Onleda. While Galvanis had been more charismatic and cleverer, Petrus might be the better fighter. What Petrus lacked, however, was the title of Heir-Incarnate, and the divine blessings it granted. Until properly anointed, he would still be weaker than Galvanis had been.

"I wish you safety and success," she said. "If I might aid you in some way, please, do not hesitate to ask."

"But we are asking," Kalath interjected. "We have a job for you, dear sister, one I don't think will stretch your capabilities too strenuously."

"Oh," she said, her throat turning dry. "And what is that?"

"The northern realm of Ierida has been leaderless since Lord Mosau's murder," Petrus said. "The same goes for Tannin after the Ax of Laha-reed overran Fort Lionfang. Rather than appoint new regents this close to the six-hundred-year ceremony, Lucavi has decided to appoint regent-temps instead."

"And I suppose I am to be one of those regent-temps?" she asked.

"Heavens no," Kalath said. He rocked his chair far enough back to reach another bottle next to the book pile, then popped the cork with his thumb. "You're Thanet's most precious and important Anointed; you could never handle that responsibility *and* be regent of a realm. You're going to Thiva with the new regent-temp, Agustin Sallo. Agustin came along with us on our boats and is new to Thanet. He'll need someone to help . . . settle in, shall we say?"

Sinshei tugged on her hair so hard, pain spiked across her skull. So that was their game. They would send her off to Thiva so she could not participate in the hunt for the Vagrant. Oh, she could protest to her father . . . but she knew how that would end.

"I suppose such matters should be resolved if we are to have a smooth six-hundred-year ceremony," she said, smiling sweetly. "How long will I be needed there?"

"Oh, I'm sure it will take some time," Kalath said. "A few weeks, at the minimum. We'll send a messenger your way if things change."

"And my duties here as Anointed One? I must attend the faith of those in the capital."

Petrus pushed up from his seat and casually tossed the lone book he held into the hearth.

"We've seen the middling faith of the people here. A few weeks' absence will change little. Lucavi's presence alone will accomplish more in days than you did in years."

The dismissal burned deep in Sinshei's breast, and she wished she could summon her gleaming blades. Petrus was strong, yes, but how did all that muscle compare to her swords of faith? She'd cut down Galvanis. She could do the same to Petrus and Kalath...

"Father's presence will indeed foster faith in those too stubborn to believe in what they cannot see," she said, sidestepping the insult. "When does Agustin leave for Thiva?"

"Tomorrow morning, of course," Kalath said. "Why do you think we summoned you with such urgency?"

Her sweet, practiced smile spread wide.

"But of course," she said. She glanced at Petrus in particular. "I bid you both well."

And I hope the Vagrant guts you like a fish on your way to North Cape.

Sinshei happily left for her room and was not surprised to find Soma waiting at her bedroom door. He leaned against the stone wall, his spear casually resting beside him within easy reach.

"How went your meeting with your father's more distinguished spawn?" he asked.

"They're sending me to Thiva to clean up the mess left by Jase's death," she said.

"And keep you from attempting to capture the Vagrant."

Ever a sharp one, her bodyguard. She pushed the door to her room open.

"I will not be gone long," she said. "Remain here, my eyes and ears on my brothers, if at all possible. Also, arrange another visit with the Vagrant. Petrus prepares a surprise march to North Cape tomorrow, and it would be an excellent chance to ambush him unawares."

Soma snatched his spear and attached it to the hooks built into the back of his armor. A smile lit his handsome face.

"As you wish," he said.

Sinshei stepped inside her room and then immediately pulled back out to call after the retreating paragon.

"Oh, and summon Signifer Weiss, would you?"

She had just finished picking her fifth and final outfit when she heard Weiss knocking on the door.

"You requested me?" the scarred man said, perfectly calm and pleasant as ever.

"Indeed, I did," she said. "How go our plans for the purge?"

He shrugged.

"They are ready," he said. "I need only permission to show them to the God-Incarnate."

Sinshei clasped her hands behind her, her fingers twirling her long hair. The Signifer had proven himself cunning and resourceful, and together they had prepared a spectacle to win over her father's admiration. Her plan had been to unleash it the day of his arrival, before finding out her loathsome brothers had accompanied Lucavi on the journey.

"For reasons beyond my control, I must leave for Thiva," she explained. "Make sure you do not reveal them, nor put them into motion, until my return. Is that understood?"

He dipped his head in respect.

"Of course, Anointed One. I have not prepared so thoroughly just for one of your brutish brothers to take the credit. I eagerly await your return."

She closed the door, wishing Soma could show her a fraction of that respect or decorum. Before she could resume packing, a series of heavy knocks interrupted her.

Gods, what is it now? she wondered, and flung her door open. To her surprise, Bassar stood before her, his face a perfectly unreadable mask.

"Is something amiss?" she asked. "I have much to pack and prepare for my journey."

"It is your departure that brings me here now, instead of when better prepared. I have been researching the events that led to Galvanis's death, and I have stumbled upon a matter better handled by Vallessau's Anointed. Upon reading the various reports and testimonies, I have encountered an... oddity."

Sinshei's heart leaped into her throat. Had Bassar pieced together what truly happened? Did he know she had lied in her report about finding Galvanis executed at the base of the sapphire altar?

The castle was quiet, its people asleep. His sword, always drawn, rested so casually upon his shoulder. His face gave away nothing.

"And what is that?" she asked, wishing she could summon her faith weapons without raising suspicion.

"It involves one of the paragons who accompanied Galvanis's arrival here, Dario Bastell. He has lied, Anointed One, I am sure of it. What I do not understand is why."

Sinshei slowly, carefully released her long-held breath. The tension eased from her limbs. She could only pray the bodyguard did not notice. Intrigue replaced her wariness. Her access to the Vagrant meant access to the Heretic. If Dario was hiding something, she might be able to play both sides...

"Tell me everything," she said. "And spare no detail."

CHAPTER 7

DARIO

Please," Dario whispered. The long hours had broken his resolve. The silence of his bedroom stabbed him incessantly. "You gave me succor once, in the shadow of Onleda's conquest. Will you not comfort me now?"

Dario knelt beside his bed, his head bowed in prayer. It was his twelfth hour doing so. No food. No drink. No sleep. His bladder ached, and he stank of sweat, but this was not his first time enduring such a trial. He had done similarly when his brother vanished in the wake of Vulnae's fall. In the ruins of the captured city, in the same temple where they had slain the heathen goddess Velgyn, Dario had pleaded for his missing brother's salvation.

Back then, Lucavi had heard and blessed him with a promise.

You are beloved, and I am with you always, honored son. Fear not the path your brother walks. Mind your own heart, and walk with my truth proudly cherished. My eye is ever upon the lost.

Dario had bathed the temple floor with his tears. Wherever Arn went, whatever his doubts, they would be forgiven upon his return. A place of honor awaited him come the Epochal War in the eternal lands beyond.

And now, all these years later, Dario heard only silence.

Two rapid knocks startled Dario to his feet. Little jolts of pain arced through his back at the sudden movement. He was naked from the waist up and wore only a simple pair of trousers. He ignored his desire to dress. Those knocks…Could it be? Had Lucavi himself come after hearing the earnestness of Dario's prayers?

"Come in," he said.

It was not Lucavi, but instead his daughter, Sinshei, looking as beautiful as ever in her crimson dress. Her bound hair, decorated with gold lace, shimmered behind her like a cloak. Dario tried to hide his disappointment. He suspected he failed.

"How is your hand?" she asked. If she cared for his lack of clothes, she showed no outward sign.

"Healing," he said. He flexed the fingers of his bandaged hand. Its pain had been a thorn in his mind for the entirety of his prayers. The wound was a direct result of a clash between him and his heretical brother. They had directly opposed each other, strength against strength in the ultimate test of their convictions.

It had been Dario's hand that failed, his bones that sundered into pieces.

"Let me see."

Sinshei unwrapped the thin cloth. The skin was puffy and swollen. Deep purple bruises marked his knuckles and joints where the bones had broken. Dario had popped them back into place himself. The innate gifts of a paragon should have healed them within a night or two. That they hadn't was…troubling.

"It could be better," Sinshei said after a moment. Her dainty fingers were dwarfed by his meaty ones as she gently poked and prodded. "But it could also be worse."

She rewrapped his hand, apparently satisfied with her investigation. Dario stood there awkwardly as she did. He shouldn't be so curt with her. What if Lucavi had sent her in proxy to answer his prayers?

"Why have you come?" he asked. "I doubt Thanet's Anointed would bother checking on a lone paragon's wounds without reason."

Sinshei stepped away, and her violet eyes drilled into him. Dario knew little of the woman, but what few times he'd met her had left him deeply unimpressed. Her station and birth insulated her from much of the world. When she prayed for others, it rang hollow. When she spoke to Thanet's people of the troubles her divine father would solve, there was no understanding there, only regurgitation. Even Arn's prayers during their training had sounded more genuine.

"Signifer Weiss has been gathering testimony from all involved in the incident that led to Galvanis's death," she said. The "incident" was the ambush of Cyrus Lythan and his allies underneath the castle, with Arn used as bait. The Heir-Incarnate had vastly underestimated the Vagrant's strength, and many paragons, as well as Galvanis himself, had paid the ultimate price.

"Aye, I know," Dario said. "I've spoken with him."

"Indeed, you told him of your fight and your injury," Sinshei said. She crossed her arms. "And yet others describe things you neglected to mention. You told Weiss you fled your brother after sustaining your injuries. Others, though, tell a different tale."

She stepped closer.

"The Heretic let you live. I would like to know why."

Dario looked away. Something about her gaze unnerved him. It was too curious. Too...hungry.

"You would question my little brother's sentimentality? He did not have it in his heart to kill me."

"He has killed many times before, including fellow paragons. Why would he spare you? You interrogated him while we held him prisoner. Perhaps your words found a place in his heart?"

Dario couldn't help it. He laughed.

"No," he said. He lifted his injured hand. "His faith has not wavered. My foolish brother instead saw hope in me, that I might join him in his heresy. That is why he let me live."

Sinshei stepped closer. Her hand touched the side of his face, an act of love to some, but to Dario, an unwanted connection. That gaze, it saw too much. Perhaps she was not so oblivious as he first thought...

"You fear he is right, and that terrifies you."

"That's absurd."

"Is it? The bruises on your hand say otherwise."

He wanted her hand gone. He wanted *her* gone. Twelve hours of prayer, and this was his reward? The touch of her fingers was like ice to his warm flesh.

"Arn has nothing to offer," Dario said, deciding he must firmly reject these doubts. Showing weakness to the daughter of the God-Incarnate was not acceptable. "He speaks of other gods, of sins and deaths, and of the cost of our campaign across Gadir. They are childish protests, nothing more. There is no substance. He would tear down the three pillars and replace them with doubt, and that, I cannot abide."

Sinshei's hand retreated.

"And yet you still wonder. Answer me, paragon, and answer true. Do you believe Lucavi's conquests to be justified?"

Damn this woman. Would she not just accept his answer? He stepped closer, daring to use his height and size to intimidate her.

"I have walked battlefields strewn with corpses numbering in the tens of thousands," he said. "If I was one to doubt, I would have already broken. My faith is strong. My heart is true. Question me no more, Anointed One."

In response, the diminutive woman reached out, as quick as a viper. Her fingers closed around his injured hand and squeezed. Pain shot through him as her fingernails dug into his swollen skin. He clenched his jaw but dared not resist. To do so would show weakness.

"I question because I see the truth within you," she said. "Doubt lingers in your heart. Your brother's actions, they have awakened questions, but instead of answering them, you deny them. You bury them deep. Why, Dario? If you were unafraid of the answers, why pretend them unworthy of your time? If you were so confident in Lucavi's truth, why not pit it against the lies spoken to you…unless you fear Arn spoke no lies. Unless you believe the campaigns you waged, the bodies you walked over, and the cities you laid low were not worth the reward."

She squeezed harder, with strength no one of that size should possess. It felt like his bones were grinding together.

"And what if they were?" she continued. "What if there is truth mixed with the heresy, to make it all the more potent? I do not wish for blind servitude, paragon. Walk in wisdom, and see the world exactly as it is. I would share that wisdom with you, if you are brave enough. Are you brave enough? Strong enough?"

These were not the words of an Anointed. No daughter of the God-Incarnate should speak so poorly of her father's campaigns of conquest and valor. Dario pushed his damn brother out of his thoughts and finally turned his full attention to Sinshei. What game was she playing?

"What is it you wish of me?" he asked.

"Walk the streets of Vallessau. See the fruits of my father's labor. When you have taken its full measure, come to me and give me your honest answer."

Some strange game was afoot, and he did not yet know the rules. Best to play along until he knew, and truth be told, a walk outside the castle was alluring after twelve hours of prayer locked in his room. He dipped his head to her.

"So be it."

Dario walked some nameless street of Vallessau. He'd briefly checked the market nearest to the castle, found its crowd tame and its wares unappealing. There were no clothes sewn with the clasped hands of the God-Incarnate. No strangers hummed familiar hymns. His walk took him past the docks and their many boats. No painted hands on their prows, no names based on the famous paragons of the first age.

Ringing bells distracted him. Dario followed the foot traffic. Children looked dour, and their parents not much better. Though he wore no armor, size alone revealed Dario as a paragon. Fearful eyes glanced his way. At the church, a squat square building with smashed windows, a red-robed priest greeted all arrivals. Dario waited outside, and when the sermon began, he listened through one of those broken windows.

It started with a song brought from Gadir, one of praise to the God-Incarnate for his blessing and mercy. The voices that sang along were so weak and quiet they could not overcome the clapping and stomping of feet meant to accompany it.

"Ashraleon be praised," the priest said when the song finished, exuberant and excited as he invoked the name of the first God-Incarnate. His energy was the antithesis of that of those gathered. Dario didn't even have to look inside to confirm it. The lack of faith was a suffocating cloud, and he fled it for the docks.

Hours of praying had left his stomach empty, and he ate a gifted pie (not purchased—no merchant or baker would ever be foolish enough to demand coin from a paragon). It was filled with freshly caught fish, chopped onions, and a leafy green he didn't quite recognize but appreciated the sweetness of. He came back for a second helping, pretended not to notice the baker's annoyance, and then continued his meandering journey.

From there he walked the outer road along the northern edge of the city, steadily climbing higher into the portions carved into the surrounding Emberfall Mountains. On a whim, he greeted the men and women he passed.

"Lucavi watch over you both," he told one couple. Forced smiles were his only reward.

"Yeah, same to you," said a young man with holes in both knees of his trousers.

Paragons were the pinnacle of faith in the God-Incarnate, yet these people held no admiration, only fear. They were conquered people, true, but Everlorn's priests were made for the hard work of winning over such hearts. Five years should have been enough time to plant seeds and see the first sprouting. Yet if he closed his eyes, Dario could almost see the aura of faith settled over the city of Vallessau. It was weak and pale. Not shining and gold, like that which had enveloped his skin as he preached his faith to his wayward brother, Arn.

Weak and pale. Not unlike when Dario prayed that morning.

He opened his eyes. The street had emptied of everyone but an older woman, her hair tied under a bonnet. Her limping gait was far too slow to avoid his approach.

"You," he said. "Do you attend the church's sermons?"

"I attend every time the bells ring," she said. Her gaze was wary, her hands trembling.

"Every time the bells ring," he repeated. "Then list a single scripture from Drasden's Coda. One scripture. That is all."

Her eyes widened and started to water.

"I... forgive me, my memory, it isn't, it is..."

He grabbed her shoulder. Her bones were thin. She felt like paper within his strong grasp.

"Something easier, then," he said. "Much easier. Every child on Gadir can answer true. What is the name of our first God-Incarnate, he to whom all our sermons open with in prayer?"

The woman had no answer, and they both knew it.

"Please," she said. "My leg, it hurts on these walks. I wish to go home."

"You wish to go? Then, go!"

He shoved the woman. She landed hard on the street. Dario stood there, fuming. Awkward, unwelcome guilt bubbled in his chest. Why should he care if she was injured? Why care at all about these people's hollow faith? They would all be dead soon, sacrificed to herald the arrival of the seventh age.

But then again, if death awaited, their faith was all that mattered. The preparation of the eternal soul ranked above all else. That was why preachers shouted from the corners. That was why they forced the people into churches. This faith, given to them in their final years, had to mean something. A place in the afterlife on the side of the righteous as they waged the war that would follow in the heavens, conquest after conquest, felling heretical gods, freeing their faithful, and uniting all of eternity.

And yet, for the very first time, the idea of that war did not excite Dario's imagination. It exhausted him. He endured the blood and the bodies, for in his heart, he believed in a promise of something more. But if that something more was endless blood and bodies...

There are true miracles that go far beyond destruction, fire, and the strength to win on the battlefield.

So Arn had insisted when refusing to take Dario's life.

What would you offer me instead? Dario wondered. *What did you see that I did not?*

"Strange to hear a paragon so invested in the faith of the people," a woman said behind him. He turned about, a cutting remark on his tongue, yet he did not speak it. The interloper's beauty shocked him. Though she wore a plain gray wrap, the cosmetics upon her face surely cost a small fortune on this distant island. Her lips were painted red. The coppery color of her skin was highlighted with black along her cheeks and jawline. The orange powder upon her eyelids complemented the earthy brown of her eyes. Her hair was tied in interlaced knots, so intricate and numerous it would take multiple hours to complete. It was a style he hadn't seen since . . . well, since his homeland of Vashlee.

"We may be the sword of the God-Incarnate, but we of the Legion serve the same goal as the other pillars," Dario said. "The salvation of all Gadir."

"Yet we are not upon Gadir."

Her voice was like a fine wine, deep and sultry. The plain garb she wore was comical on one so beautiful and wealthy, for Dario knew that to link the many dozens of braids together in hair as long as hers was the work of at least two servants. This stranger knelt beside the elderly woman, who wept from Dario's outburst. The tears slowed as they embraced. She whispered something too soft for him to hear, but its calming effect was undeniable.

"What is your name?" he asked her. Might she be some noblewoman he had not learned of? Perhaps a wealthy trader who was beloved by the commoners? She spared him a moment to answer. A smile was on her face, but it did not reach her eyes.

"I have none. What is yours, paragon?"

He grunted. So it'd be that type of game, would it?

"Dario Bastell, Paragon of Fists," he said. "Champion of Vashlee and dutiful servant of the God-Incarnate of Everlorn."

The woman did not seem impressed.

"Titles, roles, and power," she said. "You have it all. A fine use of it, I must say, to badger an old woman on her way to the market."

She kissed the elderly woman on the temple, and then together they stood. The older woman whispered thanks, shot a fearful glance toward Dario, and then shuffled away. He let her go. His attention was now reserved solely for this interloper. They were alone, the road somehow vacant despite the midday traffic.

"You mock my interest in Thanet's faith," he said. "But it is of paramount importance. We hold no higher quest, and so I ask, what of you? Have you accepted the God-Incarnate's blessing into your heart and repented of your sinful ways?"

Her shoulders pulled back and she held her head high.

"Your God-Incarnate held my devotion once. He has only himself to blame for its loss."

Dario clenched his fists. Something about her defiance unnerved him, but it also sparked anger. This tiny woman, whom he could break in an instant, showed him not the slightest fear or respect. She denied his God-Incarnate. She made a mockery of his inner turmoil.

"Then come with me to the God-Incarnate's Haven," he said, and made a great show of offering his hand. "Confess what cost you your faith to our priests, and find balm within the church for your soul."

"Did it soothe your own heart, paragon? Did your confessions heal your wounds, or open them further?"

He examined her face, struggling for a name, but none came to mind. Surely he had never met this woman before. He could not imagine forgetting one so striking. So why did she speak with such familiarity?

"You pretend at knowledge, but you are wrong," he said. "I am a paragon of Everlorn. I am our empire's inspiration for this far-flung island. You allude to turmoil and wounds that are not real. They are your imaginings, woman, and nothing more."

Still that hint of a smile played on her lips. The orange powder about her eyes seemed to have deepened somehow, turning red.

"Imaginings? No, Dario Bastell, they are not imaginings. I see the truth in your heart and the cruelty of your mind. You are honor twisted; you are pride fed fat. Who you are, who you truly are, cannot inspire me, for it is a fate I would never desire."

He grinned at her, all his frustration and confusion coming together into one single, ugly expression.

"Tell me, then, stranger whom I have just met, who am I truly?"

The placid expression faded from her face and revealed a weight that could crush mountains. Her gaze held him prisoner. Her words were condemnations he was powerless to stop.

"Before me, I see a man aflame, and though he smiles, he is burning."

The exact words Arn had spoken to him while imprisoned. Rage lit anew inside Dario's breast, and he reached for this unknown woman's throat. He would strangle the answers out of her if he must.

"How?" he asked. "How do you—"

He grabbed air. She was gone. He spun in a circle, searching, but there was no sign of her. It was as if she had never been.

"Will you plague me with illusions now?" he asked the cursed island. His gruffness was a show put on for no one. Her words wormed through his mind, unnerving him.

Dario jammed his hands into his pockets and walked back to the castle, a plan steadily forming in his head. His brother had previously contacted him through a letter delivered by some street urchin, the words written in the ancient dialect of their homeland of Vashlee. Dario suspected he could send a similar message in kind.

"Fine, then," he said. "I'll do exactly as you said, Sinshei. I'll find out the answers to my questions. I'll take the full measure of my brother's heretical truths. But if I find Lucavi wanting or the empire of Everlorn built on shifting sands..."

He thought of the strange woman's words and the fierce chill of her gaze.

No.

He couldn't finish that thought. Not now.

Perhaps not ever.

CHAPTER 8

KELES

Keles shifted her weight from foot to foot as she hid behind a thick ash tree. She wanted to keep loose and ready, for she would have only a few moments' warning before Petrus's procession arrived. It would do no good to tighten while sitting down, the weight of her heavy armor be damned. The night was young, and it crawled along at a miserably slow pace.

Two hundred soldiers, three paragons, and a son of the God-Incarnate, Petrus vin Lucavi. It was an impossible amount for their group to handle, and yet here they were, lurking in the forest for the coming ambush. Sinshei had informed them of Petrus's coming departure, and runners had come bearing numbers once they exited the city gates earlier that night.

I don't care how many accompany Petrus, Cyrus had insisted after Sinshei's information reached them. *Away from Lucavi, he's vulnerable, and surprise will be on our side. Give the order. Let the Vagrant take his due.*

Keles glanced at the sky. The trees covered the moon, but she could still see the stars on this clear night. She stared at them and imagined Lycaena watching from behind their sparkling canopy.

"You were with me when we slew Galvanis," she said. "Will you still be with me now?"

Deep below the castle, in a forgotten vault full of the heirlooms of her overthrown bloodline, she and Cyrus had battled Everlorn's Heir-Incarnate. Lycaena had filled her with power matching the storied paladins of old. With that power, she withstood blows that had broken gods. Yet since that battle, she had not called on Lycaena for aid, nor wielded her sword in any meaningful capacity.

To wield that power forever or to wield it never again—which frightened her more?

"It is late to be out hunting," a woman's voice said, startling Keles from her thoughts. She brought her gaze down from the sky to the stranger before her, who smiled with her arms crossed and her head tilted to one side. Her voice was husky, her tone playful. "Though by your armor and weapons, I suspect it is not deer you seek."

Something was immediately wrong about this woman. Though she wore the faded blouse and trousers of a dockworker, her black skin was immaculate, and her hands free of calluses and scars. Her hair was looped into a single braid that hung all the way down to her shins. Most startling were her eyes, a shade of violet, striking in their beauty.

"Aye, it is late," Keles said, measuring her every word. "And yet here you are, as well. I see no bow in your hands. Do you hunt for a different sort of game? Perhaps one forbidden after the Uplifted Church's arrival?"

It was one of Keles's few guesses as to why she would walk the road north from Vallessau at so late an hour. She could be a night woman, forced outside the city walls lest she hang from the Dead Flags.

"Forbidden?" The woman laughed, her white teeth brilliant in the dim light. "In some ways, yes, I am forbidden, yet at the same time, these loyal priests and magistrates brought me with them. I am ever unwelcome, and ever at their side." She swept her arms wide in an exaggerated display. "Truly a most bothersome fate."

The twelve scars on her left arm, cut in neat rows and matching in length and width, immediately drew Keles's eye. A ritual, perhaps? Not one she had heard of. This stranger also implied she had arrived with Everlorn's boats, but her Thanese was flawless, without a hint of a foreign accent.

"How did you find me?" Keles asked, still wondering if this was a trap. Mari and Stasia were lying in wait closer to Vallessau. Cyrus lurked in the treetops farther ahead. Between them, filling both sides, were Arn, Eshiel, and the priest's followers. Any of them should have noticed this woman's approach.

"You are not quite so hidden from the road as you believe, Keles Lyon. The starlight reflects off your armor, which is far darker than the night itself. It will scare off your prey, if they are sufficiently alert."

Keles dropped her right hand to her sheathed sword. This woman might appear to wield no weapon, but danger radiated off her in waves. Danger, or perhaps divinity. A priest of Everlorn in disguise?

"You know my name, but I do not know yours," she said, still trying to sound calm. "Would you care to share it, so we might be strangers no longer?"

The woman closed her eyes and tilted her head back as if listening to something only she could hear.

"Tonight, I am Nora," she said. "Will that suffice?"

"Well, Nora," Keles said, careful to keep her voice low. The drumming rhythm of the crickets and rustle of night birds would disguise her voice, but if Petrus's party deployed advance scouts, there was a chance they could overhear the conversation. "What brings you to me?"

Nora paced before her. The leaves underneath her feet made not a sound when she stepped on them. Her violet eyes never left Keles.

"You dance and dance about what you truly desire, don't you, Keles? I see your hand on your sword. I sense your fear at my arrival. You look for others accompanying me, and you scan me for a weapon. Tell me, of your many guesses, what do you suppose I am? Assassin, spy, priestess, or whore?"

Keles drew her sword and pointed it at Nora. Faint light shone off its steel, the blessing of the Butterfly. The woman didn't even flinch.

"I suppose none, if you are so brazen to announce them to me."

Nora tsk-tsked at her.

"Wrong again. I am one of the four, I assure you. As for your question, well..." The easy smile on her face hardened into something fierce. "I sought to judge the measure of Thanet's Returned Queen. I have already spoken with the Vagrant. I hoped to have a better encounter with you."

Cyrus spoke with you?

Keles found that hard to believe. Surely he would have mentioned meeting someone so enigmatic. Though perhaps she had donned a disguise and pretended to be a simple follower.

No. That felt wrong. He would sense... whatever it was that was different about her almost immediately.

"I do not appreciate being judged by strangers," she said.

"I am no stranger. Have I not given you my name?"

"Nora is not your name."

The woman smiled, and it revealed all other expressions before it false. This was her true smile, and it was unbearable. It was pained, and it carried such an unbelievable sadness, it struck Keles in the chest and threatened to suffocate her. Lycaena help her, who *was* this woman?

"No," said the stranger. "It is not."

The repeated hoot of a tawny owl interrupted them. It was Stasia's signal that Petrus's group was in sight. The ambush would soon launch in earnest.

"One of the sons approaches," the woman not named Nora said. She gazed over her left shoulder, as if she could somehow see him through the trees. "Will you slay him, Returned Queen? Is that within your power?"

Keles lowered her sword. This stranger showed no fear of it anyway.

"No riddles, no games," she said. "Why have you come here?"

The woman spun to face her. The light of her violet eyes flared as if the moon shone behind them. White fire flashed along the scars of her arm. She stood tall and proud, a picture of defiance and resolve. Keles knew without a doubt she looked upon the most beautiful woman she had ever seen.

"I would see death come to one who has fled its embrace for far too long," the stranger said. "Many have tried. All have failed. Yet still I search. I could aid you, Keles, if I deemed you worthy of it. But to trust in you is to trust in the strength of your goddess, and I doubt all slain divinity, no matter how great their love or dedication."

The heavy sound of marching grew nearer. Petrus and his accompanying soldiers would soon arrive. The ambush would follow, but first, Keles had to settle this mystery.

"You speak of slaying Lucavi," she said. "What aid could you offer in that?"

The woman held a dagger. She'd never moved to draw it. The weapon simply appeared in her grasp.

"You speak with the betrayer," she said. "There is but one task for which I was made."

The woman moved, so quick, so silent. The dagger vanished, and her bare hands pressed to either side of Keles's face.

"You are scarred, and those scars have made you strong," she said, her voice cutting to the bone. Her violet eyes held Keles prisoner. "I sense it in you. The will. The fire. I do not trust what the prince is becoming, but perhaps you will be the bank that guides the shadowed river."

Keles wanted to pull away but could not. She wanted to speak, to ask questions, but remained silent. Whoever this woman was, she was no mortal. The hands upon her face, they belonged to a goddess, but who? From which broken, sundered nation on Gadir had she come?

"Slay the brothers. Prove you can spill the blood of the God-Incarnate, and I shall believe Thanet home to miracles."

And then she was gone. Keles gasped in a breath as if she had been held underwater.

Get yourself together, she thought. She had to put the strange woman out of her mind, for their prey neared. The Ahlai sisters would attack the soldiers, drawing their attention away from the head of the procession. Keles and Arn would focus on the two accompanying paragons, hopefully allowing Cyrus to engage Petrus one-on-one. It was a shaky plan and relied more on brute force than Keles preferred, but it could work. Arn could go toe-to-toe with any paragon, and if Lycaena was with her, so could Keles. As for the Vagrant?

She remembered the way he had pointed his blood-wet sword at Galvanis and spoken with a voice as cold as the Crystal Sea.

I am the only god who will watch you die.

The ambush's opening salvo, however, would belong to Eshiel and his followers.

"The goddess has come!" she heard the priest shout from afar. "Stand in the presence of her fury!"

Keles closed her eyes and finally offered Lycaena a prayer.

Be with me, and do not let me falter.

When she opened her eyes, she saw fire, and the rage of the goddess unleashed upon the forces of Everlorn.

CHAPTER 9

STASIA

I hope your followers are up to the task," Stasia whispered to Eshiel as they spied on the road. The priest's clothes were plain and brown, his shirt scratched from crawling through the brush in preparation for their ambush. His eyes were closed, his hands resting in his lap. He might have seemed asleep if not for his soft, constant whispering. She never understood the words, but she knew it to be a prayer to his Butterfly goddess.

The whispers ended, but his eyes remained closed.

"After our display at the docks, you insult Lycaena with your doubts."

"Sorry, I was busy helping kill the Heir-Incarnate at the time."

She'd certainly seen the aftermath, though, not that she'd admit it to the cocky priest. Five warships, shattered and burned by the prayers of Lycaena's faithful. *Eshiel's* faithful, though she suspected he would protest any distinction between the two. Four of said followers were with her and Eshiel on the west side of the road, five more on the east to accompany the Lioness.

Stasia heard the procession's approach long before she saw them. Some two hundred soldiers, all heavily armored, and accompanied by a supply wagon, were the opposite of stealthy. She waited, just to be sure, for the first of the torch-bearing soldiers to come around the gentle curve, and then put a hand to her mouth. She'd learned multiple bird calls over the past two decades, and she imitated Lahareed's tawny owl. An ear native to Thanet would recognize the difference, but she doubted any Everlorn soldier would.

"There's the wagon," she whispered, elbowing Eshiel's arm. Any fears she'd had at being overheard were long gone. The rattle of platemail, along with the tired but jovial chatter of the soldiers, would easily drown her out. "Do your job."

Eshiel clenched his hands into fists and stood. The movement should have alerted the soldiers, but they were foolish to carry so many torches, leaving them blind to the night.

Flames flickered around Eshiel's fingers, first faint, then a swirling glove.

They would not be blind for much longer.

"The goddess has come!" he cried at the top of his lungs. His voice thundered across the forest, silencing the soldiers. Stasia felt its depth in her bones. This was no normal voice. He pointed to the soldiers, his hand opening. Nine more little fires lit up along either side of the road. The first signs of panic gripped Everlorn's forces.

"Stand in the presence of her fury!"

Ten butterflies of pure crimson flame leaped from his fingers to soar overhead. They circled once, taking flight over the mass of soldiers. With perfect coordination, they snapped still, their wings dissolving. Their bodies fell, and the moment they touched the ground, the power within them unleashed.

"Gods help us," Stasia said as explosions blasted craters into the dirt and sent soldiers tumbling. Fire washed over the men in waves, torching their skin and drawing out screams. The light was blinding, but Stasia could not look away. Where was this rage when Everlorn first invaded? Or had it taken Lycaena's murder to awaken such viciousness within her?

"Just one goddess," Eshiel said. He lifted his arms heavenward, smiling as flames returned to his fingers. "The way is ready, Ax. Have your fun."

Smoke replaced the fires. Stasia lifted her axes but was beaten to the fray. Not by her sister, as often happened, or by Arn and Keles farther down the path. No, the swarming darkness flowing through the burning soldiers spoke of another power.

Cyrus emerged from the shadows like a phantom of nightmares. Ash swirled about him but did not touch his body. His skull shimmered pure white, lit by stars that had no right to reach him amid the trees and smoke. Those nearby screamed. First in fright, then in pain.

Was this always your hope? Stasia wondered of her father as she vaulted from the brush. She crashed into a nearby soldier, burying steel into his chest in a splatter of gore. It was pale in comparison to the fury Cyrus unleashed as he cut his way toward the front. His feet danced, his swords flashed, and everywhere he moved, blood flowed.

The roar of the Lioness marked Mari's arrival from the opposite side of the road. Stasia cut her way through, eager to meet her sister's tooth and claw with her axes. What had been two hundred dwindled to one hundred within moments. As Cyrus moved toward the front of the squad, the remaining soldiers tried to regroup, only for more burning butterflies to soar from the forest. They did not explode like last time, only crashed into hapless soldiers in fiery bursts.

Everlorn's attempt at organization quickly fell apart, only to be scattered further by the Ahlai sisters' simultaneous arrival in the thick of them. Fifty or so soldiers gathered together, and Stasia leaped into them with savage glee. She ducked underneath frantic sword strikes, bashed her weight about to knock her foes apart, and cleaved through any exposed opponent with her axes. Her arms moved with steady energy, one after the other, pounding dents into shields and snapping blades foolish enough to block.

The Lioness was just as vicious. She reached Stasia's side amid an accompanying surge of burning butterflies, the glow of the fire adding a frightening aura to her gray fur and bone plates. Her wings stabbed through shields, and her claws cared little for their armor. Stasia grinned at her sister as soldiers fled in all directions.

"No mercy," Mari growled. "Keep them broken."

"My pleasure."

Stasia sprinted for the nearest soldier, but it was growing harder to find men willing to face her. Though Lycaena's followers were content to remain hidden in the dark forest, the same could not be said for Eshiel. The priest waded into battle, a flaming whip in one hand, a burning sword in the other. He cut and lashed through soldiers, his fire so great it seared through metal armor as if it were cloth.

Stasia crossed her axes to block an overhead chop, pushed the weapon aside, and then cut its wielder down. A worrisome sight from the corner of her eye had her race to take the head off a soldier who'd spotted one of Lycaena's worshipers. The soldier dropped in a heap, his head spinning through the air. The believer, a tiny blond woman, stood tall despite the gruesome sight and the blood that spurted across her chest and face.

"Her grace upon you," the woman said, and lifted a hand. A ball of flame shot from her palm and over Stasia's shoulder. Stasia turned to see it strike the face of a soldier come to stab her. The man screamed as his flesh burned and his eyelids peeled. When Stasia cleaved the veins of his throat, she considered it a mercy.

"Some grace," she muttered, yanking her ax free. Enough of these soldiers. Mari alone could handle them. She turned and sprinted along the corpse-strewn road toward the more important battle—that of the paragons.

As planned, Arn fought one and Keles the other. Unlike they'd planned, both struggled hard to achieve victory. Arn faced off against a daunting paragon in white. The man wielded a gigantic ax in two hands, his pauldrons shaped to resemble bull heads and his helmet sporting two long horns. Though they were of similar build, the opposing paragon used his enormous weapon to his advantage, refusing to let Arn close the gap.

Keles fared little better. Her opponent wielded a sword and shield like her, only both were of vastly greater size and weight. Try as she might, she could not get around the enormous slab of steel. Her sword would ping off it, and in return, he would chase her away with his own blade. Brilliant light flared off her shield with her every block.

Stasia had but a split second to decide. Arn was a former paragon. If anyone could withstand a duel, and know the limits of his foe, it would be him. Legs pumping, she flung herself at Keles's opponent with her axes raised high above her head. No hesitation, no warning cry offered, but the paragon sensed the coming attack nonetheless. His shield snapped to the side, blocking her dual swing. The two axes pounded into its surface with an ear-splitting screech of steel scraping against steel.

"Coward!" the paragon shouted at her. He shoved her away, then swung at Keles. The paladin absorbed the blow with her shield. Golden light sparked off it, Lycaena's blessing keeping the smaller woman from being knocked asunder. Keles kept close, within the reach of her sword, and then Stasia crashed back in, all her weight flung into her swing. This time, when the paragon brought his shield to bear, Keles was ready, and she thrust her sword through the crease in his armor at the knee, driving it in deep.

When the paragon tried to brace his weight, his leg buckled. Stasia's axes blasted the shield inward, twisting it so it pressed awkwardly against his chest. Another swing, and she clipped his helmet, failing to take his head off as she desired. The paragon howled, and she held back a scream as his frantic retaliation cut a thin groove across her side. That bit of blood meant nothing compared to what Keles inflicted upon him. She wrenched her sword free, pivoted until directly behind him, and rammed her sword into the small of his back.

He whirled in place, off-balance from his bad leg, and struck her with his shield. Keles toppled, but the reprieve was not worth it. The paragon wore incredibly heavy armor, and his armaments were equally heavy. He tried to turn back to Stasia, to bring his sword to block, but his clumsy movements were not fast enough. Stasia buried one ax into his forehead, breaking through his helmet to strike his skull, while her other ax chopped deep into his throat. The paragon gasped at her, blood gurgling, eyes widening, as death came to claim him.

No time to enjoy the kill. A scream from Arn drove her over the body of one paragon to assault the other. The pair had been wrestling, but the paragon had managed to swing his ax, thankfully from an awkward angle, given that it was only embedded in Arn's arm instead of cutting the limb off entirely. As Stasia closed the distance, Arn rocked the paragon onto his heels with a blow to his jaw, then grabbed the ax with his good arm. Locked together, they fought over the weapon, both bracing their legs and gritting their teeth as they pulled. A game Arn would lose, but he needn't play it long, not when Stasia descended with her axes raised high.

This time, she took off her foe's head with the opening swing.

"Took you long enough," Arn said as he collapsed to his knees and clutched his bleeding arm. Stasia knelt beside him, trying to see how badly he'd been hurt.

"Where's Vagrant?" she asked as he pushed her away.

"Up ahead, chasing Petrus," Arn said.

"Which is where you're needed," Keles said, joining the pair. She sheathed her sword and put her hands on the bleeding wound. "Heretic will be fine with my prayers. Now, go help, before it's too late."

Stasia glanced back at her sister. Of the initial two hundred, perhaps thirty or so remained, and the Lioness was busy tearing through them with wild abandon. They would be of no concern, and with the two paragons dead, that left only Lucavi's son.

"Hang in there," she said, patting his back with her blood-wet ax.

"I've survived worse," Arn grumbled, but the paleness of his skin and the depth of the wound robbed his protest of weight.

"Shush," Keles ordered. "Let me pray."

Stasia trusted the paladin to know what she was doing, then turned toward the northern stretch of road, determined to go to Cyrus's aid. Their battle raged not far away, but it was hard to make them out from such distance. Moonlight illuminated their outlines. Sparks from their colliding weapons lit their faces. She ran until her eyes had adjusted to the dimmer light away from the soldiers' torches and Lycaena's fire.

Though her weapons were ready, she slid to a halt and froze in place. Despite knowing she should help, despite knowing a paragon was never to be underestimated, she could only watch Cyrus.

No, not Cyrus, she thought. *The Vagrant.*

Shadows formed a pool around Petrus, as if he had stepped in a pond of purest darkness. They rippled with his movements. The paragon flung his enormous ax about, the tremendous weight and size capable of crushing a man with a lone blow, but he never came close to scoring a hit. Cyrus skidded along the shadowed surface like a fish within water. Whenever Petrus swung, Cyrus dipped underneath and resurfaced behind him. Each and every time, his swords found creases in the behemoth's massive plate armor. Blood dripped upon the shadows, adding to the ripples.

"Stand and fight me!" Petrus hollered after another attack whiffed. "You are but a fly biting at the ass of a horse!"

Cyrus reemerged, and for the briefest moment, Stasia believed him made of pure shadow, his cloak an extension of his body and his skull a white lantern lighting the night with its grin.

"That makes you the horse's ass," Cyrus said. "Or is that Horse-Ass vin Lucavi?"

Petrus's entire body heaved with his breathing as he lifted his ax.

"So cocky," he said. "They say you're a god now. Are you too cowardly to prove it?"

Cyrus stabbed both his swords into the dirt. Stasia couldn't fathom what he was doing. Why this show? Why put on such a display with so few to view it?

Maybe it's not a show, she thought, as he crossed his arms and tilted his head to one side. *Maybe that's who he is now.*

"Do it, then," Cyrus said. "Strike me down. Show me Everlorn's worth."

Stasia lifted her axes and prepared to sprint, thinking Cyrus was giving her an opening. The gathering shadows behind Petrus showed no such plan. Even as the paragon lifted his ax, a second Cyrus took shape unseen.

"I am the heir to an empire," Petrus shouted. "I will be a god!"

He swung overhead, with enough power to break boulders and tear apart the strongest of steel. The ax blasted right through Cyrus's body, cleaving it in half, yet it was not meat and bone, but shadow that dissipated like mist. The form behind him grew solid, became real.

"Pathetic."

Petrus spun, his eyes bulging as Cyrus lunged. His hand closed about Petrus's throat. Stasia's mouth dropped. Cyrus's swords remained embedded in the dirt, but he didn't need them. He simply tore Petrus's throat open in a single pull. Blood poured free like a river. The dying paragon's legs buckled, and he collapsed to his knees. Cyrus stood before him, and he lifted his hand to gaze upon the blood that covered his fingers.

"You are no god," he said. "You are heir to nothing. You are but a corpse who now wears my crown."

Cyrus clenched his hand into a fist. The blood hissed into smoke and ash. A gash opened across Petrus's forehead, the skin peeling down to bone of its own accord. Petrus gargled something unintelligible, collapsed onto his back, and lay still.

Stasia clipped her axes to her belt. The world felt strange about her, the forest too dense, the darkness too deep.

"Cyrus?" she said. He turned toward her, and again that skull, that grin…but no, it was him again. His cloak was but a cloak, his clothes expertly woven fabric. When he smiled at her, he looked boyish and young.

"Easier than killing Galvanis," he said. "You did well, Ax. We all did."

"Aye, we did." She turned her attention back to the others. The fight was over, the last of Everlorn's soldiers slain. Arn was on his feet, one hand upon the Lioness's back to brace his weight. The big man saw them, waved once, and began limping toward Vallessau. Eshiel and his followers were with him, and they cheered and rejoiced at what, for many of them, was their first battle.

Keles, however, was far more experienced, and her mood much more somber, as she trudged over.

"Soldiers, two paragons, and one of Lucavi's children." She shook her head. "Unreal, what we can accomplish now."

"We'll make it real, in time," Stasia said, and grinned away her exhaustion. "Right now, a warm meal and an even warmer bath sound divine."

Cyrus slid his swords into their sheaths.

"Go on without me. I'll catch up."

This time it was Keles who put forth a forced smile.

"If you insist."

The pair walked the road home. Up ahead, Mari padded alongside Arn, growling at him from far enough away that Stasia could not hear the word-lace's translation. Beyond were Eshiel and his followers, singing praises as they led the way back to Vallessau. Only one person was missing, and concern had her glance over her shoulder, to the remnants of the battle.

Cyrus quietly moved among the bodies. His head was low, his shoulders hunched, his stance resembling more a vulture's than a man's. Any desire to celebrate left her, replaced with a squirming unease that had no name or explanation. The sight was one she struggled to put out of her mind as she and Keles hurried to catch up with the others.

Cyrus, walking among bodies that had been burned, clawed, or cut down with Stasia's axes.

Cyrus, with his bare hand, his bare touch, carving upon them all his bloody crown.

CHAPTER 10

LUCAVI

Lucavi stared down at Bassar, refusing to accept the words he'd heard. Such barbarism could not be true.

"Tell me you jest," he said. The bodyguard had interrupted his reading in the castle's library, or what was left of it after his two sons made kindling of large swathes of tomes. Little was useful on an academic level, but there remained a few untouched histories of Thanet. The reading calmed Lucavi. It grounded him and made Thanet feel real.

This news, though; this was not real. It could not be.

"Forgive me," Bassar said. "I've tried to keep the news quiet, but rumors spread like roaches. I suspect the entire island will know within days. The Vagrant will ensure it."

"The Vagrant..." With the receding of his shock came anger and sorrow. It felt like his bones were twisting inside his skin. "Why must this island torment me so? First my beloved Galvanis, and now Petrus? Tell me, Bassar, and tell me true. Did he suffer? What did these vile islanders do to my son?"

Bassar did not flinch when offering his answer.

"The Vagrant did as he always does, my god. Once Petrus's throat was opened, the Vagrant cut a crown across his forehead. There was no torture, if knowing so grants you some sliver of comfort."

"The Vagrant," Lucavi repeated. The very word felt sour on his tongue. "You speak as if we do not know his name. The deposed prince, Cyrus—he did this."

Do you see? Ululath whispered within Lucavi's mind. Always the quietest, and the cruelest. *This is why all royalty must be excised in conquest, right down to the very last babe. Thanet was spoiled, and now we suffer the price.*

"The prince did the deed, yes," Bassar said. "But the island knows him as the Vagrant, and they will keep that name, and use it when they spread their tales."

Lucavi lifted his book, his thumb wedged to mark his page. What had he been reading? It felt so pointless now. More than ever, he vowed to raze Thanet to the ground for her crimes. Not a soul would remain. Those who did not give their lives willingly would do so screaming. No violence could ever compensate for this overwhelming loss.

"Vagrant. Prince. Cyrus. What does it matter his name? He's murdered my sons, Bassar. My precious, glorious sons."

A hollowness overcame him. It was strange, and unwelcome. His throat twitched and tightened. His eyes watered. Six hundred years as this incarnation, and not once had he shed tears. But had he ever known such a loss? Yes, he had fathered sons and daughters, and they had aged and died during his first few centuries of reign. Born too early to inherit the essence of the eternal god of Everlorn. Yet that was proper, and expected. This? This was...and so soon...

"Is Kalath even ready?" he asked. It was a fear he would voice to no one except Bassar. His most loyal, devoted Bassar.

The divine guard stood, and he offered his hands. Lucavi accepted them. Their hands intertwined, and Bassar pulled him close. His presence was a calming beacon. He dipped his head, and Lucavi lowered his own so their foreheads might touch. Bassar's voice softened.

"Tremble not before these uncertainties. Your legacy will echo in the histories of Everlorn as the greatest of the incarnations. Under your name, the whole of Gadir was unified. Do not falter here at the last of your steps."

Lucavi closed his eyes, and then he slid his arms around his guard. No tears for his grief, but this would suffice. He breathed out his sorrow.

Bassar was a block of muscle in his grasp, but that tension eased with each passing breath. It had been so long since Lucavi had been held. Not since Valshei burned for her transgressions against him. She had been his final consort, and Sinshei, his final child. Given the great disappointment both turned out to be, he saw no surer sign that his time of coupling and children was at its end.

So very long, but this comfort, however meager, was what he needed.

A needed comfort, Ashraleon said with such savagery it was nearly a snarl. Ashraleon the first, the progenitor, always the quickest to judge. *Be better than this, for though you are vin Ululath, you are also vin Ashraleon. I will not have my legacy diminished.*

Lucavi withdrew and stepped back. The voices of the others echoed. Drasden, Aristava, and the fourth God-Incarnate, Gaius, all chiming in with their own requests.

Be better.

Be stronger.

Be worthy of us.

"With Petrus's death, Kalath must accept greater responsibility," Lucavi said. He wiped at his tunic as if it were dirty. "He has spent much of his life spoiled, but he is Heir-Incarnate now. There is much to do to prepare him for that role."

"I thought the one who brought you the Vagrant's head would become Heir-Incarnate."

"And I will honor that promise," Lucavi said. He brushed past Bassar, who stood as perfectly still as a stone statue. "Which is why Kalath must now take up his sword."

Lucavi found Kalath where he always found him: drinking in the feasting hall. A dozen men and women accompanied him. They were young, attractive, and, based on the many spilled cups and the raucous nature of their voices, exceedingly drunk. One woman in a flimsy green Thanese dress (all light and flowing and with far too much fabric around the shoulders) sat on Kalath's lap, his hand casually draped over her breasts.

The rest surrounded him as if he were their king. Not an inappropriate level of respect, but Lucavi was in no mood for it.

"I would speak with my son," he announced. "Begone."

The crowd scattered, many tripping over themselves in their inebriation.

"I'll come for you later," Kalath told the woman on his lap. She smiled, but the way she looked fearfully to Lucavi revealed it as a lie.

"I hope so," she said, and hurried off with the rest.

Lucavi did not hide his glare. Inside, Drasden echoed his disdain.

Kalath views worldly pleasures as greater than the spiritual rewards one obtains from self-control and abstinence. Without, we are but beasts.

"Know you of your brother's fate?" Lucavi asked once all the others had left. Kalath refreshed his glass from a pitcher, slumped in his chair, and sipped at it. When Bassar circled the table to hover behind him, he pretended not to notice.

"Given your tone and demeanor, I suspect it is not a kind one."

"The foul prince Cyrus ambushed him on the road to North Cape. He is dead, Kalath. You are now the eldest born of my bloodline."

Kalath's eyebrows lifted.

"Dead? Truly? What a surprise. I thought him smarter than that."

The callous barb dropped Lucavi's jaw.

"You would insult the recently deceased?"

"This island is crawling with our soldiers. Petrus went nowhere without a paragon escort. If he's dead, then one of two possibilities remain. One, our foes are greater than we have ever faced. Quite a feat, for even gods cannot stand against us. The other option is that Petrus was a fool and got himself killed by walking into a trap."

Kalath finished the rest of his glass.

"I know which one I find more likely."

Lucavi withheld his initial reprimand. Kalath had always excelled at getting under his skin.

"With his loss, it falls to you to fulfill his duties," he said instead. "The title of Heir-Incarnate awaits you. All of Everlorn shall have need of you. In these pivotal days, you must serve the greater good, not drown yourself in wine and pleasure yourself with whatever whore is willing to cast herself atop your lap."

Kalath refilled his cup and swirled its contents.

"You do not present an attractive alternate to the wine and the whores, dear father."

Bassar smacked the cup from Kalath's hand. The scarlet liquid splashed across the blue tablecloth. Any other paragon would suffer dearly for the act, but Bassar held Lucavi's deepest trust.

"Why is it you speak with such contempt?" the divine bodyguard asked. "Your lord offers you the greatest gift imaginable, and yet you sneer?"

Kalath reached for the spilled cup, then changed his mind and slumped in his chair.

"Galvanis was meant to be god," he said. "And he was everything I am not. Petrus, as foolish as he could sometimes be, still wielded a sword like a master and knew how to command the loyalty of those around him. What am I to them? Certainly not their betters. And certainly not a god."

"I offer you eternity," Lucavi said, truly befuddled. Stubborn as his son often was, he had never spoken in such a manner.

"Am I not promised eternity when I succumb to the grave?" Kalath asked. "Besides, you offer me not an eternity, but six hundred years. I hardly want the years I currently have. An extra five hundred or so fails to appeal."

Such insolence is not worthy, Ashraleon said.

Such insolence is the arrogance of youth and the blindness of privilege, the ever-patient Drasden argued. *He never expected worship. Let him learn its taste.*

It matters not how or when he learns, Aristava said. Of all the Incarnates, Aristava was the mediator of the myriad opinions. In some ways, Lucavi felt the most kinship to Aristava, for he sought peace and understanding, whereas the others seemed to enjoy the chaos that could erupt when they argued. *Once God-Incarnate, he will have our wisdom, whether he seeks it or not. Given the worship of Everlorn, and our guidance, he will* become *worthy.*

Lucavi rubbed his eyes, and he realized that Kalath was staring at him expectantly. Did he seek a rebuttal? Or was he waiting for condemnation? Lucavi gave him neither.

"Whatever your fears, or your reluctance, you will become worthy," he said. "Set aside your addiction to worldly pleasures, take up your sword, and earn what I cannot give you."

Kalath pushed away from the table and stood. The pitcher of wine toppled, and its contents ran over the edge to drip across the floor.

"You want me hunting the Vagrant?" Kalath asked. "He who murdered my betters?"

Lucavi gave him his sincerest smile.

"If you succeed where they failed, then they were not your betters."

The faintest of smiles tugged at the corner of Kalath's lips. His bleating about being inferior to his brothers was true, but it hid a deeper desire. He wanted to be better. He just believed it impossible.

Then convince him nothing is impossible to the God-Incarnate, insisted Aristava.

He does not fear you, argued Gaius. Lucavi disliked Gaius the most. He viewed might as the solution to every problem, no matter its size or delicacy. *Convince him not of his own worth, but of the blade you hold over his neck if he continues to wallow in avarice.*

"I'll keep that in mind," Kalath said, and he dipped low in a half-hearted bow.

"Do more," Lucavi said. "Hold faith. In me. In yourself. The mantle of God-Incarnate is heavy, but it is not beyond you, my son. If you seek help, my paragons are at your disposal. The prince cannot escape you, not if you put your whole mind to the task."

With that, he dismissed his son. Kalath exited the feasting hall, leaving Lucavi alone with Bassar. His bodyguard looked at the spilled wine and shook his head in disgust.

"When the time comes, I will serve him as loyally as I have served you," he said. "But I do not look forward to the prospect."

"You speak as if I will be gone. We are one, Bassar. Should Kalath inherit us, and you speak with him, I shall hear. My words will still pass his lips."

"They may be your words, but they will come from different lips, my god. It will take time to adjust."

Lucavi waved away the concerns. His foul mood had been made no better by Kalath's indifference. Memories of Petrus mixed with those of Galvanis into a swirl that threatened to drag him down into misery. If he stayed in the castle, the present would be lost to the past, and he would drown. He had to do something to escape.

"The six-hundred-year ceremony," he said. "Are preparations ready?"

"We've been shipping wine nonstop since our arrival," Bassar answered. "And half the deliveries are already complete."

"Not the wine. The people. How prepared are their hearts?"

His bodyguard shrugged.

"I am unfit to give an answer, my god. This is a matter for Thanet's Anointed One and the church."

Except Sinshei was in Thiva, and Lucavi trusted her not at all. What faith in him existed on this island was tenuous and weak.

"Fetch me my magistrates," he said. "I am in a mood to test that faith."

An hour later, Lucavi stood upon the raised dais of the God-Incarnate's Haven, what had once been Thanet's Twin Sanctuary to their heathen gods. Soldiers guarded the entrances. Four paragons patrolled the outside. Waiting inside were twelve Thanese members of the Uplifted Church. Lucavi had requested his magistrates bring him the most faithful of their congregations. A few wore expensive, colorful clothes and flowing skirts, while others were clad little better than beggars. A fine mix. The twelve knelt with their heads bowed and had done so since he entered the sanctuary.

On a table behind Lucavi was an enormous wineskin and twelve empty cups.

"This ceremony is most holy," Lucavi said. "Everyone, leave us. Only magistrates and paragons may bear witness." He smiled at the dozen assembled before him. "And of course, you twelve, chosen for your faith. Do you feel my blessing upon you? Do you feel my love, you who have accepted my salvation and turned your backs on your heathen ways?"

The twelve mumbled and whispered their acknowledgments. None of them looked up from their prostrations. Excellent. They understood their status. Lucavi gestured to the magistrate in charge. He was a young man, his face known to him. Names were difficult for Lucavi, especially those of the living. He could not rely on the collective wisdom of his previous incarnations, but instead this aging, six-hundred-year-old flesh. But this man, he had been given an important task once, many years before...

"Castor Bouras," Lucavi said, the name finally coming to him. That's right. The magister responsible for humbling the Antiev god, Rihim. "Pour them their cups."

The red-haired man bowed low.

"I am honored," he said.

The wineskin was made of fine leather, and sewn onto its sides was the iconography of all previous God-Incarnates. Lucavi gazed upon them as Castor uncorked it. The names floated over him, warm and reaffirming. The books of Aristava. The fires of Drasden. Gaius's ax. Ululath's broken chains. Lucavi's was the newest, a white sword crowned with thorns around its hilt. There was no symbol for Ashraleon, for his praying red hands were forever the symbol of all of Everlorn.

One by one, Castor filled the cups. The scarlet liquid was a red so deep it resembled blood. It was no coincidence, but a decision made thousands of years ago. Let these heathen nations who spilled the blood of Everlorn drink of it in kind, and suffer the consequences.

Once the drinks were poured, Lucavi positioned himself beside the table and swept his arm wide.

"Come, and receive your gifts."

The twelve came forth in twos and threes, all bowing their heads. Castor handed them their cups and softly admonished them to not partake until ordered. Once they were all prepared, Lucavi approached the first, an old man with sunbaked skin.

"Drink," he ordered. The man did so eagerly, little trickles of red sneaking down his chin. Lucavi stepped to the next. "Drink. Drink."

One by one, he gave the order. Come the true ceremony, he would not be able to do so. Magistrate proxies would speak for him, diluting the power. But here, it could fall upon him—the act, and the reward.

"Not yet," he said to the last of the twelve. The woman's faith was keenest in his mind. He could see her belief like a golden mist settled across her face and chest. She held her cup, confusion on her face.

"Have I caused offense?" she asked, and her dread was true.

"No offense," he told her, and turned his gaze to the remaining eleven. All had finished their wine, and they stood holding their cups in an awkward daze. "I seek confirmation of your faith."

The first, a young man at his mother's side, began to cough. He spat a bit of bile out of his mouth. The mother reached for him, but her own movements halted as her stomach clenched, and she doubled over in pain. Others cried out pitiful groans. The oldest of them vomited, but it was not bile that trickled to the sanctuary floor, but blood.

The final woman watched them in horror. The crying intensified. The blood flowed. Lucavi towered over her, and when he spoke, the power of his voice stole her attention away.

"Look not to them," he said. "Look to me. What is your name?"

"Dasha," she answered. Her voice shook. Behind her, the last collapsed face-first into his own vomit. Lucavi brushed his fingertips across the woman's cheek. Though she trembled, her belief held strong. Her eyes did not leave his.

Faith built of sermons is a fragile faith, Drasden said, always the most studious of the lot. *But faith persevering over the evidence of one's own eyes? There is none greater.*

Lucavi enveloped her hands in his and lifted the cup to her lips.

"Drink," he ordered. "And step proudly into my paradise."

Dasha never hesitated. She drank the wine to its last drop and then lowered the cup. Her face flushed, and faith radiated off her. The first of the cramps hit. Her arms curled. Her chest hitched.

"I love you," she said, reaching out for him. Lucavi let her touch his face. He ignored the blood dripping from her fingers. Another hitch, and then she collapsed, vomiting blood. He carefully stepped aside so none touched his boots. His eyes closed. A smile crossed his lips.

"Such faith," he whispered. It floated like mist to seep into his chest, a mixture of brilliant, sparkling gold and streams of red like powdered rubies. It awakened his mind. It filled his veins with lightning.

You know but a taste, said Ululath, Lucavi's father, in the quiet darkness of his mind. *When they offer themselves to you in the thousands, it is nigh unimaginable.*

Take no pride in the sacrifice of the heathens, Ashraleon spoke. *Do not grow drunk on their ephemeral faith. This act is a necessity, the price this world must pay if its inhabitants are to know perfection.*

Lucavi knelt over Dasha's corpse. His hands cradled her head. With but a thought, shimmering gold light flowed from his hands into her. The gold rotted away at her flesh, which peeled like paper within a furnace. Her blood boiled into mist. Her bones crumbled into ash. The other eleven, they would burn on a pyre, but Dasha deserved a better fate as reward for her love. And then, come the breaking of the world and his departure from the mortal realm, he would meet her again. He would see her smile. He would hear her shout those same words to him, this time for eternity.

I love you.

"Let no evidence remain," he ordered Castor. Already he felt the jolt of energy fading from him. Despite Dasha's tremendous faith, it had been little more than a drop of oil cast into a fire. For the necessary blaze required to pass on his essence, and the essence of the Incarnates before him, it would take so much more.

Priests and magistrates rushed to gather the bodies. Lucavi watched Castor gather the cups, and his curiosity built. Yes, he had believed the young man to be one of great potential. That was why he had given him Rihim to humble, was it not? But what had happened to Rihim?

Bassar had told him, hadn't he? Yes. On the day they arrived on Thanet. He forced the fog to part within his mind, the name "Rihim" his guide stone.

"Castor," he said, gesturing to the magistrate. "Come to me."

The young man set down the cups and hurried near. He knelt with his head bowed and his face to the floor.

"Look to me, so we may speak," Lucavi said.

Castor did so, and Lucavi took a moment to admire him. He was handsome, his soft features common across much of the northwestern portions of Everlorn. His hair was neatly parted and flowed like a red river to either side of his face. His nose was sharp and tilted upward. His lips, full for a man. Lucavi reached low and put his fingers upon those lips. The warmth of his breath was pleasant.

Do not forget his failure, Ashraleon said, his voice sudden and loud like a thunderclap. *The Humbled perished.*

Lucavi jerked his hand away. Memories of Rihim came to him. The fierce panther god of hunting had been one of Lucavi's finest treasures to come from the conquering of the bothersome twin countries of Antiev and Miquo.

"Explain to me your failure," he said. "I gifted you Rihim to bring to this heathen island. In return, I come in your wake to hear of his execution."

Castor flung himself to the floor.

"Rihim was a weak and wretched thing," the magistrate said. "He mourned the loss of his wife to such an extent that it left the whole of him brittle and broken."

"But is it not the role of magistrates to make strong the brittle and the broken?" asked Lucavi. They were Drasden's words, and they came easily to him. "And so we named the Uplifted Church that all may know its divine purpose. Mankind is a wretched creature crawling in the dirt, but he must not remain there. Salvation is waiting in our praying hands. Be faithful, and be lifted."

"And I dedicate my life to that noble goal," Castor said. "But Rihim wanted nothing more than to wallow in dirt. I can break a god's pride, but I cannot put within him a desire to live. He sought death, and at the teeth of the Lioness, he found it."

The Lioness? Lucavi frowned.

"The Lioness helped slay my beloved Petrus," he said. "And she was there when Galvanis fell. She and her ilk are the greatest insults to Everlorn I have faced in my lifetime. Stand, young one, and let me look upon you."

Castor obeyed. Lucavi put his hands on the man's shoulders. Yes, this beautiful young magistrate would accomplish wonders. Lucavi had been right to see promise within him, but promise and potential were seeds not yet sprouted.

"You will find the Lioness," he said. Not a request. A statement. "As you did with Rihim, you will humble her with your scriptures and your knives. For the cost we have incurred, she will repay in glorious kind. Do you understand me, Castor? Do you hold faith?"

Tears ran down Castor's face. He reached shaking hands to touch Lucavi's own.

"I do," he promised. "Even if it takes my entire life, I shall reward your belief in me. Amends shall be made. They must be made. Let the heathens and the humbled quake at the sound of your name, for there is none greater than you, my god."

Lucavi kissed Castor's forehead. All was not lost. He still had his faithful. His youngest son lived, and even if he were half the man Galvanis had been, Kalath would have six hundred years to rise to the occasion.

"Then let it be done."

CHAPTER 11

ARN

Arn arrived at the empty boatwright's workshop, just as the message requested, to find Dario waiting for him. His brother paced the center of the shop, between the skeleton of a skiff and a smaller, more complete rowboat. He looked haggard, his eyes dark from lack of sleep.

"I'm pretty sure coming here means I am a fool," Arn said. "Did I just walk into another ambush?"

Arn expected arrogant bluster or cold indifference but received neither. To his surprise, Dario's mood was deeply melancholic.

"No Humbled lurks in the rafters, if that's what you are wondering," he said. "I only wish to talk, and I suppose I should thank you for trusting me. I would not have, after our last meeting."

Arn cracked a smile. Making light of the absurdity was the only way Arn knew to process it. Their "last meeting" had been their duel deep below Vallessau, which had nearly ended with Arn taking Dario's life before he relented at the last moment.

"No, you were quite insistent I made a mistake letting you live. I don't regret it, by the way. It is good to see you again, even if you still want me dead."

"I never wanted to kill you," Dario said simply. He shuffled his feet in place and crossed his arms. When he spoke, his words echoed in the wide building. "I always wanted to save you, Arn. Not just you.

Everyone. Even with the bloodshed and death, I saw things from a grander perspective. Was it wrong to kill one person if it saved three? Did a shorter mortal life matter in the face of eternity?"

Arn had never seen his brother so troubled. He put a hand on his shoulder. To no one's surprise, Dario shrugged it off.

"Why am I here?" he asked.

"Petrus is dead," Dario said simply. "Your work, I assume?"

Arn grinned. In less than two days, news of that victory had spread throughout the entire island of Thanet.

"Yeah, that was us. Have you come to congratulate me or condemn me?"

Dario refused to meet his eye. It was...unsettling. Arn had always viewed his older brother as a bastion of reason and certainty. When others doubted or wondered, Dario would have an answer ready. Even when facing death, he had held firm to his beliefs. What had changed? What planted that germ of doubt?

"Dario?" Arn asked as the silence dragged.

"Tell me about Velgyn," Dario said suddenly. "Her death affected you so profoundly, yet I know her only as the three-tailed beast that murdered our brethren. I saw a monster. What is it you saw?"

Arn's initial reaction was to refuse. His brother, in his cruelty, had destroyed the tip of Velgyn's tail, which Arn had kept as a charm after abandoning the Everlorn Empire. To take that last remnant and then ask for knowledge of her? Infuriating. Yet Arn saw no deceit or dishonesty in his brother's eyes. The request was genuine. He saw no regret, either, but perhaps that would come in time.

"It was hard to learn, at first," Arn said. "Our priests came and did what they always did, outlawing all tracts and discussion of the slain gods, and here I was, a foreigner from Vashlee."

It had taken months, and the spilled blood of many Everlorn soldiers and priests, to convince the hidden followers. Arn decided to skip over that part.

"Velgyn presided over the seasons," he continued. "Onleda's summers are long, their winters short, and so their miles upon miles of vineyards flourish. The wine trade has sustained their people for centuries. But one late frost? One early summer heat to shrivel up and dry the shoots? It could lead to an entire year of loss, and so Velgyn watched over them and their crops. Winter would not bite once its time was done. Summer would wait its turn. Onleda prospered, and they loved her for it."

"They loved her for giving them prosperity," Dario said. "Everlorn could give them that same prosperity, and yet they view us as the aggressor, blind to how their love of Velgyn empowered their goddess in return. It is a trade, with gain on both sides. How is she any different? How is what she offered better than the simplicity of the God-Incarnate?"

It was an argument made round and round in Everlorn's highest circles. If the gods existed to protect, bless, and guide humanity, what need was there for multiple gods? If the God-Incarnate was the strongest, the one most capable of ruling his followers, then all others were unnecessary. Let the strongest and wisest guide the world. Was it not cruel, some even argued, to allow distant children to live and worship heathen gods unworthy of their adoration?

For so very long, Arn had believed it. The lie was an easy one to swallow as he marched alongside his brother in the army of Everlorn.

"I don't know how to explain it," Arn said. "I've witnessed the worship of the faithful in their hiding places. The traditions they cling to, they are not the same as ours. Not better, not worse, but their own, and that identity gives them meaning that Everlorn could never offer."

Dario approached the shipwright's current project, a little skiff meant to carry fishermen. He brushed his fingers along its rough sides.

"And these rituals, have you participated in them yourself? Do you speak from experience?"

Arn scowled and looked away.

"No," he said. "To have slain the goddess and then participate in worship of her? A cruel jest. I watched, and I learned. I did not partake."

"Then you speak in ignorance. I should have known."

A little flutter of panic birthed in Arn's chest. No, he was losing Dario, losing him right when he was at his most open. He had to convince him, somehow, someway. Words might be his weakest weapon, but he would wield them nonetheless.

"It is not ignorance," he insisted. "It is wonder, and joy birthed over centuries. The acts and prayers are not rote. They're grounded. If you would only listen, you would understand."

"Fine. I am listening, Arn. Tell it to me."

Arn debated as memories flashed through him. There were many different prayers and rituals to Velgyn, but one in particular had left the deepest impression.

"On the night before the first day of spring, the children craft dream leaves," he began. "They take the leaves of the poplar trees that grow in their southern reaches and bind them into little balls using twine. They pray over them, together, families and friends and congregations. Come nightfall, they hold them in their hands when they sleep, careful not to crush them."

Arn emulated the act, his hands curling together to form a circle.

"I was staying with a family, and they had three boys," he continued. "With these dream leaves, you could ask for anything, anything at all, but it had to fit within the leaf. Most children asked for sweets, and sure enough, they'd wake with little cakes or honey drops inside. But the oldest son of that family, he told none of us his dream. And then that morning, he came to us, shaking. He refused to unravel the leaf until we were all present."

How to convey the moment? How did one, with mere words, tell the joy and heartbreak and love that had erupted with that unraveling?

"This was two years after Vulnae burned. The boy had lost his best friend in the slaughter, *our* slaughter. He did not dream of sweets, or a little nugget of silver to sell at the market. He wanted to see his friend again, and so...he did. When the leaf opened, a droplet of water lifted from its center. It spread, and grew. It took shape. It became him, his friend, smiling, laughing, and it spoke. He...he said he missed him, and loved him. Was waiting for him. And then the water broke in a splash, became mist, and was gone."

Something caught in Arn's throat, and he had to clear it.

"Velgyn, two years after her death, used a piece of her waning power to give a faithful child that moment. It cost her, it must have, and she gained nothing from it but the joy it delivered. And yet she did it. She gave comfort to those we brought misery."

"You expect that to impress me?" Dario asked, though his stubbornness sounded forced. "Little games and illusions?"

Arn thought of the smile on that little boy's face as he opened his leaf to discover a message from his deceased friend. And Arn remembered, so keenly, the ache in his breast at having not made a similar dream leaf. If only his shame and guilt had not paralyzed him. He would fold no leaves with hands stained with Velgyn's own blood.

"Little wonders," he shot back, furious to hear the deeply personal moment diminished to a mummer's trick. "Amid the dreary, the dull, and the tedious, even the lowest, poorest, hungriest soul might be greeted by the divine. I learned a new way to judge, Dario. A truer way, if you want to see a man's soul. Shit on legacies, wealth, and victories in wars fought by others. If we are to be judged, let us be judged by how we treat the least among us."

"The least among us?" Dario said. "Have you forgotten our purpose? We are paragons. We do not fight for ourselves. Our lives are not our own, for we are symbols of a better path. Through our faith, and our dedication, we provide a beacon to Everlorn. We are the example for all others to follow."

Arn laughed, surprised by his own bitterness.

"When a lame man asks for aid, you do not show him how to walk. *You carry him.* We paragons do not help people. That was not our training, nor our purpose. We kill. We conquer. That is our lesson for the lesser. The greatest of Everlorn are nothing more than murderers."

Dario's hesitation felt like a victory. Arn's smug confidence lasted but a breath before his brother responded.

"And who have you helped in ways other than murder?"

The retort was like a quick uppercut to the jaw that left Arn reeling.

"I protect people. It's not the same."

"Is it, though. Murder? Protection? So different, we argue, despite the corpses at both our feet. Is it all just perspective? I see horrors, and I want to scream, but a crimson color bathes all the world. With this much blood, this much death, someone here must be a monster."

There was something almost...pleading in his question that worried Arn in a way he never anticipated. It reminded him of when he was on his knees in the mud, confessing sins to Velgyn channeled through Mari.

"Who is it, then?" Dario asked. "Is it you, or is it me?"

Monsters, Velgyn had called them. Monsters, as Dario slew children fleeing the thatched hut. Monsters, as Arn crushed the goddess between his fingers. He had tried so hard to earn her redemption and had put a knife to his throat in preparation for the ultimate sacrifice. And yet Velgyn wanted none of that. She asked him to live with joy and leave his sorrow behind. His time of winter had ended.

But what of Dario? What secret guilt brought his brother here, asking for answers he would have once dismissed as heretical?

"There are monsters in this world," Arn said. "But they need not be us. Everlorn's stories of foreign gods are lies. They called them villains, and we swallowed the tale. We named them savage beasts, and we forced them to play that role when our armies came marching. But they were always so much more. They were wondrous, and beautiful. They cared, and loved, and molded their people into ways unique and different than we would ever know."

"How could you know that?" Dario asked. "You, who have seen so much less of the world than I?"

It was all because of one person. One person who had given him the courage to confront his past. The woman who understood gods better than any mortal alive.

"Please, stay with me a while longer," Arn said. "I want you to meet my friend Mari."

CHAPTER 12

MARI

Mari followed Arn through the dark streets, her nerves on edge. Something bothered him, that was for certain, yet he refused to tell her the whole truth.

Could you help me with something? he'd asked after waking her with knocks on her bedroom door. *I can't explain now, but it's important, I promise.*

She'd dressed in a hurry, guessing he had some new grim confession to share concerning his life as a paragon. It seemed the closer their hearts grew, the more fearful he was of his past.

He led her to a bricked alcove, a dead end at one of the walls that lined the eastern cliff overlooking the poorer stretches of Vallessau below. A man was waiting for her there. She didn't recognize him at first, for he lacked his armor and his gauntlets. His similarity to Arn was uncanny, though, and when he looked her up and down, judging her without speaking a word, she finally made the connection.

Mari turned to a red-faced Arn. Her voice could not have been colder if she'd tried.

"Arn. What is he doing here?"

"I'm sorry," he said. "I thought you could help."

"I sense Arn used deception to arrange this meeting," said Dario. He grinned, and it might have been charming on one so handsome if not for how ugly she knew his soul to be. "I assure you, this deception was not my idea. Apparently he thought you would refuse if you knew the truth. As for why I am here, I gave Arn a chance to explain himself and justify this heretical path he walks. In turn, he assured me that you would be far more capable in answering."

Mari grabbed Arn by the collar and yanked him so that their backs were to Dario.

"Does he know I'm the Lioness?" she whispered.

Arn's eyes widened.

"No, no, I never told him anything," he insisted. "I only said you understood gods better than I."

Mari let him go. Indecision rooted her feet to the cobbles. Part of her wanted to let Arn fix whatever mess he had landed himself in. It was a small, petty part of her, and one she rarely indulged. The temptation was strong this time. She blamed the late hour.

When she faced Dario, another part of her wanted to change into the Lioness and rip the bastard's face off. He certainly deserved it. Arn had told her of his time while imprisoned, and how Dario had charred away the Velgyn charm through the sheer heat of his faith in the God-Incarnate. Against such feverish belief, what hope was there in reaching the man?

Still, *something* had brought Dario here. To Mari's sight, which was attuned to all things divine, there was a strange aura about Dario. It differed from the obnoxious gold that coated paragons of Everlorn. Oh, that was still there with Dario, too, a second skin atop his tan flesh. But this second presence was shadowed and blue. It lurked, and she wondered if Dario even realized it was there.

Curiosity got the best of her. She put her hands on her hips and gave the paragon her best attempt at compassion.

"All right, I will listen," she said. "Tell me why Arn, in his *infinite* brilliance, brought us together."

"I already did," Arn said, voice low. He sounded like a scolded child. "To help, remember?"

"'Help' is vague," she said, challenging Dario with her gaze. "I'm here. Forget what Arn promised you. I don't care about that. I want to know what you, a paragon of Everlorn, are hoping to hear from me."

Mari knew little of Dario beyond their brief skirmishes when she was the Lioness. He was an incredible fighter, equal to his brother, but what had struck her most was his certainty. The man had walked in the light of the God-Incarnate with a belief so strong it was blinding.

"I have spent my whole life within the glory of Everlorn," said Dario. "I have seen the cities we have built, the trade we have fostered, and the grand cathedrals erected to mark our ever-growing faith. There is a cost to this, of course. I am not ignorant of that. Invasions are not clean nor kind. But Vashlee was one of the first to submit to Everlorn's spread. We did not rebel. We did not resist. And in return, our populace knows roads, bridges, bountiful harvests, and a fair share of the spoils brought by our conquests. It is a fate so many would declare a horror, and yet I see none."

Mari's jaw clenched tightly shut. She had heard a thousand variations of this speech, and it galled each and every time.

"But kingdoms war," he continued. "They did before the God-Incarnate's rise and they will continue even if the God-Incarnate were slain, so let us put that aside. It is the heathen gods that my brother insists I do not understand. He speaks of wonder and miracles, and yet to my eyes, they pale next to the glory of Everlorn. The blessings they offer are little tricks and games compared to the magnificent change we bring with our traders, builders, and teachers. What was chaotic becomes unified. Where we spoke different tongues, we now unite with one voice. Where faith was conflicted, we worship in unison. So what is it that the heathen gods can truly offer?"

The desire to unleash the Lioness manifested deep within Mari's breast, and she had to choke it down like bile. It left her throat burning and her hands clenched tightly into fists.

"You speak so much," she said. It took all her willpower to keep her voice steady. "Yet you say so little. What do you want of *me*, paragon?"

Dario shrugged.

"I want to understand why the monsters we slew on the battlefield did not deserve the fate we dealt them. I would hear the wisdom that the Uplifted Church supposedly silences. Convince me the faith I hold is wrong. Arn insists you helped him walk his new path. If it is within you, I would ask you to do the same for me, so that I may, at the least, see what this new path even is."

The shimmering blue aura around Dario floated off him like mist. Mari's rising anger granted it easy passage into her mind. It was divine, as she suspected, but not of worship and love of the God-Incarnate. This dread, this pall, was of another. It breathed into her and set her lungs aflame.

"You broke the bones of mere soldiers who could not stand against you," she said. The words spilled out of her, and she knew they were not her own. "You crushed women and children between your fingers, for they did not worship like you. You marched for a machine whose only glory is slaughter and whose only work is eternal bloodshed."

Tingles spread across her face and eyes. Her vision sharpened. Her words deepened. This lingering presence was much too weak to inhabit her as a true whispering, but enough remained to give him a voice. Doing so risked revealing herself as the Lioness, but in that moment, she could not bring herself to care. From across the eternal lands beyond, anger burst free within her breast, and at last she knew his name: Lorka, the falcon god of Onleda.

"You come now seeking wisdom from the beaten? You would walk over the bodies of the innocent and demand the *slaughtered* explain your sins? We need not justify ourselves to you. We need not debate the worth of our lives. You are the murderer. Do not come to me seeking wisdom. If you must, come pleading for forgiveness. For mercy."

Dario was a battle-worn paragon, and he did not cower before such an outburst. He stood tall and proud, hiding his true emotions. But oh, she could sense them. His fingers trembled. The muscles of his neck constricted hard enough to reveal veins. His legs rooted to the ground, braced as if anticipating a storm.

And if Lorka's presence were stronger, his life more recently lost, perhaps a storm was what she would have given him. Instead she offered words.

"Let the stars fall upon you, Dario Bastell," she said. She lifted her hands to the heavens, and she could almost feel those distant celestial orbs. Perhaps it was a trick of the light, but to her, it seemed they trembled. Oh, to be a true lord of the air and sky. How majestic had Lorka been in life? How great his wings and how beautiful his passage, if the very stars bowed to his presence?

"Let the sky swallow you. Let the darkness bury you whole and tear out your eyes with its crooked fingers. If you cannot see a truth so blinding, then you deserve to walk in emptiness."

At last, Dario showed fear.

"Lorka?" he said. "How? I was there. I saw you die."

Mari feared rage would overwhelm her, but it never did. Already the slain god was receding to the exalted lands beyond the mortal realm. Such hate and anger could not endure in that place, and she felt only its faintest traces.

"And I saw my beloved children fall by the thousands," she said, speaking the final words of the falcon god. "I heard them give up their last breaths amid the mud. You came to conquer, and my strength was not enough. How could it be, before such hate? I give you nothing, paragon, you who have taken, and taken, and taken. Life. Land. Faith. Peace. You who burn cities, deserving of nothing and yet gorging on stolen bounty."

Mari closed her eyes, and a calm settled over her.

"I fly among the stars now, and my beloved sing upon my wings. I care not if you repent. The bleak realm awaiting you, that supposed paradise of your God-Incarnate's creation, is everything, *everything*, you deserve."

The divine presence faded. The stars stilled. Arn looked shocked and uncertain, whereas Dario trembled with anger. It filled Mari with a perverse satisfaction, knowing she had denied the paragon whatever easy resolution he'd sought from her.

"I came here seeking understanding from those who believe differently than I," he said. "And yet I receive not wisdom, but condemnation. What a waste of my time."

"And what a waste of mine," Mari said. "Arn told me of how Vulnae burned. You were there when the city fell. You watched its gods be slain, Lorka the falcon, Puthora the viper, and the kind, three-tailed

Velgyn. What can I give that you do not already have? No one else can make you open your eyes, not when you alone are the one squeezing them so tightly shut."

Arn reached for his brother's arm, some sort of plea already on his lips, but Dario pulled away. His eyes were wild. His sneer was cruel.

"Blind, all three of you call me," he said. "Yet I possess wisdom you do not. This island is doomed, and damn me for considering I die with you."

The paragon stormed off in a huff. Mari glared at his back, not daring to look away. If she did, she'd see Arn, and right now she feared what she might say to him. He feared it, too, for he shifted his weight from foot to foot and struggled for an agonizingly long time before breaking the silence.

"Mari, I—"

At last she whirled to face him. Her finger jabbed at his nose.

"Next time," she said, cutting him off, "you will trust me with the truth. Is that clear?"

He withered before her stare.

"No secrets," he said. "I promise."

"Good," she said, turning for home. "Of all your promises, make sure that's the one you keep."

CHAPTER 13

SOMA

Once the city was awash in darkness, Soma left the room he pretended to sleep in and walked the ramparts surrounding the castle. When alone, it was an easy hop to the ground, and from there, he traveled east to the sea. He avoided the docks, for with all those ships, sailors, and soldiers, there would be no chance for privacy. Instead he veered north along the sand, following it until reaching the cliffs that nestled around the city.

He stepped to the sea, and the sea parted. Along that cliff, hidden beneath the waves and forgotten by those who lived in Vallessau, was a set of stairs. Regardless of the tide, the waters covered them, but those steps had not been made for the current occupants of the city. They had been made for the most faithful of the Serpent, to whom the sea would forever bow in servitude. Soma walked the steps, curled around the cliff to the opposite side, and exited upon the weathered sands there.

Now free of sight from the docks, Soma stripped off his armor. Next went his clothes. Only his spear would come with him, a reminder of the death that had nearly claimed him. He had no need for the paragon guise. Tonight, he would visit his faithful. Soma faced the moon and lifted his arms. Its light washed over him, peeling away his false human flesh to reveal the sapphire scales beneath. This mortal visage, shed as easily as his armor and clothes, had saved him during his centuries upon Gadir, but that only made him hate it all the more.

I should never have to hide, he thought. *And so very soon, I never will.*

Soma dove into the water. His legs kicked, at first separately, and then together as scales linked and split flesh became whole. Once his tail was complete, he swirled it back and forth, propelling himself much faster than any set of legs could accomplish. The water was dark and cold. The seas of Thanet, his beloved bride, stolen from him by the Lion.

Oh, how good it felt to be home.

There were many fishing hamlets lining the coast of Thanet, but it was to one in particular Soma swam. Its people were old, much older than the residents of most villages. Neighboring towns considered the people there odd, their buildings quaint and poorly kept. Traders tended to ignore the hamlet on their routes farther north to Thiva. Soma had first visited it when accompanying Galvanis on his hunt for the reborn Lycaena.

"No one goes to Whitesand if they can avoid it," one of the accompanying priests had said when he mentioned his planned detour.

"That solitude means they may hold many secrets," he'd responded. "And I would learn what they know of Thanet's gods."

When King Cleon drove Dagon's worshipers out of Vallessau, many came to Whitesand, where they could still be a short trip away from their friends and family while safely beyond the eyes of those in the Twin Sanctuary. In that little fishing hamlet, Soma found swirls cut into the baseboards of homes. Doors were marked with lines that represented the Serpent, asleep beneath the sea. Fish-scale necklaces and bracelets adorned the people. They had been wary of Soma, and his questions were met with abrupt, and often rude, answers. Though he had pretended at stoicism, inside he had been elated.

Tonight, he would reward them. The moon was full, the tide low. If they were true believers, they would come to the sea and offer their prayers while kneeling upon the sand. And they did, he knew they did, for he could feel their prayers. They settled like whispers on his mind, asking for blessings, for patience, and for him to look upon their little home with love. Some sought miracles, while others a bountiful harvest of fish when they set sail the following morning. No matter how small or grand, the requests touched his heart. If he could, he would grant each and every last one.

Soma veered eastward, out of the deep and toward the shore. There had been a time when he could have answered those prayers with ease. Altars to the Serpent had decorated nearly every seaside village. Every boat had launched with a prayer to Dagon on their sailors' lips. While Lycaena graced the land with a blanket of blooming flowers and flowing fields, Dagon had cradled Thanet within his arms, guarding that beauty from storm or hurricane. Seas calmed for captains who held firm in their faith. No children would drown or be lost to the waves if they wore one of his scales about their wrists.

The first true hurricane had come in Dagon's absence, while he lay impaled beneath the waves. Howling winds battered down homes, and the sea rose to drown whole streets. Oh, how he had felt the people's fear then. It stirred him within the depths, waking him from endless dreams.

And then Endarius's priests had twisted that fear to their own ends. *Behold the fury of the Serpent*, they had shouted to any who listened. *Behold the proof of the evil we banished. Weep for your dead, and pray for your beloved, for Dagon would drag you all to his depths to suffer.*

Dagon had claimed no such lives. He had delivered no misery or suffering while he recovered within the deep sea. But the blame had come nonetheless, perversely strengthening and changing him at the same time. Part of him embraced their hate and fear. Part of him rebelled, for he knew his true nature, even if others would deny it to further their own ends.

Soma's serpentine body brushed sand. He had arrived. The waves parted. He slithered out of the sea to the shores of Whitesand, moonlight reflecting off his glistening body. To the eyes of the gathered men and women, he knew his scales glowed a brilliant shade of blue.

"Dagon," said the eldest and closest to the water. Already tears had begun to fall from his eyes. "It is. It is you." He dropped to his knees and offered his hands. "I never thought it would be in my lifetime. Pray, lay your hands upon me. Prove to me you are real, and not the dream of a dying mind."

There were more than thirty men and women in attendance, along with a smattering of children near the back. Two men held baskets of fish, cut open and offered in sacrifice. The women held lanterns. All eyes were upon him, accompanied by gasps of shock and scattered tears. Their faith wafted off in thick waves, and Soma breathed it in greedily.

Soma put his scaled hands atop the elder's own.

"Feel my scales," he said as the elder's shaking fingers clutched him tightly. "Hear my words. I have returned to you, my faithful. My absence may have been long, but not once did you leave my heart. When you were persecuted, I wept for you. When you were hated, I bled for you. Through their hate, you endured, until this glorious hour, come at last."

He looked to his followers, such a small collection, and yet so fierce in their faith.

"I am home."

The elder backed away, tears in his eyes. The people dropped to their knees, each reacting in their own way. Some cried out his name. Others wept, a lifetime of hope and faith rewarded at last. Joy and sorrow mixed in equal measure. Their faith was like a warm wind blowing against the embers of Soma's being.

"Rise, my faithful," he said. "Rise, and know that now is the time to be strong. You are my prophets and disciples. You are my witnesses, my unerring truth. Spread word to all of Thanet. From every shore, cry out my arrival. Cry out that Dagon lives!"

Soma jabbed his spear into the sand.

"The hour has come at last. Hold faith, for Thanet shall be free, and your true god will sit upon the throne."

CHAPTER 14

STASIA

After scoring such a significant victory in killing Petrus, Stasia received the order from her father to reassess the situation on Thanet, starting with the closest thing to an army the people commanded. Two days of trekking through the Broadleaf Forest later, she and Clarissa were greeted by a surprisingly animated Commander Pilus.

"It is good to see you again," Pilus said, clasping Stasia's hands. "And to come with such triumphant news! Another child of the God-Incarnate, slain? It makes one believe our rebellion stands a chance."

Stasia slid the enormous pack off her shoulders. It hit the soft ground with a thump.

"I keep hearing Thanet is an island of miracles," she said, stretching. "I'm starting to believe it myself."

The camp wasn't much, especially compared to her previous visit with the commander. No trees were cleared, and the ground was uneven and tangled with roots. Where once tents had been in even rows, now they were scattered about wherever there was room. Smoke wafted toward the canopy from multiple fires, and the smell of roasting meat set a rumble in Stasia's belly.

"Forgive the poor conditions," Pilus said, catching her wandering eye. "This encampment is far more rudimentary than when I last played host."

"I'm used to worse," she said. "I daresay even Clarissa is learning."

"What I'm learning is that you won't let me help you even when you clearly need it," Clarissa said. "You could have let me carry my own clothes."

Her wife held no pack, all of her gear loaded into Stasia's. She'd claimed it made good training during the tedium. The real answer, which Stasia refused to give, was that she feared burdening Clarissa with any amount of baggage would slow their already glacial pace. She loved her wife to death, but she had the stride of a child...

"The Ax, taking on more than she should?" Pilus said, and he winked at Clarissa. "Heavens forfend."

"Yeah, yeah," Stasia said, pushing past the old charmer. "I smell food. Tell me you have food."

"Not as much as we'd like, but enough for all to eat," Pilus said, following. "And not that it looks like you're going to ask, but yes, you may have a share."

The food was fine, but the company finer. Stasia, Clarissa, and Pilus sat separate from the rest of the soldiers, who numbered two hundred or so by her estimation. This was at Stasia's request, for she did not want the commander to soften his answers to protect his soldiers' morale.

"At one point, I thought myself leading the beginnings of an army," Pilus said. He'd finished his little bowl of stew and sat sipping a bit of beer from a cup. "Now we find ourselves more akin to bandits, robbing only the vulnerable. Lately, that hasn't been much, either. So many soldiers came with Lucavi from the mainland." He gazed into the distance. "So many. But, if it gives you confidence, know that this is far from the total forces I have trained on Thanet."

"Where are the rest of your soldiers, then?" Stasia asked. She sat cross-legged before the campfire, enjoying the warmth on her travel-sore feet.

"Split up and on the run, mostly northwest of here, near Ialath. The empire's been hunting us with paragons, so we've had to stay on the move. Thankfully those muscle-bound warriors are not the stealthiest, and we know the land far better than their advance scouts. So far they've not ambushed us, but it is only a matter of time until we either run out of places to hide or lack the food and salt to maintain us while doing so."

Stasia rolled her empty cup between her fingers.

"My father was worried this might be the case," she said.

Pilus straightened in his seat atop the felled log.

"The losses we suffered from Jase's betrayal were tremendous, but do not question our resolve. Even now, we fight. We kill their scouts, and we ambush their patrols when the numbers are in our favor. My soldiers bear the bloody crown across their foreheads, and they give their lives to put the proper prince upon his throne."

Stasia winced at that. Clarissa noticed, and she shifted awkwardly beside her.

"Except it's not his throne," Clarissa said. "He's offered it to Keles Orani, the one they've named the Returned Queen."

Pilus finished off his beer.

"Yes, so we have heard, but most of the people here, they've been fighting for years with the Lythan name in their hearts. Learning that long-lost Cyrus is the Vagrant, as the rumors always suggested? It means a lot to them, even if Keles used to be the Light of Vallessau. Though I'll admit, taking the head of Galvanis is a bloody good start to..."

He stopped at the approach of one of his soldiers. The burly man still wore his armor and a brown cloak meant for camouflage.

"Forgive my intrusion," the man said. "But there's another transport making its way through the path."

"One of the big ones?" Pilus asked, lifting a bushy white eyebrow.

"Aye," the soldier said. "And they've a paragon escort."

Pilus thought for a moment, then gave his orders.

"Tell the others to prepare for battle, just in case."

"Find yourself a target?" Stasia asked as the soldier retreated deeper into the woodland camp. Pilus leaned forward and tapped his fingertips together. There was no hiding his excitement, nor the eagerness in his eyes.

"Ordinarily we let any imperial transport through if it is guarded by a paragon," he said. "But ordinarily, the conqueror of Fort Lionfang is not with us. Would you care to repeat your prior miracle, Ax, and lead my soldiers into battle?"

Stasia glanced at Clarissa, curious to see her wife's reaction. Their travel here had been draining, and nothing was forcing them to take this opportunity. Clarissa, however, was a picture of cold calculation.

"Every dead paragon is a significant victory," she said. "If you think you can do it, Stasia, then do it."

Stasia grabbed her axes from where she'd rested them beside her.

"I've led your soldiers once, and I'm willing to do it again," she said. "And ambushing a transport out here in the woods? Now we're fighting *my* kind of fight."

Pilus's ear-to-ear smile lasted but a moment before he turned to his camp and started issuing orders.

"Get ready to move out," he shouted to them. "We've imperials to slaughter."

Stasia clipped her axes to her belt and then dug through their belongings for her shin guards and vambraces. Clarissa kept by the fire, watching her prepare.

"Are you going to stay here?" Stasia asked, tightening the leather strip that secured the thin plate of metal over her left shin.

"I don't want to distract you while you fight," she said, crossing her arms and hunching lower. "I want to help, and yet there's not much I can do, is there? I guess I'll wait for you to return."

Stasia pulled the vambraces on, one after the other, and then clanged them together. The sound, a portent of coming battle, set her pulse to racing.

"Even here, you'll be helping," Stasia said, and she bent down to kiss her wife. "Because you'll be what I'm fighting to return to by this night's end."

Hours later, the camp feasted again, this time overwhelmed with jovial laughter and copious drinking.

"If you're going to accompany me to all these battles," said Stasia, "we should get you a sword."

Clarissa laughed at Stasia's suggestion.

"Me? A sword? Have you seen these arms?" The pair sat by a little fire on the edge of Pilus's encampment. The celebration raged behind them, a veritable feast given the supplies they'd looted. Clarissa waggled her arms as if they were thin reeds blowing in the wind. The ambush had gone swimmingly, with Stasia falling from overhanging branches to decapitate the lead paragon before he even knew a battle was to be had.

"You'd gain muscle quickly enough," Stasia said. She poked her wife's bicep. "I mean, you'd have to. Arms that skinny, any gain is inevitable."

"You're mean after a battle, you know that?"

Stasia forced herself to laugh long and loud. Painful memories from after Lord Agrito's death threatened to reawaken, and she wanted none of them.

"That just means the fight was too short," she joked. "I never got a chance to let out all my frustration."

Clarissa's turn to poke Stasia's bicep. Sarcasm dripped off her every other word.

"There must be a lot of frustration built up in there for you to be so strong. Does my lovely presence weaken you? Mayhap I should deny you my touch when I know another battle is on the horizon."

Stasia grinned at her.

"I've known soldiers who believed that denying themselves pleasure before a fight made them stronger. I've never been one of them. If I'm going to die, I'd rather have a good fuck before I hit the grave."

Cries of "Ax" from farther within the camp interrupted them, earning a roll of Stasia's eyes.

"What?" she asked, finally turning around. Two dozen men were gathered around one of the enormous casks they'd seized, still on its cart. Several laughed, and one beckoned the pair closer.

"We're cracking this thing open," shouted the soldier holding the spigot. "Only seems right you take the first swig."

"The last thing I want tonight is to get drunk with you lot," she shouted back.

Multiple men protested, but she laughed them off.

"Fine, then," the spigot holder said. "You two lovely ladies be all cuddly over there, but if you're ready to have some real fun, well, this barrel's really, really gods-damned big."

He struck it several times with a hammer, then shouted happily when the seal broke. Deep crimson liquid poured out, and soldiers thrust their mugs underneath it, catching it in splashes that only elicited further laughs.

"It's fine if you want to join them," Clarissa said. She tucked a bit of her red hair behind her left ear. "I'd hate to keep you just for my sake."

Stasia wrapped an arm around Clarissa and pulled her close.

"I've had many, many battles to get drunk after," she said. "But ones to sit and cuddle with my wife? Very few."

"You could drink while also cuddling me."

"Yes. But put some alcohol in me, I might not want to stop at cuddling."

Clarissa kissed her cheek, and the warmth was a pleasant tingle that traveled all the way down her spine.

"Gods, you're incorrigible. I may have to *force* you to celebrate with the troops, if only for some peaceful sleep."

A startled cry interrupted Stasia before she could reply. Soldiers stood around a collapsed man, all looking stunned and confused.

"Sigwulf?" one asked. "Sig...are you..."

The soldier couldn't finish his sentence. He dropped to his knees and vomited. Stasia prayed the red she saw in it was the wine and just the wine. Another man collapsed, then another. They howled in pain, some vomiting, others clutching their stomachs and gasping as if breathing were a struggle.

Stasia rushed toward them and pushed past the gathering soldiers.

"Move," she shouted. "Move!"

Yet it was over before she even reached them. Seventeen men, all dead, blood dripping from their mouths and nostrils. Their eyes stared, red and vacant.

"Make way," Pilus shouted, his authoritative voice piercing the shock. Murmurs followed as the crowd split to let him through. He stared at the bodies, quiet, his expression numb.

"What happened here?" he asked.

Stasia knelt down and lifted one of the wine cups. It took little to guess the reason, at least for the immediate deaths.

"Poison," she said, pointing to the enormous cask of wine they had opened. She fought back a shiver. They'd invited her to join in. If not for Clarissa, she might be lying dead along with them.

"A poison this quick, this lethal?" Pilus asked incredulously.

"Did...did they know we'd capture it?" one of the soldiers asked. "Was this a trap?"

Stasia shook her head. That didn't seem right. Everlorn preferred brute strength to prove their righteous superiority. Poisoning was not their style.

"Even if they'd known, this is such a strange way to strike back at us," she said. Pilus nodded in agreement. Still, no one moved to address the bodies. The sudden brutality of the deaths had everyone locked in place.

"If not to trick us, then why?" asked another.

Stasia didn't answer. She pushed through the crowd, yanked one of her axes free, and clutched it in both hands. Two good swings split the cask through the middle, spilling the remainder of the wine across the dirt. Soldiers stepped back when it splashed near their boots, as if its very touch might harm them.

"I don't know," she said, and clipped the ax back to her belt. She glanced at the bodies. "But whatever the reason, it's one most cruel. No one should die like this."

Pilus crossed his arms and tapped at his chin.

"Bury the bodies," he ordered, suddenly snapping into motion. "And do it quickly. We're moving camp."

There was little grumbling about the extra effort and travel, not after such a gloomy affair. Stasia glared at the broken cask, her mind scrambling for an explanation.

"Ax," Pilus said, his voice low as he stood at her side. "There is something you should know."

She braced herself.

"Out with it," she said.

Pilus kicked one of the cask's splintered pieces.

"We've seen numerous transports like these since the God-Incarnate arrived. Truth be told, they're a near weekly occurrence, and always heavily guarded. Because of your help, tonight's was the first we felt comfortable ambushing."

Stasia hated where this was going, and so she guessed the worst possible outcome.

"And these transports," she said. "Do they all carry casks like this one?"

Pilus's look of dread was answer enough. She stared at the bodies, bathed in crimson from the spilled wine and their own blood.

"Who are they for, Pilus? Who is all this *for*?"

CHAPTER 15

ARN

Arn walked alongside the heavy-laden cart and scratched at his face, wishing it didn't itch so much. He'd made the decision to grow out his facial hair in an attempt to disguise himself for missions like this. Ever since his capture, posters bearing his crude likeness had been nailed to signposts throughout the city. The scraggly beginnings of a beard were most unpleasant, and why Arn preferred to keep clean-shaven.

"Something wrong?" Mari asked, happily walking beside him. She wore a plain skirt and a loose shirt, the clothing cheap and light in case she needed to become the Lioness.

"It's fine," he muttered, and adjusted his wide-brimmed hat, a style popular with the local fishermen to protect them from the sun. The hat was a new purchase, and it fit so poorly that Arn swore his head must be bigger than anyone else's upon Thanet. He felt like an oaf, and his disguise probably fooled no one. "I'm just worried I'll be caught."

Mari slid her arm around his elbow and walked as if they were a couple instead of the protectors of the wagon ahead of them.

"You're a bit noticeable, true. I'd have brought Stasia if she weren't off meeting Pilus, but we make do with what we have."

"Story of my life. Everyone, settling for dumb old Arn."

He grinned to show he wasn't serious. She elbowed him anyway.

"Right now, you're my pretend husband, so pretend you're worth someone as amazing as I am. And keep your eyes forward. That wagon won't survive even a cursory inspection."

"As you insist."

There wasn't much to watch. They timed the delivery to early morning in the hopes of making their driver seem like one of dozens come to the docks to trade. If a soldier did seek an inspection, Arn and Mari were there to chase them off, at first with mere distraction, then with violence if necessary.

Arn pushed his hands into his deep pockets, feeling the openings of his gauntlets hidden there. There was no reason to suspect the delivery would go amiss, but life in Vallessau had grown steadily more difficult for Thorda's resistance. There were just so many soldiers everywhere, patrolling the streets both day and night. Even this delivery, bringing Thorda's crafted armor and weapons to a house near the docks so they might be smuggled to Pilus by boat, had everyone nervous.

The two men pulling the cart slowed, and one of them waved a signal with a flash of fingers near his waist. Soldiers up ahead. Arn quickened his pace a bit and gazed down the low decline toward the docks.

"Just four," he said.

"That's not bad."

Arn briefly hoped the soldiers would leave the cart be, but then one wearing a word-lace flagged them over. The two men halted, and they stretched their sore muscles as the soldier asked what they were transporting. Arn didn't even need to hear to know the attempts at deflection were not working.

"I think we're needed," Arn said.

Mari withdrew a tiny bottle of alcohol from one of her skirt pockets.

"How good is your acting?" she whispered as she handed it to him. Arn flicked the cork off with his thumb, splashed a bit on his hands, and then poured the rest on his tongue.

"I suppose we'll find out."

The pair passed the cart on the same side as the four soldiers, and though Mari made a show of stepping around them, Arn barreled right into the closest one. He bounced off, pretending he couldn't easily overpower the man, and instead staggered on uneven feet.

"Watch yourself," the guard shouted in Eldrid, unaware Arn could understand the foreign language. He drew his sword and pointed with it. "Fucking drunkard."

The soldier with the word-lace turned, and he readied his own sword.

"You've started drinking this early?" he asked. "Are you Thanese truly so slovenly?"

"Sorry, sorry," Arn said, taking an uneasy step back. "But that's where you're wrong. I didn't *start* drinking. I still am. It's been a night, hasn't it, uh..."

Shit. He hadn't prepared an alias for Mari. He stared at her, and his panic must have been obvious, but she smoothly stepped in.

"That's enough, you," she said, patting his chest. "Let's get you home and into a bed."

"Drunkards and whores," the first said, again in Eldrid's tongue. He shook his head. "I say we arrest them both on principle."

The second put a hand over his word-lace, which ceased the magic from functioning momentarily, not that it mattered to Arn.

"He's big, and drunk. He'll get violent. Just run a sword through him while I keep him distracted." The hand fell from the word-lace. "Woman, leave, and be thankful that I pretend to not know what you are. As for you..." Another emphatic jab with his sword toward Arn. "Stay where you are. You assaulted a soldier of Everlorn. I would have your name and place of residence."

Arn glanced at Mari, who'd also understood perfectly.

"I'll see you when you get home," she said, stepping away. Up ahead, the other two soldiers argued with the men pulling the cart. They'd been told to stall as much as possible, and if they were forced to prove their goods legitimate, two of the crates were filled with hooks and line. The men had already opened one, to the soldiers' complete dissatisfaction.

Arn slid his hands into his pockets and the gauntlets within. Well. They did need to create a distraction.

"Name's Dario," he said, figuring he might as well have fun with the matter. "Dario Digger."

"A digger, are you?" the word-lace wearer asked. "There even work in that?"

"I dig graves," Arn said, tracking the movements of the other soldier. Waiting until the man was perfectly behind him. "And there's always dead men to fill them."

Arn spun and caught the wrist of the soldier thrusting for the small of his back. A tug, and he continued the thrust onward, right into the belly of the soldier with the word-lace. Arn smashed in the head of the other with a single quick blow.

Up by the cart, the two soldiers spun and drew their weapons at the sound of battle. Arn clacked his gauntlets together, but even that was a distraction. Mari arrived as the Lioness, leaping down from the nearest rooftop with her claws out and wings slicing. The first died in a tremendous spray of blood, his armor doing little to prevent the opening of his throat and rib cage. The second tried to flee and died with Mari's teeth around the back of his neck. A shake, and his spine snapped.

The roads were quiet but not empty. Screams of surprise and horror marked the battle, and amid the sudden commotion, the two men lifted their cart and hurried toward the docks.

"Follow me," Mari said, her growl translated by her own word-lace. "I saw a patrol when I changed."

It was dangerous, for paragons might arrive at any moment, but Arn decided a second attack would better disguise the reason for the fight. He chased after Mari, the pair dashing parallel to the docks. Sure enough, a squad of six soldiers lazily marched through the street. Panic put a nice fire under their steps as Mari and Arn barreled toward them without warning. The men were outmatched and unprepared, and they died in bloody fashion. Arn followed in the Lioness's wake, tossing men aside as if they were playthings. There was hardly much for him to do, for Mari was savage in her assault, and far more reckless than he liked.

The six were dead in moments, all but one, who faced a growling Mari. His sword swipe missed as the jagged tips of her wings tore into his sides. He flailed as they lifted him up into the air. His second swing struck her shoulder, hard enough that Arn saw blood. He panicked at the sight, even though that little crimson blot was nothing compared to the terror Mari unleashed when her wings ripped the man in half.

"We're done here," she said, licking her face. "Follow."

They raced away from the gruesome scene, Arn trusting Mari to better know the streets. Thankfully it was still early, and easy enough to go unseen as they made their way east and up one of the inclines to the next rung of buildings carved into the mountains. Mari chose a gap between two homes, slipped inside, and then beckoned Arn to follow with a tilt of her head.

"Are you all right?" he asked, inspecting the hit on her shoulder. The bone plate there was scratched, and the skin along the upper side cut and bleeding. She rubbed against him before continuing deeper into the alley.

"You're cute when you're worried about me."

She suddenly halted in place. Somehow the gray of her fur paled. Her claws dug deep into the ground, cracking stone with their might as her entire body shuddered.

"Mari?" he asked. The light of her word-lace shimmered blue, translating her growl.

"I'm fine. It's fine. I'm..."

The fur receded. The bone armor dissolved away like mist, as did her wings and tail. Naked, she collapsed to her knees, and Arn immediately moved to catch her. She fell limp into his arms. Though his coat was heavy and lined with hidden chainmail, he shifted it to cover her in an attempt to preserve her modesty. She shivered against him, her face pressed to his chest. Her breathing slowed as what pain she felt eased away. The silence lingered, not entirely unwelcome.

"So," she said at last. "Did you enjoy the view?"

He gave her a squeeze.

"You scared me, Mari. Nothing to enjoy about that."

She snuggled tighter against him.

"All right, then. Maybe next time will be better."

He laughed and shifted so his back was more comfortable against the home they hid behind. The patrol had been small, and the supplies safely delivered. No reason to be in a hurry, especially if Mari needed rest. The worrisome part was that she'd never needed rest before.

"What's going on with the Lion?" he asked. "Did you do something to anger him?"

Mari's fingers traced along his ribs.

"We don't necessarily agree on much, but that's not what is happening. Faith in him is weaker than it should be. Perhaps the people here never fully embraced him, even after all these years. But I feel it also, far back in Mirli, Endarius's first home. The people there... they remember him, but only as a story. A creature who fled. They've denounced him, and the dogma of the Uplifted Church has taken hold of their hearts."

Her fingers halted. He felt her tremble.

"Imagine it. The people you once guided, who once worshiped you in return, now serving the God-Incarnate and calling you a villain."

"Then perhaps he shouldn't have left."

"And so he dies in Everlorn's invasion." She shook her head. "I won't judge him, nor second-guess his actions. All I know is that it wears away at him. He was the first to fall here, while Lycaena lived on and fought for two more years. It makes his presence here... tenuous."

Arn didn't like the sound of that. Would Endarius abandon Mari? Or would his blessing become too weak for her to do much more than become some little kitten?

"You'll be all right, won't you?" he asked. "If he leaves? If his faith dwindles?"

Mari did not reply. Her fingers resumed their travels across his chest. Despite the worry it put into his belly, he let the matter drop. He would not force the issue if she did not want to answer. This closeness was more than they'd had before, and he sat perfectly still, feeling awkward and uncertain. At last, he removed the gauntlet from his right hand and gently stroked her brown hair, enjoying the feel of it through his thick, callused fingers. Her face turned toward him, and she buried her nose against his body.

"You snuggle like a kitten," he said.

"And you're petting me like one," she said. Her fingers stopped their tracing to dig her nails momentarily into his skin. "And blame Endarius. I've spent too many years as a Lioness to avoid picking up a few habits."

He leaned his head back and stared up at the sky, content with the comfort of her presence. Little daydreams flitted through him, hopes he rarely dared entertain. What life would be like if the war were over and they could be in peace. What Mari would be like, free from the influence of any gods. What, together, they could be, and do…

"Will you ever trust me?" she asked, pulling him from his thoughts. The words, they were so soft, so frightened in their tone, he almost did not hear them.

"Of course I trust you," he said defensively.

Mari pulled back enough that she might look him in the eye.

"But you don't," she said. "When you get worried and confused, you strike out alone. You try to solve it yourself. When you lost Velgyn's pendant, Cyrus had to force you to let him come along. When you feared Dario's presence on patrols, you lied about it to my sister. And when you needed me, when you thought I could help, you didn't even ask, not if I would, not if I agreed, not if I even thought it was the right thing to do."

Arn looked away, unable to meet her gaze. What could he say to that?

"I don't…Mari, I'm sorry. I don't know what I'm doing half the time. Better to ask for forgiveness than for permission, you know?"

"No." She shook her head. "No permission, no forgiveness. I want your trust. I want your belief that somehow, in this grim world of ours, we can together make a bit of light. When you falter, you reach for me to catch you, and I will do the same. Is that so wrong of me to ask? Is that too naïve a hope?"

May all the gods damn Arn for eternity, he saw the first budding tears in her eyes.

"I am not my sister," she said. "I am not reckless with my heart. Please do not make me regret this."

Mari's eyes were more beautiful than a sunset, their red more vibrant than any rose. He never considered himself the best speaker, and words felt insufficient against such fears. Only one answer made sense to him. He bent down, slowly, carefully, ever observing her reaction. She tilted her head up to him, and his heart skipped a beat. Their lips touched, gently at first, his approach still so tentative. Mari surprised him with a sudden lunge, deepening the contact. Her hands were upon his chest, her fingernails digging into him as she closed her eyes. Arn let the kiss linger, the soft touch of her lips erasing his fears.

At last, she pulled away, and her eyelids fluttered as she caught her breath.

"You're supposed to ask first," she whispered.

"Ask before what?" he said, and grinned at her.

Mari shifted her weight until she was sitting directly atop his lap facing him. Arn fought back a groan, so very keenly aware she was naked atop him.

"You're lucky you're handsome," she said, and kissed him a second time, quicker, more eagerly. It felt like she was stealing the breath from his lungs, his heart raced so fast.

"Am I?" he asked when she pulled back again.

Mari slowly, carefully grinded against him, the rotation of her hips leaving him clenching his jaw and tilting his head backward.

"Yes," she whispered into his ear before her teeth closed around his earlobe. "For at least today, you are very, very lucky."

CHAPTER 16

KELES

Keles walked with her face covered and her eyes on the road. Her sword was hidden underneath her cloak, but she was forced to leave her striking black armor stashed at her new home. Sinshei had done her best to suppress reports of the Returned Queen, as they called her, but it was only a matter of time until the Uplifted Church heard too many rumors to dismiss them outright and she became a wanted woman.

A smile crossed her face. It would not be the first time.

Rain had fallen for much of the day, and so Vallessau had a familiar, if slightly unpleasant, smell to it. She knew it well. Wet cloth, damp wood and stone, stirred-up filth from runoff, and above it all, the scent of the sea blowing in on the wind. Beneath gray clouds, she arrived at the remains of the prison.

Why do you invite me here, Eshiel? she thought as she passed through the broken door. *Is it cruelty, or callousness?*

The squat structure was made purely of stone, all hard corners without the need or desire for a pleasant appearance. The floor of the entryway was covered with the splinters of broken tables and chairs. Three rats scoured the far corner, and they eyed her warily.

The Vagrant had done his work at some point in this prison. Past the entry were the cells. Each and every one of the doors had been broken from its hinges. No repairs had been made. It was cold and sparse and served no purpose. In time, perhaps squatters would overtake it, but for now, there were far better and more pleasant homes left empty for anyone to bother with so dismal a place.

Keles shivered as she walked past the cells. No sign of Eshiel. He'd sent a note to Thorda requesting that she meet him here just before dark, but it seemed she had arrived early. A strange mix of dread and nostalgia propelled her forward, to the final cell in the corner. Its bed was packed straw bound within a sheet. She touched the sheet. Damp. Cold. She remembered it so well. Her fingers traced a path to a little hole in the sheet, and then slipped inside.

There. Still hidden.

Keles pulled the ring free from its hiding place. It was simple enough, a thin silver band lacking any ornamentation. She lifted it up to catch what little light filtered through the thin slits of the prison windows. Carved into the ring's surface were little swirls meant to represent the wind, and dancing upon that wind was a single name: Lycaena. The night they had crowned Keles a paladin, they had given her that ring and bade her join Vallessau's war against the invaders. Oh, to have that faith again. Only sixteen, and convinced she could sway the course of an entire war.

Keles clenched the ring in her shaking fist. Her breath caught as she closed her eyes. When captured during the failed attempt to save Lycaena from execution, Keles had been brought here, to this cell, and spent a month in isolation. Her only visitors had been priests and magistrates of the Uplifted Church, come to spout their doctrine. They'd stripped her of her armor, her weapons, her symbols, even her clothes, so that she slept naked and cold.

All but this ring. She'd hidden it in her mouth during her shackled trip back into Vallessau, and then within the bed upon her arrival. This cell. This damn prison. Keles felt the walls closing in on her. The world was too dark, the light from the windows too blisteringly bright.

It was here I lost her, she thought. *It was here, right here. Not on the podium. Not before the crowds.*

Keles had no idea she was crying until the first tears slid down her cheeks. Every night, when she should have been sleeping, she had withdrawn the ring, clutched it to her chest, and prayed with all her heart to her goddess. She had begged Lycaena for comfort and warmth in the cold darkness of the cell. She had asked for guidance in the face of these trials, for wisdom to answer the questions of the Uplifted Church, and above all, for courage in the face of martyrdom.

"Every night, I sent you my prayers," Keles whispered. She forced her hand open and stared at the ring. "Did you lack the strength to answer them? Was the trauma of your execution too fresh, or did too many cry out in despair for you to hear my own?"

At the end of the month, Sinshei vin Lucavi had arrived. Her offer had been simple, and one given to all captured at the execution. Come the forsaking ceremony, all Keles must do is publicly denounce Lycaena, swearing her allegiance to the God-Incarnate, and her every crime would be forgiven. The Anointed One had been so sweet with her words, so seductive with her promises. It would be a new beginning for Thanet, and for all her people.

"Do not die for a slain god," she had said. "You need not be buried with her. Live within the new."

Keles dropped to her knees. The night after Sinshei left, Keles had spent hours pleading to Lycaena. Hours, asking one question. That was it, one simple question.

What should I do?

Despite her tears, despite her earnestness, she was given no answer. Afterward came her rage. *Would you deny me?* she had asked the silence. *Am I not worthy? Send a moth, a butterfly, a hint of fire or rainbow, anything, anything!* She was the Light of Vallessau. She had given up her childhood to learn the art of war. She had marched at the front of armies, her gleaming blade cutting soldiers in twain. Sixteen. She had been sixteen when she first killed a man. Did none of that matter? A short lifetime of sacrifices, and her reward would be silence?

Or maybe there was no reward. There was no one left to reward her. Sinshei's words were true. The goddess was dead. Before a crowd of thousands, Keles had forsaken Lycaena, but it had been here, when the light of morning shone upon her cell, that she first cast aside her faith.

Keles's old anger returned. Her hand shook as she held that ring, her mind returning to the past, remembering the isolation, the desperation, and the despair. Keles had given *everything* of herself that night in prayer.

"Why?" she asked this new silence. Lycaena was with her. Lycaena had always been with her. It was time to demand her answer. "Why did you not come to me? When I begged for you, when I pleaded for comfort, why did you not answer me?"

She stood and drew her sword. Light washed over it, proof of the goddess's power. It was with her now, but then?

"Why did you leave me?" she asked, sheer anger pushing her words through the sorrow threatening to choke them down. "Why did I suffer alone when all I needed, all I ever wanted, was a single word from you? A single whisper, to prove I wasn't alone. To prove that I was not abandoned, and a fool, and about to die for nothing."

Keles dropped both ring and sword to the stone floor. She stared at them, feeling hollow. Some queen she would be. Cyrus proudly declared her the union of Thanet's true gods, the beloved of Lycaena and the heir of the bloodline of Dagon's chosen. Yet she knew nothing of Dagon, and her love of Lycaena was tainted by this betrayal. They had turned their backs to each other, Lycaena within this cell, and her before the city at the forsaking ceremony.

"Will you not answer me even now?" she asked.

Keles grabbed her sword, and then after a moment's hesitation, she reached for the ring.

The metal dissolved at her touch. The silver ran like water across the stone, swirling and growing. Fire sparked across its surface, adding color. Red. Orange. It lifted, growing taller, molded by invisible hands. Wings spread wide. A dress flowed to every corner of the cell. Keles fell to her knees, her head bowed as she struggled for the proper words.

"My goddess," she whispered. "I do not know what to say."

The intensity of her colors paled, and yet Lycaena seemed to become more real in the process. Keles did not understand what she was, or what she had become, but she knew the goddess was here, with her, even if only in a phantom form.

Lycaena lowered herself until she was on her knees before Keles. Her wings fluttered and curled around her like a cloak.

"Do you recall my final words?" she asked.

"Of course I do. I will never forget them. Beauty in all things."

Lycaena smiled.

"Beauty, even amid despair. Beauty, even among the conquered and the broken. I saw beauty in you, Keles Orani. I saw faith so strong it could set the world aflame. And you suffered for it. You fought for it. You lived a life I would never ask of my people, and in my name, you dwelt within a cell awaiting execution. You begged to me for an answer, and so I looked into your heart. Do you know what I found?"

Keles shook her head, dreading the answer. What condemnation would the goddess offer? Somehow, she must have been found wanting. What else would explain the silence? She waited, tense, for her human frailties and faults to be laid bare.

It never came.

"I found a desire to live," Lycaena said. "How do I grant you that desire when your faith in me was so strong, and your love for me so pure? I could not order you to abandon me. I could not force you to speak a lie to be spared the noose. And so I gave you the only thing I could give you, my child. I gave you my silence."

Keles's entire body shook.

"And you think it a kindness?" she asked.

Lycaena lowered her gaze, and her phantom hands clenched.

"Do you think me blind to the suffering of my children across Thanet? Thousands fought in my name. My love led to their deaths. Do you think me immune to doubt? To sorrow? When the blade cut my throat, I almost abandoned this world entirely and passed to the eternal lands where my faithful await. I stayed, out of my love for those still struggling. I stayed, for those who held faith in me. And here you were, one whose passion was unmatched, whose trust never wavered, and you pleaded with me, your goddess, to order your death. To tell you your life was worth forfeiting. That your faith in *me* was worth dying for."

Lycaena looked up, and to Keles's shock, she realized it was the goddess who now wept silver tears.

"I wanted you to live, Keles. I wanted you to live, and know love, and experience joy. I would sacrifice all your prayers, and all my pride, to see it done. Was I wrong? Was I foolish? I do not know. You may not believe me, little one, but I was beside you in this cell. I heard your every prayer. I listened to your every cry. I watched your heart break, and with every passing second, I yearned to reach out and take your hand. I doubted, and I feared. I saw the cost of relinquished faith, and it broke me."

The goddess's image, already translucent, faded further. She wrapped her arms around Keles, and her touch was so soft, so gentle, it felt like the wind's caress. Her words quieted, and by the end, they were but a whisper.

"Turn away from me, and I shall forever love you still. If you are to grant me your faith, may it be because of that love, and nothing else."

Fire swirled around her, consuming her body and dress to leave behind only a single hovering butterfly. Keles stared at it, and in that moment, she knew Lycaena would forever have her devotion. Whatever mistakes either had made in the past, whatever choices and their dire consequences, they would together forge Thanet's future. Keles would trust in the goddess willing to confess her own doubt to the mortal woman who had so briefly abandoned her.

The butterfly shimmered and broke like embers on the wind, leaving behind only the whisper of the goddess's voice.

And now comes another whose love transcends. Heed his words, for I have shown him the truth, for which his heart was prepared.

"Keles? Keles, are you in here?"

She turned to see Eshiel Dymling finally entering the prison. He cut a handsome look in his deep red robes and tattooed head. That he'd not been arrested by Everlorn soldiers on his way over was a minor miracle in and of itself. Keles tried to remember her displeasure at the chosen meeting place, but the vision of Lycaena robbed her words of any ire.

"I am," she said. "But I would like to know why."

He didn't answer at first. His attention was on the cells, the bars, the awful beds, and the pitiful sliver of light through the windows. He had dwelt in a similar cell, she realized, and undergone a far worse fate. His body still bore the scars.

"Their true face," he said, bitterness overcoming his every word. She took a step back in shock. His rage was immense, and for the briefest moment, she feared it directed at her. "This was always their true face, and I brought you here to remind you of it. Sinshei has lied to you, Keles. She has lied to us all, playing us for fools as she orchestrates a betrayal unfathomable in its cruelty."

"I don't understand," she said. "Explain yourself."

"Lycaena has sent me dreams. They were vague at first, and what I understood, I did not wish to believe. Yet the Butterfly is unceasing, and with every passing night, they grew clearer. I relive the memory of your uncle, Rayan, in his final moments. I confront Galvanis vin Lucavi. My bones break, and his sword pierces my stomach. And then, as I lie there bleeding, Galvanis gloats over me. Our island is doomed, he vows. Not a single soul on Thanet shall survive a coming sacrifice. The entire island will be slain, to be replaced by boats full of Everlorn loyalists. No one spared. No one saved."

Keles knew she should be furious at hearing such truths, but her insides felt drained and hollow after her encounter with Lycaena. All she could muster was tired resolve. Everlorn could not be trusted. Everlorn could never be trusted. Was she truly so surprised?

"Perhaps Sinshei will prevent it if named Heir-Incarnate, or after she becomes Goddess-Incarnate?"

Eshiel shook his head.

"If that is true, then why has she not told us of this sacrifice? Why keep secrets from we who would elevate her to godhood? Whatever the answer, we cannot trust her. This offer she makes to us is a lie. Thanet will not be free. You will not be queen. Whatever throne she gives you, it will be one of bones."

Keles remembered the sense of honesty Sinshei had conveyed when telling her story of Galvanis and her mother. She remembered her insistence on making the world a better place, and how freedom and reformation would come to the people of Gadir should she become God-Incarnate.

Gadir, perhaps, but what of Thanet?

"The Lucavi bloodline is monstrous," she seethed. "I thought Sinshei free of its curse. Perhaps I was only a fool."

Before either could continue, the soft thudding of footsteps alerted them to the arrival of a third.

"Hardly where I expected your scent to lead me," said the Lioness. She walked the lone aisle between the cells, her bone wings curled tightly against her sides. She sniffed at Eshiel. "Is everything all right?"

"As well as can be hoped for," Keles said. "What brings you, Lioness?"

"We've discovered the other divine brat has been sneaking out at night. We know where, and we're going to kill him. Thorda wants you with us for the attempt. Would you join us?" She turned. "Your prayers and fire are welcome as well, Eshiel, if you have the strength for it."

Eshiel grabbed Keles by the wrist before she answered, and he pulled her close so he could whisper.

"It is a cruel jest to aid Sinshei when we are uncertain of her motives."

Keles needed only a moment's debate before she shook her head.

"Kalath's death is still a blow to Everlorn, and even more vital if we must win our freedom on our own."

"But surely we must tell..."

"When the deed is done," Keles interrupted. "I would have us first focus on the task at hand. Will you trust me, Eshiel?"

The older man bowed his head.

"Of course. My life is ever yours, Light of Vallessau."

Keles pushed past him to Mari. Given her Lioness form, her sharp ears likely overheard their conversation, but if she was curious, she gave no outward reaction. Keles was thankful for that kindness.

"How much time do we have?" she asked.

"An hour, at most."

Keles had her sword with her, but that would not be enough.

"Then let us hurry. I need my armor for the battle ahead."

CHAPTER 17

VAGRANT

From what they'd learned, the alehouse was considered one of the best in the city and, as of the past year, was frequented exclusively by imperial soldiers and tradesmen. It was also one of the few places in Vallessau still attended by night women, the priesthood turning a blind eye to the pleasure of Everlorn's faithful.

"There," Lioness said, she and Cyrus lurking on the rooftops across the street. Together they watched a man stumble out of the alehouse. He paused at the bottom of its stairs as if sick, then lifted a hand. A single finger flashed briefly before he actually did vomit. A convincing display. When the vomiting was done, the man held up three more fingers, then used them to wipe sweat from his brow. Done, he staggered away.

First floor, third door. That was where they'd find Kalath.

"According to Sinshei, he's supposed to be hunting me," Cyrus told Mari as he summoned his skull face and felt the cool silver of the crown about his brow. "I think he's about to be more successful than he hoped."

Mari winked, an amusing sight given her current form.

"I'll make sure you get the killing blow. I'd hate to steal your fun."

Signal given, Cyrus waited for the next phase of the plan. Given Kalath's apparent desire to sneak away instead of performing his God-Incarnate-given duties, his retinue was light. Six soldiers had accompanied him to the alehouse, along with three paragons. One of those paragons was outside keeping watch. The other two were inside, presumably guarding Kalath's room.

Step one was getting the outside paragon's attention. For that, Thorda had called in one of the cells still positioned within Vallessau, organized before Jase's disastrous treachery.

Halfway down the street, the first fire burst into life. Twelve men, all wearing black masks and red crowns painted on their foreheads, tossed torches and bottles of alcohol through the windows of a building. They moved quickly, hitting the second. The nearby alehouse wasn't meant to be a target, just close enough that the paragon on watch would see and intervene.

"Sargon, Themis, get out here," the paragon shouted, banging on the door of the alehouse before pulling a gigantic ax off his back. He gave chase without waiting, bounding down the street after the arsonists, who fled at his approach. Little did the paragon know Heretic lurked in waiting. Between the advantage of surprise and the twelve friendly soldiers, Cyrus trusted Arn to handle that fight.

The other two paragons emerged. Before they could follow the first, a voice called out to them from the opposite end of the street.

"A strange place to find loyal paragons of Everlorn," Eshiel shouted, fire enveloping his hands. "But I suppose it will make it easy to celebrate your demise."

Keles kept hidden in the alley beside Eshiel, preparing her own ambush along with soldiers and Eshiel's faithful. When the paragons attacked, they would find themselves immediately outnumbered. It would be a brutal fight, but Cyrus put his trust in them. He had to, if they were to attack Kalath.

The two charged Eshiel with weapons drawn, eager to claim the head of the troublesome priest. Cyrus couldn't help but grin. Ah, paragons, ever reliable in their zeal.

"Our turn," Cyrus said, rising to his feet. "Stay sharp. I don't know how strong Kalath will be, but if he's anything like his brother, it'll be a tough fight in close quarters."

"My claws work just as well in close quarters as they do on a battlefield."

Cyrus hit the ground running, the fall not even jarring his knees. He crossed the street in an instant, never slowing when he hit the door.

It shattered before his might. Screams followed, confused shouts from soldiers deep in their cups. Cyrus assessed the situation in the blink of an eye, noting the locations of soldiers, their tables, and who else among them was likely an innocent visitor to the establishment.

And then he went to work.

Soldiers died without a chance to raise their swords. He dashed from table to table, dancing atop them in a flurry of steel and cloaks. More screams joined the first as blood sprayed across the floor and stained the clothes of the servers there. Only two escaped his initial wrath, but their foolish attempts to flee were halted by the Lioness's arrival. Her jagged wings cut their throats, killing them mere feet from the door.

"After me," he called to her, dashing through the exit of the commons and around the corner to the hallway containing the bedrooms. The third door was his destination, and it seemed the noise of battle had alerted those within. A frightened woman with a ruffled dress exited, and she startled at the sight of him.

"Please don't kill me," she said, her eyes widening. "We can't refuse, you know that, we can never refuse."

"Go home, woman," Mari said, padding around the corner. "You need not witness this bloodshed."

Her eyes flicked between the two.

"Thank you," she said, and then fled past them. Cyrus positioned himself before the closed door. Surprise was lost. Time to take this carefully.

"You ready?" he asked Mari. She stood aside. At her nod, he kicked the door open and dashed inside with weapons up to block an attack that never came.

The room was enormous and must cost a small fortune to rent each night. Kalath leaned shirtless against the back wall, looking like a softer, more handsome version of his older brothers. He wore no armor, just a pair of dark trousers. His only weapon was a spear, which leaned against the wall beside him.

"The Vagrant, I presume?" he said. "My father would have me hunt you. For the supposed wisest being alive, he is often a damn fool. It's enough to shake one's faith, wouldn't you agree?"

Cyrus slowly approached, his weapons up and ready. Petrus had been a beast of a man, all too happy to use his superior strength to his advantage. This son, however, was different. Too amused. Too… unimpressed.

"It seems you have a decent head atop your shoulders," Cyrus said. "A shame I'll have to remove it."

Kalath flipped his spear once and then jammed the butt into the ground. His smug grin faltered for only a moment.

"I know. Come do it, Vagrant. I will not fight you."

Cyrus paused.

"Careful, Vagrant," Mari whispered beside him.

"If you think a trick will save you, you are wrong," Cyrus said, thinking the same. To his surprise, Kalath laughed.

"You are the slayers of Galvanis and Petrus. I am no fool. They were both far superior to me in battle. My only hope is my bodyguards, and I suspect they are already dead. But even if I could defeat you…" He shook his head. "I do not want the reward it would earn me."

That surprised Cyrus. He had assumed Sinshei the only child willing to turn against the father, but if Kalath did not wish to become God-Incarnate, then perhaps Everlorn's ranks were more traitorous than anticipated…

"It is a strange man who would refuse godhood," Cyrus said, careful to keep his weapons raised.

"Perhaps you think it strange, given you have accepted the same gift, but I grew up in Lucavi's shadow. I have seen what it did to him. What it *still* does to him."

Mari paced a circle around Cyrus, her wings tucked tightly against her body.

"What are you doing?" she whispered, her low growl helpfully translated by her word-lace. "Kill him."

"I have to know," he whispered back. "What if we can secure another ally?"

Mari snorted, her opinion so obvious the word-lace did not bother to translate. She repositioned herself behind him, her red eyes glaring daggers Kalath's way.

"If you refuse the God-Incarnate's gift, then perhaps I have no need to kill you," Cyrus said, testing the waters.

"Father doesn't tolerate failures," Kalath said, and he shrugged. "Oh, perhaps he'll forgive me. You did slay Galvanis and Petrus, after all. But he has never considered me worthy of his power, and if I do not bring him your head, I suspect it will be my own that is forfeit. No, it is death or godhood, and I'd rather have death."

Death over becoming God-Incarnate of Everlorn? Cyrus tried to imagine what it would be like to have that kind of power offered to him, and then refuse. It would take tremendous willpower, perhaps even more than he possessed. Kalath certainly didn't seem like the noble sort, and the stories that made their way out of the castle painted him as a lecher.

"Why would you deny him so?" he asked, genuinely curious. "What is it that disturbs you so greatly?"

Kalath lifted his spear a bit and jammed the butt back down, cracking a deeper hole into the floorboards.

"You haven't seen it," he said, looking away. "It hollows him. The other God-Incarnates reside within his mind, and they never cease enforcing their will. My desires? They won't matter. I could fight them, but would I win? Could I win, if every day of my life, six former gods whisper their disdain? I would not be a god. I would be a puppet, held up by six hands, and I refuse, Vagrant. What little pride I have will not accept that travesty."

Cyrus glanced back at Mari, dying to have a moment to discuss this with her. What would it be like to have not one voice, but multiple, all with their own histories and beliefs regarding the purpose and shape of the Everlorn Empire?

Nightmarish, Cyrus suspected. Perhaps Kalath was not so strange to refuse, after all.

"If you find Lucavi as monstrous as we do, then come with us," he said. "Join us, and help us overthrow your father and put an end to the line of God-Incarnates."

"Do not mistake me," Kalath said. A grin spread wide across his lips. "You slew my brothers, who, if alive, would have spared me the curse of godhood. I could have lived many more happy years in their shadow, but instead my father's eyes are upon me, and he will not accept failure. I die to him, or I die to you. I consider neither of you my friends."

So much for obtaining another ally. Cyrus readied his Endarius blade for a thrust.

"Then I will give you the quicker, painless death," he said. "Close your eyes, and lift your head."

Kalath obeyed. He stood there, proud, and with spear in hand.

"I cannot kill you, Vagrant," he said, his eyes still closed. "That, I know."

He exploded into motion, a predictable betrayal. Cyrus's swords were already up, ready for the thrust, but it never came. Kalath flung his spear with the strength of paragons. Not at Cyrus, but past him. The Lioness.

Mari screamed as the spear pierced her ribs. Cyrus saw red. His fury was all-encompassing. His swords pressed together to pierce Kalath's abdomen. A twist, and he ripped the swords out to either side to empty the man's guts. This would be a painful death, slow and agonizing. The bastard deserved no better.

Kalath collapsed to his knees, entrails spilling out. Yet despite the pain, he laughed.

"Can't kill you," he said, his skin losing color as his breathing turned rapid. "But I can... I can... hurt... you."

Enough. Cyrus cut out his throat with the Butterfly blade, then zipped it back in the other direction to carve a bloody crown upon his forehead before his body collapsed completely.

"That you are his child is proof of your damned god's wretchedness." He banished his skull face, spat on the corpse, and then summoned it anew. Finished, he turned about, immediately relieved to see Mari had pulled the spear free with her teeth and dropped it to the ground. Blood dripped along her side, but he'd seen her survive worse.

"I'm sorry," he said, approaching her. "You were right. I never should have listened to..."

Her eyes were glazed over. Her legs trembled beneath her. The blood, there was more than he realized, so much more.

"Mari?"

The Lioness collapsed, her fangs dulling, her claws retracting, her fur receding. Cyrus's every thought ceased as he caught her limp body. The wound in her side still bled. It hadn't healed. Why hadn't it healed?

"Mari," he said, unable to fight off his growing panic. "Mari! Mari, please, wake up."

But she could not hear him. Her eyes had rolled back into her head, and from her pale lips, he heard the first whisperings of a prayer. She no longer occupied the physical world.

The land of the divine had come to claim her.

CHAPTER 18

MARI

Mari was intimately familiar with this dark place, and yet she shivered with fear all the same. There was no sky above, only darkness. There was no floor below her, only emptiness. Whatever invisible surface she knelt upon, it was cold and firm like stone. This was the realm of gods.

"You are bleeding."

Endarius's voice rolled over her like thunder. She met his overwhelming presence. Unlike the smaller gray bone form she took, here in this place, the Lion shone with all his former glory. His fur was the golden hue of wheat. His feathery mane rippled with a rainbow of colors from an unknown wind. To even meet his gaze now took great effort, even greater than during her first encounter with him, where she pleaded for his aid.

Then, he had been full of rage and pride at a mere mortal offering such a contract. This time, she saw only disappointment and surrender.

"Better I bleed than your followers," Mari said. She touched her side and felt it wet and sticky. The wounds she suffered when transformed healed when she returned to her mortal human body, but here in this place they formed true upon her naked figure.

"But it is not you who bleeds," Endarius said. "It is I."

A flash like thunder, and the Lion's body changed. His wings snapped. His fur peeled back. Blood splashed across his fur as each and every wound

Mari had suffered as the Lioness inflicted itself upon the dead god's form. Her heart ached at the sight. Each one was an error on her part, a dodge too slow, an attack against her made unseen. Some she remembered, such as the broken wing suffered when fighting the Humbled known as Rihim. Most others were a blurred history of nearly four years of struggle.

"Would you not endure them if you lived?" Mari asked. She stood and tilted her chin. "I give you the chance to do as you would. I let you fight. I let you rage. Is that not enough?"

Before the Lion spoke, she knew the answer. This always happened in every conquered land. The reasons changed, but never the end result.

"Not yet a decade passed, and yet I feel the prayers of my followers dwindling like a fading storm," he said. The wounds he suffered as part of their communion faded away, hidden once more behind a visage of beautiful glory. "My paladins are slain. My priests are few, and they hide, scattered and afraid. Even my faithful, my few remaining followers, have turned their hearts to others. Out of fear. Out of ignorance. They pray to the Butterfly, or the God-Incarnate of Everlorn. Not to the Lion. Not to me."

Mari stood with her fists clenched at her sides. She knew where this was headed, but she had to stop it; somehow, she must *stop* it.

"Such self-pity is unbecoming of the Lion I know," she told him.

The darkness shifted red as Endarius roared. There! There was the rage that had fueled him after his death, only it did not last. The crimson eternal turned dark. The roar did not even echo.

"Spare me your ignorance," he said. The light left his eyes. His gold fur paled. "The end of a brief mortal life is swift. Your souls flee your flesh with such haste, you are but stars falling upward to the sky. You lack understanding. You lack choice. It is a fitting end for the confused, frail creatures that you are."

He stepped closer. The wounds she had suffered returned to his body, freshly weeping.

"But you are not gods. I am. I linger. I listen to the prayers, and I drown in their sorrow. For a time, it was enough. But how could you fathom the pull of the hereafter? I feel it, little Miquoan woman. It is a hook in my flesh. It is a rope tied about my throat. A few hundred offer me their prayers upon Thanet, and yet in the paradise I have prepared, thousands upon thousands call eagerly for my arrival. They shout my name with joy instead of mumbling it in fear. To remain here is a burden, and to give you my strength, a tribulation I will suffer no longer."

"Please," Mari said. "Don't do this."

The Lion looked over his shoulder to the endless horizon.

"You don't know. You don't see."

But Endarius was wrong. She did see. For a full second the darkness parted to reveal rolling fields of grass. She saw scattered trees, their trunks curved and winding heavenward, their bark so dark it was nearly black. An endless number of oases blossomed amid the grass. And everywhere, everywhere, there were people. They strolled the lands, laughing, singing, and holding hands. Some were young, still children, others old with gray in their hair.

The joy of it escaped that vision like a wind, and as it flowed across her, Mari's eyes swelled with tears. There was such peace in that place. Such bliss. With each god she whispered it was the same, always the same. Who would choose to remain in this broken world when that realm awaited?

Mari would. She always did. And this time, she would demand the same of Endarius.

"No."

The Lion's mane bristled. His attention returned, and his eyes narrowed.

"Do my ears deceive me? Who are you to protest?"

Mari mustered all her willpower to remain calm before that growing rage. If only she could awaken it further...

"We made a pact," she said. "Together we would save Thanet. We would take our revenge against Everlorn. Do you already surrender? Was your rage truly so shallow?"

Stars burst across the darkness. In all directions, the horizon shone with a piercing light like a blue sun rising.

"Despite my misgivings, I gave myself to you," Endarius roared. "And yet what do I see? My faithful dead. My island conquered. Nothing is changed. No one is freed. I am forgotten. You have inspired no faith. You have given no remembrance. The blood on my tongue does not sate, Mari Ahlai. It is bitter, and I want it not. Let me go to the paradise of my faithful. It is there I shall greet my remaining worshipers, and welcome them with open wings and a joyful sound."

Mari couldn't stop her growing panic. If she lost Endarius now, then what use would she be to the rest? Without his strength, she could not fight. She could not kill.

"No," she repeated. The connection between her and the Lion was like a rope, and she grabbed it in her mind. "I won't stand idly by while my friends and family bleed for your island. I won't relinquish you when there is so much left to be done. I don't care how badly I fail. I don't care what wounds I suffer, or what mistakes I make. I will fight, Endarius. I will fight for those I love, for those who are strangers, for anyone, everyone, just to make this suffering stop. So we might finally know peace!"

Endarius closed the space between them. His claws pierced the ground as if it were glass. The cracks spiraled outward for thousands of miles, as if all existence were a mirror, and he, its destroyer. Their eyes met, and she felt him pull against her in turn. Withdrawing his power. Revoking the communion. She expected rage, and she saw it at first, but it did not last. Pity replaced it, and that was so much worse.

"Yes," said the Lion. "You will fight. As a woman. As a human. Naught else. You are the Lioness no more."

And then the darkness shattered. The connection between her and Endarius severed clean, and in its wake she felt fire burn through her body. Her vision turned white. Her ears filled with the noise of rushing water. The Lion bounded away, to a splitting horizon that promised a paradise the mortal world could never know.

Amid it all, she screamed and screamed, a protest that meant nothing, stopped nothing. A lone word on her lips, howling as she was robbed of her feral strength.

No.

No.

No.

The Lioness no more.

No.

CHAPTER 19

VAGRANT

Cyrus knelt over Mari, hating himself. Hating his swords. Hating his shadows. Hating the Vagrant because for all its power, it was useless here.

"Mari," he whispered, cradling her head in his lap. Her whole body shivered, and her fever was terrifyingly hot. He'd covered her nakedness with his cloak and pressed his left hand against the spear wound. Slaughtered Kalath lay nearby, the blood of the God-Incarnate's son spilled to the alehouse floor, yet that meant nothing to whatever illness gripped the younger Ahlai sister. Over and over she whispered a single word, whose meaning he could only guess. She spoke as if trapped within a dream, and it took all her willpower to force out that lone syllable.

"No. No. No."

"Whatever you're fighting, keep fighting," Cyrus said. "You're strong enough, Mari, I know you are."

Regret bunched in Cyrus's chest. If only the Vagrant were more than a murderer. Thorda had created him to take life, not save it. If only...

Cyrus's thoughts were broken by the door opening.

"All guards are gone," Arn said, stepping side. Behind him were some of Pilus's soldiers, scouring the alehouse for survivors. "Is Kalath dead or...Mari?"

Not Lioness. Mari. Perhaps the breaking of protocol endangered Mari, but Cyrus did not have it in his heart to be angry. How could he, when the anguish in Arn's voice was so visceral? Arn rushed over, then slid to a stop. He stared down, hands flexing, arms shaking.

"What happened?" he asked. "Why isn't she fine? She's always been fine."

"She was stabbed," Cyrus said.

"So what? She's been stabbed before. The wounds, they go away when she transforms back." Arn swallowed. "Don't they?"

Cyrus lifted his hand to show him the blood. It was the only answer he knew to give. Arn paled at the sight, and his eyes widened.

"A healer," he shouted. The word-lace around his neck flared with blue light to project his translated voice. "A healer, is there a healer here, a surgeon, a witch doctor, whatever you people call them?"

"Calm yourself," Cyrus hissed. Soldiers gathered near the door, and he feared they might see Mari's face.

"You have no need for one," a woman said, stepping through the door. "I am here."

Cyrus's mouth dropped open. It was the raven-haired woman from before. He'd not anticipated ever seeing her again. The paint was gone from her face, but instead of a plain outfit and bare feet, she wore a startlingly blue dress that reminded him of those his mother wore to state gatherings. Here in this blood-soaked alehouse, her fine beauty seemed all the stranger. She moved with purpose, neither asking for nor needing permission to carefully sit beside Mari.

"What are you doing here?" Cyrus asked. Something was amiss with this woman. She ignored his question completely.

"Disperse them," the nameless woman said, gesturing at the soldiers outside. "I would work in silence."

"Work?" Arn asked. "So you can help her?"

She nodded, and that was enough for Arn. He bellowed at everyone to move their asses, clapping his gauntlets together for emphasis. Meanwhile, the woman casually lifted Cyrus's hand so she might look at the wound.

"Deep, but not fatal," she said.

"I don't think the wound is the true problem," Cyrus said, debating how to even begin explaining the nature of Mari's gifts as a god-whisperer.

"No," the woman said. "It is the god leaving her. Mortal flesh struggles to part with the divine once it has felt its blessed touch."

Cyrus's mouth dropped open. How could this woman possibly know that? Just who was she? Her hands pressed against Mari's side, and she bowed her head.

"Rest, and know peace," this stranger said. "You are deserving."

The wound closed. There was no light, no divine spark, just a closed, scarred strip of flesh where there was once blood and gore. Arn gasped, and Cyrus sucked in a hiss of air. Relief warred with confusion as the woman leaned back and made washing motions with her hands. Mari's blood caked, dried, and fell off like dust.

"The physical aspect will cause her to suffer no longer," she said. "As for the withdrawal of her divinity, that will take time. I've comforted her as best I can, and subdued her fever. The rest must be done through her own strength."

"Then she'll be fine," Arn said. "Mari's the strongest person we know."

"Aye, the Lioness is," Cyrus said, frustrated that Arn now twice revealed Mari's identity yet sympathetic to the error. He couldn't shake that moment when Mari transitioned back into her physical body. The way she had screamed…

"Who are you?" he asked, withdrawing from the painful memory.

The woman leaned back on her haunches, met his eyes, and smiled. That smile nearly broke Cyrus. Wave after wave of sorrow and exhaustion struck him square in the chest. He felt the weight of years, no, *centuries* crash down upon his spine. Her gaze was a vortex, and it pulled him into her, threatening to drown him. He saw vile acts flicker like embers within the darkness, innumerable horrors committed upon countless women, gathering and gathering until they became this raging inferno.

Before she even spoke, Cyrus knew she was not human. It felt like she had dropped a veil, and now her divinity rolled out from her with undeniable power.

"No one," she answered. "And yet far too many."

Cyrus stood, carrying Mari easily in his arms despite her weight. It was a feat he'd have struggled with a year prior, but the Vagrant was now known for his strength.

"You have my thanks, unknown goddess."

Again that smile, tired and guarded and beautiful.

"There you are," Keles said, she and Eshiel arriving together. She startled the moment she saw the nameless woman.

"Nora?" she asked, her eyes widening. Cyrus glanced over at her.

"Nora?" he repeated.

"A false name, yet true at the time," the strange goddess said. "I have spoken with many of you before today, taking your measure."

"Not sure I like the idea of being judged," Arn interrupted, and he reached out. The pain in the bigger man's gaze was enough for Cyrus to relent. He handed Mari over, letting Arn cradle her against his chest.

"I come not to judge but to give answers," she said. She brushed her hand through her raven hair. "About the truth of this island, and the God-Incarnate's desires for it."

Arn and Cyrus shared a look.

"She helped Mari," Arn said, and shrugged. "That's enough for me to trust her."

When Keles showed no objection, either, Cyrus relented.

"Very well. Come with us. We need to get Mari home, and once we do, you can spill your secrets."

No smile, but there was a twinkle of amusement in her dark eyes.

"Careful with secrets, Vagrant. Carry too many, and you will break beneath the weight of truth denied."

An hour later, the entire group gathered in Thorda's lounge. The nameless woman had said not a word the entire trip. Stasia and Clarissa had returned during Kalath's ambush, which was a welcome surprise. Cyrus had not known what to expect when Arn arrived carrying Mari in his arms, and was struck by the tenderness Thorda displayed.

"Take her to her room," he had said. "I will prepare her some soup. Fear not, Arn. She has endured this before, and she will do so again."

It was nice to see the man still had a heart somewhere buried beneath the stone. None of that was visible now as they sat in chairs and on couches surrounding the nameless woman. Thorda had not asked her name, or why she had come. It seemed he had sensed her divinity the moment she stepped through the door.

"I know you are eager for my answers," she said, turning to address them all. "But I am not the only one come to speak. Eshiel? Stasia? You bear pieces of my truth. Please. Share them."

The two exchanged glances.

"I suppose I shall start," Eshiel said. "My dreams have been troubled with visions, visions sent to me by Lycaena. They are many, some kind, some cruel, but the most troubling, and most common, is where I relive Rayan Vayisa's final moments."

Cyrus winced at the image the name conjured, that of his confused friend bleeding in Keles's arms.

"At some point, the God-Incarnate plans to sacrifice the entire island," Eshiel continued. "Every last native man, woman, and child will die in his name."

Cyrus's entire mind blanked. It couldn't be true. Lucavi wanted to convert the people. He didn't want them slaughtered. To murder thousands upon thousands, after all this time and effort...

"That fucking bastard," Stasia said, breaking the silence. "When we ambushed Everlorn's supply train, we found an enormous cask of wine. Our fighters cracked it open to celebrate, but the people who drank it?" She shook her head. "They were poisoned to death. And according to Pilus, that cask was but one of many that have shipped out from Vallessau since Lucavi's arrival."

"They're going to force people to drink it?" Arn asked.

"Or have them drink it willingly," Thorda said, his tone dark. "An act of faith. The culmination of a culture steeped in conquest and sacrifice."

Rage replaced the blankness in Cyrus's mind. Such a monstrous crime could not be allowed.

"This is madness," he seethed aloud. "Is subjugating us not enough? Why a slaughter?"

The nameless woman paced the room and stopped in front of Thorda's chair beside the roaring fireplace.

"Know you who I am?" she asked him.

Thorda stared at her for an uncomfortably long time.

"You have many names," he said at last. "But Everlorn's faithful call you the Nameless Whore, the deceitful wife of the first Incarnate, Ashraleon."

Cyrus lowered his gaze to hide his surprise. He knew little of the Nameless Whore beyond the occasional curse or sermon from Everlorn's preachers. She was the supposed master of the hell created by the God-Incarnate to punish all who refused to grant him their faith.

"Nameless She?" Stasia said, rocking backward in her seat. "It's... it's you? Here? You're real?"

"I am real in many ways," She said. "I am the culmination of so very many beliefs, conflicting as they are. If you do not believe me, then tell me, Stasia, what color is my hair?"

"Brown," Stasia said after a pause. "Am I wrong?"

"I see red," Arn offered.

"Black," Cyrus said. "You appear as we expect you to appear, don't you, Nameless one? Beautiful and mysterious. I suspect none of us see the same eyes, nor the same face."

The woman smiled his way, and for once it did not threaten to break him with its exhaustion.

"You are learning," She said. "But regardless of what I have become, I was indeed the wife of Ashraleon, or at the least, I bear her memories. I know the truth of the God-Incarnate's creation, for I alone still live to remember it."

CHAPTER 20

SHE

Nameless She looked upon this gathered group, each and every one of them a hero in their own right. The Vagrant, She knew only by story, and had sought him out for that reason. Eshiel wielded faith as fierce as any man or woman alive. Arn was a former paragon, and She knew the incredible strength required to abandon Everlorn. Stasia and Thorda Ahlai were strangers to her, as was the daughter asleep down the hall. She knew them well, though, oh so well. She had walked the lands of the recently conquered many times. She knew their handiwork. Hope wrapped in a bloody blade. It never worked, but not for lack of trying.

Everlorn was just too great a monster.

"I do not know if I am the real woman once married to Ashraleon, or if I am the collective of the prayers and beliefs formed by the Uplifted Church," She said. "I remember little of the years immediately after the God-Incarnate's creation. Who I am now, and what I have become... that began several hundred years after. That is when my walk began."

She slowly turned, taking the measure of her audience. They did not trust her, but they *wanted* to trust her. Killing the sons had instilled hope within them, but now they knew the true scope of the pending nightmare.

"The story of Everlorn's founding spread by the Uplifted Church bears some truth to it. Eldrid was invaded, yes, but that invasion was in retaliation for Ashraleon's war. When our defeated armies returned to Eldrid to lick our wounds, our vengeful foes gave chase."

She could still see the returning parade in her mind's eye. The people of Eldrid had lined the streets to support their soldiers, but it had been a cold day, the cobblestones swept with snow. There had been no joy in the cheers. Some even cried out in anger. The faces of the soldiers told the true story. They were ragged beneath their white armor. Blood and dirt stained their pristine cloaks. Even their horses seemed to walk with heads hung low. They had numbered less than a third of what they had been when they proudly marched out at the start of the war.

"We were a small nation, overlooked and deep in the north. We worshiped no gods. Why, I cannot say, but I believe we were cast out from an even older nation lost to time. So when our home was invaded, we had none to turn to but our king. And Ashraleon, well..."

She closed her eyes, remembering the man he had been before the prayers and sacrifice. Nothing of her life prior to her betrothal remained to her, no names, no faces of her family. Had She been betrothed from the day of her birth? Arranged by her parents as a child? Had She come from a noble family, or had She been of a lower class and swept up into Ashraleon's arms? Only guesswork remained, and She had long tired of the attempts. None of it mattered. Only what came after.

"People loved Ashraleon," She said. "He was handsome and wealthy, but that wasn't all. He moved through life as if he was owed the world. At the games of politics, none could challenge him within our court. He poured our treasury into building an army, and his first campaigns knew only victories. They were but a taste of his true dream, one I believe was sincere. Everlorn would become mighty, and his name forever remembered."

She let herself fall back into the pieces that remained of her marriage within her fragmented mind. A great ruler needed a perfect bride, of that She was certain. Her beauty had impressed. Her grace and elegance were sufficient. But had he loved her? She didn't know. The stories the Uplifted Church told claimed Ashraleon had loved her deeply, but in her heart, She felt only coldness, and in her memories, an impenetrable distance.

"So the bastard's been wanting to conquer Gadir from the very beginning," Arn said when her silence ran long. "But you're making it sound like he was just... you know... human. A king, like any other."

Finally, She opened her eyes and gestured to Vagrant.

"Do you find it odd that a human might become a god, when the evidence of its possibility sits among us?"

The young prince's entire body locked still. His face... for the briefest moment, she saw his true face. The skull flashed across his features, and though it grinned, she sensed its seething rage.

"I do not appreciate the comparison," he said. "I have become what I must to save my people. Or will you claim Ashraleon did the same?"

She laughed, and the way everyone recoiled only deepened her amusement.

"Save them?" She said. "No, prince, my former husband did not seek to save them. Ashraleon believed himself infallible. He thought fate promised him an empire. That he failed to conquer our neighbor broke him. Enemy soldiers marched for his head, and it terrified him. He was a man, yes, but he was also king, and young, and convinced that death was a thing that came for others, not himself. To lose it all was inconceivable, and so he ordered preparations made. Eldrid would not be taken from him. It would be sacrificed."

"The poisoned wine," Stasia said. Her fingers drummed her thighs. Her face had gone pale. "It was used from the very beginning, wasn't it?"

Nameless She nodded.

"He kept it quiet, the preparations handled only by his most fanatical followers. He stoked hatred of our neighbors to justify it. Too many would rather die than be punished for their crimes, and they cared not if others must die with them. But when I learned..."

Most of her memories from that era were hazy, but not this one. This betrayal was her one act that had scarred deep, carving itself upon the very psyche of Everlorn. The God-Incarnate, no matter his name, would never forget, nor would he ever forgive.

"The entire castle was locked down, and I was forbidden from leaving. I wish I remembered more. I wish... I hope I tried to inform others. Eventually I planned a way out of the castle, but the one maid I trusted informed Ashraleon. He confronted me. He was so angry, so shocked, that I would not stay. We fought, and I hurt him, I did. I thought I even killed him, but I was so scared, I ran. I wanted out of Eldrid, out of Everlorn. I didn't make it far beyond the city, though. Our nation was overrun with enemy soldiers, and they brought me to their king."

So strange, that one particular memory of meeting the foreign king in a wide yellow tent flapping in the chill wind. She could remember the words spoken when She knelt on cold wet grass at his feet, but not the face of the one speaking, nor his name. To have so much of herself defined by the belief of others was troubling, if She dwelt on it, which was why She rarely did.

"I was to accompany him to the siege of Eldrid, not as a prisoner, but as an honored guest. I suspect he hoped to use me as a puppet to replace Ashraleon afterward, but then I told him of my husband's plan. I begged him to hurry, to get to the capital before the sacrifice could be completed. And to his credit, he did believe me. I rode at the front of his armies, to the walls of Eldrid. But we were too late. As ever, I am too late, always walking in destruction's wake."

Even on the other side of the walls, it had been horrendous, in some ways even more so than bearing witness. They could only hear the pained cries of the dying and the scattered screams of those who refused out of fear or anger. Attacking soldiers rushed the walls to overcome Eldrid's skeletal force patrolling the ramparts, but they were too late. Nothing would stop the mass suicide.

"I sincerely believe Ashraleon himself meant to drink, and die with his people," She said. "Perhaps it was cowardice. Perhaps it was a belief that, even at his absolute lowest, fate would still deliver him an empire. And so he lived, as thousands upon thousands died in his name. A sacrifice worthy of a god, and so a god he became. With that newfound power, he took to the field outside Eldrid and challenged his aggressors."

Another brutal display She had been forced to watch. Nothing could stop Ashraleon. The ground quaked with his every step. His skin had shimmered the color of the sun. His sword cleaved through steel and armor as if it were cloth. The God-Incarnate was terrifying in every age, but never had he been so terrifying as in that one, single battle.

"We have seen the power ten Seeds can give a paragon with their sacrifice," Thorda said. "I cannot imagine the power a man would wield if granted the blood of tens of thousands."

"But why keep doing it?" Stasia asked. "He gained his power, and then he founded his church. Their worship alone should keep him strong. Why spend all this time and effort on places like Thanet?"

This was a question She had pondered extensively as well.

"Because too many lived that remembered Ashraleon as he was, a human king, born of human parents. His divinity could not be denied, true, but neither could his birth. Everlorn was but a shadow of what it would become, and many neighboring nations remembered the original family line. If I were to guess, he could not convince himself of his true immortality. And that is what he wants, more than anything. Immortality. To carve his name so deeply into our world it may never be washed clean. Perhaps he thought another sacrifice done in secret would empower him further, but in this, he erred."

That first time, it had been done to a small nation north of Eldrid, longtime nomads who built magnificent hide structures whose heat even the tundra could not penetrate. Ashraleon had been so patient with them, living among them for two decades, healing their wounded, teaching their children, and attending the funerals of their parents. They were coddled, protected, and told they were the cherished future of Everlorn.

And then came the sacrifice.

"I witnessed it," She said. "As I always witness it, each and every six centuries, as penance for my failure. Thousands upon thousands gathered together in the God-Incarnate's audience. Tens of thousands more in other cities, walled in and surrounded by soldiers and paragons. Some sing. Some pray. Everywhere, there is fear. And then the ceremony begins."

She shivered. The number of people was far, far too great for all to drink at once. The deaths came in waves. Prayers and songs gave way to screams of pain. Children crying as their parents forced them to finish their cups. Intermittent sobs as soldiers patrolled alongside priests, urging more to drink. Those who refused were cut down. Many who resisted at first broke before the horror. Far better to drink and hold on to the promise of the God-Incarnate than to acknowledge the senseless slaughter. Far better to drink than be impaled upon the spear or cut down by the sword. Or worse, acknowledge the entire faith you built your life around was a lie.

"My husband remarried and chose his newborn son, Aristava, to be his heir. He cast his power, his memories, his entire self, into him. But this is where he erred. What had once been the paranoid fears of a human turned god became codified into his very identity. The lifespan of an incarnation, even the great and original Ashraleon, was now set at six hundred years. It is no longer optional. He *must* continue passing himself on to his heirs."

"So then we kill his heirs," Eshiel interjected. "All of them. Leave him with no one."

"Sinshei claimed this would accomplish nothing," Cyrus said carefully. "Did she lie?"

Nameless She shook her head.

"If you slay his heirs, you will doom another nation to suffer as Thanet has suffered. When God-Incarnate Drasden lacked an heir he trusted, he still performed the ritual, a desperate measure he hoped would extend his own life instead of granting it to another. It delayed the transition by two decades, but at great cost to his strength. Those two decades, though, were enough time for him to birth his son and heir, Gaius. The sacrifice was held again, dooming tens of thousands more to poison."

"And so Lucavi comes here to do the same," Keles said. "Distant and isolated Thanet. He robs us of our gods, strips us of our faith, and then forces a new doctrine down our throats until the poisoned wine may replace it. Sinshei's promise was a lie. I would be no queen if she became Goddess-Incarnate."

Nameless She tilted her head to one side. Interesting. Sinshei vin Lucavi was making plans to usurp the title? That did explain why the Vagrant's group focused on killing the other two heirs. She had thought it pragmatic, a chipping away at easier targets before making a move on the God-Incarnate himself. No, instead they worked at a doomed plan.

"I do not know what the Anointed One promised you, but if Sinshei is to become Goddess-Incarnate, then Thanet must be sacrificed. If you would become a queen, Keles, then it would be a queen of graves."

Oh, how familiar the rage she saw in young Keles's eyes. The betrayal. The realization that Everlorn would break and slaughter anything and anyone to continue its spread. That even its supposed reformers viewed the rest of the world from a gilded seat in the heart of Eldrid.

"Sinshei has much to answer for," Keles said, and her every word dripped with venom.

Nameless She closed her eyes and pictured Sinshei in her mind. It took but a heartbeat for her to locate the woman. After all, one must guard one's heart against the Nameless Whore, lest She bring her temptations. Sinshei's heart was far from guarded. It bled with ambition and lusted for power.

"If you wish to speak with Sinshei, then you are in luck." She shook, her body shivering as if it could slough off all the memories and horror She'd been forced to relive. She smiled at Keles, and it hurt to see the way the younger woman flinched. "The Anointed One is on her way to Vallessau even as we speak."

CHAPTER 21

SINSHEI

Sinshei's work in Thiva was not finished, but nothing would stop her from returning for the announcement of Kalath's death.

"Such a tragedy," she said to the pair of paragons guarding the city's eastern gate. The night was dark, and the gates closed. "I heard the horrid news on my ride here."

One of the paragons opened the gate, while the other patted her horse and lowered his voice so the nearby soldiers would not overhear.

"Paragon Hiram, at your service, Anointed One," he said. His hair was closely shaved, and his head bulky and square, so his reddish face looked like a sentient brick. "It is good to see you back. The city is unstable after Kalath's unfortunate death, may Lucavi rest his soul."

Sinshei dipped her head, feigning sorrow instead of her true elation.

"Thanet tests us cruelly," she said. "It is lucky my work was finished when it was, so I might be here to console my grieving father."

In truth, she'd received a note from one of her loyal priests, detailing the confession of a soldier forced to attend Kalath's drunken revelries. Hours after sending a message to the Coin sharing the detail, she'd packed her things and followed, trusting the Vagrant to succeed.

"They stab and ambush like cowards," Hiram lamented. "But they will receive their reckoning soon enough. Where is your bodyguard? Shouldn't Soma be with you?"

Sinshei could only shrug.

"I sent warning of my return," she said. "I thought he would be waiting here for me."

The two paragons exchanged a glance.

"The city is not safe," said the second paragon. "Let us escort you to the castle. We have lost two sons. I will not let our carelessness result in the loss of a daughter."

Hiram walked several paces ahead of her horse, his gigantic sword drawn and lazily resting across his shoulders. That posture hid his true caution. The man relentlessly scanned the road ahead. The hour was late, the streets quiet. The path they traveled led directly to the castle, with no unnecessary turns or side streets. It seemed Hiram had decided speed outweighed unpredictability when it came to their safety.

The second paragon walked beside her, holding the reins to her horse in his left hand. His skin was a rich brown, his hair long and dark. He was big even for a paragon. Though he spoke the imperial tongue without need of the word-lace around his neck, it carried a heavy accent she could not place. A paragon of spears, judging by the weapon strapped to his back.

"May I have your name, paragon?" she asked.

"Seeq."

"Seeq? An interesting name. Where are you from?"

The paragon grunted.

"How is a woman born in Aethenwald not tired of such a question?" he asked. "Though I suppose everyone knows where *you* are from, vin Lucavi."

Sinshei twirled the end of her hair and debated rebuking him or apologizing. Both were deserving responses, so she considered it even.

"Answer the question, paragon."

The giant man shrugged, his eyes never leaving the rooftops as he answered.

"I am Seeq, the first paragon uplifted out of Lahareed," he said.

"Where I walk, my people shall follow. The sinful and stubborn cling to the past. I shall show them where our future lies, and it isn't in the arms of the goddess who abandoned us or the squabbling lords that left me hungry and homeless."

Up ahead, Hiram gave an order to halt. Seeq pulled on the reins, and his free hand reached for the handle of his spear. For the longest time, neither said a word. It seemed the paragons never even breathed. Sinshei remained a perfect visage of calm, not difficult, given the circumstances. The two paragons feared an ambush from the Vagrant. They didn't know the allegiance she had created, or that the murders of Lucavi's children were her own orchestrations.

The two nearest lamps flickered and died. She looked to one just in time to see shadowed tendrils snuff out its flame.

Seeq drew the spear from his back and handed Sinshei the reins.

"Do not panic, and do not flee," he said softly. "They may have an ambush prepared ahead. You are safest beside us."

Ax struck first, lunging from a rooftop with her two-handed namesake weapon lifted high. Hiram planted his feet and spun, his enormous sword rising to meet it. Sinshei knew of the Ax of Lahareed's reputation, but she was still shocked to see the way Hiram's elbows jarred and his feet scraped across the stone. The Ax, she was only human... wasn't she?

Their weapons parted, and each pulled back for a retaliatory swing. A ball of flame smashed into Hiram's chest before he could strike again, flung by Eshiel marching down the street with his hands raised. Flame circled his fingertips, evidence of the damned Butterfly's power. Ax seized the opportunity, striking at the distracted paragon with a blow straight to his chest.

Hiram blocked, but only barely. Another surge of fire was his reward. His armor, blessed by the prayers of priests, held strong, but the paragon's flesh was another matter. Already burns marred his face, ugly patches where the flames had curled across the steel to reach his skin. He roared, and when he swung his sword, even Ax had to retreat against Everlorn's might.

But then Everlorn's might was used against itself as the Heretic leaped out from an opposing alleyway. Sinshei cried a warning, and though Hiram turned, he still absorbed two blows from Heretic's gauntlets before he could block. The sound of breaking metal shrieked along with cries of pain. Sinshei prayed to her father, summoning two swords and two spears into existence on either side of her.

What madness possesses them? Sinshei wondered. Did they not know it was her, and only meant to attack the paragons?

"Go," she shouted at Seeq. "I can defend myself. Now, go, lest you watch Hiram die."

Seeq ignored her. His eyes were still on the rooftops. Searching...

The Vagrant landed in a shimmering burst of steel, his feet already dancing beneath him as his swords slashed. Seeq met his charge instantly, the distance between them closing in a flash. His spear twirled about, batting the swords back with the reinforced metal of its handle. Between every few blocks the paragon would thrust with blistering speed. Normal foes would be impaled, but the Vagrant was far from a normal foe.

Sinshei watched the exchange, and though she had her divine weapons, she feared to use them. God-Incarnate help her, they were both moving so fast, she was not certain she could strike the proper target. Past them, Hiram batted his sword back and forth, now purely defensive against the combined onslaught of Heretic, Ax, and Eshiel.

She had two paragons on her side, and yet Sinshei knew it was not enough. This was a battle she would lose.

Sinshei flicked the reins despite Seeq's advice. Her horse bolted forward, past the chaos, past the flailing axes and spinning swords. She heard Seeq shout behind her, heard him scream in pain, but she paid him no mind. Whatever had come over the Vagrant's group, she would investigate it later, once safely at the castle, guarded by Soma and in the presence of her father.

Shadows deepened ahead of her, and from the very night sky dropped the Vagrant. His grinning skull glowed in the night, a phantom white that chilled her blood. That same light cast across his swords, as if they were carved from the moon.

How has he changed so much? she thought as she pulled back on the reins, halting her horse. Godhood seemed to be taking root at a terrifying pace.

Vagrant stood and tilted his head to one side, amused.

"Why do you flee, Anointed One?" he asked.

Sinshei pulled hard left, turning her horse about. Seeq had been right—there was no escape. If the paragon still lived, if she could...

And then she saw the shield rising to meet her. The hard surface easily knocked her from her saddle. She hit the ground, a thousand curses jumbling about her discordant mind.

Damn it, Soma, where are you when I need you? she thought as, bruised and bleeding, she rolled to a halt. A shadow loomed above her, shimmering blue.

"Hello, Sinshei," Keles said, and then cracked her boot into Sinshei's mouth before she might utter a single word. "Welcome back to Vallessau."

Another kick to her stomach, denying her breath. No words. No prayers. No defense. Keles knelt down, one hand latching around her throat, the other readying a gag. The burning light upon her blade paled in comparison to the rage blazing across her face.

"I have questions. For your sake, pray you have answers."

CHAPTER 22

SOMA

A high moon, looking like a silver coin in the sky. A rising tide. A shared prayer. Soma relished all three as the song washed over him.

Forever old, forever found, we behold the sea, the villagers sang. Most were elderly, but a few were young, including the freckle-faced woman whose voice carried over all others. The praise seeped into Soma's blood. He stood up to his waist in the sea, his arms raised above him and his head tilted to the stars. The villagers gathered around, shaking seashells or clutching crudely painted imitations of his sapphire scales. Their voices quieted, so that their youngest and best singer finished the song alone.

"As ever was, as ever will be," she sang. "To the sea, we crawl on our knees."

The prayers filled Soma with strength, and he breathed it in with a smile. This power was so much cleaner, so much purer, than the stolen faith granted him during the paragon sacrifices. The first time had been the hardest, living in constant fear during his training that someone would sense the divinity hiding underneath his human flesh. But once the ten Seeds gave their lives and he had been granted the title of paragon, it grew so much easier. Paragons were expected to bear auras of divinity. They just did not know how true Soma's was.

A new song began, and Soma listened as the past haunted him. Instead of re-creating his life from scratch every time his agelessness became noticeable, he began the Ordiae family line. He formed sexless marriages and encouraged his wives to satisfy their desires elsewhere. Soma would bear no child of mixed mortal blood, like the gods of some nations did. Let the humans rut.

Eventually his wife would father a son, and once that son was old enough, his family would depart from the castle for a lengthy journey afar. Every single servant would be replaced. Every painting taken down. So odd, the Ordiae family, so eccentric, but that was to be expected of the powerful and wealthy, was it not?

And then Soma would dispose of his family, shift the flesh of his face, and come home in the guise of his own son. Once more he would return to the Bloodstone for training to become a paragon. Once more he would kneel naked in a ring of Seeds in the bowels of the Bloodstone and accept their brutal sacrifice. This was how he maintained the proud line of god killers, working his way up the hierarchy of Eldrid, earning their trust until, at long last, he could attempt his goal: the assassination of God-Incarnate Lucavi.

Soma tried to hide his bitterness from his followers. Centuries after washing up on Gadir, Soma disguised himself from head to toe in black, swapped his spear for a sword, and made his attempt while Lucavi held solitary vigil in the Cathedral of Solace. Soma had dropped from the ceiling with all his power, all his might, thrust into a single blow.

Lucavi had looked up just moments before the hit. Soma's blade struck true, and yet...

The god's skin had denied him. Despite all of Soma's strength, he managed to carve only a single, shallow cut that bled a few scarlet drops before it sealed. Lucavi's shock at receiving that blow had been Soma's only saving grace, for as Lucavi howled at the pain, perhaps the first pain he had felt in hundreds of years, Soma fled the premises, burned his clothes in a fireplace, and donned his paragon armor to join the search for the mysterious "assassin."

But failure did not mean ending his quest. Instead, it led to more research. It was within forbidden vaults kept so secret that even paragons would be executed for trespassing that he found detailed reports of the six-hundred-year ceremonies. He read of the need for heirs and of the great sacrifices required. Most importantly of all, he read of how the existing God-Incarnate would cut his own throat to give his life for his heir.

An heir that, for the briefest moment, would still be human as the power flowed from one to the other. Soma needed only be in the room when it happened—which meant the heir must trust him unconditionally.

The singing halted, pulling Soma back to the present. The young singer, the woman whose voice had risen far above others in both power and beauty, approached him. The waves pushed against her, yet she pushed back. She was so small, the water rising above her chest so that she struggled to reach him. Soma fell into the ancient prayers Thanet offered him, and within those memories he found hers. Katelyn. Her name was Katelyn. Oh how she had prayed, and so recently. For comfort. For guidance. For a moment in a quiet, dark night to feel anything but alone and abandoned. Her auburn hair was tied back from her face with blue ribbons, exposing her brown eyes. They were wide. They were filled with tears.

"Dagon," she said, fighting the tide. The rest of the village stayed back, some with hands to their mouths, others glaring with disapproval. "I..."

More old prayers of hers came to him. Soma offered his hands, and she accepted.

"Katelyn," he whispered, surprised by the sudden weakness in his limbs. Her words were all he heard. She'd had a lover, a man who traveled to Vallessau with hopes of fighting the invading empire. When he did not return, she traveled to the city. She walked its streets. She collapsed beneath the Dead Flags and shrieked to an uncaring sky at the sight of her lover hanging by a rope, shrieked until soldiers forced her to leave.

Katelyn's soft hands upon his scales. Her eyes, staring up at him. A thousand prayers, all offered when he was but a story, a promised mystery of her elders, but now he was here. He was here, and she knew not what to say. He felt her questions. He felt her need. To be loved. To be remembered. To ask for answers, reasons for her suffering and her loss.

How could he tell her the pain she suffered was of his own doing? After failing to kill Lucavi, Soma had studied the God-Incarnate's children and deemed Sinshei the one most amenable to his influence. He protected her from rivals and obeyed her orders, steadily building her trust. When the young woman had been frustrated with her assignment of choosing the sacrificial nation for the six-hundred-year ceremony, he had come to her, so helpful, so convenient, to tell of her of the small, isolated island of Thanet.

Would any of this soothe Katelyn's trauma? Would it matter if he told her that the end goal—an empire broken and its God-Incarnate slain—justified the loss of those she loved? Guilt stabbed Soma, foreign and unwelcome, and so he pushed it away. Guilt was beneath him. The choices of gods could not be second-guessed.

And then she smiled.

"Thank you," she whispered, and the dam broke. She collapsed against him, her face to his chest, and wept. The tears were harsher than any seawater. Soma wrapped her in shaking arms, closed his eyes, and to the shock of even himself, wept along with her.

"When I was lost, you were my light," he told her. Centuries peeled off him. Memories of war and conquest slipped away like discarded chains. Soma held this young woman, blessed with a thousand memories of old. The first festivals. The cheers of sailors. His visits inland through rivers, always a surprise, always a delight. Worship, prayer, love gifted and given, until he could only curse Endarius, curse the empire, curse everything that had taken it from him.

"Thank you, precious child," he whispered to her. Hundreds of years of hiding and pretending ended, and he let his heart be naked. "Thank you, beloved one. Thank you for reminding me of all that I have lost. Thank you for holding me in your heart while I was so far away and unworthy of your devotion. I heard your prayers, even if I was not there to wipe the tears from your eyes. I heard your lamentations as those you loved were taken from you. And yes, I heard your cry in the deep, dark night, when it felt like the dawn might never come. But dawn did come. It always will."

Katelyn gently pushed away, now floating in the water. She looked up at him, and seeing her love, her relief, filled Soma with a hate so savage it shocked him with its power.

This is what was taken from you. This was the purity of purpose that was lost.

Never again.

Never again.

"To the mother sea," Katelyn said, half a song, half a confession. "Where all are welcome, and all may forever be."

It was a new song, one composed after his departure, but it felt good. It felt true. Soma lowered himself into the water and let loose his voice. The waves carried it as ripples across the surface, his words breaking upon the shore with the power of the unending tide. It would be his final message to them, one they would repeat as they traveled across his island.

"My children, Thanet shall not be broken. It shall persevere. To this end, I swear upon the moon, the stars, and the ocean depths."

It was an outlandish hope, foolish and impossible, but one he must cling to as he swam back to Vallessau. His sapphire dream: Everlorn toppled, the false gods removed, and a single faith restored. A world where he could comfort those who desired it.

A world in which he could finally relinquish the hate he felt for humanity and instead cherish those who came into his arms with a song on their lips.

CHAPTER 23

VAGRANT

Cyrus sat on the edge of Mari's bed and gently touched her face with the back of his hand. It'd been two days since killing Kalath and capturing Sinshei. Two days since her collapse. She was warm, so very warm. Even in sleep, she turned and moaned. Whatever discomfort she suffered must be intense. It twisted Cyrus's gut that he could do nothing to aid her.

"I must say, you've missed a lot," he said, keeping his tone conversationally pleasant, as if she were listening to him while they sipped cups of tea. "Sinshei's betrayal, and then her capture? Meeting the Nameless woman? Learning of the sacrifice to come? I don't envy you when you wake up, Mari. That's going to be a lot to take in at once. Some of it's good, though. We're still fighting. If only our task wasn't so damn difficult, I might even feel good about it. You'll see, when you wake."

When you wake, he repeated inside, refusing to believe anything else could happen. It didn't matter her fever. It didn't matter her pain. She would overcome it. Losing her now was not... It wasn't allowed. The world could not be so cruel.

He took one of her hands in his. His fingers closed over hers, as if in prayer. If only he could offer her more, but this, this was at least something, wasn't it?

"I once knew a bird, a blue little bird," he sang, with a cracking voice that lacked the soft beauty of Mari's. It was years ago now, but he had never forgotten the rhymes. "And every morning, I would watch it fly, fly, fly..."

When Cyrus finished, he found Arn approaching from the den. He had a bowl of broth in hand, and he blushed at seeing Cyrus.

"Time for her to eat," he explained.

"Is the conversation going any better out there?" Cyrus asked as he moved aside to let Arn in. The big man chuckled.

"Nope."

Though the resistance had killed Kalath and captured Sinshei, the mood was tense within the den. Stasia was drunk on the couch, Eshiel and Keles together at a small round table, and Thorda, as always, in his rocking chair near the fire. There was only one topic of conversation, the one that had dominated their discussions for the past two days: Sinshei's fate.

"I say we cut her head off and be done with it," Stasia said, emphasizing the idea with a swipe of her glass. "That two-faced cunt promised us freedom while plotting to murder us all instead. There's no getting around that fact."

"We did not capture her for emotional satisfaction," Thorda said. "She is the daughter of the God-Incarnate. Between her knowledge and her position, she makes a valuable hostage."

"Strange how we saw no reason to take Petrus and Kalath hostage," Cyrus said, taking his preferred spot in the corner.

"A hostage was not what we needed at the time," Thorda countered. "Yet with this newfound knowledge, we face a difficult challenge. To cast aside any potential a hostage brings us would be foolish."

"We all heard Nameless She," Keles said. "Lucavi needs an heir. Sinshei will be valuable to him."

"We also heard he can postpone matters to father a new heir if he must," Stasia said. Her speech was slurred from drinking so heavily. "And that's assuming we trust the Nameless goddess in the first place. She might be playing us like everyone else keeps playing us."

"I see no reason to doubt her," Cyrus said, frowning.

Stasia waved her free hand aimlessly above her.

"She shows up out of nowhere, helps us capture Sinshei, and then vanishes again. Real trustworthy. She's got a grudge against Everlorn, yeah? So maybe we're tools to get even."

Thorda stood from his chair and cleared his throat. The mood in the room, already tense, turned icy. After all that had happened, Thorda was still their leader, and if he had reached a decision, little could be done to change it.

"We do nothing but talk in circles," the older man said. "If what we understand of Lucavi and his sacrifice is true, nothing will prevent it, which means there is nothing he can offer us in exchange for Sinshei's life. What gains to be made are slim, but there is still some potential from her as a hostage and not as a corpse. Therefore we keep her until we know better, or a consensus may be reached among us."

There wasn't anything to say that hadn't already been said, so the group remained quiet.

"Very well," Thorda said. "Then let me address the true reason I've gathered you all here." He withdrew a little scrap of paper from within a secret pocket of his robe and held it aloft. "Given our recent victories, Commander Pilus has messaged me his desire to march on the city of Ialath. He hopes to free it from the imperial garrison, and he requests the Vagrant's aid in doing so."

Ialath was on the far northern side of the island, fairly far from Vallessau. If Pilus succeeded, it'd be difficult for Lucavi to send reinforcements. He'd have to go by fleet, or through multiple forests bisecting the island should he go by land. Either put the troops in danger of ambush. No doubt Pilus had similar thoughts in mind.

"Freeing a city of such size would be a great victory," Cyrus said. "Especially if Lucavi cannot reclaim it before the six-hundred-year ceremony."

"A fact Pilus does not yet know," Thorda added. "But he must be told. His connections are invaluable in spreading the word in what few weeks we have left." He looked Cyrus's way, his expression guarded. "This is your choice, Vagrant. My orders are not yours, as you have made abundantly clear."

After so many skirmishes and ambushes, the idea of full-on warfare excited Cyrus in a way he did not expect. His grin spread wide.

"Oh, I'm going," he said. "I wouldn't miss such a battle for the world."

"That's because you've never fought in one before," Keles said, all eyes turning her way. "I have, Cyrus. Everlorn is fiercest when their might is gathered, and their paragons can turn the tide of an entire battle. What you've experienced, what you've fought, is so much smaller in scale than true warfare. Are you certain this is wise?"

"If Pilus believes he can win, then I trust him," Cyrus said. "He's given me no reason to doubt him before."

Keles stood.

"I thought as much. Then I'm going with you."

This time it was Eshiel who protested.

"Are you certain?" he asked. "Do not forget your time as Vallessau's Light..."

"And I will not be returning to that role, either," she snapped at him. "I will not be coddled and protected in the rear guard. I will lead as a queen should. The fate of our island hangs in the balance. Let us be bold, not timid."

"I would have it no other way," Cyrus said. "But what of everyone else?"

Thorda crossed his arms and assessed the others.

"I suspect Arn will not leave Mari's side," he said. "And truth be told, I am reluctant to spare even you, Cyrus. Right now, we must spread word of the six-hundred-year ceremony to every corner of this island. What casks of wine we can find, we break. What preparations there are for the ceremony, we disrupt. Every city. Every village. Every seed of resistance I have sown—it must now bloom, if Thanet shall have a future."

He shook his head.

"I pray that it will be enough."

"It will be," Eshiel said. He stood and bowed to them all. "Know that my own followers, and those loyal to the Butterfly, shall ever be on your side. I will organize their travels so that no village, no matter how small, is left ignorant of the coming poison."

"Will the people believe them?" Cyrus asked.

The priest shrugged.

"Whether they believe or not is up to them. I can only give them the truth and let them do as they wish with it."

"The aid is much appreciated," Thorda said. "What of you, Stasia?"

She lifted an empty bottle.

"I think I need more wine. And I'm not leaving here, or Clarissa. Vallessau's got casks of wine stashed for the ceremony somewhere in this city, and I'm going to find and break them all."

With that, it seemed the plan was settled. Keles followed Eshiel to the door, saying her goodbyes. Cyrus followed Stasia into the kitchen, and when she grabbed another bottle of Thanese wine, he held out a glass he retrieved from a cupboard.

"A toast to your coming victory in Ialath," she said once it was filled. She clinked the bottle against his cup, then drank heavily.

"Do we have more wine, or should I ask you to save me some?" Keles asked, joining them.

"I've begun thinking I should learn to appreciate beer over wine," Cyrus said, and then winced. "Sorry. That's a terrible joke."

Stasia smacked him in the chest.

"Cyrus and terrible jokes?" She sauntered back to the den, leaving him and Keles alone. "A combination I'd have never guessed."

He laughed, but the humor was forced. He didn't like the way Keles was looking at him. Too much concern. Too much worry.

"We've killed three of Lucavi's children and captured a fourth," he said. "Whatever challenges are ahead, we can handle them."

Keles crossed her arms and frowned.

"No matter Pilus's confidence, we will be facing highly trained, highly skilled opponents. Among their number are paragons and priests who are trained to slaughter gods. If Pilus's estimations are wrong, can we truly sway the battle with just the two of us?"

Cyrus drained the last of his wine, set the glass down, and then flashed a grin with his true face.

"With what I am becoming? I think the two of us can take on the world."

CHAPTER 24

LUCAVI

Lucavi stood upon his balcony; he had not moved in hours. Or was it days? No. The sun and moon had circled only once. Rain had come and fallen upon him. His legs would not move. His gaze would not shift. He had stood here, lost in his own mind, ever since he'd been informed of Kalath's death and Sinshei's capture.

"I will drown you all in blood," Lucavi whispered to the city. Vallessau. An untamable huddle of stone and wood built upon cliffs encircling a calm port. "I will purge you with fire. I will cut every man's throat and hang every woman and child by their feet so the sun bakes them and the crows eat them as they scream and writhe and suffer for what they have taken from me."

Yet still he could not move. His feet were bolted to the balcony. His glare pierced the city, and he imagined the cowards with their skull masks holding his daughter hostage. What were they doing to her? What acts of vileness would they perform as a way to humiliate him? Was Galvanis not enough?

The city was red to his eyes, red with blood, red with fire, red with wine. Soon. So very soon. Let them all drink. Let them sputter and gag as their throats closed and their stomachs hemorrhaged. Let them die, their last words a prayer to his name. It didn't matter if they spoke it genuinely or pantomimed it at his soldiers' orders. They would die; oh, how gloriously these people would die.

"Lucavi?"

He turned. Bassar stood at the entrance to the bedroom, one hand still on the opened door. His voice may have been calm, but his face revealed his worry.

"Yes?" Lucavi asked.

Bassar crossed the carpet to the bed and pulled off the top blanket.

"You're naked, my lord. Did you stand out in the storm?"

Had he not dressed? No. Lucavi supposed he hadn't. But what purpose were clothes, what meaning the rain, when he was invincible? What mattered this tiresome charade at humanity when he was anything but? He was a god. The prayers flooding his ears told him so.

Bassar wrapped him in the blanket. Lucavi watched him. The paragon kept his eyes respectfully to the floor, and it wasn't until the blanket was tied that he looked up. Something in his eyes piqued Lucavi's curiosity, like an anchor attached to his mind, dragging down his thoughts from above to the here and now.

Lucavi knew what was in those eyes.

Knew what must not be.

"Forgive me for my trespass," Bassar said. His hands were still on Lucavi's arms, holding the blanket tight. No gloves. Lucavi felt the warmth of his fingers. "I sought to give you time, but if we are to act, it must be soon."

"Act," Lucavi said. He swallowed. His throat was thick for some reason. "How, pray tell? How does one act when... when..."

It hit him. All at once. Like a sledge. Like an earthquake.

Galvanis. Petrus. Kalath. Taken. Murdered. And now Sinshei, claimed like some final trophy. The last of his loins. His journey to Thanet should have been one of glory, but now he had lost his sons, his beloved sons. He slumped forward, and Bassar caught him, holding him in his embrace.

Lucavi shuddered. From the moment he set foot on Thanese soil, he had been denied a chance to grieve, but it came to him now as he sank into his divine bodyguard's arms. He shed tears no one could ever see. A low sob trembled from his throat, wordless, moaning, dragging on and on, as if to pull the entrails from his body, his every bone and fiber to splay out across the carpet. He wailed, and his mind went black, and finally, finally, he wept for all he had lost.

Bassar stood still and silent. He was a pillar, and Lucavi leaned upon him even as he feared the burden would crush him. Tears flowed down his face to fall upon the paragon's armor. They were red, same as the crimson hands of prayer that marked Everlorn's flags.

Silence. If only he could have silence. If only the voices would not speak, but they would, Lucavi knew they would; it was only a matter of time.

Lucavi, said Ashraleon, as if he were listening, but of course he was listening. He was always listening. *We have given you your solitude, but your duty now compels. Stand tall and strong. My compassion has reached its end.*

Compassion. As if the first God-Incarnate knew the meaning of the word.

"I suppose it is selfish to grieve at my loss when all of Everlorn sacrifices daily in the quest for our grand unification," Lucavi said. He looked down at Bassar and felt imprisoned by the paragon's golden eyes. His look... there was so much there unspoken, and deep within, Lucavi was terrified he would speak it. Terrified, for such a confession would never be private.

"It is not selfish," Bassar said after a pause. His thumb wiped across Lucavi's cheek, banishing a tear. "How could it be selfish when your people grieve along with you? When we return to Eldrid, I shall ensure statues are built to honor your sons and placed in prominent positions within the Bloodstone."

Lucavi smiled.

"Thank you," he said. A hundred urges filled him. To embrace Bassar fully. To place a kiss upon his immaculate forehead. To rage and weep and grieve for his lost sons. To scream to the heavens his complete and utter hatred toward the voices that would never leave him be.

He refused them all. Instead he pushed Bassar away.

"Leave me," he said. "I would have my solitude."

Solitude.

Alone, among the God-Incarnates of old and their loathing of everything that he was.

CHAPTER 25

VAGRANT

Three days of hard travel brought Cyrus and Keles to the fields outside the city of Ialath. They'd passed the remnants of Fort Lionfang the day before, granting Cyrus an appreciative look at Stasia's handiwork. From there they skirted the northern tail of the mountains known as Lycaena's Cocoon and followed the road toward Ialath until they were several miles out. Then they headed northeast, toward the blue waters of Lake Respa. Miles of red cedar surrounded its borders, and within camped Commander Pilus's growing army.

Keles's army, Cyrus told himself as he passed through the tall grass. His belongings were gathered in a rucksack on his back, and he shifted its weight for the dozenth time that day. Pilus had done so much work, but he sought no crown for himself. He had fought for Cyrus's parents in his younger years, and after their execution, he had come out of his retirement from military service to lead in the dark days that followed. He was a man who cared about Thanet's freedom first and foremost. A lucky man to have, Cyrus knew. Infighting and political power grabs could quickly undermine what progress they had made.

"Have you any guesses where we should go?" Keles asked as they stopped for a break to stretch their legs and drink from their canteens. The lake was in sight, albeit distantly. On the far side loomed the cedar trees. After days of hard travel and sleeping out under the stars, the idea of going for a swim was greatly appealing. The tall grass scratched at Cyrus's legs, and his clothes stank of sweat and dirt from the road. It seemed the sun shone all the hotter when they were away from the sea, a thought Keles had laughed at when he suggested it, but she didn't deny it, either.

"Pilus's note was hardly the most detailed," he said, and gestured broadly. "All he said was he'd be in this forest. I suspect they will have scouts near the lake, plus men sent to draw water from it. I say we sit and wait to be found."

Keles removed the tight cloth band that tied her hair, shook her head, and began tying it anew.

"I never thought you fond of sitting and waiting."

He grinned at her.

"All right. I'll confess. I had every intention of going for a very long, relaxing swim. Scouts noticing us was just a convenient possibility. That a problem?"

Keles finished tying her hair and then wiped away a few errant strands still sticking to the sweat on her face. She hesitated, an argument of some sort on her lips, and then laughed.

"No," she said. "I smell like a farmer's boot. A swim sounds divine."

They were hardly the only ones with such an idea. They walked a well-worn path to Lake Respa's southern tip, and by the time they arrived there were two dozen kids laughing and swimming naked in its waters. A man with graying hair slept nearby in the grass, a wide-brimmed hat laid over his face to block the sun. Cyrus suspected he was in charge of wrangling the kids back to Ialath. Farther northeast, he saw some dozen men fishing with thin rods and catgut line, while across the lake itself, multiple rowboats traversed its surface, the men and women tossing and dragging nets.

"Busier than I thought it'd be," Cyrus said as they approached.

"Were you hoping for somewhere private?" Keles asked as she picked a spot within sight of the water and dropped her rucksack there.

"Quieter, maybe." He winced at the screech of the children. Gods, it sounded like they were murdering one another. Given the noisy splashes, he couldn't rule out that possibility, either.

Keles pulled her shirt off and dumped it atop the rucksack. Cyrus immediately glanced away, self-conscious though she still wore a thin undershirt…one that hid little given the travel sweat that soaked it.

"Well?" she asked as she stripped off her trousers. "Changed your mind?"

There was no denying the mocking playfulness in her grin. Cyrus forced himself to meet her gaze and look nowhere else, less in fear of offense and more because if she caught his eye wandering she would be far too amused.

"Of course not," he said, removing his own shirt. She was already halfway to the water by the time he set it down. He watched her leave, and a bit of his excitement faded. She was so much stronger than he remembered, her every limb flexed with muscle. Dagon's gift, given by the traitorous Sinshei. And across those muscles were scars, far more than he would have ever guessed. The price she paid for her time as the Light of Vallessau.

What you've experienced, what you've fought, is so much smaller in scale than true warfare, she'd said, and he wished he'd not dismissed her so cavalierly.

"You coming?" Keles asked, submerged up to her waist in the lake's pristine waters. Her smile had grown into a smirk. "I thought you were dying for a swim."

"Still am," he said, neck growing red. He sprinted toward the lake and leaped with far more strength than he intended. He vaulted over Keles to the depths beyond, to the astonishment of the children. They did, however, see the splash he made, and when he came up for air, he heard their cheers and laughed.

"Sorry," he said, and grinned at a now-soaked Keles. "You know me. I had to make an entrance."

They set up camp hours later on the far side of the lake, closest to the trees. It wasn't much, just a small fire between their bedrolls, but Cyrus trusted the smoke to attract attention. Sure enough, as the sun began to set, the fishers docked their boats, the children staggered home, and a gruff man emerged from the woods. He was dressed like the other locals, with brown trousers, a white shirt open at the front, and a dark felt hat. Unlike them, he had a sword prominently sheathed to his belt.

"Hey there," he said. His face was covered with a beard that grew down to his neck, and he scratched at it nonchalantly. "You two love-birds weren't planning on staying the night here, were you?"

"Would that be a problem?" Cyrus asked.

"We don't take kindly to anyone hanging around the lake at night. It's not safe, if you take my meaning."

Cyrus glanced at Keles, and she nodded in the affirmative. He stood, and when the man's hand drifted toward the hilt of his sword, he stifled a laugh.

"You're right, it isn't safe," he said. "Not for soldiers and spies of Everlorn, but we are neither. I am the Vagrant Prince, Cyrus Lythan, and over there, lounging by the fire, is Returned Queen Keles Orani."

Keles gently waved at him in greeting. The man stood frozen in place for a good three seconds.

"Bullshit. Prove it."

Cyrus closed his eyes, then opened them again, this time bearing a new face.

"Will this suffice?"

By the man's panicked curse, Cyrus suspected that was a yes.

His name was Tobias, he informed them as he led Cyrus and Keles through the red cedar forest toward Commander Pilus's encampment.

"It's not far," Tobias explained, keeping to a well-worn path trod by countless feet. "We want to be close enough to Ialath that we can move out and reach it quick if need be."

"Who is regent here?" Keles asked. "And how has he not noticed an enemy army so close to his doorstep?"

"The regent for the realm of Pilion is some stuffed-up noble from

Gadir," Tobias explained. "And he hasn't noticed because he's holed up a hundred miles away in Raklia. That, and we don't want to be noticed. We know the land. They don't."

Cyrus suspected it wasn't quite that simple. No doubt the swimmers and fishers of Lake Respa held suspicions of the army's proximity, and he'd even wager people brought supplies from Ialath to donate or trade. But thankfully it seemed they were loyal to Thanet, or at least distrusting and resentful of the imperial occupation.

It wasn't long before another pair of soldiers blocked the path.

"We bringing visitors, Tobias?" one of them asked.

"Of the kind you wouldn't believe," their guide said, and he grinned wide. "I bring you the Returned Queen and her escort, the Vagrant."

Cyrus didn't bother waiting for questions, explanations, or the inevitable doubt. Instead he bowed his head a moment, lifted it, and grinned his true grin.

"If we could speak with your commander," he said. He thought he'd be amused by their reactions but was taken aback when the pair suddenly dropped to their knees.

"You're here," the younger of the two said, swiping his fingers across his brow. "You're real."

The worship rolled off them, and while it was not unwelcome, it made Cyrus uneasy. He wasn't sure what to say.

"He is," Keles said. "On your feet, the both of you. We'd like words with Pilus."

They were all too happy to oblige. At their beckoning, Cyrus and Keles traveled into the camp proper, a sprawling mess of tents, ditches, and fireplaces. A few trees were cleared to make space, but mostly the soldiers set up in the gaps as best they could. Cyrus kept his hood up and his face low, not wanting to make any further commotion as they passed men and women clearly tired and on edge. The younger man ran ahead, no doubt to give warning to the commander. Their destination was the largest tent, pale green and with its flaps pinned open. Within was a long table with several chairs. Eating alone was Commander Pilus. At their approach he wiped his hands on the tablecloth and then stood.

"This is a welcome surprise," he said, offering his hand over the table.

"And a welcome reunion," Cyrus added, shaking the man's hand. "I've not seen you since one of the Coin's little parties."

"Forgive my rudeness," Pilus said, turning to Keles and bowing his head. "I should have greeted Thanet's Returned Queen first. However, I must express consternation at your lack of retinue. A queen should travel with guards, advisers, and maidens."

"And when I sit upon a throne in Vallessau, perhaps I shall have all of those things," Keles said, taking a seat at the table. "Until then, I think Cyrus here is more than capable of keeping me safe."

"That I am," Cyrus said, sitting beside her. "But I make a terrible handmaiden. I cannot braid hair to save my life."

"We all must make sacrifices," Keles said, and she winked.

Cyrus and Keles accepted drinks from a soldier who came over carrying cups and a pitcher. An ale of some sort. He drained half his cup as Pilus settled into his chair opposite them. The soldiers hurried away, leaving them in relative privacy. They were still visible to the rest of the camp, and many eyes were turned their way. Cyrus thought about asking for the flaps to be shut, decided against it. Those gazes... they were filled with hope and adoration. Let them look. It fed him in a way that he could not deny.

"I suppose we should discuss the coming assault," Pilus said.

"No, not yet," Cyrus said, deciding it best to just come out with the dire news. "Do you remember the poisoned wine you discovered when Ax was with you?"

Pilus's pleasant demeanor darkened.

"I do," he said stiffly. "We feared there would be more poisoned caches beyond that one. Was I right?"

"You are," Cyrus said. "Because come the six-hundred-year ceremony, Lucavi plans to have each and every citizen of Thanet drink and be sacrificed in his name."

The commander stiffened as if stabbed. His lips quivered until his teeth were bared.

"He would exterminate the lot of us like unwanted pests," he said.

"Eshiel is spreading word to every village throughout Thanet as we speak," Keles said. "The ceremony must be avoided at all costs. We can only pray that the people believe us."

Pilus leaned forward with his elbows on the table. His hands clenched into fists, and he rested his forehead against them as he gazed into nothing.

"We have but two weeks to inform the island," he said. "That isn't enough time, not near enough."

"We'll find a way," Cyrus said, trying to be hopeful. "What resistance groups we have will find and destroy the poisoned wine, and those ceremonies will not go unimpeded, I promise you."

Pilus slammed his fists to the table, hammering the wood loud enough that nearby soldiers quietly glanced in their direction.

"I am glad you have come, both of you," he said. "Together, we will crush the occupying forces of Ialath."

"I agree with the desire, but time is not on our side," Keles said. "Will you be able to form a proper siege?"

"It would be no siege," Pilus said. "There is no way for us to cross the span between here and the city without being noticed miles in advance. They will ride out to meet us in the fields beyond the walls, of that I am certain. Cowering within would belie their supposed might and superiority."

Cyrus frowned. It was a gamble, but then again, nearly every paragon he'd met was absurdly arrogant. He suspected Pilus was correct about this, but that begged other questions.

"How many soldiers can you muster?" he asked. "And how many defend Ialath?"

"I command two thousand soldiers," Pilus said, and there was no disguising his pride. "It puts us on near even footing with our estimates of their force, which is a thousand and five hundred. Yet I have set in motion plans to greatly hamper their defenses. Several dozen men and women loyal to Thanet are stationed inside the city, many of them hunters skilled with a bow. Once our army arrives, and Everlorn's eye is directed outward, those loyalists will strike at the defenders on the walls. We shall slam the city gates shut behind the empire's army and then pelt their forces with arrows. They shall have nowhere to retreat and no safety for their back lines."

The plan was flimsy, with multiple chances to fail, but that was to be expected when fighting against such an overwhelming enemy. What Cyrus didn't like, however, was how one key aspect of the defense had gone unaddressed.

"Soldiers and perhaps even priests, I trust you to handle," he pressed. "But how many paragons are among their number?"

"Three, one of them being their commander. They are mighty, I know, but we killed one at Fort Lionfang through overwhelming numbers, and I trust my men to do the same here."

Cyrus shook his head.

"You have a minor numbers advantage, and you gamble on a paragon's pride. Even with the aid of your trickery, your troops could not have withstood the might of paragons on the battlefield. Without us, you would be slaughtered."

Pilus did not back down.

"Then it is good we are not without you. But if we free Ialath, then we need not fear for her people, nor the poison that is most certainly stored somewhere within the city's vaults."

Cyrus stood from the table and pushed away his half-empty cup. Keles did likewise.

"Keles and I will handle the paragons," he said, a plan already forming in his mind. "When did you plan to march out?"

Pilus stood, sensing their little meal was over.

"It will take much of the day to reach there, so I had planned for us to leave tomorrow night, a few hours prior to dawn. That way we can battle at midday when the sun is high."

Cyrus shook his head, his ideas solidifying. Keles would lead the soldiers into the fight and deal with the initial brunt of the paragons' assault. But if she endured, and allowed him to fight unhindered elsewhere...

"Do you trust me, Commander Pilus?" he asked. "Do you trust me with the lives of your men and the fate of your battle?"

The older man crossed his arms and stared. A lengthy internal debate later, he answered.

"It is a foolish man who relies on trust to carry him through desperation...but I am that desperate, and that much a fool. I have long feared the deaths we would suffer, even in victory. If you are what they say you are, Vagrant, perhaps you may grant us a miracle."

Cyrus grinned. It was good to hear such trust put into him, such faith.

"Then march at dawn, if not later. I want us to arrive with the setting of the sun."

Pilus didn't even try to hide his disapproval.

"The night is a dangerous time to hold a battle of such size," he said.

Cyrus grinned again, this time with his true face.

"Dangerous indeed, but for who?"

CHAPTER 26

LUCAVI

Lucavi sat on the bed, his eyes closed, his mind awash with the prayers of his faithful on Gadir. They were so many, tens of thousands at any given moment. He could dip into each and every one, if he wished, isolating them to their unique voice, but he preferred not to. Better to let it wash over him like a comforting wave. The praise and worship of the many, granting him the necessary strength to face the day.

A knock on his door pulled him from his dreamlike trance.

"A visitor," Bassar said from the other side. "Signifer Weiss would like to speak with you."

Lucavi rose from the bed, smoothed out his tunic, and then pressed a hand to his forehead to help still the turmoil of prayers and bring him more focused into the now.

"Come."

Lucavi stared at the newcomer's face as Bassar escorted him inside. His dark hair was cut close to the scalp, his face heavily scarred from ancient burns. The man had been Imperator Magus's Signifer during the first years of Thanet's conquest, and from what Lucavi had gleaned, he did his job immaculately. He carried a surprisingly thick stack of papers in his arms, and he cradled them with a love normally reserved for newborns.

"I thank you for granting me this audience," Weiss said. "I was ordered to wait, but Anointed Sinshei's capture demands haste over prudence if we are to bring her back safely."

Lucavi arched an eyebrow.

"You believe you know where she is being held?"

Weiss shook his head.

"Not so precisely, my god." He held out the stack of papers. "But I believe that if one casts a wide enough net, even the most slippery of fish can be caught."

Lucavi scanned the first few papers. The information was mostly meaningless to him, just lists of names, locations, some values in Everlorn's gold coin standard, and scattered bits of half sentences. Next to many names were two different marks, one a red X, the other a black Y.

"What is all this?" he asked.

Weiss beamed with pride.

"The collective work of Sinshei, myself, and a few assistants, meant to be a shared gift given to you to mark your arrival. Within I have cataloged every single household in the entirety of Vallessau, with information taken from our patrols, our taxes, and church attendance rolls. With that, I have cross-referenced all confessions delivered to our soldiers as well as those to our Uplifted priests. Taken together, it is as near perfect a picture of this heathen city as one can draw."

Lucavi tapped on one of the Y's.

"What then of these marks?"

"Those I harbor suspicions of are marked in black Y's to signify a need to remove them from their current environs, break up their families, and put pressure on them to obey lest further sedition occur."

"And the red?"

Weiss shrugged nonchalantly.

"Named in confessions, caught disguising their assets, or run afoul of soldiers. They are the ones I have deemed worthy of a traitor's fate."

Lucavi flipped through several more sheets, seeing a shocking number of red and black X's and Y's. Was the city truly in so dire a state?

Of course it is, said Drasden. *Do not the deaths of your sons prove as much?*

Still, the scope of what Weiss was suggesting...

"You would order a purge of the entire capital," Lucavi said, honestly impressed by the grandiose strategy. "Nearly every family would be affected in some way."

Signifer Weiss bowed low before him.

"I propose doing what must be done to bring this troublesome city to heel. Know that, under my guidance, this will be an orderly and strategic cleansing. Many Imperators have tried similar tactics in other nations, with a goal of fostering fear and broken will, but it is always done sloppily, and mostly at random. Not so here. I present you with information, and I ask that we use it. And if Sinshei is held captive, I suspect she will almost certainly be in one of the places I have marked with an X."

Lucavi remembered his vision of Vallessau drowning in blood. Yes, this was much cleaner than his own emotional desires. He put a hand on Weiss's shoulder and bade him rise.

"You have done well," he said, offering back the papers. "My entire army is at your disposal. This island, it looks to be a poor sacrifice, but we must weed out what rot that we can. Perhaps fear, and freedom from vile influence, will fix these heathens. Pull them out by the root, and if fate is kind, we will find my daughter during the cleansing."

The Signifer took back his papers, cradled them against his chest, and beamed with pride.

"Your will be done," he said, bowing low before hurrying out of the bedroom. Bassar watched him go with his arms crossed behind his back. He seemed hesitant about something.

"My lord..." he said, then shook his head. "What would you have me do?"

Lucavi dared not look into those golden eyes. Ashraleon's words echoed within him, forever taunting.

Stand tall and strong. My compassion has reached its end.

"I would have you do your duty," Lucavi said. "Break the will of this wretched city until they return my daughter to me. Let us prove, once and for all, that their time for taking is at its end."

CHAPTER 27

VAGRANT

Thanet's army marched toward Everlorn's, and seeing it, Cyrus knew Pilus had been a fool to think he could win on his own.

Perhaps things are more desperate throughout the island than you know, he thought, studying the forces before the gates of Ialath. Their foes were highly trained, and they arrayed themselves in perfect lines thirty rows deep. Their armor was polished to a shine, and their matching tabards bore the red hands of prayer.

By comparison, Pilus's soldiers were much more haphazardly dressed, and they carried no consistent tabard or standard. Only one mark unified them—the painted red line across their foreheads. Seeing it everywhere gave Cyrus a warm sensation in his stomach. He was not the only god the soldiers worshiped, though. Before they ever marched, Keles had gathered hundreds around her for prayer.

We walk in the light of the goddess of beauty and grace, she had told them, her head bowed, her eyes closed, and her armor immaculate. The Returned Queen in all her majesty. It had filled him with pride, and even a twinge of jealousy. The soldiers did not look upon him like they did her. There was no hiding their love and adoration. She had walked through their number, encouraging them, telling them Lycaena would embrace them should they fall. Some even wept when she put her hands upon their shoulders and told them to be brave.

Cyrus looked to the nervous soldiers to either side of him. No, they held no love for him, but it was not love he needed. He needed them to believe he was death come for Everlorn, and each and every bloody crown upon their foreheads blessed him with that conviction.

"We are in luck," Keles said beside him. The pair were at the forefront of the army, which at Pilus's request had come to a halt a quarter mile from the enemy. She pointed. "I see all three paragons have come to play. The city shall be relatively undefended."

"It also means the start of the battle will be ferocious," he said. He studied her, comforted by her hard resolve. "Will you be able to endure it?"

"Lycaena is with me," she said, and drew her sword. "I shall not falter here and now, when my people need me most."

Cyrus smiled at her.

"I believe you."

They waited together until Commander Pilus, having spent the past few minutes checking on his lines and shouting orders and encouragement both, joined them. He looked dashing in his well-worn chain armor. A horn hung loose from his belt by a strip of leather. If he was nervous about the coming battle, he showed not a hint.

"We are as ready as we will ever be," he said, one hand on his hip, the other resting atop his sword hilt. "So is Everlorn, I see."

"You were correct in your estimates," Cyrus said. "You outnumber them by several hundred, but the paragons will make a mockery of that advantage. Your soldiers must remain disciplined. The moment a single line breaks, it will become a bloodbath."

"Isn't that what you two are here to prevent?" he asked.

Cyrus drew his swords. His pulse quickened. The faith of the soldiers filled him, and it was a strange intoxication.

"Doubt neither of us," he said. "Give your order. Let us crush Everlorn on the field of battle."

Pilus removed the horn from his belt.

"Lycaena be with us," he muttered, and then lifted the horn to his lips. He blew a single long note that was then matched by two others farther back. The signal to march. The soldiers lurched forward, uneven at first but then forming a cohesive line. Horns sounded from afar, and

Everlorn's men approached the same. The clasped hands on their tabards seemed to glow crimson in the dying light. A wave of hate. A force of conquest. Cyrus gazed upon them and let it fill his heart with rage.

You will know, he thought as he clutched his swords tightly. *Our fury. Our defiance. Before death comes, you will see the doom of your faith.*

Another horn. Their pace quickened. The sounds of footsteps and rattling armor became a thunder. A march became a charge. Cyrus ran at the forefront, his swords out, his skull grinning. The transition was so easy now, even easier than donning a mask. He let the army see his approach, let the paragons press to the front to meet him...and then shadows swallowed him whole.

The light of the sun was all but spent, and the city of Ialath filled with many dark corners. Cyrus reemerged upon the walls of the city with his speed intact. There were twenty soldiers up there on the ramparts, maybe thirty at most, and they were not ready for the savagery of Thanet's newest god. He tore through them, his feet pounding, his swords cutting through weapons held with trembling hands. His slashes opened throats frantically crying for aid. None would be coming.

Above the gates, he disemboweled the soldier guarding the stairs and then severed the ropes attached to the pulley, dropping the city's iron gate with a heavy thud. Goal achieved, he sprinted back up the wall to gaze out upon the battle.

Sight was poor with the setting sun, but dim light meant little to Cyrus. He watched the soldiers slaughter one another, and for much of the battle line, Thanet held the advantage. That would soon end, though, given the destruction the paragons were unleashing. Two worked together to form a bulwark none could break, and with every swing of their enormous weapons, multiple men and women fell in a mess of blood and broken bones.

The third charged directly for Keles. Even from afar, Cyrus could see her. To his eyes, she shimmered with divine light, an outline of blue and red swirling together, the blessing of Dagon and Lycaena both. She met the paragon wielding an enormous sword with her shield raised high. Cyrus held his breath as their weapons made contact. Suddenly the entire battle mattered not, just that single moment.

Her shield flared with rainbow light. Her cloak lifted behind her, splitting in two to become wings that were of such brilliance they lit the night with their glory. Cyrus shook his head. He never should have doubted her.

"You spared us the hard part," a man shouted. Cyrus turned to see archers rushing up the stone steps to either side of the gate to join him upon the ramparts. Only a few soldiers had remained on the far side to resist, and they were quickly brought down, their bodies riddled with arrows. The one who had shouted at him was a grizzled man, bald on the left side of his head from scars left by a wicked burn. He readied an arrow. "But don't you have somewhere to be?"

"I do," Cyrus said, and directed his gaze to the paragons. Not yet. Soon. "Let your arrows fly, and do not fear hitting me."

"Hitting you?" the man asked as several dozen men set down their quivers and lifted their bows. In answer, Cyrus leaped off the wall toward the battlefield, soaring with his cloak rippling behind him and his weapons curled downward like the talons of a hawk.

Cyrus had faith in Pilus's men to hold strong against the paragons. They would fight, and they would die, but they would not break their lines so long as they had life in them. But these soldiers of Everlorn? They who waited at the rear for their moment to rush to the front? How would they fare when they faced not a paragon but a god?

Cyrus landed behind them, unseen, unprepared for. Two men died instantly, stabbed through the neck before his feet even touched ground. He ripped his swords free and then spun through the trio beside him, his off hand cutting open a soldier's throat, his main hand batting aside a panicked defense to stab through ineffectual chainmail to pierce the heart. The third swung even as he screamed in fright. Cyrus sidestepped the attempt with ease, and he did not strike back. He wanted the fear. Craved it.

The first volley of arrows fell upon the back line. The screams of the wounded caught the attention of large portions of the army toward the rear. Then they saw him, calm, still, laughing as that third soldier fled instead of attempting another swing. Only then did the Vagrant speak, and his voice carried through the entire battlefield.

"I behold the dead."

Swords and spears turned his way. Another volley landed, and amid its destruction, he laughed again. The battlefield was so crowded, so dark. The Anyx ring burned on his finger. This would be his playground, and their grave.

Cyrus sank into the ground. When he reemerged, he was in the center of an entire squad. Their screams of fright became screams of pain as he tore through them. He held no blade back for parry or defense. His speed was beyond them. The darkness protected him. Bare steel shattered when brought up to defend against his hits, for his own shimmered with the light of the moon. All the while, arrows fell like rain.

Yes, the dark voice screamed inside his mind as he carved a trail of slaughter through their number. *Yes, embrace it, embrace everything you are meant to be!*

Cyrus dominated the battlefield as if within a dream. With every passing moment, every brutal kill, it seemed time slowed further. His opponents swarmed him, but he knew their attacks before they made them. His body twisted, swords lashing out to cut exposed throats and slice off hands holding weapons. He ended his spin to face a pair of spears thrusting for his chest. He batted each aside and then dropped to his knees, falling into shadow, reappearing yet again several dozen feet away.

Pilus's soldiers had been pushing, and Everlorn's reinforcements were rushing to plug holes in the line. They were not ready for the Vagrant.

At last, his savagery earned him the attention of his true foes. A paragon of axes rushed toward him like a charging bull decked out in heavy plate. A cry to Everlorn was on his lips. His raised ax could fell a tree in one swing.

Stop fearing them. They are men, not gods.

Cyrus waited until the last moment to sidestep. He felt the wind of the ax upon his face, saw its force ripple the hood of his cloak. The ax buried into the dirt, then tore chunks free as it twisted its arc to aim for Cyrus's waist. The paragon bore divinely blessed muscles, and his speed was otherworldly, but to Cyrus it all seemed slow and clumsy.

The paragon's superior might had rendered practice unnecessary. He'd grown sloppy, too used to mortal enemies.

Cyrus punished him for that ignorance. He leaped right over the ax, his legs curling to his chest, and then he kicked. His heels crunched the paragon's nose in with a wet splatter. He rolled the moment he landed, avoiding another hit, and then came up swinging. His swords cut brand-new lines across the paragon's cheek.

"You're nothing," the paragon howled. "A false god, one who will break before me."

"Do you not understand?" Cyrus asked as he ducked underneath a swing and then slashed both his swords across the paragon's chest. The metal crumpled, and blood dripped from where he scored a shallow cut. "There is nothing false about the suffering of my people. Every day, they die for me and what I represent."

"You represent nothing," the paragon seethed as he tried and failed to push Cyrus away. "You are blasphemy."

"I am your death," Cyrus told him. "And the people cry out for it every day and night."

"Enough talk!" the paragon screamed, and Cyrus was all too happy to oblige. He hopped backward, avoiding swing after swing, while watching for an opening. It'd come. His opponent was overwhelmed with anger and blinded by fanaticism.

There.

Cyrus dashed forward during an overhead chop, the windup much too high, the strength miscalculated. One sword cut through the armpit, the other at the waist, and then he circled, carving into the paragon as if peeling the skin from a piece of fruit. Blood flowed in twin rivers. Cyrus let go of his swords, dropped underneath the paragon's retaliatory swing, and then came up with his fists crunching the paragon's throat. He staggered, and again Cyrus danced about him, making a mockery of the dying man's slowness. His fingers closed about his hilts, the weapons still embedded in flesh, and he ripped his swords free while twisting to maximize the damage. The paragon howled in pain, a howl that ended abruptly when Cyrus's blades crossed over his throat.

One major threat down. Between Cyrus's assault on the rear, the barrage from the archers on the walls, and their initial numbers advantage, Everlorn's army was crumbling rapidly. Many had turned to retreat, only to find the gate closed to them. They died, easy pickings for the archers. Others tossed their weapons and scattered east and west.

Of the remaining two paragons, the one with the sword still battled Keles, but her shield and sword beamed with light, and her cloak rippled with Lycaena's blessing. Cyrus trusted her to find victory, and so he turned to the other paragon, who was surrounded by Pilus's men.

This one wielded a shield and spear, and his armor was even thicker than normal. Pilus's soldiers were hacking away at him, but they struggled to find openings. In time, they would win. Even paragons would fall before hundreds of enemies, but how many would they take with them in death?

Cyrus saw his opponent, saw a paragon exhausted and overwhelmed on all sides, and knew victory was already his.

Take it, the dark voice howled in his mind. That voice, his voice, the voice of the Vagrant, was the only thing he could hear. *Take what is yours.*

Cyrus sprinted past the wounded and vaulted over the dead. When he neared the ring of soldiers surrounding the paragon, he crouched low and leaped. Gravity held no sway over him. He soared high into the air, slowly turning so that his eyes never left the paragon.

The moment Cyrus's feet touched ground, he plunged both swords directly into the man's gut. The paragon gasped as the weapons punched into his lungs. He tried to retaliate, but already the Thanese soldiers were upon him, cutting at him and bashing away his spear.

Cyrus met the gaze of the dying paragon. He saw shock and disbelief. Cyrus ripped his swords free, pulling entrails out with them. He saw pain and death.

Once more into the shadows, the sun now completely set and the carnage lit by the moon and stars. He reappeared near Keles, stepping out from a trio of crumpled corpses.

The sword paragon was already dead. Keles stood triumphant over his body, one heel up and resting atop his chest, her sword raised high.

"For Thanet!" she screamed. "For your goddess! For your queen!"

Cheers accompanied her, the cries of the victorious. When at last she noticed Cyrus's presence, there was something in the way she looked at him that he did not understand. Or perhaps did not *want* to understand.

"Vagrant," she said, the name spoken with surprising reverence. "We did it. We won."

Cyrus looked to the battle, to the fleeing Everlorn soldiers, to the numerous dead. He smelled the stench of blood and vacated bowels and heard the screams of hundreds of wounded. He saw a field of corpses, sacrificed in the name of conquest, of Lucavi, of the Returned Queen, and of the Vagrant. Saw their bloody crowns.

And he laughed.

"Was it ever in doubt?"

CHAPTER 28

DARIO

It is a grim day," Dario said, eyeing the sky. The breaking of Vallessau had begun only hours before, yet already the streets were stained with blood. The sky above was blackened by both storm clouds and pillars of smoke.

"It is a cleansing day," Bassar said. He checked his scroll, then pointed. "There, the home with the white door. The owner, Mallus, is condemned. After that, do you see that large building painted red? Search it while I take care of this place here."

Dario disliked the way Bassar ordered him around so readily. His role as divine bodyguard gave him certain privileges, but they involved his protection of Lucavi. They did not apply in battle, and Dario most certainly saw this "cleansing" as a form of battle. Still, to complain would risk revealing his dour mood, and his conversation with Sinshei had already made it clear that the church was aware of his shaky faith. The last thing he needed was to risk adding his own name to a list with a red X beside it.

Dario knocked on the first door. He noted claw marks cut into the wood as he did. Endarius's blessing. They should have been removed years ago.

The door crept open. An elderly man stepped out. He said nothing, only lowered his head and looked to the dirt.

"Mallus?" Dario asked.

"I am."

A single blow to the temple was enough, instantly lethal. A small mercy. Dario left him for the corpse wagons. On to the next house, the next place, the one painted red. He knocked, but no one answered. Hardly surprising. He leaned his weight back and prepared to bash it open with his heel.

The door flung open just before Dario's foot connected. A dozen men and women attacked him, flowing out the door, the windows, even two leaping down from the rooftops. They brandished simple weapons, swords, clubs, and daggers, but it was the masks they wore that turned Dario's stomach.

Skull masks, all white, all grinning.

"Collect the Vagrant's due!" one shouted as they charged. Dario's balance, precarious from his interrupted kick, was their only hope. He denied it immediately. His foot slammed the ground with all his strength, and the ground rumbled with it. Rage rose within him. He would not die here with a crown carved across his forehead.

Dario caved in the head of the first man and sideswiped the second to snap his neck. He retreated two steps, his hands up like a bare-knuckle brawler. It wasn't punches he deflected but knife thrusts, his foe a burly third man with a drunkard's gut attempting to reach his exposed face. The steel of his gauntlets easily held against the knife, and Dario rewarded the man with a blow to his belly. The man heaved as the punch lifted him off the ground and left him collapsed, unable to breathe.

Three dead in as many seconds. The ambush was already faltering. Dario's finely honed instincts took over. All he saw were grinning skull masks, and for that he was thankful. They inspired no fear in him. Instead, it made them become a single entity to be put down. They were not names on a list, not families to be broken apart. They were enemies. They sought to give him a bloody crown, and so he gave them his fists in return.

No more retreating. He crashed into them, relying on his armor to keep him safe. He grabbed limbs and broke them like twigs. His elbows and knees were as lethal as his fists against such meager opponents. A punch, and ribs shattered. Pivot on his heels, and then another strike, the might of a paragon obliterating mortal meat and bone. Panic replaced their anger, but they did not flee. They were committed. They still held hope.

And for that Dario broke them. Spines. Jaws. Skulls. He caught a thrust aimed for his eye, the woman's wrist mere paper between his fingers. He crushed it when he made a fist and then flung her over his shoulder at the home they had hid within. She hit the boards with a wet smack, dropped, and lay still. Dario turned, searching, searching, but that was the last of them.

The noise of battle was replaced with sudden, stark silence. Dario stood gasping air, but not from exertion. His heart hammered against his ribs as he stood in the center of the bloody remains. It was a painting of war, and he its magnificent artist. His blood cooled, but his mind would not stop burning.

"Look upon the work of my hands," he said, quoting Aristava, "and by them, let me be judged."

When Dario participated in the scouring of Vulnae, he had walked streets choked with smoke. The dead burned in such high piles, the ash had floated for miles like dirge clouds. That sight had broken his little brother. Why had it not broken him? What was it Dario had seen instead?

He looked to these bodies, slain bearing the mask of the Vagrant.

And why did he not see it now?

"Look upon the work of my hands," he repeated, and this time he did look. He dared *see.* A dead man in his thirties, who had cowered within the home clutching a knife. A man who knew there was no chance to overcome the forces crusading through his city. Dario saw calluses on his fingers, stains on his sleeves, a hole in his shoe that needed repairing. Dark hair curled back, tied with a ponytail, a vibrant blue...ribbon? From whom? Who had given him the ribbon? The man's mask had ripped free in battle. Behind it was a large nose, wide lips, two moles on his neck, and a butterfly drawn in ink upon his cheek.

"Look upon the work of my hands."

For faith in a slain goddess, the man lay dead, his spine snapped in half. Who had he been? A sailor? A tradesman? Some merchant, perhaps? He had no business in battle. What was so precious to him that he would fight this inevitability? What could these heathen gods possibly offer that was worth this sacrifice?

Each life was a story, but Dario was their final chapter.

"The work of my hands..."

The world about him gained a clarity that frightened him. Details he so casually ignored now shone vibrant. Two children staring from a nearby window, their eyes wide with fear. The smoke rising from the west. A flock of crows already descending on Dario's previous kill two houses down. A dead old man, condemned on a list. Mallus. His name had been Mallus. Dario hadn't even hesitated. The crows pecked at his eyes and drank the matter leaking from the skull Dario had split in half.

Eyes open, he could only see. Nothing would shut them. He heard the suffering, too. The crackle of fires. The screams, some of pain, some of fright. And crying, so much crying. Deep wails as loved ones were torn apart, some headed for prisons, some for nearby cities, and some to die on the cobblestones. Smells joined in. The burn of ash. The stench of shit and piss from the corpses. Covering it all was the deep, throat-coating scent of blood. This was only one street, one specific moment, but it was being relived everywhere across Vallessau, magnified a thousandfold as the armies of Everlorn did their work. This was terror. They unleashed terror.

Lorka's words entered his mind, unbidden and with such force it stole his breath away.

The bleak realm awaiting you, that supposed paradise of your God-Incarnate's creation, is everything, everything, you deserve.

"Is this it?" Dario whispered. "Is this the truth I refused to see when Vulnae burned?"

What had he told his brother then? He couldn't remember. This was needed, wasn't it? That had been his argument. What did suffering in this mortal life matter when compared to the rewards of the eternal? They were saving souls. They were preparing eternities. The now must give way to the future. The heathens might weep, but when they were spared the torment of the God-Incarnate's hell, they would rejoice.

Spared the torment.

The God-Incarnate's hell.

The work of my hands.

"Are you well, paragon?"

Bassar casually strode to join him, his task the next street over apparently finished. Blood dripped from the shining edge of his sword.

"I'm fine," Dario said, pretending to misunderstand the question. "A few stubborn Thanese tried to ambush me, but they were nothing I couldn't handle."

The paragon grinned, but his smile never reached his eyes, which were always guarded.

"But of course," Bassar said. "If you are done with your fun here, I have another address for us to check."

Dario stretched his fingers, the gauntlet's metal groaning and his knuckles cracking.

"Fun?" he said, unable to bite his tongue. "These men and women were meant to be saved and brought into the God-Incarnate's loving arms. I take no *fun* in their deaths. It is a loss, sad and unwelcome."

"Perhaps you view me as cold," Bassar said, resuming his walk. "But by my eyes, they tried to murder you for sharing Lucavi's love."

"Love we brought with ships, soldiers, and paragons," Dario said. "Look around you, Bassar. Their neighbors lie dead in the streets. I doubt they sense much love here."

Bassar halted immediately. He glanced over his shoulder, his golden eyes startling in the night. It felt like catching the attention of a hawk moments before it dove on its prey.

"You repeat the words of heretics, Dario Bastell. Has your heart been compromised by the plight of these islanders? Or do the pleadings of your brother bear weight in your mind, as we all feared?"

Dario's pride would endure no such barb. He closed the distance between them in a single step and grabbed Bassar by the top of his silver armor. All the while, he paid keen attention to the placement of the divine bodyguard's long blade. It stayed on his shoulders, ready but not yet brought to bear.

"I have served the God-Incarnate loyally since I was in the crib," he said, pulling Bassar closer, challenging him with his gaze. "My every word, deed, and, yes, life taken, is done to exalt his name."

"Yes, but do you *love* him?" Bassar asked. He grabbed Dario with his free hand, the space between them shrinking even further. They were so close, their noses nearly touching. "Do you ache for his success? Do you wake every morning yearning for others to see him as you see him? For others to feel that same love, that same adoration, and give it in return? Is he God to you, Dario? Beyond Everlorn? Beyond life itself?"

"From the moment I set foot on this island I have had my faith challenged, even by my own brother," Dario said, low, breathless. "I will not have you do the same. My faith is beyond reproach."

He tried to shove them apart, but Bassar held strong. Their armor clattered as they pressed together.

"If you feel it true, then you know why we do what we must. If you feel this love, then you want all the world to feel it. To share it. We face an impossible task, but our blood, and our strength, shall make it possible. All of us will play our part. Even the dead."

At last, they separated. Bassar stretched his back and shoulders, the movements rattling his sword against his armor.

"Come now," he said. "Sinshei awaits, and our search must continue."

It was raining by the time Dario and Bassar arrived at the next location. A mansion. The crowd within was far greater than Dario had anticipated. Servants greeted them, looking fine in their suits despite the late hour, but they numbered nearly three dozen, far more than any one mansion should require. Different pins on their vests, he noted. Marking who they served, perhaps? A group of older men came rushing into the foyer, and women trailed after. Neighbors, by Dario's guess, multiple families coming together for supposed safety in this single house. Some were dressed in their finest, while others looked like they'd been dragged straight from bed.

"Is this everyone?" Bassar asked. He paced the group as more and more entered, women in simple but pretty dresses and men so young that acne marked their faces.

"This intrusion is unacceptable," a woman shouted. Dario assumed her the lady of the house. Her face was radish red, her words fiery, but her anger clearly hid her fear. She looked to be in the later stages of her life, but she pushed away a guest trying to hold her back as if she were still young and spry.

"We've complied with every request, given every tithe!" she screamed at Bassar. "You can't do this. Even Regent Gordian approved, he promised, he promised—!"

Bassar flipped the sword from his shoulder, looped it about, and buried it to the hilt in the woman's chest. Scattered screams and gasps came from those in attendance, but the loudest was from two children, a young boy and girl in loose, rumpled sleep clothes. An old woman held each of their hands in a vise grip. Her skin paled, and her jaw locked tight. Dario could almost feel the hate rolling off her.

None of that seemed to affect Bassar. He twisted his sword ninety degrees, then cut through the spine. The lady collapsed when he pulled his sword free. Her blood flowed across the fine limestone tiles in a steadily growing pool.

"We come looking for the God-Incarnate's daughter, Sinshei vin Lucavi," he said, the word-lace at his throat flaring to translate it for all present who did not speak the imperial tongue. "If she is here, confess, bring her forth, and you shall live. Servants will not be blamed for the deeds of the masters. But if Sinshei is here and you hide her, well..."

He flicked a few stubborn drops from his sword onto the lady's corpse. "Then all here shall suffer her fate."

What followed was a cacophony of pleading, promises, and assurances that Dario's word-lace struggled to translate. He grimaced at the headache it caused. From what he could tell, they were insisting Sinshei was not there, meaning this was another waste of time. He marched for the exit. Let Bassar deal with it, then.

Yet the front door did not grant him freedom, but instead a host of soldiers led by none other than Signifer Weiss himself.

"Oh good, you are here," he said. "I anticipated the people of this manse might pose an issue. Did they?"

Dario gestured to the corpse on the floor.

"Does it look like they posed an issue?"

Weiss's face twitched, and he arched an eyebrow.

"One easily overcome." He snapped his fingers at the soldiers accompanying him, at least two dozen by Dario's count. "Gather everyone, no matter their age. Many neighbors took refuge here, which is convenient. We can check off a lot of names at once."

Dario started past him, only to be stopped by the Signifer.

"Will you not aid me, paragon?"

"We're looking for Sinshei," Dario said.

"And have you searched the building for her? My notes suggest their sympathies for the Vagrant are very high."

Dario didn't bother hiding his annoyance.

"No, not yet," he said. "I guess I can start."

Yet after twenty minutes, Dario found nothing. As expected. The people here were afraid, one could easily tell that, but they lacked the zeal of true believers. They carried no skull masks in their pockets. They still thought compliance would save them, and so they complied and pretended not to see the corpse splayed out on the tile.

Still, Dario made a show of searching, tossing beds, kicking open any locked doors, and elbowing a few walls for secret passages. When finished, he returned to the foyer, but Bassar was nowhere to be found.

Did he run off on me? Dario wondered.

"Where's Bassar?" he asked one of the soldiers processing the Thanese. So far they'd been organized into two groups, with a third still waiting.

"I don't know," the soldier responded. "Signifer Weiss is upstairs. Maybe with him?"

Dario nodded and climbed the stairs. This night seemed destined to never end. He wanted nothing more than to climb into his bed and sleep away the next few days. That sleep would be a long time coming. He glanced out a window. The fires seemed to be spreading. The sight of them reawakened a discomfort he'd been trying to suppress.

Was his brother out there fighting? There were far too many soldiers, and accompanied by paragons besides. It'd be hopeless, but since when did that stop Arn? Dario looked at one fire and imagined his brother burning within it. He thought of Bassar's sword buried in Arn's gut, bleeding him out with nary a tear shed.

Doctrine and law insisted Arn deserved such a fate. He was a heretic, a betrayer, and a murderer of Everlorn's soldiers, priests, and paragons. And yet Dario could not stomach the thought. For all his brother's faults, there was no malice in them. He truly believed he was doing the right thing. How did Dario combat that? What wisdom did he lack that could convince Arn of the proper way?

Dario exited the stairs and found the Signifer standing alone on a second-story balcony.

"Is Bassar not here?" he asked.

"He is not," the Signifer said. "I suppose you found nothing? A shame." He lifted his notes, scanning them in the lamplight. "Might you accompany me further? I've taken upon myself the most dangerous of locations, and I would appreciate another paragon or two to protect me. So far the Vagrant has not shown himself, but surely it is only a matter of time."

Dario glanced at the papers. That stack was but a slice of the whole given to multiple magistrates and priests at the start of the purge. Names upon names, addresses, church attendance, tithe amounts... it was as if Weiss had found a way to measure every person's faithfulness to the God-Incarnate. All of Vallessau, shrunken down to sheets of yellow Thanese paper. Such a task had to have been in the works for months.

"Why do all this?" he asked.

"To find Sinshei, of course," Weiss said, tugging at the sleeve of his coat. "I thought that obvious."

Dario scoffed.

"You were working on that list long before she was captured. What's the point? We're putting in all this effort to cow a populace that will be sacrificed down to a man come the six-hundred-year ceremony."

Weiss tilted his head slightly to one side, as if confused by Dario's line of inquiry.

"Do farmers deny food to their cattle because they are destined for slaughter? Of course not. Our God-Incarnate deserves the finest sacrifice as capstone to his legacy. That means a properly obedient and faithful populace."

Dario stared at the diminutive man. He'd not known him prior to arriving on Thanet, but what few interactions they'd had painted him as a calm, intelligent man, not one prone to religious fervor.

"You don't carry the faith others do," Dario said. "Nor do I believe you hold much love for the God-Incarnate. You're deflecting, Weiss. Tonight is your night, one you worked for months in preparation for. Why?"

The Signifer glanced down at his notes, and finally he grinned. Just a small one, tugging a little curl at the sides of his mouth.

"If you must know, paragon, my love is for Everlorn. There is a cleanliness to it that heathen nations lack, and it is a joy to watch them transform. As for tonight, well?" His smile spread, fuller, purer. "Through reports, numbers, and rumors, I have exposed an entire city, digging through all its falsehoods and deceptions to find the deep roots of its treachery. I am *good* at what I do, and I take great pride in that, as do all the best in their fields."

Weiss tucked his papers into his left arm and leaned upon the balcony railing with his right, gazing upon a city choking in death.

"Whether these people die tonight, tomorrow, or in the ceremony to come, it matters not. What matters is that I saw them for who they are, even when they thought to hide it. So much emphasis is put upon the might of paragons as justification for Everlorn as the one true empire. Yet in the shadows are people like me, proving that we are more than our strength in battle. We are smarter than them. More ruthless. More willing to do what must be done."

He stood and waved as if he were a grand conductor upon a stage.

"Look upon the work of my hands," he said, and laughed. "To think I once resented Imperator Magus for bringing me to this far-flung little island."

Weiss left him upon the balcony. Dario stood there, alone, confused, angry, and conflicted with too many emotions that he could neither understand nor identify. Nothing about tonight was any different from what he had done before. The casualties of Vulnae's invasion easily surpassed tonight's. Dario had cleansed whole villages before, piling their corpses and burning them so the ash clouded the sky as a warning.

The brutality. The death. It had been *justified*. Surely it still was, wasn't it?

If you cannot see a truth so blinding, then you deserve to walk in emptiness.

"No!"

Dario smashed his fist upon the balcony railing, shattering the stone. Rubble rained down to the courtyard below. He bared his teeth like a cornered animal. No, this was the danger of heresy. This was the venom that seeped into your veins. He had to be stronger. He had to hold faith. The God-Incarnate was righteous. He was just. Through his guidance, all would be redeemed and made to believe. Salvation was their goal. This misery was born of kindness, once you looked upon it from the proper point of view.

"We are the knife that cuts away the rot," he said, closing his eyes. "We are the fire that seals the bleeding wound."

He fell to his knees. He cast off his pride and humbled himself before his god. From the lowliest child to the mightiest paragon, all must kneel. This doubt, this awful, burning, clawing doubt, must be defeated.

Help me, O Lord, he prayed. *Be with me, and guard my faith. Keep me strong. I need you, Lucavi. I need you now more than ever.*

Not silent this time, but aloud, a heartfelt prayer whispered to the night. If he gave everything, if he revealed his weakness, perhaps he could love Lucavi the same way Bassar did.

"Please, God, show me the way. Grant me the truth, and the strength to see it. Open my eyes. Open my heart. Wisdom, give me wisdom, and courage, I beg."

Dario held his breath for an answer that did not come. No touch of the God-Incarnate upon his heart. No whispers, no golden glow of faith emanating from his skin.

Only the smell of blood and ash upon the wind.

CHAPTER 29

STASIA

Stasia crashed through the squad of soldiers with fury even the thunder could not match. Her axes cleaved their ranks, easily puncturing their armor. Screams filled her ears, but they were diluted, distant. Blood flowed, but it gave her no satisfaction.

Hopeless. Everywhere, every direction, every fight, hopeless.

Two men tried to flee, only to have their chests and skulls crushed upon Arn's arrival. Stasia stood amid the gore, six soldiers of Everlorn bleeding out in the rain in the middle of one of Vallessau's gods-forsaken streets. She looked to the nearby house and its broken door. More bodies within. Stasia and Arn had arrived too late.

"We've got to hit the bigger groups," Arn said, wiping a bit of blood from his gauntlet onto his heavy coat.

"Bigger groups have priests and paragons," she said.

"We can take them."

"Fast enough that they can't call for reinforcements?" Stasia shook her head, and she kicked one of the bodies. "They're swarming this city like ants. After killing Lucavi's children, we should have known they would retaliate. This is on us. Too complacent. Too confident in our victories."

Arn nudged her with his elbow.

"Don't give up on me yet, Ax. They're desperate, that's all. Keep on fighting. That's all we can do. That's what everyone else is doing."

It was true. Stasia and Arn had raced throughout Vallessau, seeking smaller, isolated groups of enemies to ambush. Every now and then they found the remnants of a battle, where a cell of Thorda's resistance fighters had been stationed. The Thanese bodies outnumbered Everlorn's by far. Rain fell upon black cloth, washing away the chalk skulls the men and women had drawn upon them.

The Vagrant's mark, their hope and strength. The Vagrant, who was not here to help them when they needed him most.

"You're right," she said, unable to fight off her bitterness. Maybe it was the rain. Maybe it was the terrifying number of captured and dead. "We fight, and we fight, until we're dead, or there's no fight left in us. The war will be over, Thanet sacrificed, all for a new God-Incarnate and a new age, while we suffer and die."

Gods help her, she missed her sister. She missed Rayan. She even missed Cyrus. These soldiers who lay dead at her feet, did they know what they died for? Did they know the misery they spread? Did they even care?

Arn put a bloody gauntlet on her shoulder. She glared, then bit down her retort. His expression was too honest, too sincere. It'd be like kicking a puppy.

"Let's go," he said. "People need us."

Stasia twirled an ax between her fingers.

"You're right. Come on."

She trudged down the street while visualizing a map of the city in her mind. They'd mostly moved at random, seeking what prey they could find, but the chaos of the night had mostly kept them near Thorda's safe house. If she wanted to start making more significant progress, they'd need to go where the purge was currently focused, which was higher up toward the homes built into the cliffs. She turned at the next intersection. If she followed the road up for about a quarter mile, there'd...

A lone woman rushed toward Stasia. Her thin coat was drenched, and her dress sticking to her body. Stasia's mind froze in shock.

"Clarissa?" she asked, bewildered. "What are you doing?"

Her wife barreled into her, her arms wrapping about Stasia's waist.

"You're safe," she said. "Thank Lycaena."

Stasia clipped one of her axes to her belt and used her free hand to lift Clarissa's chin. Their eyes met, and she offered her grandest, falsest smile in defiance of the horrors of the night.

"Of course I'm safe," she said. "Why aren't you home?"

Clarissa pushed away and wiped a bit of wet hair from her face.

"My mother," she said, thoroughly out of breath. "They came for her."

Stasia didn't think her mood could worsen, but renewed hatred coursed through her veins. Arn arrived before she could speak, an arm raised above his head to shelter his face from the rain.

"What's going on?" he asked, nodding toward Clarissa.

"It's my mother," Clarissa repeated. "So many of my friends were being raided, it's... it's like they know, somehow. They know too much. I didn't feel safe in my house, so I ran to hers, only they... they'd already arrived."

Stasia's mouth went dry.

"Is she...?"

Her wife shook her head.

"They're relocating her somewhere outside the city. I followed them for a time and overheard them talking. They're heading toward the west gate. Please, Stasia, you have to help her. You have to free her. I don't know where they're taking her, or why, or what they'll do when they get there."

Stasia kissed her forehead.

"We're going to run, and I need you to keep up, all right?"

Clarissa nodded.

"Anything. Just save her, please. I know you can."

Stasia readied her axes, pondered a moment, and then struck them together to form a great ax. Visions of bloodshed filled her mind as she withdrew the pole from the pouch she always carried and slid it in place, extending the weapon's reach. When this furious, she wanted to lash out with single, powerful hits.

"Wait," Arn said, trudging alongside her as they started west. "What about the raids? The soldiers? Our fight?"

"What fight?" Stasia asked, whirling to face him. "We have no

Vagrant. No Lioness. No plan, and no army. This shit is hopeless. So I'm going to make sure at least one person I care about survives. You want to be useful? Go home, and make sure Thorda and my sister aren't targeted by these raids."

Arn clenched his fists.

"You think Mari's in danger?"

Stasia gestured wildly around her, to the empty street, the distant torches, and the thundering rain.

"We are *all* in danger," she said, and headed for the gate. Clarissa fell behind almost immediately, forcing Stasia to slow down. Her poor wife looked exhausted. How many streets had she run, first to track Adella, then to search the chaos and bloodshed for Stasia? Her hair was matted to her neck and face, and her chest heaved with frantic breaths.

"I know you're tired," Stasia said, and she offered her hand. "I know everything hurts. Hold on to me, keep your legs moving, and do your best to ignore the pain. Can you do that? For Adella?"

Clarissa took her hand.

"Leave me if you must, just get past the gate to save her."

Stasia shook her head.

"I'm not leaving you," she said. "Not now, not ever. Now, run."

They raced through the dark streets, two shadows amid the rain and blood. Twice they passed groups of men and women rounded up by soldiers, but Clarissa breathlessly insisted that they keep going. Her mother was past the gate, she was certain of it, and so they went. The going was surprisingly easy, for the purge was like an enormous wave of soldiers, priests, and paragons washing over the city. Once they were in its wake, there was only the sound of the rain and the weeping of those left to mourn the taken and the dead.

That changed when they finally reached the western gate. It was open but guarded by two dozen armed soldiers. Stasia observed it from where they crouched behind an overturned cart, trusting the shadows to keep her hidden.

"We need to get past," she said. Clarissa looked frighteningly pale, and her entire body lifted with her every breath. Stasia felt pity at her exhaustion but forced the emotion away. No time for that now.

"Can you take them?" Clarissa asked.

Stasia bit her lip and glanced around the cart.

"That's a lot," she said. Stasia scanned the walls, then took Clarissa's hand. "Come on, I think I see a way."

The soldiers were gathered at the open gate, and the light of their torches and the falling rain would blind them to much of the night. Nearby were steps that led up to the ramparts of the wall that sealed off the western half of the city from the forest path. They had been left unguarded, and it was easy enough to sneak up unnoticed. Beyond them stretched the forest of ash trees that grew to the city's very edge.

"How do we get down?" Clarissa asked. Stasia grinned as she whispered back.

"Hold on to me."

Once her wife had wrapped her hands about her waist, Stasia held her snug with her left arm and readied her ax in her right, keeping it low near her ankles. Together, the pair leaned closer to the wall's edge. Leaned, and then stepped off.

The moment their fall began, Stasia swung her ax above her head. It slammed into the stone, cut a groove, and then caught. Stasia held back a scream as both her weight and Clarissa's pulled on her right arm, but their momentum halted with the pair halfway down the wall.

"Hold on to my leg, and then drop," Stasia ordered. Clarissa nodded nervously, then did as Stasia said. She stretched her arms out, hanging from Stasia's extended ankle, and then let go. The fall was still a good ten feet or so, but doable without injury. Once Clarissa landed, Stasia ordered her to move. The last thing she wanted was to hurt her wife during her own landing.

Stasia now had the trickier part: dislodging her ax. She grabbed the handle with both hands and swung her weight so her feet pressed to the wall. She gathered herself, counted to three, and then flexed her entire body.

Out came the ax, then came her fall, much more awkward than Clarissa's. Stasia twisted as she fell and flung her ax aside so it wouldn't land atop her. The muddy ground was a poor welcome, as were the bushes that grew along the forest's edge. She cried out as she rolled twice before coming to a halt.

"Are you all right?" Clarissa asked as she rushed over. Stasia pushed herself to her feet and tried not to imagine how many scratches and bruises she must sport.

"I'm fine. We need to reach the road, or we'll be hopelessly lost." Now cut off from the light of the city, and with the sky clouded over, it was shocking how dark the night had become.

By keeping the wall to their right, they were able to stumble through the brush until they reached the forest road that cut through the Emberfall Mountains.

"If they're marching at night, in this weather, then they'll have torches, and lots of them," Stasia said. "We go until we see them, all right?"

Clarissa nodded. Or at least, Stasia thought the black and gray blob where her wife's head was nodded.

Step after unsteady step, they followed the beaten road as it turned to mud. Forget the element of surprise, what Stasia would give for a torch of her own. Mud clung to her boots, and twice she stumbled off the path and into the brush, but at last she saw the distant flicker of torches. Stasia released Clarissa's hand. Four soldiers formed the rear, pushing and urging the people onward. Up ahead, two more torches led the way. Six in total, against only her great-ax? Stasia grinned. She liked those odds.

During her resistance in Aethenwald, she had been known as the Killing Rain. This darkness, this downpour, filled her with a sudden nostalgia for her younger years, when she was far more brash and reckless. She'd failed in Aethenwald, of course. Failed there, like she failed everywhere. The bitter truth added speed to her step, and when she leaped upon her prey, they stood not a chance. Her ax tore through two of them before they knew they were under attack. One drew his sword, shouting a warning for those up ahead. She cut his throat in reward. Torches fell from dying hands. In the growing darkness, she flashed her teeth at the last soldier, felt an animal savagery take hold. Instead of fighting, he fled.

Stasia caught him easily. Her ax plunged into his back, severing his spine. Screams followed, ghostly images of panicked faces. Stasia ignored them. Pushed ahead, to the front, to the last two escorts. They had their weapons drawn, but there was no disguising their fear when they saw her approach, her ax wet with the blood of their comrades. Exhilaration gave fuel to her attack. This chaos was where she thrived. The soldiers had but a heartbeat to recognize her weapon and prepare a defense before her ax arrived. The first foolishly lifted his sword to block. Her ax smashed through the thin blade to bury deep into his chest, the Ahlai-made steel easily parting his chainmail. Stasia dug her right heel into the mud and twisted, using her still-embedded ax to fling his body at the other soldier. They connected with a tumble of armor and limbs. Her final foe pushed the corpse away, stumbled in the mud, and then frantically thrust upon realizing how exposed he was.

He missed. The rain, the dark, the chaos; it was all too much. She was home within it, but this soldier, alone and afraid, was not. She cut him down, and it almost felt like a mercy. If only this dead soldier could be all of Everlorn. If only something good could come of this damned night.

Movement behind her. She turned, readying her ax, but it was only Clarissa. Her red hair was matted from the rain, and so far from the torches, her face was shadowed and hidden. How much had she watched? Stasia didn't know, nor was she sure it mattered.

"We need you to lead," Clarissa said, closing the distance between them.

"Lead? Why?"

Clarissa gestured back at the rest of the prisoners.

"Most of us can't go back to Vallessau, but my mother has relatives in Kritia, sixty miles from here. The soldiers had some food and water we can take. The people are ready, but they won't leave yet. Too many are refusing to go without you. They don't feel safe. So...will you? Come with us?"

Stasia looked back to the city, ablaze with Everlorn's cleansing fires. Sixty miles, on foot, with many of the travelers elderly? They'd be on the road for at least two days, perhaps three. She tried to think of a reason to stay, to believe there was hope in fighting, but they were woefully unprepared, and their strongest fighters were scattered to the winds. That hope was thin and fraying. Her absence would not be felt, for what could they even accomplish while her sister recovered, and Cyrus and Keles were off aiding Commander Pilus at Ialath?

No, this was where she could do the most good. Stasia leaned her ax across her shoulder and smiled wide. Pretend the night was young, and lacking the horrors. Beam with confidence despite the desire to crumple down into a small ball and weep. Be strong, for those who needed her to be.

"I don't know the way," Stasia said. She offered her hand. The rain had already washed away most of the blood. "Which means I can't lead, but you can, Clarissa, and I'll be right alongside you every step of the way."

CHAPTER 30

KELES

They asked Keles to pray over so much as the night wore on. Over the injured. Over groups of soldiers asking for future victories. Crowds of men and women shouted at her as she walked the narrow streets toward the docks, where, in the distance, multiple imperial ships fled for safer harbors. They hailed her as a hero, her stand against the paragon of swords growing more epic with each retelling. *Pray for us*, begged the people, and so Keles prayed.

They asked Cyrus to pray over nothing.

"This is necessary," he said as soldiers lined dozens of men and women into a city square. Pilus had chosen the location with care. All around were the poles of the Dead Flags, currently empty, the bodies cut free the moment the city was captured.

"I know," Keles said, her voice cold. "Do not think me soft, Cyrus."

"On your knees!" Pilus shouted at the prisoners. They were a mixture of lords, soldiers, and Everlorn appointees, all foolish enough to allow themselves to be captured alive. Excited Thanese troops beat and kicked those who at first resisted, until all were on their knees. The surrounding crowd, numbering in the thousands, howled with glee. People were crammed together as tightly as possible to bear witness, with hundreds more climbing up to the rooftops of the surrounding homes for a better view.

They did not know what they were about to witness, not entirely. It would be an execution, yes, but it would also be a dire message.

Pilus joined Keles and Cyrus beside the rows of prisoners.

"We're ready," he said.

Keles slowly breathed in and out to steel herself.

"Bring the wine."

They'd found the enormous cask hidden in the castle, and over the past hour had loaded it up onto a cart. At her order, they wheeled it into the square. Pilus's soldiers readied dozens of cups but did not yet fill them. Keles climbed atop the cart so she might be seen better. Her every lesson at proper demeanor comforted her as she felt the eyes of the crowd upon her.

"People of Ialath," she shouted. "People of Thanet! You have suffered greatly beneath the boot of Everlorn, but you know not yet the crimes they would commit!" She pointed to the cask beside her. "This wine was prepared for you, as it was prepared for every town and city across our island. It is your gift for the coming celebration. It is the true reward for any who would give their hearts to the God-Incarnate instead of our beloved Lycaena."

Keles drew her sword and pointed it at the prisoners.

"Give them their drink."

Soldiers broke open the cask and filled the cups. Keles thought the prisoners might resist, for surely they knew the fate awaiting them, but they calmly accepted their drink.

Better to die quickly of poison than endure what the people would do to them, she decided. She couldn't blame them. A hush fell over the crowd as they watched the prisoners drink. One doubled over, clutching their stomach. Another coughed, then another. A few in the crowd screamed at the first bloody pile of vomit. Fear became rage as the prisoners collapsed, retching and clutching at their stomachs and throats. Cyrus walked among their corpses, one by one marking them with their crowns.

Keles stood tall and projected her voice with every bit of strength in her lungs. These words would carry, and be shared all across the entire northern coast. If Lycaena were kind, they would save untold thousands from a similar fate.

"Behold the promise of Everlorn, and the death it brings!"

Afterward, Cyrus stayed close to Keles as they passed through crowded streets to attend an impromptu feast thrown to celebrate the city's liberation. It didn't matter that more soldiers might return to retake the city, or that other ships might sail from Vallessau or Raklia. For now, in this moment, the city and its people were free. And yet, the Vagrant remained quiet and composed.

"You need not stay with me," she whispered at one point. The feast was in full swing, with fish freshly roasted over hastily constructed fire pits, the meat mixed with walnuts and honey broken out from imperial storehouses. She tried not to grimace at the sight of Everlorn's appointed mayor swaying from a pole in the distance. Fishermen were carrying the pole throughout the streets while chanting their praises to the heroes of Vallessau, the Returned Queen and her Vagrant.

"I know," Cyrus said. "Let them look upon me while the victory is fresh. Do not worry. I have my own business to attend, and I will attend it before the night is through."

Except that made her worry all the more.

More drinks. More prayers. More smiles for Keles and frightened looks for Cyrus. She heard their whispers, saw the respect and fear in their eyes. He did not wear the skull face, yet all sensed it. His faint smile. His polite nods. This was not the real him; not anymore, not after what they had witnessed.

After two more tiring hours, it seemed Cyrus had had enough, and he leaned close to whisper his farewell. "Enjoy your accolades."

The rowdy crowd parted for him. It seemed even the drunkest among them were frightened to lay a finger upon his cloak.

"I need rest," Keles told Pilus, who had dutifully joined her at the long table. It was a ridiculous setup, the tables stolen from the mayor's home and dragged outside before the docks. Even when she had been the Light of Vallessau, she had never been given such treatment.

"Nearly every home will open its doors to you and offer you a bed," Pilus told her. "Have you an idea where you will sleep?"

"I'll find a place," she said, not wanting to lie. Tired as she was, it wasn't bed that awaited her. Following Cyrus would be difficult if he wished to go unseen, but she need not chase his exact steps, not if she was right about his destination.

Keles pushed through the revelers, who were much less reluctant to make way and much more eager to praise her skill, her victory, and yes, her beauty. Thankfully the late hour served her well once she was beyond the docks. Her dark platemail blended well into the night, and if she moved quickly, those still out and about were much too preoccupied with their feasting and drinking to notice.

The moon was high and the clouds sparse by the time Keles reached the outer wall. Archers stood guard at the gate, laughing and eating off a shared plate. They startled when they realized who she was.

"Lady Keles," said one, wiping his hand on his leg so he could salute her.

"Have you seen the Vagrant pass this way?" she asked them. They exchanged glances.

"We did not," one answered. Keles pressed on anyway.

"No, you probably wouldn't."

The task of sorting the dead would begin in the morning. She herself had done a preliminary search, aided by a few dozen others, for those who were injured and could be saved. They had been the first she prayed over, the sealing of sword wounds and mending of broken bones. The dead were left as they were. An honorable pyre would be built for the Thanese. The soldiers of Everlorn would be stripped of valuables, loaded onto boats, and tossed overboard, where they could bloat and rot and be eaten by creatures of the sea.

That was daylight work. But tonight? A few hours before the dawn? Cyrus had his own task to perform. Keles saw him standing in the center of the corpse-strewn battlefield. His hands were at his sides, and his head tilted so he might stare up at the stars. He did not move. His back was to her, and she could not see his face through the hood of his cloak. If he spoke, or sang, or wept, she could not hear it. He was so very still, as if listening to a voice far, far away.

"You don't need to be here for this," he said without turning.

Keles halted several feet away. Her hand drifted to her sword hilt without thinking, and the realization made her uneasy.

"And yet I am," she said.

At last, Cyrus turned. His brown eyes shimmered in the night. The light of his grinning skull shone brighter than any star. The teeth did not move when he spoke.

"Then you know I must do this. What I am...it is not just what Thorda made me. It's what the people believe. It's what they want, what they *need*."

"I did not come to judge you."

"Then why are you here?"

Keles tried to see past the bone to the young, easily embarrassed man he'd been when they first met. She wanted to take his hand and remind him of their talks, of his parents, of their time dancing while her uncle Rayan stomped the floor and strummed his lute. To embrace the human in him and feel him embrace her in return.

Her feet remained still, as if the ground clutched her in its grasp.

"I didn't want you to be alone," she said. It was the best she could do.

Cyrus laughed softly. He returned his gaze to the stars and lifted his hands.

"I have never been one for crowds, you know that. Solitude suits me better." Light shimmered across his gloves, crimson in color. "I wish you didn't have to see this, Keles."

The hair on her neck stood on end. She felt divine energy growing around her, like the tension in the air before a strike of lightning. Her heart began to race, and she could almost feel Cyrus's will pushing her away like a physical force.

"Don't," she said. She didn't even know why.

Cyrus's feet lifted off the ground, pushed up by darkness solidified. Not far, just a foot or two as shadows swelled below him. The night around her felt like it was cracking, and behind it lurked something even darker. Something cold and deadly.

"I felt it on the battlefield," he told her, his voice a whisper and yet audible to her ears. "The belief in me, it's growing." Soft red light began to glow across the corpses, deep and somber, like the oldest of embers. "Not just among the Thanese. Those of Everlorn fear me, too. They hear the stories and see their dead. It's not worship. It's belief, but more...primal. Elusive. Dreadful. They know what I come for, and they know I will take it. They believe, deep down in their souls, nothing can stop me. And it *horrifies them.*"

Keles clenched her jaw. She would not cry out. She would not scream at the writhing corpses and the unearthly light pulsing like veins across the blood-soaked ground.

Cyrus closed his hands into fists. No more whispers.

"I am their fear made real," he shouted. "I am their nightmares made manifest and given blades. They would fight me, deny me, but their fear only makes me stronger. Victory is inevitable. I will have my vengeance. I will have my kingdom."

The crimson glow swelled across the battlefield like a river. Cyrus stood upon nothing. His cloak billowed in a wind unfelt. His gloves opened toward the stars, and his scream could be heard for miles.

"I will have my crown."

The sound of tearing flesh filled Keles's ears. The forehead of every single corpse, Thanese and Everlorn both, ripped open from temple to temple. Blood poured forth, but it did not run down their faces to pool upon the earth. It floated upward, little droplets so dark they looked black. Toward the space above Cyrus and his lifted arms.

The blood gathered into a perfect sphere, vibrated, and then exploded outward. It rippled with energy. It pulsed with crimson light. Keles closed her eyes and whispered a prayer to her goddess.

Is this the god with whom I shall share our land?

When she opened her eyes, the visage of the Vagrant hovered high above the battlefield. A grinning skull composed of blood, slowly turning so all within the city might bear witness. Keles looked upon it and refused to be afraid. She would not let the Vagrant alone lay claim to this victory. Keles lifted her hand, taking comfort in the presence of her own goddess, strong and renewed within her breast.

Lycaena's fire flowed from her fingertips. It swirled into the sky to set the blood aflame. The skull burned, its crimson color fading into white, then nothing at all. All who witnessed would remember, and believe. Tales of Ialath's freedom, and the Vagrant's skull, would spread throughout Thanet. By the time the duo returned to Vallessau, it would be one more legend added to their names.

The presence of the divine drifted away, but the Vagrant remained, and as he lowered to the ground, the last of the blood and fire swirled down to be absorbed into him. He sagged the moment his feet touched earth. It was as if Cyrus's physical body could not handle the weight settling over him, invisible and crippling. He looked to Keles with a face of flesh and eyes wet with tears.

"There is no other way," he said, his voice cracking.

Only now could Keles embrace him. The distance between them vanished, and she held him against her as he closed his eyes and slowly breathed in and out. She remembered their first meeting at one of Thorda's awful gatherings. She remembered their dance on his birthday, and the time they had sat and watched the moonlight shine upon the harbor. The distance between them had seemed so much greater, and yet filled with such potential.

Those moments felt a lifetime ago. He was no longer a young man fighting for his kingdom, nor she a paladin who had cast aside her faith. There was only the Vagrant, and the Returned Queen.

"It is still your choice," she whispered.

"What choice, when only I can carry the burden?" he whispered back, and despite trembling in her arms, he stood and pushed her away. "I will not refuse it, no matter how terrible a road I must walk."

Cyrus left her there on the battlefield to slowly stumble back to the gates of Ialath. Keles looked to the hundreds of bodies stretched out in all directions, their foreheads sliced open.

"I believe you," she whispered to the boy she might have loved and the god she would never worship. "And that, more than anything, is what I fear."

CHAPTER 31

SHE

Nameless She walked the city of Vallessau without fear of soldiers, priests, and paragons. As a woman with a thousand faces, She would forever be a stranger. She was guided by a vague sense of direction, of *need*, without any conscious effort. Everywhere she looked, she saw the city's scars from the horrid purge the night before. Burnt homes. Smashed doors. Blood on the cobbles, dried beneath the unrelenting sun.

"There is no limit to your cruelty, is there, Ashraleon?" she asked as she stopped before a fountain. Once, it bore a roaring Lion carved into its stone. Instead the statue was broken, and hanging from its remains were three corpses, strangled by the rope that held them.

She pretended not to catch her own reflection as she left. It was a blur on the water, lacking any discernible features. She could not even see her own face. Her body, if She looked upon it while naked, was hairless and without any blemishes, moles, or wrinkles. It resembled more a doll than a human body, and the sight deeply discomforted her. She needed to neither eat nor sleep. Perhaps She even *was* a doll, a living and breathing approximation of the woman She had once been. The only detail She could be certain of was her skin color, a pale shade resembling Ashraleon's. She doubted it had been her own in her mortal time. It felt more like a collective agreement among the people of Gadir, and even that shade had shifted to become paler over the last few centuries.

At the next crossroad, high up in the outer rungs of the wealthy districts, She looked out across the city. She saw the ashen remnants of fires and riots. She saw the warships forming a perimeter around the docks. And above the castle, She saw a storm cloud brewing, a familiar mixture of hate and desperation visible only to the eyes of the divine. It floated from distant Gadir to settle over the castle like a hurricane's eye.

It follows you everywhere, She thought. The hatred of millions. The rage of the conquered. *Do you feel it, Ashraleon? Do you know how many pray for your death?*

She turned and resumed her walk, not knowing where but trusting these seemingly random choices to lead her true. She sensed the pain before She heard the vomiting. It sounded like a woman attempting to retch out her entire stomach. The sound guided her to a small street dead-ending at one of the walls built against the surrounding Emberfall Mountains. There She found a freshwater well, and the source of the pain. A young woman was on her knees, her hands weakly clutching the stone well to keep herself upright as she vomited yet again. The bile was white, and lacking substance.

"What is wrong?" She asked, kneeling beside the woman. She looked young, best guess not yet into her twentieth year. Her hair was a lovely shade of brown, bordering on a deep bronze. It was tied back and knotted with a green and blue ribbon She suspected secretly referred to Lycaena in some way. Her face was flushed, the red threatening to overwhelm her many freckles.

The square was quiet but for a lone man watching them out of curiosity. With a quick glare, She easily withered him. A foul look crossed his face, and he left.

"I'm fine," the woman said, glancing once and then turning to stare. It was a look She was well familiar with. No matter the circumstances, when people saw her and her beauty, they immediately doubted their initial impression. They had to look again, to confirm. It passed quickly, followed by the woman's face turning pale. "I'm...gods, I think I'm..."

Another round. There was a specific smell to it, strong enough to power through the acid. She suspected the cause before the woman even explained it.

"Daylily flowers," she admitted. "I was told, if you ate enough on an empty stomach..."

"Hush, now." She pressed the back of her hand to the woman's forehead. Feverish. "What is your name?"

"Elodie."

"The flowers are killing you, Elodie, yet you knew they might, didn't you?"

Elodie froze in place. Her shoulders went rigid, and when she looked back, coldness had come to her eyes.

"I had to. You don't know."

Oh, but She did. She knew it so well. She turned her hand and placed her palm against Elodie's cheek. A whisper, and the power flowed. To Everlorn, she was the Nameless Whore, but to the conquered? To the people who watched the Uplifted Church rip apart their culture by the foundations? To the women who lost their businesses, their homes, even their marriages should they be wed to another woman? The Whore became Nameless She. A symbol. A martyr. A trust that the world was not so simple as Everlorn decreed, and a belief that the woman the church deeply hated, slandered, and vilified was so much better than they claimed.

To those people, She was hope. To them, She was comfort. Healing flowed from her palm and into Elodie. The fever abated.

"I don't understand," Elodie said. The coldness had left her, replaced by guarded confusion.

"You do not have to. Lie still. Let me work."

Next She pressed her hands to Elodie's stomach. Though much of the flower had come up with the bile, more remained inside, working its poison. She could picture them in her mind, little yellow petals mashed to a pulp.

You are unneeded, She thought. *Begone from her.*

The petals shriveled to black and then crumbled away. Elodie gasped, and comfort came almost instantly. The woman gaped at her. By now, she'd know something wondrous was happening, an event she could not explain. Time would erase it, though. It always did. People forgot. They misremembered. The many miracles She worked faded like morning mist or were attributed to other gods and goddesses. Such was her lot.

What deeds people did attribute to the Whore were never of her own doing. This was the cruelty She lived day in and day out. Her gifts, unremembered. Her crimes, never hers, but thrust upon her by the Uplifted Church. But the look of relief in Elodie's eyes gave her the strength to keep going. The woman lowered her voice, as if to give confession.

"One of their soldiers," she said. "I don't even remember what he looks like. He...and then the moons came and went, and my blood didn't come."

It was a painfully familiar story. She moved her hands lower, to Elodie's abdomen.

"Is that still your wish?" She asked. Elodie paused to think, then nodded.

"He took enough from me. I won't let him take more."

"Then let it be done." She closed her eyes and let the magic flow. "The guilt. The fear. Be free of it. Your life, I return to you."

There was no gasp this time. Just calm, quiet tears. Nameless She stood, wiped the dust from her knees, and then gently brushed Elodie's bronze hair with her fingers.

"Goodbye."

"Wait, please," the woman said, grabbing her by the wrist. "Your name. I must know."

She smiled, wishing She had a better answer, one that would give the woman comfort. Instead She pulled her wrist free.

"I have none. Farewell, Elodie."

Ever since arriving in Vallessau, hidden on one of Lucavi's many boats, She had chosen this place close to the docks, preferring the smell of the brine over the more common city filth that hovered like a cloud over the streets higher up. Her "home" was little more than a shed. Four walls, a straw bed, and an emptied-out dresser. Whether its contents had been stolen, or taken with the former owner when they fled, She could only guess. Her own possessions were few, and She stuffed them far into the back of the lowest dresser drawer. She opened it now.

Inside were a book, a quill, and a capped inkwell. She laid them out before her and opened the book. More than half of it was filled with writing, the same sentence again and again, page after page, with only a single variance.

Tonight I am Arianna.

Tonight I am Nora.

Tonight I am Keles.

She uncapped her inkwell, dipped the quill within, and set to writing while sunlight remained.

Tonight I am Elodie.

Elodie waited for the ink to dry. She stared at the name, letting it burn into her. Come morning, it would leave her. She would not remember it even if she tried. When she read her own writing, her memory of choosing this name, of allowing herself to become it, would fade from her. It would look foreign, feel foreign.

The writing was her proof. For a time, She had a name, and one of her own choosing. Ashraleon and his children could do so much to her, but they could not wipe away this ink.

"Elodie," she whispered, liking the feel of it on her tongue. She gazed over the other names, feeling another minor thrill of victory. No, she could never remember choosing them, but she remembered the people they came from. Arianna was an older woman Elodie had met the first day she arrived, full of fire and cursing out soldiers under her breath as Everlorn's fleet disembarked. Nora had been a baby with a cough whom Elodie had prayed over to the comfort of her mother. And Keles, well, there would be no forgetting the woman who would name herself Queen of Thanet.

Names of people, names of memories. Names that, for a day, had also been hers. Though she could not remember calling herself them, the rituals she created saved her. Each day, a person met. A name stolen. Everlorn might call her Nameless, but she would deny them in every way.

The remnants of the previous night's fire were in a little circle of stones in the center of her home, half-burnt logs resting atop some ashes. Elodie crisscrossed some smaller twigs over a larger branch she snapped in half. That done, she set her hands upon it and closed her eyes. With but a thought, her hands shimmered red, and then her little fire burst into life. Elodie felt neither relief nor pleasantness from its warmth. The fire was a needed tool, little more.

Night came. The stars twinkled into view, and she watched them through her window. Had she enjoyed a life of quiet contemplation when she was human? Elodie did not know. Too little of herself remained, and what was left was shaped by the stories and beliefs of the Uplifted Church. Her only certainty was that, come the dark, she would retreat alone, always alone, into hiding.

Elodie had years upon years to dwell upon this fact. "Whore" they called her, and yet she never felt the desire for intimacy, nor any need for it on a carnal level, despite the jokes and drawings people made of her. Oh, how wild some artists' and storytellers' imaginations ran. They would have her perform sex acts no physical body could accomplish, at least, not one with a proper skeleton.

It was never about the sex, she knew. The fear was of corruption and defilement. She seduced not bodies, but minds. It put a smile to Elodie's face. Yes, she had most certainly done *that* over the years. A woman with a thousand faces could whisper the most damning words into the ears of those willing to listen. Elodie had fostered resentment among regents, stirred up crowds, and even been the first to cast stones to ignite riots against Everlorn occupation. She had done it all, and more, never to be remembered. Nameless. Faceless. Church and history would remember only the Whore.

There was one aspect the people most certainly believed, and oh, how deeply they believed in it. Elodie winced as the compulsion stirred. It was a sickly need roiling to life deep within her belly. To fight it was to lose. Centuries had taught her this.

"Tonight I am Elodie," she whispered.

Elodie thrust her hand into the fire.

At times, she felt whole. Other times, she felt ready to split in half, a thin piece of paper ripped apart by callous hands. During the day, she would heal, pray, and comfort as the Nameless She to whom the conquered, if not worshiped, at least extended their sympathy. Come the night, the Whore would awaken, and she must cut, and she must burn. The sinful must be punished, but Elodie refused to let anyone else suffer at her hands. She would not become the vile thing they desired her to be. Only herself. Only Elodie.

The fire would not be enough. It was never enough. It only bought her time. After the first two hours, she pulled her arm free. Already the skin healed. Fire was ever her servant.

"Tonight I am Elodie," she said again, and withdrew the knife tucked into her sash. There was no object in all the world she was more familiar with, not an inch upon her body that its edge had not met. Elodie set it against her left arm, closed her eyes, and slowly breathed out. The foul beast must be fed.

Elodie cut a slash across her arm, just shallow enough to draw blood.

The Nameless Whore, inflictor of wounds.

Another cut beside the first, equally shallow.

The Nameless Whore, punisher of the sinful.

A third, curling deeper, piercing into muscle.

The Nameless Whore, the sickly, hateful, eternal giver of misery.

In the pictures, she laughed and grinned as she did her work. In the stories, she cackled and recited the many sins that justified the flesh she burned, the bones she broke, and the blood she spilled.

In this little shed on the distant island of Thanet, Elodie sobbed silent tears as the pain overwhelmed her body and the rot in her mind guided the movements of her blade. Nothing would make it stop. Nothing would make it stop. Nothing would ever make it stop.

Hours.

Passed.

When morning came, She put away her dagger and held her arm over the fire. Her blood dripped upon the logs, and She held still until the last of it fell. The wounds healed quickly, a rare benefit of her divine nature. Even the scars would fade in time, if She let them. She rarely did. The fire and the blade always awaited the rise of the moon.

Once her wounds were closed, She used the underside of her dress to wipe away the drying blood. Then She reached for her book and opened it to the last page.

Tonight I am Elodie.

Elodie? Oh yes, the woman who ate the daylily flowers. So scared, and yet so brave. It might seem strange, but She prayed for this Elodie. Not to any god or goddess in particular, but more of a hopeful desire cast into the world like a message stuffed in a bottle and thrown into the sea. Should any divinity hear it, and possess the power, perhaps they might send a bit of their compassion her way.

She stored her book and scattered her fire so it would dwindle out completely. Her face was wet with tears, and She dried them with her sleeve. She gazed down at the blood on her arm, and for the first time in centuries, She dared allow herself to hope.

"Do you know you inflict this cruelty upon me, Ashraleon?" She asked the silence. "Would you regret it even if you knew? No, I doubt you would. But the end comes. You are so far from your home of Everlorn. You're comfortably nestled within the souls of your children, cradled by Aristava, Drasden, Gaius, and the like, but I will rip you free. I will remind you of who you are. I may be nameless, my past stolen, but I remember you, Ashraleon. I remember your sins so very, very well."

She flipped through the pages, seeing the thousands of names.

"I have endured so much of what you forced upon me," She said, and a thrill surged through her to chase away the horrors of the night. At last, She smiled. "Your hate, and your spite, will be your undoing. I will embrace your claims. Here on this forgotten island, I shall become the monster you believe me to be."

CHAPTER 32

SINSHEI

Sinshei's hands were bound behind her back, thin ropes wound about each and every finger. From the moment she'd awakened, they'd gagged her with a tightly knotted cloth. Its rough fabric rubbed against her tongue every time she swallowed, stripping it raw. She ached with thirst. Her stomach had knotted from hunger. Her captors fed her so rarely, and always with a blade at her throat, daring her to summon her divine weapons in the brief moment she was able to speak.

Not yet, she always told herself. *Trust in your father. You will be found.*

And yet the days passed, dark and dreadful. She lay in a dark cellar, the cold stone her bed. In the corner was a pail for her to relieve herself in. At least they were kind enough to let her shuffle about the room with twin ropes about her ankles instead of just pissing herself.

Mostly, she slept.

The door opened, and she stirred. In the dim light, she surveyed her captor. It wasn't Ax or the Vagrant, nor even the former paragon, Arn Bastell. She shuffled up on her knees, curiosity chasing away a bit of her grogginess. Her visitor was the Coin, only he no longer hid his face beneath a hood. The door shut behind him with a thud.

"Hello, Sinshei," he said, and his voice was colder than any Eldrid winter. She sat up straight, attempting to be dignified even in her distinctly undignified setting. Her resolve waivered when he laid his eyes upon her. Those eyes, red like fire, red like blood. They seemed to glow in the dark cellar. There was no disguising this old man's hate. The only light came from a small lantern, which he set down beside him.

She did not attempt to respond to his greeting, given her gag. Instead she gave him a mocking smile. Pretend at a strength she currently lacked, that was her only defense.

"Deciding your fate has been...contentious," he said, glaring down at her. "I do not blame those who wish for your death. You deserve it, most certainly. I have argued to spare you. Not out of kindness. Not pity. I claim it is for the potential knowledge you possess, and how it may aid us."

She never saw him draw the knife. It seemed to appear in his hands, small, polished, and impossibly sharp.

"A believable lie," he said, kneeling before her. "But we both know you are useless as a hostage. You bear no knowledge, and you will garner no worthwhile ransom."

Then why are you here? she wondered. *Why let me live?*

"Clever, manipulative Sinshei," he said, slowly twisting the knife handle between his fingers. "That's what you thought, isn't it? That you could whisper lies and half-truths to achieve your ends. That you could kill those who denied you, even your own brothers. Perhaps you viewed that as strength. Perhaps it even is, in the twisted world Everlorn has birthed."

He knelt before her, his expression hardening.

"Yet you fail to see how little your machinations mean to the immovable heart of hate that is your father. While you've been trapped down here, Lucavi has brutalized the city. He has slaughtered good men and women, for crimes both great and small. He has burned their homes. He has torn apart their families. And do you know the saddest part about it?"

He gently brushed a bit of her dirty hair away from her face. The loving act felt so much more insulting than his words.

"He didn't do it for you. He did it for his sons. For his pride."

His beard and hair were white, and his face wrinkled. He looked so tired, so old. Had he appeared that way when he first entered the cellar?

She didn't think so. Something strange felt afoot, a heathen magic she did not understand.

His knife pressed to her throat. She held perfectly still. The Coin's control was masterful. Not a drop of blood drawn. No pain felt. Not yet.

"Your father does not love you, Sinshei," he said. "Your father is a beast that knows not what true love is, and what scraps he does understand, he does not portion to you."

Slowly, carefully, Sinshei tilted her head upward, exposing her throat. Her eyes bore into his, showing her resolve. Daring him to make the cut.

I know my father, she thought. *I know his failings. I need no such truth from you.*

The Coin leaned closer. She felt his warm breath on her cheek, and strangely, it smelled of smoke and oil.

"I am old, so much older than I should be. I belong in a grave, yet I deny the need. I deny my daughter. Look what you have wrought upon me, Sinshei. Look what your father has inflicted."

Sinshei felt lost in a dream. In the Coin's eyes, she saw his truth. She saw forests burning. She saw treetop villages overrun with soldiers. She saw a man hanging before a crowd, his face hidden behind a mask eerily similar to the Vagrant's.

The knife trembled, and at last, the first drop of blood trickled down her neck.

"If only he did love you," he said, and his deep voice matched the trembling of his knife. "If only he felt the same for you as I do for my daughters. If he cared for you, if his entire world revolved around you, then I could *hurt* him. I could torment you, peel away your flesh, shred your eyes, break your bones, make you scream, make you beg, and he would *care*. He would suffer, just like I have suffered all these long, long years."

Sinshei could not move. She felt trapped by his hate. There was a world within the man's irises, if he even was a man. Fields of battle. The smoke of forges. Faces trapped in trees whose trunks reached the heavens.

The knife twisted, scraping its edge along her skin as if granting her a shave. It pooled her spilled blood along its edge, and then he held it before her. The tip turned, pointed straight for her eye. This was it. One thrust, and her life would end. All her hopes, her dreams of becoming Goddess-Incarnate, would end in some wretched cellar.

"The Ahlai name will not die here, you hear me?" the Coin seethed. "We will live. We will thrive. The sins of Everlorn are legion, but they will be repaid in blood, even if it takes centuries. At last, I have my Vagrant. At last, true death comes for your father. And I pray, daughter of Lucavi, that I will be there as you look upon the corpse of your god and weep tears for him that he would *never* weep for you."

But she already wept. His hatred and sorrow overwhelmed her. If she were not gagged, she might have begged for his forgiveness. Such indomitable will. Such boundless hatred. Tired and groggy and starved, she could only endure, and wait for the killing thrust. There was no doubt in her mind he was ready. It was why he had come down here. It was why he had brought the knife.

The Coin gently rubbed a callused finger across her cheek, wiping away a tear.

"That you would weep," he said softly. "Do you fear death, Anointed One?"

Sinshei sat up straight, and she leaned forward until the knife he held pressed once more to her throat. She could not speak, but she stared into those burning eyes of his and spoke the words in her mind nonetheless.

I fear only my own failure, and it will not come at your hands.

The knife lowered. The Coin cupped her face with his free hand. She knew, somehow, he heard.

"The sacrifice nears, but it will not crown a new God-Incarnate. It will not extend the life of the current. It ends here, Sinshei. Finally, at long last, it ends. Whatever grand plans you believe await you, they are delusions and lies. You will not become a goddess. Consider it pity, or cruelty, however you would define it, but I will let you live so you see it with your own eyes. Very little brings me joy, but in that, I will take some measure of bitter solace."

The knife vanished into his robe. He exited the cellar, and when its door shut, she was swallowed once more in darkness. Sinshei slowly breathed in and out, taking the time to settle her heart. With the Coin's absence, she felt far more herself. The tears she shed were from exhaustion, nothing more. She held no sympathy for the man who would slaughter her family and deny her the godhood she deserved.

Once prepared, Sinshei propped herself up on her knees. Her pulse quickened. Strangely, she was more afraid now than when she faced the knife. She prayed to her father so rarely. What need for it was there when she could kneel before him and ask in the flesh? What prayers she did offer were often the rote praises sung in songs and commanded during sermons within the Uplifted churches.

Head bowed, eyes closed, she humbled herself as she had never done before.

My father, I beg of you, hear me amid my despair. I know not where I am. I know not what they would do with me. I have only a name. Ahlai. Ahlai. Ahlai. Please, seek it out, and save me.

"My Lord?"

Lucavi opened his eyes and looked about. He was at a grand feast within the castle, surrounded by petty nobles and greedy merchants come from Gadir filling the chairs. Why? Oh yes. To build morale after Weiss's purge. To ensure loyalty come the necessary sacrifice. The now, it was so hard to remain in the now, especially when his daughter's voice whispered in his ears. Bassar was beside him, outwardly calm but clearly worried by the gentle shift of tone in his voice.

"Ahlai," Lucavi muttered, tasting the name on his tongue. It felt familiar, but from where? How many years ago?

Miquo, answered Aristava. Upon hearing the country's name, Lucavi felt a shock ripple through him. *Thorda* Ahlai, the merchant whose companies' forges were some of the largest suppliers of weapons to the empire's war machine.

"It can't be," Lucavi said, ignoring the guarded stares of others seated nearby. "He swore upon his husband's corpse."

"I'm sorry," Bassar said, lowering his voice further. "I do not understand. Is something amiss?"

Lucavi clenched his fists, bunching the white tablecloth between his fingers. More and more memories came to him, tumbling free from crowded corners of his mind. The other God-Incarnates shouted their fury, adding to the cacophony. Of the nation's god-whisperers. Of Rhodes Ahlai's rebellion. Of the skull mask he fashioned to hide his identity.

"Find Signifer Weiss," he ordered his divine bodyguard. "Tell him I want to know everything of Thorda Ahlai and his connections to Thanet."

CHAPTER 33

STASIA

"Are you sure we don't need to take Adella farther?" Stasia asked. "Kritia is much too close to the capital. I'd hardly call it safe."

"It's safe enough for now," Clarissa said. She sat by the creek bed, drying her hair with a pale gray cloth. They'd both taken a dip at her mother's insistence. It'd been their first chance to bathe since fleeing the city, and Stasia had welcomed the chance. "Everything we've heard indicates that the purge was isolated to Vallessau."

Stasia dipped her toes in and out of the chill water.

"Lucavi's timing could not have been more perfect. The one time Cyrus leaves the city, and that's when the bastard finally snaps."

Clarissa stood, grabbed her nearby dress, and tossed her cloth to Stasia.

"Besides, Mother won't be staying here," she said. "The purge started in Vallessau, but you're right that it may spread. She'll be traveling with a group farther west, and it should be safe enough."

"We could still accompany her. Is anywhere truly safe on Thanet come the damned sacrifice?"

"She doesn't want to keep you from Vallessau," Clarissa said. "And neither do I. You're needed there. We both know that."

Stasia wiped her face dry, then grabbed her nearby shirt. She'd soaked it in the creek before bathing and wrung it out as best she could. The cloth clung to her wet skin when she put it on, clammy and unpleasant, but she ignored it. This wasn't her first time frantically fleeing a city without adequate preparation.

"Good, you two girls are done."

Both turned to see Adella descending the beaten path from Kritia to the creek. She carried a wicker basket overflowing with clothes in her arms.

"Helping out, are we?" Clarissa asked with a smile.

"People here were kind enough to give us food and lodging despite us arriving in the middle of the night," the older woman said. "It's only right I repay their kindness. That, and we all should try to look our best for the ceremony."

"Ceremony?" Stasia asked. She avoided meeting either's gaze by pulling on her trousers. "Is there time for something like that?"

"There is always time," Adella said. She set the basket down on the grass and pulled out a bar of lye soap from a small pouch resting atop it. "We've a long journey still ahead, and I won't see either of you for some while. We all could use Lycaena's blessing."

Stasia hopped on one foot so she could pull the other trouser leg up. The motion was mostly an excuse to turn aside to hide her grimace. Fantastic. A Lycaenean ceremony of some sort.

"I suppose we could," she said, then winced again. She'd done a terrible job of keeping the hesitation from her voice.

"Of course we could," Adella said, and whether she detected Stasia's hesitation or not, she hid it well with her own exuberance. She began scrubbing the clothes, perhaps with a bit more vigor than she'd shown before. Stasia bit her lower lip and wished that, just occasionally, she was capable of tact.

"I'm going to head back, see if I can find a bite to eat," she said, deciding the wisest course was to immediately exit the situation. She knelt down, gave Adella a giant hug, and then trudged back to Kritia. Clarissa followed, and once her mother was out of earshot, she grabbed Stasia's wrist.

"Is something wrong?" she asked.

"Nothing, it's nothing."

"Clearly not."

Stasia spun on her.

"Fine, but it's not a big deal, I promise. I just don't want to upset your mother when I don't go to tonight's... whatever it is."

"A star-fire ceremony," Clarissa said. "And she won't be the only one disappointed."

Stasia took in a sharp breath and then slowly let it out. She'd erred. Too selfish, too focused on herself; she'd thought of Adella's request solely as an annoyance to be avoided. It had never occurred to her how Clarissa might take that rejection.

"Oh. I see. Lycaena's not exactly my goddess, though."

Clarissa crossed the space between them, her blue eyes peering up at her with a sharpness rivaling the edge of Stasia's axes.

"Please, this is important to me. I've demanded so little of you and have never asked you to attend one before. I am asking now. You don't have to participate, but I want you there at my side. When I pray for you, I want to feel your hands in mine and to know you hear it, too."

Guilt gnawed the interior of Stasia's rib cage. She gripped her left wrist, fingers twirling her silver marriage bracelet.

"I'm sorry," she said. "It's only... I'm not good at this religious stuff. I always feel awkward all throughout. It's more of—"

"Mari's thing," Clarissa said, finishing her sentence. A faint smile lifted her lips. "You're more predictable than you know, Stasia. I've done a lot for you. Can you do this one thing for me?"

It was such a simple ask, and Stasia berated herself for turning it into an argument. She put her hands on her wife's shoulders and kissed her forehead.

"Of course," she said. "When does it start?"

Come nightfall, the crowd gathered atop a hill several hundred yards beyond the last house of the village. About twenty men and women were in attendance, along with a handful of children beside their parents. Their faces were lean with hunger (the past few years had been good for no one on Thanet). What finery they possessed, they wore, be it jewelry or laced skirts and vests. The women had on ornaments crafted of freshly bloomed roses as well, which Stasia rejected. Clarissa shot her a look but said nothing.

I promised to attend, Stasia argued silently. *That is all.*

An older man named Mikel led the congregation, his dark skin wrinkled and his white beard expertly trimmed. He wore a brilliantly colored scarf wrapped about his neck, the fiery yellows, oranges, and reds blooming vibrant even in the starlight. His deep voice sang as people climbed the hill in scattered groups.

"Come, children, the rain falls heavy. Come, children, the night falls deep. We weep, the stars fall. We laugh, the fires burn. We sing, and life blooms anew."

Others joined in, the harmony pleasant enough that time passed swiftly. Adella matched him in volume, her voice so beautifully pitched Stasia wondered if she'd had professional training sometime in her life. She'd never mentioned such during their many conversations over dinners (Adella sang far better than she cooked, Stasia lamented in hindsight). Or perhaps it was merely a lifetime of singing these same songs, granting perfection over the course of decades.

Mikel invited Adella to his side halfway through the first song, and together they led the rest gathered in a loose circle. Clarissa slipped her hand inside Stasia's, gently swaying, and Stasia at least mouthed along the words to not feel so awkward.

"I thank you all for coming," Mikel said when the last of the songs ended. "Both those familiar to me, and those of you passing through our village. Truly, we are blessed, for have you ever seen a sky so clear in all the world?"

Murmurs of affirmation. The sky did seem beautiful, though Stasia could not personally agree, for it paled in comparison to the crystalline canopy she and Mari had seen during their travels across the desert to Lahareed.

Her cheeks flushed. Gods help her, was she going to nitpick every little thing this village elder said and did? What was wrong with her?

"Lynetta, if you wouldn't mind passing out the butterflies?"

A red-haired girl stepped into the center of the ring, carrying a little basket. One by one she stopped before an attendee, curtsied, and then handed them a handcrafted butterfly. When she came to Stasia's trio, Stasia bit her tongue, deciding how to politely decline.

The girl curtsied again, then offered the butterfly. Its base was a little nub of some waxlike substance, and its wings were carefully folded and cut from Thanet's distinct yellow paper. All in all, it was barely larger than Stasia's thumb. The girl's smile wavered when Stasia did not immediately accept.

Damn it, fine.

She scooped up the paper butterfly. Such a little thing. Why make a fuss?

"Thank you," Clarissa said when Lynetta moved on.

"Sure," Stasia said, keeping her voice low. She lifted it closer to her face. It wasn't wax that formed the crude base, but something darker. "What do I do with it?"

"These butterflies are our messengers to Lycaena," Clarissa explained in a whisper. "When Mikel tells us to begin, we shall whisper to them our deepest prayers. They'll remember them all, and then we set them alight to the stars, to carry them ever onward."

Stasia glanced at the little paper and wax construction in her hand.

"Set them alight how?"

Clarissa grinned.

"If you don't know, then enjoy the surprise."

They both hushed, for Mikel had resumed speaking. It was definitely a sermon. Stasia had attended enough ceremonies throughout Gadir to recognize one when she heard it. He spoke of Lycaena's love for her children and of how she ever watched over them. There was particular emphasis on her presence, always referenced as a physical yet unseen thing. It was meant to counter the scar caused by Lycaena's execution.

The goddess once walked these lands with these people, Stasia thought. *Then Sinshei beheaded her, and Lycaena's presence became only spiritual. Will it be enough?*

She looked to the children, some paying respectful attention, others shuffling from foot to foot and staring at anything other than the elder.

Or will they all be sacrificed to Lucavi, sustenance for the God-Incarnate to consume in his desire to live another six hundred years?

Stasia did her best to shake that grim thought out of mind.

"Confess now your heartfelt needs," Mikel said. "Hide nothing from she who already knows your deepest concerns. Confess, and be unburdened. All shall be heard."

Stasia lifted the little paper creation to her lips. Talking to it felt weird, and despite not knowing anyone there besides Clarissa and her mother, she felt a heat of embarrassment. After all the nations she'd visited, and her many talks with Mari, she knew the power these rituals possessed. It was one thing to know it, and another to believe it. Would these words actually reach Lycaena? And even if they did, what did it matter? Stasia held no love for the goddess. She did not care for any blessings or guidance. She walked her own path. She always had.

Clarissa's hand tightened around Stasia's. The tension was enough to pull Stasia from her self-absorbed thoughts.

When I pray for you, I want to feel your hands in mine, and to know you hear it, too.

Stasia's wife was true to her word. Hand in hand, with eyes closed and the faint hint of building tears, Clarissa confessed her heart.

"Dearest Lycaena, keep my wife safe when the world comes crashing down. When she's fighting, when she's in danger...I can't be there. I can't protect her. So please, Goddess, I am begging you. Protect her. Love her, even if she loves you not. Do not take her from me. Let me have this happiness. Let us *both* have this happiness. Please. Please, Lycaena. I love her. Let it last. Let it be."

A lump swelled in Stasia's throat. She couldn't shake feeling responsible for her wife's fears. These battles Stasia fought, they were necessary, they weren't even choices...but that didn't erase the risk.

Mari insisted these rituals held power, and so Stasia whispered softly, so softly that even her wife would not hear.

"I am not yours, but she is, Lycaena, and so to you I pray. Grant her happiness. Grant her peace. As for me...I'll try to be worthy of it."

Heads lifted as the prayers ceased. Mikel stood in the center of their ring with his hands lifted. His eyes turned to the sky.

"To the stars we send our fire," he said. "Give your messages to the heavens."

One by one the people held their butterflies above their heads, the wax bodies resting on their open palms, and Stasia did likewise. Mikel paced about the interior of their circle, suddenly fierce with energy. He moved and turned like a trapped animal. The words flowed faster from his tongue.

"To the Butterfly we cry! To the Goddess we sing! Heartfelt we pray, joyful we rise, and now with hope in our breast we cast our hands skyward."

He clapped his hands together.

"Hear us!"

The gathered people immediately echoed him. *"Hear us."*

Mikel spun, arms raised, energy rising. His hands clapped, the impact forming faint sparks that showered like embers.

"Hear us!"

"Hear us!"

Wind blew across the hill, sudden and startling in the calm night. The wing tips of the paper butterflies fluttered, and Stasia felt the hairs on her neck stand on end as the familiar aura of the divine swelled about her. It was like when Mari first communed with a god, only instead of sharply focused on her sister, it smothered over all present like a blanket of lightning.

Mikel stomped his feet and twirled in their center, his hands clapping one final time.

"Our beloved, our cherished, our living goddess, hear us!"

Sparks billowed from his now-burning hands, settling upon the black, waxlike bodies of the butterflies and immediately setting them aflame. Instinct cried out for Stasia to drop hers before being burned, but she could not move. The aura of magic paralyzed her. The joy of the elder kept her calm. Lycaena's fire, it would not burn.

Wings fluttered. The children gasped in wonder. The burning manifestations of prayers and butterflies took to the skies, scattered at first but then coming closer together, unifying into a circular pattern as they rose and rose, as if their destination were the very stars.

Adella resumed singing, soft and low. Stasia couldn't even make out the words, but her heart knew them. Her gaze locked to the heavens. She felt loosened from the ground, and for the briefest moment, the most terrible ache cut through her breast. Was this what her sister experienced when she communed? Was this the true peace that gods brought? Not the savagery she witnessed time again by gods defending their realms, nor the vengeance of those slain and given new life through Mari's gifts. A wonder. A peace. A relinquishing to that which was vast, and beyond mortal understanding.

"Stasia?"

Clarissa sounded so very far away. The butterflies danced, but Stasia didn't see them as butterflies anymore. With how distant they were, those flames could be anything, fireflies, torches, stars...

Leaves. Red leaves, burning brightly, such as when the people of Miquo would prepare for an autumn ceremony. When the very last of the leaves had fallen, they would set the fires and call upon their multitude of gods for safety and prosperity through the winter months. Stasia stared at those swirling specks and felt six years old again. She held Thorda's hand, while Rhodes cradled a young Mari in his arms.

There was no hill anymore, only towering trees with trunks a dozen feet thick. Their bark was blacker than the night. The burning leaves swirled higher, bathing the trees in red. She had wed underneath such a burning sky. A Miquoan sky.

Only twenty or so people had been in attendance for the Lycaenean ceremony, but Stasia saw dozens, then hundreds, of sparking butterflies flit across the midnight canopy. They surged around her, and when she looked for the source, she found herself alone. Even Clarissa had left her. The ground was flat, and it stretched on and on to a horizon that seemed endless. Its perfection was broken only by the black trees that rose thousands of feet high to blot out the very stars.

A deep fear awakened inside Stasia's mind. This place. She knew this place, not by any experience she herself possessed, but from her talks with Mari. This was not the mortal realm but the realm of gods. It was where Mari knelt before the slain divine and asked for their power so she might exact vengeance against the Everlorn Empire.

Stasia shouldn't be here. She *couldn't* be here. This was not her place. She was no god-whisperer.

What to do? How to leave? She didn't know. Her balance was unsteady, and at last she understood why. Water, she stood upon water, yet its surface held firm beneath her weight. It rippled and splashed, soaking through her boots with an icy cold.

"At last, the heir comes before us."

Stasia spun, searching for the source of the voice. It was aged and deep, and every syllable trembled. She saw nothing but trees. Their bark was so black, so deep, that when she looked into them she felt like she could fall forever...and then a face peered back at her. His hair and beard were long and shockingly white. He hovered within the tree, as if the bark were his opened cocoon. His arms were crossed over his bare chest. When his eyes opened, they shone the fiery red of Miquo.

Though she had never met him before, Stasia knew his name. He was Aloth, the father and keeper of knowledge, and one of the few gods whose names Stasia had memorized during her limited schooling. There was no hierarchy among gods in Miquo, but of the ones who had passed on and devoted their wisdom to the god-whisperers, Aloth was the most well-known and beloved.

And now he was before her.

"Heir?" Stasia asked.

"Heir," said a woman behind her. Stasia pivoted, and with every turn she saw more red eyes opening within the trees. Dozens at first, then an audience of hundreds, come to observe...what, exactly? How had a Lycaenean ceremony brought her to this place, this moment? The woman, her eyes sewn shut and her tongue forked, continued. "Though I question your validity."

"She does not know," a third said. He was young, barely more than a babe, yet his voice carried the depth of mountains. "Her father has kept her in ignorance."

The trees muttered among themselves. Their displeasure was frightening. She relied on her strength and stubbornness to carry her through life, but her muscles and axes meant nothing in this divine realm.

"I'm sorry," she cried out to them. "I don't know your names. I don't know your faces."

The discordant chatter resumed with heightened fervor. "An insult!" some cried out. Others called her unfit, or unworthy. The forest judged her, but for what, she knew not. Or at least, she pretended not.

But of course, mocked the Soma of her past. *You are not mortal.*

"She will learn," Aloth said, and the others quieted in respect for the eldest among them. "When her time comes. We are too few, and too weak, to refuse her."

"Refuse me?" Stasia asked. "Refuse me for what?"

"Do not tell her," said the woman with sewn-shut eyes. "To do so now would defy the decision of the Forge."

Stasia's heart felt like it would pound out of her chest. The water beneath her no longer held firm. She'd sunk up to her ankles. The icy chill clawed into her veins. She wanted nothing more than to leave.

"Was it not the prayer of her father that summoned us?" Aloth asked. "Did it not reverberate through our forest?"

Thorda's words thundered across the infinite canopy, summoned by the ancient being wrapped in bark.

Gods of Miquo. Those from ages past who may only whisper, and those who yet live hidden and scattered, I beseech you. I ask naught for myself, but for my daughter. Witness her. Embrace her. Love her, and the woman she has chosen. I ask. I beg. I pray.

"Embrace her," said a woman whose eyes and ears were like those of a wolf. "Embrace she who knows us not?"

"Must we love only those we deem worthy?" asked another, he with skin akin to the brown and gold scales of a water snake. "The girl's ignorance is not of her own making. She was kept so, and for reasons not for us to question."

"Girl?" Stasia asked. Panic drove her words. She was being judged and demeaned and insulted, all for something that couldn't be real. It couldn't be—her father, what Soma said, the very idea of divine blood in her veins, it was madness.

"Girl," Aloth said, and the word cracked like a whip. She dropped again, the black water rising above her knees. "Child. Little one. You are nothing before we who have watched centuries pass like rainstorms. Long have we sought to look upon you, but the time has not yet come. You glimpsed us too soon."

Too soon, echoed a dozen others.

"Too soon?" she asked. "For what? Speak plainly, damn you!"

The water was up to her chest now, stealing away all feeling of her extremities. Aloth's lips curled into a smile.

"Yes, you will be a fiery one, fitting of the Forge. I eagerly await you, Stasia Ahlai. As do we all. But until the inheritance is granted, you are not yet ready. There is still much to be done."

"Our names," shouted a young woman Stasia could not see. She tried to find her, but the water was up to her neck, and her body would no longer turn. "Behold our faces! Learn our names!"

Aloth reached out to her. Bark groaned and cracked. He was so close to her, his pale fingers reaching out to brush her forehead. The water might be ice, but his fingers were even colder, so cold they burned. Her eyes locked wide. He smiled, and she saw his teeth were stone, and the words he spoke were carved upon them while she watched.

"Welcome, and farewell."

He pushed her down below the water, into the darkness. The chill poured in through her ears and nostrils. It sealed away her eyes, but the darkness was not permanent. Little lights pierced the veil. Stars, she realized. Heat blossomed within her breast, sudden and fierce. Sounds returned, syllables, words...

"Stasia?"

Stasia startled. She stood on the hill outside Kritia. The ceremony was ended, and the last of the butterflies had flitted away. Already those with children were ushering them down the hill for their bedtimes.

Clarissa took her hands, and she tilted her head to one side.

"Is something wrong?"

Where to even begin?

"No," Stasia said. Already the memory faded from her, the faces becoming nothing but gray blobs among the trees. "Yes. I...I'll explain when I can. For now, can we go? It's gotten late."

Worry chipped away at Clarissa's smile, but her wife did well to hide it.

"Of course."

Together they descended the hill. Once they reached the bottom, Stasia glanced back. Where once there had been nothing, a lone tree now grew atop the hill's apex. Its bark was deep black, and within its embrace, she saw her father curled into a ball, weeping.

She blinked once and it was gone. Green grass. An empty hill.

But still the sound of her father weeping.

CHAPTER 34

ARN

Does it always take this long?" Arn asked Thorda as the pair watched over Mari. His little chair creaked beneath him as he shifted his weight side to side. His lower back hurt. Too much sitting. Too much waiting. A price he'd pay, because he had no intention of leaving Mari's bedside.

"This sickness?" Thorda asked. He stood with a washrag in one hand and a little tin pail of water heated with coals in the other. He wet the rag and then brushed it along Mari's forehead with slow, careful precision. "There is no preventing it, but the time varies depending on how long she spent connected to the deity. With Endarius, her commingling lasted years."

The memory of seeing Mari collapsed on the floor of the alehouse stabbed Arn's gut worse than any dagger. He hid the discomfort with another shift of his weight. If only the Nameless woman had stayed with them, to soothe Mari when her fever spiked and her pain reached such a level she whimpered amid her dreams.

"Well, she's kicked this before," he said. "So she'll kick it again. She always does."

Thorda did not answer immediately. He dipped the cloth into the pail, wrung it out, and then lifted her left arm by the wrist. Carefully, he washed her skin from the elbow to her dainty fingers.

"Taking the power of the divine into mortal flesh is always a risk," Thorda said. The heaviness to his voice ceased Arn's squirming. "Something you should know well. Not everyone survives the paragon ritual."

"But for me, or even something like what Cyrus is becoming, it's a onetime struggle," Arn said. "Why is it so different with Mari?"

"Because she herself is not becoming divine. She shares her body with the slain god, giving it life. She is a wooden bowl filled with fire and blood, and with each and every whispering, I pray she is not consumed. Her gifts were meant to be used sparingly, in quiet, prayerful moments among fellow believers. Never like this. Never in war."

And yet she did so anyway. Was it courage on her part, or cruelty on her father's? Arn didn't know, nor was he equipped to judge. His homeland of Vashlee had been an honored member of Everlorn since long before he was born.

"But it's free of her now. Endarius left her. Why then this sickness?"

Thorda switched arms. Arn suspected Mari didn't need the attention so much as Thorda desired something, anything, to do to help his daughter.

"Nothing is so simple when it comes to gods. Mari suffers to take the divine within her, and when it departs, it takes a heavy toll."

Did that mean it hurt when she transformed? Arn had never guessed. She was ever playful, even as the Lioness. Yet...yet that was a lie, wasn't it? He'd seen her on Stasia's wedding night. A swell of hurt dwelt within her, of a nature he didn't fully understand. Perhaps this was a part of it.

"She never lets it show," he said.

"She hides it well. Or maybe it isn't hidden, and she doesn't view it as suffering. I've pushed her so hard, perhaps she sees it as normal, as expected..."

This was a side of Thorda that Arn had never glimpsed before, a brief crack in the brutal façade the man maintained at all times. Arn cleared his throat and glanced away.

"We've all done the best we can," he said. "These aren't easy roads we walk. And Mari, she's a tough girl, and just as stubborn as you or her sister. If she didn't want to be a god-whisperer, then she wouldn't be one. Simple as that."

"I don't feel tough," Mari said. Arn startled in his seat, while Thorda merely smiled and set aside his washcloth.

"Welcome back to the waking world," he said.

Mari covered her face with a hand.

"Some welcome. My head hurts. How long have I been out?"

"Four days," Arn answered.

"He would know," Thorda said. "He spent nearly every hour of it at your side."

"How kind of him."

Thorda took her hands in his, the act seeming all the more intimate given Thorda's icy nature. Arn felt like a trespasser in the moment, but neither did he want to leave. Thorda bent down, gently kissed his daughter's forehead, and then released her hands.

"I will give you two a moment," he said.

Arn stared at the floor, praying the awkwardness would pass. Even harder was pretending not to see the knowing look Thorda gave him on his way out. With Thorda's departure, Mari seemed to refocus, and it felt like she truly saw him for the first time since waking.

"Hey, you," she said. Her eyelids drooped, and her words were slurred enough that she sounded intoxicated.

"Hey," he said, sliding closer. "You gave us all quite a scare."

"Did I, now?" She closed her eyes and slowly exhaled. "Well. I'll try not to do it again. No . . . no promises, though."

A sudden urge to be useful overcame Arn now that she was awake and lucid. He stood from his chair, then hesitated, unsure of what exactly he meant to do.

"Do you need anything? Blankets, pillows? Are you thirsty? Hungry? We've given you sips while you slept, warm broth, I think, but you must be starving. We've no servants here, but I can get something if you—"

"Water," she said, interrupting him. "Water would be fine."

For reasons he couldn't understand, he started blushing.

"Right. Water."

He rushed out to fetch a pitcher, glad no one else witnessed his blubbering.

Calm down, he told himself, as if that would work. His relief at seeing her awake and unharmed overwhelmed him. Twin impulses to shout for joy and collapse into tears warred within him in a wildly confusing mix.

When he returned, Mari had pushed herself up to a sitting position. He offered her a glass and put the wood pitcher on the bedside table. She sipped at it, her red eyes watching him with a welcome but uncomfortable alertness.

"So," she said, setting down the glass. "Did you really stay with me the whole time?"

Arn fought to maintain composure, but the heat in his face surely betrayed him.

"Well, not *all* the time," he said. "Your father's exaggerating, just a bit. I was worried about you; we all were."

Mari pointedly stared at the opposite corner. Stacked haphazardly were multiple pillows and two blankets, comprising the bed Arn had used for the past few days. His blush deepened. She must have noticed while he fetched her a drink.

"Are those yours?" she asked.

"Yeah."

"Did you sleep in here with me?"

Words ceased to properly form in Arn's brain. The stutter that came out flowed of its own accord.

"I mean, not *with* you, but…if you woke up, or needed help in the night, I wanted to be here for you. If something happened, I didn't want, you shouldn't…I didn't like you being alone."

She laughed. Of course she laughed; he was rambling like an absolute fool to a woman who'd just woken up from a divinity-induced coma. Arn clasped his jaw shut and put an end to the rush of words. At the least he could let her respond first. Mari, seemingly to put him out of his misery, smiled and patted his hand.

"I'm only teasing, Arn. You don't have to apologize for looking after me. It's nice to know you cared."

She was giving him a way out, he knew. He could smile and pretend everything was fine, that he hadn't sat at her bedside sick to death and unable to cope with the terror squirming in his gut. But he wouldn't pretend. He'd put up brave fronts around his brother. He'd become a false beast of vicious strength when shackled with paragon gauntlets. With Mari, he would be himself. He would be true, even if it meant revealing himself to be a softhearted, bumbling, and confused man.

"Of course I cared," he said. "I cared so damn much, Mari, I couldn't sleep or eat or think about anything at all. I was worried you wouldn't wake up. I was worried I'd never see you, we'd never speak, I'd never get the chance..."

All the gods and goddesses help him, he was crying.

A hand settled over his, and mercifully his rambling ceased. Her other hand gently pressed against his cheek and pulled him toward her.

"Come here, you big oaf," she said. Arn's resistance lasted but a half second before he leaned in. His breath caught in his throat. Their lips touched, hers soft and warm, for the gentlest of kisses.

"You're adorable," she said, withdrawing back into the pillows. Her hand, though, refused to release his.

"If you say so."

She smiled slightly, and her eyes closed. Arn lowered to his knees so he was equal to her height and leaned his head against hers upon the pillow, forehead to forehead. Eyes closed, he listened to the sound of her breathing. Her fingers tightened, her thumbs rubbing across his knuckles. As if confirming he was still there.

"Thank you," she whispered.

"For what? The water?"

It was a joke, and he was glad to see her smile.

"Of course," she said. "Just the water. Not anything else at all."

Time passed, soft and gentle. Her breathing slowed, and he suspected she would sleep again soon. Every second was one he cherished.

"So what all did I miss?" she asked after a moment.

"Plenty," Arn said, and so to pass the time, he told her of the resistance's progress, how Nameless She had come to Mari's aid, and of Sinshei's capture. Tentatively he broached the subject of the island's sacrifice on the six-hundred-year ceremony, not wanting to burden her with so much so early, but she pressed him, forcing out all the details despite her exhaustion. The anger seemed to wake her and add life to her cheeks.

"For Sinshei to lie to us so," she said, shaking her head. "Disgusting."

"I know," Arn said. "That she's still alive is..."

He froze. A feeling like warm fog rolled across his body, sickly and unpleasant. He furrowed his brow. This unease...he recognized it, but from where? And why did it provoke such a visceral response? When he heard a heavy knock on the front door down the hall, he wasn't even surprised. This vile aura, it felt alien to him, unknown, unwanted...

"Wait a moment," he said. Despite wanting nothing more than to cuddle hours away with Mari, he pushed himself to his feet and opened the door. It was not even halfway open before he shoved it closed but for a crack for him to see through. He held his breath and fought off a surge of panic. He could only pray no one outside noticed the movement.

"Arn?" Mari asked, careful to keep her own voice at a whisper. He gestured at her to wait, for despite their silence, it was hard to hear Thorda over the rattle of armor and weaponry.

The God-Incarnate's voice, however, thundered through the walls with the power of the divine.

"I confess, I never expected to meet you again, let alone on the other side of the world," said Lucavi. "What brings you to Thanet, Thorda Ahlai?"

"The needs of my business bring me all across Gadir, and even to islands beyond," Thorda answered. Arn pushed the crack open a little wider, trying hard to see. Lucavi stood in the entry, just inside the door. A paragon flanked his either side. Thorda stood before him, looking small and old before such mountains of muscle and armor.

"Except no permits were to be issued for Thanet. You bribed your way here."

Thorda dipped his head low.

"I may cross certain lines when it comes to matters of business, and for that, I ask only your mercy and forgiveness. Yet as my enterprise expands, so too does Everlorn benefit."

"Yes, your ever-expensive arms and armor."

Lucavi drew his sword. Arn's breath caught in his throat, yet somehow Thorda did not look alarmed.

"Yet perhaps this is a blessing in disguise!" the God-Incarnate continued. "You are Miquoan, after all, so surely your knowledge and connections will aid me in answering a question that was recently put before me." Lucavi twirled his sword between his fingers. "Soldiers who survived the attack on Fort Lionfang reported seeing a red-eyed woman leading the assault. Curious, no? And then there is the matter of the Lioness, who I always presumed to be a priestess of Endarius, but then Bassar here"—he dipped his head toward his bodyguard—"reminded me of your fabled god-whisperers."

The twirling of the sword stopped.

"Tell me, Thorda Ahlai, where are your daughters?"

The entire mansion fell silent. Arn could not move if he wanted. Dread iced him in place.

"Everlorn has taken everything from me," Thorda said. "You will take nothing more. If there is a hell, it awaits you, Lucavi, you and every last one of your brethren."

Lucavi thrust his sword into Thorda's gut and pinned him to the wall.

"Parasites," the God-Incarnate said. "All the world will be better when I cleanse you from it."

Arn's vision turned crimson. He shut the door completely and then put his back against it. Mari's face drained of color, and he could see the question in her eyes, the one unspoken on her lips, and he knew not how to answer. He only shook his head, yet that seemed enough. Her hands shook as she clutched the bedsheets.

Maybe they'll leave. Maybe they'll just torch the building, and we can escape in the smoke.

"Search the estate. There may be evidence of his conspirators."

All hope died. They'd find Sinshei, and once they did, and she started talking...

He didn't have his armored coat, didn't have his gauntlets. Mari was stripped of the Lion's blessing. What could they do? They had to flee, to escape, but where, how...

Footsteps nearing. He met Mari's eye, and he saw her fear. He vowed, then and there, to let nothing happen to her. It didn't matter if it cost him his life. She would survive. She must. If only there was a way out.

No window. No escape. He clenched his hands into fists and decided to hope for miracles.

The moment he heard someone touch the handle on the opposite side, Arn smashed through. Some hapless soldier yelped in shock, the only noise he made before Arn's fist caved in his skull. Arn grabbed the body and flung it forward, hitting two more soldiers rushing toward him. Down the hall, the God-Incarnate was gone. Perhaps there was hope, after all. He sprinted at the next person, the divine bodyguard Bassar, who wielded a sword so enormous he rested it across his right shoulder.

"Get out!" Arn screamed, wanting all attention kept his way. Bassar readied his sword, but with such a narrow space, he could only swing it vertically. Arn judged its angle with ease and then lunged into the air, kicking off the wall to grant him height. He collided with Bassar, his fists pounding the paragon's chest. His knuckles bled from the silver chainmail, but he forced the man to drop his sword so he could draw his arms back and block. A haphazard plan formed in Arn's mind as he uppercut twice, clipping Bassar's chin and staggering him. If he could cause enough chaos, maybe they would give chase when he fled the building. Maybe they would assume he was the only one in the room and not check. Or if they did, and Mari hid under the bed beforehand, or...

Bassar retaliated, sudden and vicious, his elbow slamming into Arn's gut. Two more punches followed, brutal to his chest, but Arn wrapped the paragon in a bear hug and then hollered out his pain and frustration. They wrestled, stuck in a deadlock, before Arn's greater strength won out. He flung them both sideways, smashing through a door and into Stasia's empty room. They rolled along the floor, separated, and then crashed back into each other, their fists leading. Arn weathered the blows. Had to stay offensive. Force all the attention his way.

"Come on," he shouted from bleeding, swollen lips. He grabbed part of the bed they'd broken and struck it against the paragon's chest. "Come on, you bastard, you think I even feel this?"

In return, Bassar rammed his head into his stomach, wrapped his arms around Arn's waist, and lifted. The two tumbled back to the hallway, breaking boards and smashing a giant indent into the opposing wall. Arn kicked the man twice, bloodying his face, and then pushed back to a stand, his fists up and ready to brawl.

Ready, until he saw Dario beside Mari's bed. His left hand pinned her by the throat. Already she struggled to breathe, her face reddening. His brother's right hand was held high in a fist.

"No more, Arn," he said. "Surrender. Neither of you need die this day."

This day, he said, as if mercy would be waiting for either of them. It was a cruel promise, but what choice did he have? That hand on Mari's throat ended all other options.

"You bastard," he said, slowly lifting his hands and placing them behind his head. He dropped down to his knees. Bassar retrieved his discarded sword and pressed the blade to Arn's throat.

"Fetch proper manacles," Bassar ordered.

Behind him, Arn heard Mari gasp in a breath of air as Dario's fingers relaxed.

"I do what must be done," Dario said. "As ever, you would not understand."

Risking the cut, Arn turned to see Mari cradled in Dario's arms. The sight of it turned his stomach, and all color drained from the world. To know, to fear, to believe that this would be the last time he saw her, held by his traitorous brother? How cruel could the world truly be? Why must it hate him so?

"I will never forgive you," he said.

There was no pity or remorse in his brother's returned gaze.

"I never sought forgiveness," Dario said, and carried her out the door to whatever prison awaited them.

CHAPTER 35

DARIO

It was common to feel fear when meeting the God-Incarnate of Everlorn. Even paragons were not immune. It was only natural, even proper, to feel a degree of trepidation before addressing the supreme deity of Gadir, and yet this went far beyond the norm. Dario stood before Lucavi's bodyguard and prayed none of that nervousness showed. He offered his fellow paragon a salute and pretended all was well.

"You are expected," Bassar said, and stepped aside, granting passage into the former king and queen's bedroom. Upon his arrival on Thanet, Lucavi had immediately taken up residence there. The God-Incarnate was ever aware of how symbols and presentation could sway the minds of the heathens. It was the same reason he gave all his decrees from their royal throne room.

Dario pushed the grand door open and entered. Once inside, he immediately dropped to one knee. Lucavi sat on the edge of the bed, a book in hand. He marked the page and then set it aside.

"I thank you for granting me an audience," Dario said, his forehead resting on his arm propped atop his right knee. A hand, warm and firm, settled upon Dario's left shoulder. He did not hear his god's approach. Stripped of his armor, and wearing only a golden robe, Lucavi was capable of surprising quietness if he so wished.

"My most loyal paragons are ever welcome in my presence," Lucavi said. "I suspect I know the reason for your coming here, but I would have you speak it all the same. Confess your heart, Dario Bastell. Make clear your request."

Dario did not look up until the hand left his shoulder. Lucavi towered over him. In the dim light, his skin seemed to glow as if from unseen candles. For an agonizing second, Dario thought to tell everything. His talks with Arn, his meeting with Mari, her granting words to Lorka; all of it. He shoved the idea aside. No, he was risking enough with this lone request. The time for confessing those secrets was not now, if it would ever be.

"You say you know my reasons, and so I will speak plainly to you, my god. I ask that you spare my brother from his execution, and instead put him into my care."

"Your care?"

The words floated over him, measured, telling nothing.

"Yes, my care," he said. "Your son, Galvanis, bless his memory, placed me in charge of my brother's spiritual salvation. I ask that you grant me the same courtesy."

"From what I understood, Galvanis let him live so he might be used as bait."

"A decision made much later," Dario insisted. He paused to control himself. Every word had to be chosen carefully here. "His detention was mine to control, and my hope was to bring him back to Eldrid as a penitent. Our souls are linked by blood and reputation, and I would save us both. This I swear."

A moment's silence. Dario stared at the rug beneath him, each and every one of those long seconds like a nail pounding into his temple.

"You love your brother, don't you, Dario?"

"I do, though I do it poorly. I mistook judgment for caring, and compassion for weakness. That, too, is why I seek to make amends. The path Arn walks, it is as much my fault as it is his."

Lucavi was still so close, he could see the God-Incarnate's bare feet from the upper corner of his vision. It was strange, to see toes and veins, even if the skin was so white and hard he could have been chiseled out of marble. It humanized him, yet showed how inhuman he truly was at the same time.

"Stand, my child."

Dario doubted he could have resisted the command even if he wished. The words pulled at his chest, and he sprang to his feet immediately. Lucavi towered over him, and while his smile was one of compassion, his eyes showed no such warmth. They were stern. Certain. They filled Dario's belly with dread.

"No, Dario, I will not grant your request. Your brother's sins are too many to be forgiven, not even if he were to plead for mercy and don the armor of a penitent."

Dario squared his jaw and met those stern eyes. He would not break, not here, not now. He could fix this. His faith would be rewarded; his service, repaid.

"There must be another way," he said. "All may seek forgiveness, is that not the promise of Everlorn?"

"Does your brother seek forgiveness? *My* forgiveness?"

Dario opened and closed his mouth. What point was there in lying? He had heard the conviction in Arn's heart. To convince him would take a lifetime, and that was exactly what Dario was hoping to bargain for. Yet the God-Incarnate demanded the truth, and so the truth he would receive.

"No," Dario said. "Not now. Not for many years, if ever."

"As I thought," Lucavi said. "Then we need not drag out the inevitable. We both know his crimes, and both know his deserved punishment. Arn must be executed."

Don't panic, Dario screamed at himself, but it was so much easier said than done. He dropped once more, this time to both knees, and lifted his hands above his head in supplication.

"Please, my lord, spare me such a fate. My joy in eternity shall taste ashen if I must watch my brother suffer in the Nameless Whore's hell. Even if it takes my entire life, I will bring him to salvation. Give me that chance, I beg of you."

Silence followed. Each second was like a needle piercing his spine. Would Lucavi grant mercy? Or would he be disappointed in Dario's weakness? On and on, the silence dragging, until suddenly the God-Incarnate answered. His voice was calm, almost curious, revealing no judgment at Dario's emotional plea.

"Answer me this, paragon, so I may know you walk in knowledge. What is the fate of my faithful come the end of this mortal world?"

This was a truth even children learned in their little school sessions in the multitude of churches across Gadir. Dario looked up so he might judge Lucavi's reaction to his answer.

"We will wage the Epochal War, conquering the eternities of the heathen gods."

Lucavi smiled. His hands settled on Dario's shoulders.

"Exactly. No soul, no matter who they worshiped in life, shall be beyond my reach in death. From the greatest to the least, they will kneel before my judgment. They may wail and gnash their teeth, but it will change nothing. In their pride, they fear this. In their servitude to weaker, false gods made in images of animals and objects, they refuse to acknowledge the obvious truth. I am humanity perfected, and so I will uplift humanity with my divine hands."

"Then where goes my brother's soul?" Dario asked. "Must I fight him again on the battlefield? Must I witness him being condemned for eternity, all for the failures and sins made during this life so short it is but a flickering candle by comparison?"

"Your brother's punishment shall not be eternal, Dario. That curse belongs only to the most cruel and wicked sort who would, even amid forever darkness, refuse to repent. You ask for mere years to grant your brother a chance at redemption. I refuse you, not out of cruelty, but mercy. I would not give you years, but eternity, dear child."

Lucavi lowered so he might take Dario's hands in his. Those pale white fingers brushed across the shining steel of Dario's gauntlets.

"Arn's every sin must be accounted for. Let him add no more bricks atop his back to weigh him down. Grant him *mercy*, my paragon, and let it be done by your own two hands."

Dario's world spun round like a kite cut free in a storm as he realized what Lucavi wished for him to do. This...this cruelty...it couldn't be true. It couldn't be asked of him.

"Mercy?" he said. His lips felt made of stone.

Lucavi stood to his full height. His hair shone like spun gold, his skin like reflected moonlight. Sapphire eyes beamed with newfound love.

"I sense the storm within you, Dario Bastell. Even now, you doubt. Even now, you wonder. Hear me, and hear me true. This is the culmination of your faith. Earn an honored place at my side when we wage the Epochal War. Rise above your doubts and fears. Spill the blood you love, and in doing so, prove my ultimate truth."

It felt like Dario's bones trembled inside his body. His heartbeat pounded in his ears, and his tongue turned as dry as sand.

"And what is your ultimate truth, my god?" he asked. "Tell me, for I do not trust my own wisdom."

Lucavi's fingertips touched Dario's chin, and though they were gentle, his skin felt lit with fever. The God-Incarnate tilted his gaze upward, guiding their eyes to meet. Deep within those irises swirled stars and constellations beyond Dario's understanding.

"Your suffering means naught before the everlasting. When the conquered weep for their dead, they see the loss of the ephemeral. I see the salvation of the eternal. All will one day learn this truth, be it by sword or by sermon. It matters not, so long as they learn."

His hand withdrew. His face hardened.

"Do you have that faith? Do you possess that wisdom, my child?"

Dario stood, and he gazed up at the culmination of Everlorn's wisdom and grace, he whom the Uplifted Church would shape the living to become. He was beautiful and terrible, and Dario felt himself withering in his presence.

It was dangerous to lie to a god, and so he spoke the painful, bleeding truth and prayed it would be enough.

"I do," he said. "I have long thought myself wise, but I walked in darkness. For the very first time, I know what you would have us become."

Never did Dario expect what followed. The mighty God-Incarnate wrapped his arms about him, embracing him against his marbled body. The heat of his divinity felt like fire across Dario's skin. Sobs choked his throat, for this was what he had always desired, and yet never before received.

"Go to your brother. Give him your love. He may not understand now, but he will. He will."

A hard road followed, but Dario promised to endure. No regrets. No second guesses. He would walk that path regardless of the blood that must be spilled and the fear that filled his heart.

"A life ended," he said, his eyes closed to hide his tears. "And a new life begun. Let it be done."

CHAPTER 36

STASIA

I don't understand why we can't use my father's name to get us through the gates," Stasia said as they waited at the shoreline. "I've never had issues with inspections before."

Clarissa lifted her lantern higher, scanning the water for the boat meant to bring them into Vallessau.

"If they ordered my mother to be relocated, there's a good chance I was singled out as well," she said. "Forgive me for wanting to remain unnoticed until I am certain there is no warrant for my arrest."

Stasia shrugged. Her fingers drummed the tops of her ax hilts. Her heels formed divots in the sand as she shifted her weight side to side. She could feel the nervous energy building inside her.

"I guess I can't complain about being extra careful," she said. "Even if it is a pain."

"Being safe is what keeps us alive," Clarissa said. "Pretty sure you tried to teach me that on our very first date."

"I also tried to get your clothes off, too. Don't put too much stock in my advice. I'm hardly a bastion of wisdom."

"Trust me, Stasia. I would never dare think of you as such."

Stasia laughed.

"You're lucky our boat is here, or I would have to punish you for that."

Clarissa only kissed her cheek and then waved the lantern high above her head to signal to the distant rowboat slicing like a shadow across the water. When the boat's lone occupant lifted his own lantern, Clarissa used the lid of hers to flash its light twice, then a long third, signaling all was well and for him to come ashore.

The man was gruff and bearded, and Stasia suspected him a longtime fisher given his ease in guiding the rowboat despite the dim light. Though his face was grim, his voice was surprisingly kind, and he talked quietly with Clarissa as they sailed around the horn and toward Vallessau's docks.

"How has the city been in our absence?" Clarissa asked him.

"Lycaena knows we've seen better," he said. "There's a chill in the air, and we all feel it. It's like..." He paused to think. "It's like we all have knives resting on our necks, and we're afraid one word to the wrong person will cause the knives to fall."

Stasia withdrew one of her axes and carefully ran her finger along the edge. Strange, there was a chip along the edge. So unlike her father's craftsmanship. Come to think of it, she'd never once known his weapons to break in battle. It was why Ahlai-crafted weapons were sought out so highly by soldiers and collectors alike. Was her old man losing his touch?

"I know the feeling," she said, putting her ax away. "It's like the air weighs too much, and you can never quite breathe. Smiles come hard, and joy even harder."

"Well it's a good thing we Thanese are a tough lot," the fisher said. "As them Everlorn people have discovered time and time again." He paused. "Is it really true, by the way? Those rumors you're spreading about the poisoned wine and the ceremony?"

Stasia grimaced.

"Painfully true."

The fisher shook his head.

"Those pig fuckers. We'll stop them, though. I know we will. Thanet won't die like they hope. Snuff your lantern, by the way. We're almost there."

The docks were blockaded, but the large imperial warships were anchored much too far away to notice a little rowboat easing toward the sands at the far southern reach of the docks. Three women and two children waited there, looking tired and nervous. Stasia helped the fisher pull his boat aground while Clarissa spoke quietly with the group.

"All aboard, now," the fisher said. Once the five were inside, Stasia pushed the boat out and then waved goodbye. She didn't know where they went, but wherever it was, she prayed they were safer than in Vallessau.

"Stasia..."

She turned, surprised by the dread she heard in her wife's voice. Clarissa looked pale, and her fists were clenched.

"What?" she asked. "What's wrong? What did they tell you?"

Clarissa bit her lower lip.

"Your home was attacked. Several of my group saw it."

It felt like the stars were collapsing all around Stasia. The gentle crash of the waves came from a thousand miles away.

"Survivors?" she asked.

"Arn and Mari were taken prisoner."

"My father?" Silence. She took a step closer. "And my father?"

Clarissa stood tall and took Stasia's hands in hers.

"I'm sorry."

The world turned flat and glassy. Shock washed over Stasia, but she forced it away through sheer will. Action. She had to take action. Move. Attack.

"Stay here," she said.

"Stasia, wait."

"I said stay here!" The words came out as a snarl. She felt like a caged animal, eager to bare her teeth. "It won't be safe, Clarissa. Stay here, or go to a hideaway."

Her wife withdrew her grasp.

"I know what you're going to do," she said. "Don't throw it all away for nothing. I need you, too, Stasia. Don't make me live without my wife."

Stasia thought of her sister in the empire's clutches. Would they torture her? Fill her mind with their ugly scriptures? Or would they publicly execute her as a message to the city?

Here hangs the Lioness, criminal to Everlorn.

"Not for nothing," Stasia said. "I love you, Clarissa. I will always love you. But I have to go."

Warring desires ripped Stasia apart. She wanted to return home. She wanted to storm whatever prison held her sister. She wanted to stay and comfort Clarissa and be comforted in return. There were too many questions, too many unknowns, and above all, her belief that somehow, someway, she could make things better. She could set it right, if only she were strong enough.

Stasia ran.

A young man leaned against the front door of her home, his head tilted and a wool cap pulled low over his face. When he saw her, he nodded and beckoned her over.

"I've been keeping watch," he said. He flashed a bit of steel sheathed to his belt.

"Have you been inside?" Stasia asked.

The man tried, and failed, to hide his frown.

"Just briefly. It's... not pleasant."

Stasia pretended he'd not said those words and they did not mean what they implied.

"Do you know where the prisoners were taken?" she asked.

"Two people were taken out of here in manacles," he said. "We don't know where, though, sorry. There were so many soldiers everywhere, what with the God-Incarnate himself arriving, we could only watch from afar."

Stasia put a hand on his shoulder.

"You've helped enough. And... thank you."

The man hesitated a moment, then nodded again.

"Yeah. All right. Good luck, Ax. And for what it's worth, I'm sorry."

Stasia didn't acknowledge him. She didn't have the space in her mind. All that mattered was her home, one of several they'd moved about in the past few months. The front door's hinges were intact. No locks broken. When the empire came, they had been welcomed. What happened? How had they been discovered? Or was it inevitable there'd be a traitor among them after spending so many years on Thanet?

She stepped inside.

Froze.

Clenched her hands into fists.

"Thorda," she whispered.

Her father lay on the floor, half propped against the wall facing the door. His robe was slick and stained red from the gaping wound in his stomach. Several intestines hung loose. Pools of blood surrounded him. His skin was pale, his body still.

So still.

But not completely.

"Stasia?" he muttered, his eyes fluttering open.

Stasia knelt beside him, coating her knees in his blood.

"I'm here," she said. Relief warred with her shock. "But you…how are you alive?"

Her ignored her question and tried to push himself up. She clutched him in her arms, only for him to resist.

"A chair," he said. "Fetch…a chair."

Stasia dashed to the next room to grab one of the chairs from the dining table. She set it down beside him, and this time when she offered, he accepted her help. His arms crossed over his waist as she lifted him, and she pretended not to see the pink, ropey strands between his fingers.

"There's not much time," he said.

"I don't understand," Stasia said. "Who did this?"

"Lucavi. Underestimated me to the last. He should…he should know. Killing a god. It's never easy."

Stasia froze. No. Not now. This was too much.

"Stop," she said, unsure of what she was even protesting.

"It's true," Thorda said. He closed his eyes, and his voice softened. It seemed to make speaking easier. "I was Miquo's God of the Forge. Its fires. Its crafts. They were mine to cherish, and to remember."

Everything was chaos. Her emotions. The world. The blood staining her clothes.

"Why didn't you tell me?"

"Not now," he said. "Ask...your sister. She will answer. But you. You must know. You've feared it, but don't be afraid. Don't resist. You are my blood. My chosen. My heir."

Would it be so terrible if you were a god?

Even when she'd discussed the possibility, it had never seemed real. They were the daydreams of others, accusations to deride her hard work and dedication. Divine blood, within her veins? Surely it couldn't be. This feeble, bleeding man crumpled before her on a chair, that couldn't be one of Miquo's last remaining gods. For her homeland to fall so far, for its divinity to be reduced to such a pittance of its former glory...

"Heir," she said. "But not yet. You've years left in you, old man."

With shocking strength, he grabbed her arm. His red eyes blazed with newfound light.

"Lucavi has Mari. Please. Save her. You must. I know you can."

"And I will," she said, fighting off sniffles. She kissed her father's forehead. It was one of the few places upon him free of blood. "Of course I will."

At that, he relaxed. His fingers released, and he eased back into his chair. His eyes focused on her waist. He reached out to brush his fingers across the edge of the ax belted there.

"Your weapon," he said. "It is damaged."

"Now is not the time—"

He ripped the ax free of its holster and held it out to her. She met his gaze and saw the strength in it, fierce and unbroken to the last.

"My hammer. It is on the forge. Fix it. Do this, please. For me."

Thorda's forge was but a small converted bedroom not far down the hall. She glanced at it. The door was broken off its hinges, no doubt from when the empire's soldiers had searched the place.

"All right," she said. "If it will make you happy."

"Thank you," he said. "My daughter. My child."

Stasia crossed the hall and stepped into the tiny forge. It wasn't much, just an anvil, a few shelves, and the waiting hammer. She stared at the instrument. Her father's hammer. How many weapons had he crafted with it? His works were revered across the land, and now she knew why.

Her fingers hesitated above the hammer. This... this would change things. Change *her.* Could she? Did she have the strength?

Her hand opened. Closed into a fist. How many lives had she taken? She was destruction incarnate, the fearsome Ax of Lahareed. She did not create. She did not build. Taking up this hammer meant becoming something new. Would it be alien to her? Or would it be a new facet of her being?

To refuse meant to be afraid, and there was no time for fear. Mari and Arn needed her. Stasia lifted the hammer. It felt cool and comfortable within her grip. Familiar. With her other hand she set her damaged ax upon the anvil. She raised the hammer.

Behind her, she heard her father retch.

Stasia slammed the hammer down upon the ax. She barely aimed. She had no thought to technique or purpose—her father had not trained her much beyond the basics at the forge. The hammer's blunt surface struck the brilliant steel. Not Thorda-made, as she had always viewed it in her mind. Ahlai-made. Her family. Her bloodline.

Another strike. Sparks flitted across the room. She watched them fall as she made her vow.

I'll save you, Mari. I'll save you, Arn. Not just you two. Everyone. I promise. I promise.

Another hit. Another. She struck with strength lacking control. Faster, wilder, beating her ax with the hammer as sparks flew and heat grew within the steel. Reforging a weapon her father had once perfected. There would be no oil, just the first of her falling tears. Lift the hammer, then bring it down.

Her father crumpled from his chair.

Again. Again. Strike the blade. She saw faces in the steel. Soma, laughing. Sinshei, scheming. Lucavi, murdering. The steel, which shimmered orange from the heat. Strike. Strike. Not her father's hammer, but hers now, hers, the heir to a faded, desperate divinity. She was screaming. Sobbing. Raging. The muscles in her back and neck stretched and grew. Strike. Strike.

Become Goddess.

Her every will channeled into one final blow. Her entire body rose with the hammer, her legs stretching, her arm curling. Down came the hammer, and with its contact, the ax head burst into flame. She lifted it by the handle and watched it burn. Though its fire trickled toward the hilt, it did not harm her, for how could it? Its heat was her own rage. Its oil was her very tears.

Stasia removed her other ax, set it upon the forge, and then clipped the hammer in its place on her belt.

"I know who I am," she whispered to the silence. She did not fight the tears trickling down her face, nor deny the many whispers she felt brush across her spine like a cold wind. Prayers for safety, for confidence, and for luck come the next battle. Wishes and fears, some spoken, most held silent as these men and women clutched Ahlai-made steel. In time, she hoped she would grow accustomed to their presence.

Stasia returned to her father, found him silent and still. She lifted him back into the chair with her free hand, fetched a blanket from his bedroom, and then laid it over his body. The desire to speak, to eulogize, came over her, but that had never been their way.

"For the trials you faced, and the life we lived, you did your best," she said. This would have to do. "And what failures you made, I forgive you of them. Remember me, Father. Watch over me, and please, hold faith. I'll bring her home. I promise."

Stasia pressed her burning ax to the blanket, setting it aflame. Next she brushed the curtains, and then the furniture. The fire spread, slow at first, then faster, hotter. It rippled across the walls. It clawed at the floor. Smoke billowed out the windows. Any sane person would flee the inferno, but no such fear dwelt in her heart.

Within it all, Stasia stood before the consumed corpse of her father. The taste of embers coated her tongue. The blood on her clothes dried and cracked. What tears she shed evaporated away. She stood tall amid the fire, her ax in one hand, her hammer in the other. The heat washed over her, purifying her. The roar of the flames was a defiant song in her heart.

Let her father be the first sacrifice to her godhood. Let this house be the first forge she kindled. And within it, bathed in embers, let her own body be the first weapon crafted in her name.

The Goddess of the Forge stepped out to the cold night street and exhaled ash onto the wind.

Waiting for her, her hands clasped behind her back and her head bowed, was a fellow goddess, Nameless and beautiful. Her face was a mystery, blurred and ever shifting to Stasia's newly blessed eyes.

"I know where your sister is being held," She said. "Follow me, Stasia, if you would save her."

CHAPTER 37

MARI

From a warm bed to a cold dark cell in mere hours. Mari would question which god she offended, but that answer seemed obvious. The chill did not bother her too badly, though the sweat coating her body from her broken fever added to the bite. The manacles around her wrists were tight and kept her hands bound to the wall above her head, but that, too, she could ignore for a time.

No, the worst was the gag they had tied over her mouth, a thick knot of cloth that was rough against her tongue. They feared what she could do and seemingly thought muzzling her would prevent her from taking the form of the Lioness.

They think I'm still dangerous, she thought. *How wrong they are.*

Mari chastised herself immediately. Now was not the time for such despair. So long as others survived, there was hope for rescue. Her sister, for one, was with her wife. Arn was in a cell near hers. Cyrus and Keles would also return to Vallessau soon, and their fury upon learning of Mari's capture would be savage. Her capture, and her father's murder...

Mari closed her eyes and leaned against the stone wall. Tears came unbidden, not the first, and she suspected not the last. It was all too much. To lose Endarius, to wake to Arn, and then to suffer such loss. No chance to say goodbye. No chance to mend the gaps that had grown between her and her father over his secrets.

For thousands of nights, she had lain in her bed dreading the possibility of their discovery and arrest. Her mind would spin countless scenarios for her to fear. Now that she faced its reality, she was surprised by how unafraid she felt. The nightmare had come at last. Perhaps there was freedom in that.

Mari giggled despite her tears. Or perhaps she was still feverish and exhausted. Whatever awaited her in death, she knew it was beyond the reach of the God-Incarnate's vile hands, no matter how many times he might insist a war in the heavens would follow his conquest of the mortal lands.

The walls to her cell were solid stone and dug lower into the earth than the walkway above, so that any entrance through the gate had to be followed by descending a rope ladder. Given her isolation, she had no warning before the door creaked open and blinding torchlight washed over her cell. Mari squinted against it, trying to identify her guest.

Immediately her heart sank. The man wore the robes of Everlorn's priests. He was surprisingly young, too, his red hair parted down the middle. Hunger shone in his eyes. Nothing good would come of his arrival.

"Hello, Mari," the man said after descending the rope ladder. His voice was perfectly smooth and controlled. It was something the priests and magistrates were taught in their churches. No matter the circumstances, the priests were meant to sound calm, collected, and in control. They were the men and women with the answers, if only the conquered populace would be willing to ask them the questions. "I am Magistrate Castor Bouras. I do not believe we have met."

"I'd have already killed you if we had," she said into her gag. She had to force down another giggle. Yes, her fever was definitely returning. Her face felt flushed, and it was hard to think straight. The delirium accompanying it felt nice, though. It made it easier to deal with the cell and the manacles and the gag.

Castor knelt on his haunches before her. Mari met his gaze, unafraid. She'd seen his kind before. Highly educated, bursting with confidence, and completely inflexible in their beliefs. No doubt he wanted something from her. The question was, what?

He'd tell her, though. Oh, he most certainly would. These types could never keep their mouths shut.

"I have a few questions for you," he said. "Though I would first tell you what I know so you may not waste both our times with lies or attempts at stalling. We know you worked with your father in fostering rebellion. We know you are the Lioness, and your sister the Ax of Lahareed." He shuffled closer. "Most interestingly, we know you are a god-whisperer of Miquo."

Indeed, and if Endarius were still with me, I'd rip your throat out and have myself a drink of your blood.

Instead she smiled. If this priest wanted answers, then that was the one thing she would not give him. Even if it led to torture.

Seeing the way he smiled back, she knew that was indeed what awaited her.

"I'm going to remove your gag so we might discuss," he said. His left hand settled on the knot behind her head, and then he hesitated. He raised his other hand, palm open. A quick prayer left his lips, and then a golden dagger shimmered into view. "But know that I will tolerate no foolishness, nor any attempts to escape. Even if you did kill me, two paragons wait outside. You would never escape."

Aye, but I'd at least have taken you with me, she thought, wisely keeping it to herself. Given her grim life, she had attended many meetings when men and women were prepped for the possibility of torture and advised of pitfalls to avoid. Denigrating your captors was one such mistake. The insults might seem fun, or harmless, but it meant you were communicating with them. Insults could lead to arguments. Arguments could lead to information. Better to ignore, or repeat rote, prepared phrases. Mari knew all that, and she also knew it would be extremely difficult. She might have trained to keep her mouth shut, but these priests had equal training, if not hours and hours more, on how to pry loose stubborn lips.

"There," he said as the knot fell loose. He beamed at her, as if he had done her a great favor. Mari swallowed and rolled her tongue around her mouth, trying to rid herself of the dry taste. All the while, she pretended he was not there. Her gaze remained unfocused, distant, another surprising benefit of her current illness.

"I must admit, I am excited to meet you," he said, taking a step back. The golden dagger hovered at his shoulder, never leaving. "Though I am experienced with the Humbled, Everlorn has not once captured a god-whisperer. Not alive, I should add. You are quite a prize."

She laughed. She couldn't help it.

"How wonderful," she said, staring at the cell's ceiling. She could see him from the corner of her eye. His calm smile faded for the briefest instant, and behind that mask, she saw ugliness so deep and vile it twisted her stomach. The way he looked at her...it was contempt and disgust mixed with overwhelming desire. Not for her body, she suspected, but for what she was, and what she represented. Knowledge. Mystery. Uniqueness. All of which could be used for his advancement up the ranks of the priesthood.

"I do not mean to sound callous," Castor said, that practiced smile returning. "Nor pretend that you are not bound as our prisoner. I am merely trying to reinforce to you your value. Despite your crimes against Everlorn, and the many lives you have taken, your nature as a god-whisperer grants you a chance at redemption rarely afforded to others. Many Humbled slaughtered thousands of our soldiers before they submitted and worked to repay their debt. You may do the same, even if it is not necessarily on the battlefield."

Mari focused on a single crack that ran through the ceiling. Focus on that, and hide the horror she felt at the thought of being Humbled. She'd seen the trauma inflicted upon Rihim of Antiev. The panther god's mind had been utterly broken, his honor and love for his wife, Amees, twisted into something sick. It was only in death, and in hearing the words of his slain wife, that he gained a semblance of his former self.

Castor was unbothered by her silence. If anything, it added to his energy.

"Ah, but you Miquoans are a stubborn lot," he said. "I've read stories of your country's insurrection. Why, one of your fathers was particularly famous, wasn't he? Like father, like daughter; I suppose that was your plan. Lead an insurrection while pretending to be one of Thanet's slain gods, is that it? Only you have failed, like you always fail. It is our churches your people fill, not the Lion's. It is to the God-Incarnate they pray, not any of your heathen gods."

He knelt closer to her. His cologne washed over her, a strong mixture of citrus and bark, and it sickened her already queasy stomach.

"Yet despite the hopelessness of it, you fight on. A commendable trait, but sadly misguided. You are a remarkable individual, Mari Ahlai, but your fathers raised you poorly. Did they tell you that you had no choice? Did they insist peace was impossible, despite the peace that Miquo has been blessed with for the last decade? What lies did you swallow as a child, convinced they were irrevocable truths?"

His voice softened. His every word vomited sincerity and understanding.

"If you would but make peace with Everlorn, and share your wisdom with me, you will face a far better fate."

You walk the lands of gods, she thought, refusing to acknowledge him. *You sing where darkness meets light along the horizon. You are safe. You are not here. You are not here.*

When her silence stretched, Castor let out an exaggerated sigh.

"I feared as much. Your ferociousness was not born out of a weak will." He stood, his form looming over her. A flex of his hand, and the gold dagger zipped into orbit. "You fought Rihim, didn't you? If our understanding of events is accurate, you even killed him. You are familiar with the Humbled, then. You know what they are. What they become. But do you know how it happens, Mari?"

Castor waved his fingers. The floating dagger settled its edge against her left cheek. Heat burned off that creation of light and faith. A faint pain jolted throughout her face and all the way down to her collarbone and shoulder, as if it were injecting her with lightning.

"There are many theories as to the best methods," he said, his voice dropping to an intimate whisper. "Some are universally agreed upon. We will deprive you of sleep. We will starve you of food. The body must be weakened until the soul is ready to listen. But beyond that? Some think it best to overwhelm a Humbled with prayer. Others suggest scriptures and lessons. Pain, though. I have always found pain to be the purest, most direct form of instruction."

The dagger cut her cheek. What had been faint became searing as that jolt arced through the entire left half of her body. She did not scream, for she had no breath to do so. Several heartbeats later, he pulled the glistening blade away. She hung limp from the manacles. Blood dripped down to her chin to fall as scarlet drops upon her dress.

"Pain leads to the fear of pain," Castor said. "And eventually that fear overwhelms all other resistance. Closed eyes open at last. Stuffed ears are made clear. Obedience may be taught, and faith may be earned, but first the way must be prepared. It is no different from our soldiers storming the shores of Thanet. There will always be those who resist the God-Incarnate's wisdom, just as there will always be pride and ignorance within the minds of heretics. Both must be uprooted, and brought to flame and blade."

He slashed her again, this time quick and without warning. Mari screamed as a matching wound appeared above the first. Twin cuts on her left cheek. Blood flowed freely now, no longer just little drops off her chin.

"Your conversion is guaranteed, Mari Ahlai. The only question is how much you must suffer before you grant me the answers I seek. Spare yourself. It is your choice to make, and yours alone."

Mari closed her eyes. Ignore the pain. Ignore the blood. Retreat into memories of the past.

You walk the lands of gods. You are safe. You are not here. You are not here.

"Nothing," she said. "I will give you nothing."

His hand was on her throat in an instant. Rage replaced his seductive whispers.

"Do you think you can resist me, Mari? Do you think your stubbornness can outlast my patience, me, when I have all the time in the world to inflict my will upon you? I humbled Rihim. I humbled a *god*. What hope have you, little Miquoan girl?"

Something deep within Mari broke. Her laugh felt like it came from another, for surely it could not be hers. It was wild. Frightening. She spread her teeth wide, flashing them in the darkness as if she still bore Endarius's fangs. For the first time since Castor Bouras entered her cell, she let him see, truly see, the red in her eyes.

"I am a god-whisperer of Miquo," she said. "While you know only this mortal life, I walk the lands beyond. I kneel upon barren darkness that spans the horizon, and I bow my head before slain gods. Never am I wanted. Never am I greeted with kindness. These gods rage against me, priest. They seethe, and moan, and denounce their fate as a spirit lingering about our world without a body. I endure it, each and every time, for I know I must. For it is a price only I may pay."

She leaned forward, her shoulders aching as she stretched them to their limits. She wanted Castor to be so close he could smell the blood on her face.

"Their reasons differ, but all of these gods accept me, for a time. Some want to inspire their followers. Some want to return to life through newborn faith. And some merely want vengeance for the crimes your empire inflicted upon them and their faithful. That lingering essence, a collection of all their love and faith and belief, swarms into me. Into my fragile mortal body. And do you know what they always try to do?"

The man was enraptured. She was giving him every bit of the knowledge he desired, but in a way he never expected. He'd wanted her broken, or obedient. Whatever this was, even though it transfixed him, it inspired fear and revulsion.

"These dead gods try to become as they were in life," Mari continued. "Beautiful colors. Vibrant fur and flesh. They try to change me to become them, but I deny them, Castor, I deny them. I strip them of color and cloak them in bones, for they are dead, and I will not abide their lies. And then the change comes. My skin tears. My bones twist and bend. The presence of a deity rends, it sears, and it is everything your gleaming dagger inflicts but upon a scale you cannot imagine."

Mari might be in a cell, and Castor's hand on her throat, but in that moment, the priest was her prisoner.

"I take *gods* into my flesh, and within me, they *break*. Who are you compared to them?"

Castor shoved her back and retreated a step. In the center of the cell, he fumed and shook with his hands trembling at his sides. The frustration, the doubt, it reeked off him, and she needed no divine senses to smell it.

"You act strong now," Castor said, recomposing himself. "We shall see how strong you are after months in my care. Lucavi has tasked me with your breaking, and I shall not disappoint my god."

"Empty words," she said, and relaxed against the wall. Castor climbed the rope ladder, dragged it up after him, and then slammed the cell door shut. Mari closed her eyes and let the exhaustion take her. Finally, he was gone. She'd barely had time to herself since waking up next to Arn. Her mind wandered, and she felt the faint tug of the mystical world. She would not slip within, not entirely. This was no place or time for such a communion.

But if she focused on a name, an identity, she could still sense the divine. In conquered lands, she needed totems, altars, or symbols to connect to the various gods. They were not necessary for the prayer, but used to grant her knowledge and intimacy so she might make the connection.

Not needed, not now. Her prayer was simple, and she knew it would travel true, for who else alive might she be more familiar and intimate with than her own blood and kin?

Stasia's face hovered like a ghost in her mind, and with such power Mari knew she had inherited the legacy of their father. The Ahlai name would live on. A new god would tend the forge. Sadness and pride mixed within her, and she knew it would be many long, quiet nights before she fully understood that complexity. The loss of a father. The ascension of an heir.

A spark between them, connection made. A single emotion washed over Mari, and she smiled. No, she would not be here for months. Not days. Not even hours.

Not when the Ax of Lahareed approached bearing such rage.

One prayer, one promise, whispered to the silence of her cell.

"Come get us, sister."

CHAPTER 38

STASIA

Stasia lurked at one of the shops built near the base of the capital hill and watched the scattered patrols atop the castle walls. Her every instinct begged to attack, her body trembling with rage. But not yet.

They have locked your sister and her friend in the castle prison, Nameless She had said as they approached the heart of the city. *In cells reserved for the most dangerous or most valuable. Getting either in or out will not be easy.*

Stasia knew what cells Nameless She referred to. When Arn had been captured, but before Lord Jase had come with his lies, their group had gone over the castle layout in preparation for a potential jailbreak. The entrance was small and unassuming. It was where only the most important and delicate prisoners were taken during Thanese rule, those with noble blood, vast wealth, or ties to the two churches.

After twenty minutes, she finally saw the first strands of smoke rise from the south.

If you care for us, and all we've done, spread word to those loyal to Thanet, she had told the Nameless woman. *Set fires and cause chaos, the more the better. Help me save those I love.*

A second plume joined the first, somewhere set alight in one of the upper streets carved along the northwest portion of the Emberfall Mountains. Already she saw the commotion spread across the soldiers as they shouted and pointed.

If there is anything I have been made for, She had answered in turn, *it is spreading hatred against the empire.*

"That's right," Stasia whispered as the smoke grew. "We're mad, and we're retaliating for attacking our leader. Come get us."

A third fire, then a fourth. The fifth, though, set her heart skipping. Far near the docks, a tremendous explosion of fire billowed into the sky. Its smoke coalesced instead of thinning, becoming the shape of a butterfly that slowly floated higher above the city. A defiant message of Lycaena's fury to the conquerors, one she suspected was created by the hand of Eshiel himself. She'd have to remember to thank the priest after all was said and done. Soldiers marched out the gates of the castle, two paragons included in their number. Those atop the walls watched the fires spread across the south and east.

Stasia headed west and scaled the hill within seconds, using her ax to catapult herself higher, her feet running along the wall like a spider. Another strike of the ax, another pull, and she vaulted to the top of the wall.

Two soldiers were a hundred yards to her right, staring at the still-burning symbol of the butterfly. Stasia pulled the hammer from her belt, crouched low, attacked. Her ax cleaved the head off the man on the right. Her hammer caved in the helmet of the man on the left. Both were killed instantly.

No hesitation. No delay. Blood was drawn, and it filled Stasia's veins like fire. Her rage was unrelenting, and she let it define her very world. Nothing would stop her. Nothing would slow her down. She spun about, scanning the courtyard to the keep farther uphill. There. Not by the grand double doors, but to the side.

There was no stealthy way to reach it, and so Stasia abandoned stealth. It never suited her anyway. She would trust her strength, her fury, and the sheer audacity of her attack. From the heart of the castle, she would rip her friends and family free.

Stasia raced upon the wall, curling along the western side to get as close as possible before jumping down to the courtyard. Another duo of soldiers spotted her arrival, and they froze in disbelief. One turned to run. The other drew his sword and readied his shield. Stasia vaulted at the stationary one, landed atop his shield, and kicked off again, somersaulting over him. Her trajectory carried her to the fleeing soldier, her ax carving a line from his shoulder to his spine.

The soldier behind her screamed a mixture of shock and anger. Stasia ripped her weapon free, spun, and blocked a frantic downward chop with her ax. The sword's edge slid along her ax when she twisted it, opening up a blow from her hammer that caved in his entire rib cage.

Two down, an endless number to go. She broke into a sprint across the rampart. Four soldiers rushed at her from up ahead, shouting warnings and readying their weapons. Stasia closed the distance between them and then pivoted at the last moment to dive to the courtyard below. The distance should have shattered her legs. Human legs, perhaps, but that wasn't her anymore.

The grass was a blur beneath her as she crossed the courtyard to the prison entrance. It was a little side door carved into the keep, a late addition tucked away from where petitioners and royals would pass through the main entrance. A lone man stood guard before it, but scattered soldiers were already rushing ahead of her to join him. Eight, by her count. The fools. They needed eighty, not eight.

Never slowing, never doubting, she blasted into their group. Her ax whirled, leaving a trail of flame that washed over any who tried to counter. Her hammer was poor for blocking, but its every blow against a shield shattered the bones of the arm holding it. She twirled through them, always on the offensive, always striking. Blood flew, bodies fell, until only one remained, a frightened spear-wielder still guarding the door.

A kick of her feet, and she regained her momentum in a charge straight at him. The spear thrust for her abdomen, easy and predictable. Stasia batted it aside without slowing. She led with her right shoulder. No key. No knocking. She hit the soldier square in the chest and pushed onward, blasting into the door and shattering it off its hinges. The guard's limp body rolled across the debris, past two more guards who stood facing the entrance with weapons drawn and baffled looks on their faces.

No chance to prepare. No time to react. She bore down on them, and when one blocked, her ax shattered steel on the way to carving off half his body. The other panicked, and when he tried to flee past her, a swipe of her hammer snapped his spine at the waist. He collapsed, coughing and gasping in pain. She turned to finish him off, only to see he was not alone.

Shit.

A paragon of swords pushed through the dungeon entrance, his giant frame destroying whatever remained of the door. The entrance room was square and cramped, the sides mostly occupied by crammed shelves. The paragon's movements would be limited, but he wore bulky armor and carried a sword that likely weighed as much as Stasia. Close battle would suit him just fine.

Stasia lifted her ax and struck it with her hammer. She'd just have to make a close fight suit her as well. Fire burst forth around her ax, burning as if the head were drenched with oil. She grinned at the man. She wore no mask, and her word-lace did not disguise the red of her eyes. Fully herself, with no more need to hide. The paragon likely thought the fire of her ax a jester's trick, but oh how wrong she would prove him.

He closed the distance with his shoulder leading and his sword pulled back in both hands. He would crush her with his weight and keep his blade ready to counter whatever attack she made in defense. Stasia retreated two steps and then swung her ax in a wide arc. Flame billowed off it in a curtain, and she knew, somehow she knew, it would hover there, held in place by her sheer will. Smoke rolled off it toward the ceiling.

Between the fire and the smoke, she was fully hidden from view. All that mattered now was whether the paragon canceled his charge out of caution, or if he pushed through, trusting his strength and armor. Stasia knew which one he would do, what all paragons would do, and so she attacked accordingly. He thought he battled a random member of Thanet's resistance, or perhaps an exceptionally skilled fighter.

Not a goddess of hearth and flame, whose might could mirror his own.

The paragon blasted through the fire, screaming at the pain as its heat lashed his face and charred his skin with divine power. His sword swung in an arc, curling from right to left. Stasia met it with her hammer, and she screamed right back as the impact traveled up her arm and flooded her elbow and shoulder with pain. It held, though, by all the Miquoan gods, it held, and he had no defense against her ax as it came crashing down.

The burning head cleaved his skull in half. The paragon dropped and lay still.

Stasia yanked her ax free of the filth, shook her numb left arm in a futile attempt to restore feeling to it, and then turned. She had to hurry. There was but one hallway to travel, leading to a small flight of stairs. She dashed down the steps two at a time to the remainder of the prison. A lone soldier waited midway through the lone path between the cells, and she flung her hammer on instinct as he lurched to a stand from his little wooden stool. It sailed end over end to crack straight into his forehead. He dropped instantly.

She turned her attention to the cells. They were mere pits dug into the earth and then sealed with brick. Each entrance was barred by a gate that connected from ceiling to floor. She could see a plain straw bed down in them, along with a blanket. Fine conditions for a prison, compared to many she'd been to (and a few she'd been confined within). The very first one contained a blessedly familiar figure.

"Arn," she said as she smashed open the lock with her ax. "Can you move?"

"My hands and feet are chained," he said, and rolled onto his side so she could see better in the dim light. "So. No."

A rope ladder was nailed to the ground at the cell door, and she kicked it down to Arn.

"I can check the entrance for a key," she said, biting her lip. She needed Arn out and ready to fight. Whatever resistance she fought getting in was going to pale compared to what they faced getting out.

"Do not bother," a deep voice said from toward the entrance. Stasia turned and felt her stomach sink. Two paragons marched toward her in single file. The nearest was a green-eyed pretty boy with a spear, the perfect weapon for their cramped environment. Behind him, a paragon of fists, whose gauntlets were well suited for tight spaces. Stasia braced her legs and readied her weapons, her mind racing. Strong and furious as she felt, trying to take two paragons on at once was a death sentence. If she could avoid the spear, perhaps she could get in close and force him to use only the handle…

"You've come for Arn?" the second paragon asked before the first could attack.

"Arn and all the rest," Stasia said, feigning cockiness.

"Then I'll send your corpse to him as a present," the spear-wielder said. He pulled his weapon back to strike but never had the chance. The paragon behind him grabbed his helmet and twisted it sideways, pushing his head through the bars and wedging him in place. He bashed both his gauntlets straight down on the man's neck, snapping it instantly. The dead paragon's body hung limp and suspended within the bars.

Stasia stared at the paragon, utterly baffled. Then he took his helmet off, and she saw his face.

"If you're here to rescue Arn, let me help you," Dario Bastell said. "I've come to do the same."

No time to question her good fortune.

"Think you can get him out of those chains?" she asked.

In answer, Dario withdrew a key from a pouch at his waist.

"I'm the one who put him in them."

Good enough for her. She retrieved her thrown hammer and then passed Arn's cell to the next. Relief swelled in her heart. There was her sister, sitting calmly on her knees. No smile, but no fear, either.

"Hey there," Stasia said as she cut the lock. "Sorry it took me so long."

She didn't bother with the rope ladder. Stasia hopped down and checked the manacles pinning her sister's arms above her head. Two chops with her ax, and the metal broke. Her sister appeared exhausted, and she rose on unsteady legs.

"You look…stronger now," Mari said.

Thankfully Stasia's mind was far too focused on survival to feel any of the hurt she knew she would one day suffer.

"Then you know," she said. "But for how long?"

"Since Rihim told me. Father confirmed it."

Yes, this would definitely hurt, but not now. Right now, she would use every shred of her divinity to escape.

"Hold on to me," she said, paused a moment, and then jumped back up to the cell door, carrying Mari with her. She set her sister down, then positioned herself so Mari could lean her weight upon her while they both walked. Up ahead, Dario and Arn whispered to each other, then stepped apart.

"Trust me, don't trust me, I don't care," Dario told them all as he marched for the exit. "But if you want to live, I suggest you follow me."

"He's killed one paragon already," Stasia said, in case the others were uncertain. "We don't have the luxury of doubt."

Arn broke from his brother, and he offered Mari his arms.

"I'll take her," he said.

Stasia reluctantly accepted. They passed through the cells to the main entrance, where Dario was kicking open the shelves that lined either side of the wall. Most were supplies for the prisoners, but one in particular appeared to be Dario's goal.

"There we are," he said, and reached inside to pull out Arn's gauntlets. Mari wrapped her arms around Arn's wrist so he could release her and catch the gauntlets tossed to him. He donned them with a grim smile.

"Can you stand on your own if I need to hit something?" he asked Mari.

"I'll manage."

"She better," Dario said, sprinting out the door. "We already have company."

Stasia hurried to join him, bracing for the worst.

It was still worse.

More than one hundred soldiers formed a semicircle sealing in the dungeon entrance built into the keep. A priest flanked by three paragons stood at their head, the young bastard looking as smug as could be.

"If any of you wish for clean deaths, lay down your arms and surrender," he shouted. "Otherwise, I will be the one to administer the punishment you deserve for such bloodshed."

"Castor," Arn muttered beside Stasia.

"He came to me, too," Mari said, slowly pulling away from Arn so he might fight. She wobbled a bit but remained otherwise strong. "Kill him if you can, would you?"

Arn clacked his gauntlets together.

"Happy to try."

Stasia stood in the center of their group, watching the soldiers steadily close in. They were being careful, and they had every reason to be. With Arn on her left and Dario on her right, they possessed the might of paragons as well. She herself was the Ax of Lahareed. If only Mari could become the Lioness, perhaps they could overwhelm even these numbers.

Except Stasia was not the Ax of Lahareed, not anymore. She was greater. Despite the clear night, it seemed the world darkened. Her father's blessing felt mighty and wild and new. Whispers filled her ears, speaking in her homeland's tongue. She lifted her hammer above her head, and to her amusement, the frontline soldiers shuffled back a step.

"Gods and goddesses of Miquo," she whispered. "Did you love my father?"

The darkness grew. Trees ringed the soldiers, though they seemed oblivious to them. Time itself slowed to a crawl, for this divine plane cared not for earthly law. Faces within the bark stared back at her, and this time, she knew their names. To the left of Aloth the wise was the wolf-faced Galaa, and to his right, blind Rosara.

He gave much to keep us in remembrance, said Aloth.

His hope for our revival never broke, said Galaa. *His life was spent in penance. Yes, we loved him, little Ahlai god. The last of us. How could we not?*

The world was pitch black, yet piercing the veil, Stasia saw the hearths of Thanet's homes, red and yellow stars burning before her vision across the entire island. From thousands of miles away, she felt the comfort and pride of those who held weapons crafted by her name and her bloodline. Was this the power her father wielded in his younger years? Or was this something more?

"Not the last," she said. "Will you love me, too, gods of Miquo?"

Will you serve? asked blind Rosara.

Stasia grinned, and her teeth felt like fangs. She exhaled and saw sparks.

"I will *fight*," she said. "Give me what strength you have. Help me save my friends."

You ask for much, insisted Aloth. Bark groaned as the trees twisted and writhed. *We who are so little have little left to give. Our prayers are few. Too many of our faithful bend the knee to Everlorn.*

"Then I will come to Miquo myself. I will crush their priests, burn their churches, and cry out your names to the heavens until our faith returns. But I must live. I must slaughter the God-Incarnate and shatter an empire. *Witness her*, my father prayed at my wedding, and I demand it now."

Indeed, I did, Thorda said. His face, there, among the trees, looking younger than she had ever seen him in life. No gray to his beard, no wrinkles to his skin. Stasia took a step back as if stabbed.

"Father," she said, at a loss for words.

All the other trees withdrew into the earth, their branches closing and curling inward as if they were seeds un-sprouting. There were only the hearths, a hundred, a thousand, then tens upon tens of thousands lining the horizon from distant Gadir. She saw her weapons glint like little silver stars. It was an overwhelming nightscape, beautiful and deadly, and they revolved in orbit about the face of her father. Tears, clear as the rain, ran down his cheeks as he smiled. He reached a hand out to her, the bark splitting and cracking to give way.

My dearest daughter, this gift you bear, I should have given it to you so many years ago. Take it now. Take the strength of my fellows, the strength of Miquo, the power of the broken and the desperate. If we fade, we fade. You called upon us in your need, and we shall answer.

Stasia's throat constricted, and she fought to form words.

"I wish you'd trusted me."

His face receded into the bark. The darkness brightened, and the stars of steel and hearth blistered away.

I have always trusted you. It was the world I feared. Change it. Melt it down, and forge it into something better.

Stasia opened her eyes, never realizing they were closed. Time was as it always was. The soldiers had not moved. Arn and Dario still flanked her. Her hammer remained raised, only this time, she felt power beyond her own fledgling faith. The might of Miquo, channeled together into one last moment of rage. Stasia felt delirious with its energy, and when Castor readied his gleaming blades of faith, sensing something amiss, she nearly laughed. Her proclamation was simple, her demand, undeniable.

"Make way."

Down came her hammer.

The earth roiled and broke. Cracks split the ground, heaving rock and ripping grass and brick apart. The shock wave rolled outward, taking half the courtyard with it. The noise was deafening, the deep rumble of stone making a mockery of the clatter of plate and chain as the soldiers fell. Bones twisted. Limbs snapped. Not even the paragons could hold their ground. One dropped to his hands and knees to ride out the impact, while another grabbed Castor and protected him with his own body.

The silence that followed was almost equally deafening.

"To the wall!" Dario screamed, and he led the charge across the uneven terrain with a dexterity that belied his tremendous size. Frantic soldiers tried to stand and rebuild their lines, but they were scattered, injured, and frightened. Easy pickings for the Bastell brothers.

"I know you're ill," Stasia told her sister. "But I'm begging you to run."

The uneven ground was worst for Mari, but she did her best to scramble in the wake of bodies left by Arn and Dario. Stasia guarded the rear, punishing any soldiers foolish enough or brave enough to chase.

"No," Castor screamed, drawing her attention. He scrambled over the broken rock, three golden swords swirling above his head. "The whisperer is mine!"

All three swords flew at Mari, slashing wildly to match their wielder's temperament. Stasia flung herself in the way, batting them aside with her ax and hammer to protect her sister. One of them nicked her arm, and she swallowed down a scream at the sudden pain. Golden light arced from the blade into her, filling her mind with a horrid sensation of *wrongness*.

"Keep running," Stasia shouted, seeing Mari hesitate. She lifted her weapons. "I'll keep us safe."

The three weapons pulled back for another attack, and she braced for the hit. All three at once would be difficult, and against priests, her normal tactic was to charge them directly, overwhelming them with her strength while taking advantage of their relative inexperience in battle. Not possible here. Castor was on the opposite side of the ruined courtyard, and surrounded by soldiers.

The weapons flew, but they did not reach her.

Fire blasted into them, a great torrent that batted the swords away as if they were leaves in a windstorm. Stasia turned, shocked by the sight. Eshiel hovered above the wall, grand wings of flame bursting from his back. More fire wreathed his hands, and smoke lifted from his eyes. Amid that fire, she saw deeper colors, radiant threads of faith granted to him by his goddess that held him aloft.

"Run, Ax!" he shouted, his voice carrying across the way. "Lycaena shall keep you safe!"

A wave of his hands, and the courtyard exploded with flame, bringing ruin to soldiers attempting to cross. Never one to turn away help, Stasia ducked her head and sprinted, all while keeping her head on a swivel.

As expected, Castor refused to relent. This time his swords turned into three long, barbed spears. They were better suited for the long-range attack, but Stasia had terrain on her side. She slid down an angled piece of stone and spun at the bottom. Now that she was out of Castor's sight, he could only guess at her location. Two spears struck wide, and the third was easy to bash aside. They pulled back, paused for another strike, and then went flying when Eshiel's fire blasted them away.

Stasia used the reprieve of fire to close the remaining distance between her and the outer wall.

"Up we go!" Arn shouted, hoisting Mari onto his back, putting a foot into his brother's readied hands, and then with his aid, vaulting up to the top. Dario quickly followed, bounding far higher into the air than his bulky body should allow and then pounding cracks with his gauntlets to pull himself up the rest of the way. Stasia sheathed her weapons before following, and she scurried up like a spider, using the same handholds the brothers had made to get to the top.

Arn had already carried Mari down by the time Stasia made it up. Beside her, Dario was crouched in preparation for a leap.

"Nice timing, priest," Dario told Eshiel, who hovered just shy of the wall.

"It is my specialty," Eshiel said, two more blasts of flame soaring over the wall to burn fleeing soldiers alive. Dario saluted him with two fingers and then hopped to the ground after his brother, safely outside the castle grounds.

"Hey," Stasia said, meaning to thank him, not just for his aid here but for the chaos his followers had spread elsewhere to buy her time, but she had not the chance. Eshiel's eyes widened, his arms crossed, and then the wings curled around him to form a shield just in time to block a trio of spears launched by a furious Castor. He dropped to a crouch atop the wall, dazed, but the spears were not yet done. Stasia dashed in the way, drawing an ax and swiping it wide to bat the gleaming weapons of faith aside.

They pulled around, two of them thrusting, a third becoming a sword of tremendous size that sliced downward in an attempt to chop her in half. Stasia held her ground, instinct guiding her hands. She blocked the largest of the weapons while twisting her body and praying the spears did not score a lethal strike.

Eshiel's fire ensured they cut not at all. Together, fire and ax, they sent the golden weapons flying. Eshiel chased them with another burst of flame, scattering them so far, Castor dismissed them rather than regain control. Three new swords shimmered into existence, floating above the head of the distant priest.

"Get going, Ax," he shouted. "Before I tire!"

Stasia hated the idea of leaving him, but more soldiers were already approaching from either side of the long wall, and it was only a matter of time before more priests and paragons came to aid Castor in his attempt.

"Fine," she said, clipping her ax back to her belt. She glanced over her shoulder, for one last glare at Castor. "But you…"

Castor no longer wielded swords, but a gleaming bow twice his size.

"Get down!" she shouted, leaping at Eshiel.

The arrow flew with such speed it was but a flash of light. She grabbed his arm and pulled, he twisted toward her, and then the arrow sliced across his stomach. Blood erupted in a tremendous spray, and she felt him turn in her grip from the force of the hit. He let out a startled cry, all fire and power leaving him as he collapsed into her arms.

"Ax?" he asked as the blood flowed.

Stasia had no choice. Blindly, she fell backward off the wall, trusting the Bastell brothers to catch her.

The fall felt like a lifetime, but catch her, they did.

"How bad is it?" Dario asked as they set Stasia back on her feet. She dropped to her knees and gently laid Eshiel on the ground.

"Bad," she said, seeing the savage cut across Eshiel's stomach from the golden arrow. There was so much blood already, and she did not know how deep the cut went.

"No," Mari said. She leaned against Arn for support, his huge arms wrapping around her smaller body. "He . . . he can't. Bandage him, carry him, please, do something."

Stasia stared at the cut, a wild idea forming in her mind.

"I don't know what I'm doing, but I'm going to try," she said, putting her hands upon the wound. "Don't hate me if I mess this up, all right, priest?"

The Ahlai name was, in its own way, one of creation. It turned ore into metal into art, even if its purpose was for slaughter. It was blade and hammer, yes, but it was also the wedding bracelet around her left wrist. Delicate and beautiful. And if Stasia closed her eyes and listened, truly listened, she could hear the prayers from her long-distant homeland. Those who remembered her father, and knew him as more than a name carved upon the hilt of a sword.

Her fingers sank into Eshiel's open wound. Warm blood flowed across her hands. She closed her eyes and tried to imagine a different place, and a different time. When her blood-mother had taken her to the tops of the trees, to look upon the sunrise across the Miquo canopy. That wondrous expanse. That burning sky.

Stasia would not surrender herself to Thorda's legacy. She would not forfeit her accomplishments, nor her sense of being. The forge might one day be hers, and she might learn to wield the hammer as well in creation as she did in battle, but for now she could only be herself.

"I am a goddess of Miquo," she whispered. "I am the heat that purifies. I am the forge that makes way for creation. I am ash. I am *fire*."

Flames wreathed her fingers, and she slid them across the wound, seeing them in her mind's eye. Cut flesh cauterized at her touch. Spilled blood blackened and burned away. Tears trickled down Stasia's cheeks. She heard the prayers of Miquo. Not the soldiers who wielded Ahlai weapons or the traders who relied on them for their livelihoods, but her people, the oppressed and broken who clung to their beliefs in hidden rooms and at unseen forest altars. She heard *their* prayers, felt them as they wore masterfully crafted rings and chains and set fire to leaves while crying out the name *Ahlai! Ahlai!* when only the stars and moon might hear.

A maker of beauty. A maker of war. A Goddess of the Forge, whose purpose would always and forever be hers to choose. The wound was not healed when her hands pulled away, but it was sealed, and the blood within purified. Across his pale skin, folded across the cauterization, was the burnt marking of her own two hands.

"Not my finest work," she said, and grinned at the now sleeping man. "But I'm still learning."

"Stasia..."

Stasia turned to see tears filling her younger sister's eyes. Mari collapsed into her, her arms wrapping her in a hug as she sniffled.

"I'm sorry I didn't tell you," she said. "You deserved to know."

Stasia patted her side and gently separated herself from her sister.

"Later," she said, and winked. "We still need to get out of here."

She took her sister's hand, and together they raced after the brother paragons, who took the lead, Dario carrying the injured priest. The five kept to the main road, trying to gain distance from the castle, but it seemed escape was not yet to be.

"Not now," Stasia muttered as their group skidded to a halt. Thirty soldiers formed a line to block the road, led at the front by two paragons, one wielding a ruby-studded spear, the other a tremendous ax. They held their ground instead of advancing. Time was on their side, after all. Stasia suspected they'd been one of the groups sent to investigate the fires, and pure bad luck had them meeting on the way back.

"We can break through," Dario said, cradling Eshiel like a child against his chest. "Me and Arn first, you two in the follow-up, unless you think you can repeat your little trick with your hammer?"

"I think that was a onetime thing," Stasia said. She tensed her legs, but then halted. Shadows curled like mist along the feet of the soldiers, spreading among their number. By the time they noticed, it was much too late. Hands lunged out from the pool, six-fingered and clawed, grabbing at any nearby legs and ankles. Not to kill, only to hold in place.

The killing was reserved for the wraith that rose among them, his body wrapped in darkness, his face a grinning skull. His swords gleamed with moonlight as they did their work, carving through the group with horrifying speed. Blood sprayed wild in all directions, but none seemed to stick to the Vagrant's cloak.

Only the paragons offered a challenge. The spear-wielder dashed to meet the surprise attack, his spear spinning with skillful control to block Vagrant's initial barrage. The other tried to join him, but then Keles joined the fray, her shield sparkling with a blue light deeper than the sea, and her cloak a brilliant rainbow of color that shifted and moved as if filled with life. Her sword met the paragon's ax, and she easily held her ground.

Left alone, Vagrant made easy work of his foe and then dove upon Keles's opponent. Together, they battered his ax aside, cut through his armor, and embedded their weapons simultaneously in chest and stomach. As the paragon writhed in pain, Vagrant slashed open his throat, flipped his swords, and cut a crown across his forehead. The body dropped, but Vagrant was not done. He turned to the other men he'd killed, sheathed his weapons, and lifted a single hand clenched into a fist.

Bloody slashes appeared across the foreheads of every single dead soldier, their skin opening of its own accord. His shaking fist lowered, and when he turned back to them, his brown eyes sparkled behind the bone of his godly face.

"Did you miss us?"

CHAPTER 39

SHE

Nameless She skirted the wall that surrounded the capital hill. She pretended not to notice the blazing golden torch that was the divinity of the God-Incarnate, visible even through the stones of the castle. The night neared its end, and blood dripped from her left arm. She had cut, as She always cut, but for now, She fought the urge. There was something She must do, in this last hour before the sun began its rise.

Passing through the wall was easy for one such as her. Along the west was a small door, its wood thick and reinforced with steel. Two guards kept watch, and She approached them with her head down and gaze cast to the dirt. She wore the clothes of castle servants, and she held a full basket the moment she desired it.

"Food for his grace's faithful," she said when stopped by the guards. She made sure to speak Thanese. Neither guard wore a word-lace, and by their looks, she suspected they did not understand her words, but her purpose was obvious enough.

"Anything good in there?" the first asked in Eldrid, a gruff man whose beard was the color of coal.

The other guard peered in the basket, then shook his head.

"Just that awful bread they cook. Tastes like they mix sawdust into the dough."

She refused to meet their gaze, nor give a hint that she could understand them. Demure. Quiet. Obedient. Exactly as they would expect.

"Should we check her?" asked the first.

The second, a red-haired man who would be handsome if not for the vileness in his eyes, shrugged.

"Aye, she's a dangerous-looking one, isn't she?"

He laughed, and suddenly his hands were upon her. She flinched as if struck, though it was purely an act. There was nothing these two could do to her that compared to what She had done to herself for centuries. He pressed his side to her, his hands groping her breast, his grin inches away from her face, which She turned away from him.

"Weapons," he said, squeezing her breast hard enough to hurt. "Any weapons?"

Finally She lifted her gaze. Their eyes met. She wondered what color he saw, not that it mattered. What he *felt*, though? She knew. It flowed out of her, vicious and sharp as a blade. A thousand memories, gifted to her as prayers she never asked for. He would feel it like a cold winter morning. It would seep through his veins, make his stomach clench and his pulse race twice as fast. She would be beauty to his eyes, but terror to his heart.

"No," she said in Eldrid. "No weapons."

Just all that I am.

The red-haired guard released her breast, stepped back, and then backhanded her across the cheek.

"Get to work," he said in Eldrid, proving the words were not for her but for himself. He pretended to be undisturbed, but it reeked from him like piss. "Our god's faithful are hungry."

She bobbed her head, clutched her basket of bread, and hurried past them into the grand courtyard surrounded by the castle wall. Behind her, the two soldiers laughed. They would forget her soon, just a nameless servant, and should one mention the encounter to the other, they would not even agree on the color of her hair.

That did not ease the ache in her breast.

Once in the courtyard, she saw the aftermath of Stasia's assault. The ground was broken and uneven in large swathes near the castle entrance, and fire from Eshiel's hands had scorched portions of both stone and grass. It was dangerous to be here, so close to the God-Incarnate, but curiosity pulled her along. Here on Thanet, something had changed. The storm cloud of hate that followed Lucavi was ever present, but now She sensed something new, something small and divine that She did not recognize. Tonight, She would confirm its presence.

There was only a small gap of grass between the keep and the castle wall. It was dark, shaded from the stars and unlit by any torches. Within that darkness, she found the entity lurking. It was small, without shape or form. It hovered in the air, invisible to any mortal eye, but not to those who could see the divine. She approached this orb of darkness slowly, reverently. It did not move. It did not flee.

"I believe I know what you are," She whispered. "What you would become."

From the orb's surface stretched thousands upon thousands of tendrils, thin as spider silk, reaching out into the sky. Touching the storm cloud of hate that had followed Lucavi.

For centuries, She had seen that cloud with her divine-blessed eyes. Though its power ebbed and flowed, it was always with the God-Incarnate, and well familiar to her. This entity, though? This little thing aching to be born was new. She offered her arms, as if for an embrace, and it dove at her. The orb struck her chest, and She choked down a cry. Her mind went blank. Divine power flowed through her, and She felt those tendrils separating one by one as the entity made a new home within her breast. Her teeth clenched. She fought back against an urge to change, to become something new and terrifying.

Not a god. A wish. A desire. So powerful, yet formless and nameless.

She denied it. Nameless, She might be, but She would forever be the Whore, not what this entity would have her become. Another. There must be another.

The presence settled down within her, content with its new home. At last it spoke, and She sensed it took great effort to form those words.

Is it time?

Her fingers gently touched her chest, feeling the power, the hate, the rage and desperation of millions dwelling within her. Eyes closed, she imagined a future without the God-Incarnate, and it flooded them both with pleasure.

"Not yet, little one," She whispered, and felt it shiver. "Not until the very end."

CHAPTER 40

VAGRANT

Home was now a dilapidated storefront located along the northern edge of Vallessau. Clarissa had brought them here at night, and whatever the place used to sell, it had long since been looted. The windows were boarded up and there were no beds, just piles of blankets and pillows on the floor. Outside was dark, and all their lit candles were positioned so their glow was hidden from the outside. Secrecy was of the utmost importance now. Their names and identities were forfeit. Posters of all their faces were drawn and nailed to major intersections of Vallessau, along with absurdly high rewards.

"Should we start without the priest?" Dario asked. It seemed the entire room tensed at his speaking. "Time is not on our side."

"Our side," Stasia said dryly. Despite Dario's aid in their escape, no one was particularly comfortable at his involvement.

"Yes, our side," Arn said. He and Mari sat together on some stacked pillows. Her hands were crossed atop her blanket, her skin pale and her hair haggard. Though her health had improved significantly since Endarius's departure, she still suffered intermittent fevers and shakes. She never complained, but it hurt Cyrus to see her suffering so.

"No need to defend me," Dario told his brother. "No one forced me to come here, and no one is forcing me to stay. So long as you'll accept my help, then I'll help. After all I've done, I think I can endure a few bitter comments directed my way."

"Enough," Cyrus said, and flung open the door. "He's here."

A pale Eshiel Dymling slipped inside.

"Greetings, Vagrant," he said. He walked gingerly, and a bulge under his shirt hinted at the many bandages wrapped about his waist covering the wound he'd suffered during their escape.

As Eshiel took a seat beside Keles, Cyrus stood over the cloth map in the center of the room. One week. They had one week until the six-hundred-year ceremony began. One week until the empire attempted to sacrifice the entire island in a horrifying tribute to their next God-Incarnate.

"Now Eshiel is here, we can start," he said. "I... suppose I should be the one to go first?"

The group exchanged glances. They all knew who should have been leading this meeting, but Thorda Ahlai was now bone and ash. After their rescue, Stasia had confessed everything, of her father's godhood and her own ascension. In some ways, it was absurd, but after seeing Stasia's rage during the rescue, and the fire that wreathed her ax, it was hard for anyone to deny the story. It only impressed Cyrus further the true might Thorda Ahlai had assembled upon arriving on Thanet. A god-whisperer, a fledgling god-to-be, a paragon, a paladin, and then whatever Cyrus was becoming. No wonder he had pinned such hopes on success here across the Crystal Sea.

"Our father was ever blunt when it came to most matters," Mari said. "Just talk, Cyrus. We'll plan this together. No leaders anymore. Just us."

He nodded and then, without ceremony, began to speak. It was strange, leading the way. He stammered and paused at random intervals while trying to get his bearings. The vacuum left by Thorda's death was too large. He felt it, as they all did.

"What plans Thorda started, we must push to full speed," he said. "The sacrifice, and the poison, must be stopped. A free Thanet means nothing if her people do not live to see it." He turned to Eshiel. "How have gone your efforts?"

"There are those loyal to the Butterfly all throughout Thanet," the priest said. "Already they meet in secret with our island's people, spreading word of the coming sacrifice. The stashes of wine are often guarded, but we smash what we can and set fire to what we cannot. Come the ceremony, we will guide people into the wilds, to flee the sacrifices we cannot halt."

A good start, but just that, a start. Cyrus glared at the map as if he could take his ire out on its pale cloth. With Clarissa's assistance, they'd gathered the status of resistance groups sprinkled throughout the island, while Keles and Cyrus had positioned Commander Pilus's army.

Those numbers, compared to the cities the people were being relocated into, were painfully lacking. The markers showcasing Lucavi's forces were so very many.

"We need to stop the ceremonies in the cities," Cyrus said, stating the obvious.

"We've told everyone a hundred times what the empire is planning," Stasia said. She leaned against the wall of their little home, her hands resting on the hilts of her weapons. Beside her was the fireplace, healthily burning. "Those cities should be fucking empty."

"The horror is too big," Mari answered. Her eyes lingered on her clasped fingers. "The lie will be even easier to swallow than the poisoned wine."

"Give your people some credit," Dario said. He lurked behind Arn, pacing like a caged animal. "I've read enough reports to know the entire island is in chaos. Travel out of the cities has already been heavily controlled, and I suspect it will be banned completely in the next day or two. People are looting what they can and sneaking out anyway. As much as the church will try, most of the populace will not die in a single night." Dario grimaced. "And as awful as this sacrifice will be, the cleansing that happens after will be worse. No need for pretending at that point. They'll sweep through Thanet like a wildfire, killing who they find and burning what they cannot search. Lucavi will leave this place an island of ashes and bones."

"Which is why we have to stop it," Clarissa said, trying to remain cheerful despite the gloom. "That's what we're planning for."

Except the plans were insufficient. Commander Pilus had his meager army, and in their final discussion before Cyrus and Keles left for

Vallessau, they had agreed he should split his army to disrupt the ceremonies taking place in the three largest cities on Thanet outside the capital, Thiva, Syros, and Raklia. Pilus would order them to attack just before the sacrifice, while the bulk of the empire's forces were distracted and focused on rounding up civilians. Pilus's most recent communication made it clear that, while confident in Thiva and Syros, he could send only a token force to the more distant Raklia, and he requested more soldiers be sent to bolster their number.

But they had no soldiers to send. What forces were in place in Vallessau were spread thin to try to disrupt the nine different gatherings planned for the ceremony.

"The church is ordering everyone they can find to gather in the cities," Cyrus said. "This helps us, in a way, if we can bring our own forces to bear."

"Forces that are pitiful by comparison," Stasia pointed out.

"Yeah, well, we have gods on our side," Arn shot back at her. "That has to count for something."

It did, not that Cyrus would waste the effort to argue. His strength was growing, but they would be losing a lot of advantages. There would be no surprise ambush, no picking the terrain or forcing leaders to make split decisions. These sacrifices would be heavily guarded, and expecting attempts at disruption.

And then there was the God-Incarnate, his priests, and his paragons...

Cyrus scanned the map. Thiva, Syros, and Raklia, all with meager squads trained by Commander Pilus. Even if by a miracle all three were victorious, the casualties would be high, and there was no guarantee they would win in time to stop the sacrifices. It was a grim gamble, but what other choice did they have?

Then there was Red Glade, the largest of the cities Pilus could not reach. And that just touched on the cities. There were so many towns and villages, and each one might be visited by a single Uplifted priest and a squad of soldiers. The Thanese resistance had grown, and even those smaller places would fight back. Some would even win. But not enough. Never enough.

"There is no denying the truth," Cyrus said, unable to hold back his dread. "No matter what we do, a lot of people are going to die."

The room fell quiet. Stasia crossed her arms and frowned back at Cyrus.

"And so we give up?" she asked.

Cyrus shook his head.

"And so we let that knowledge guide us here. Of all the paths available to us, which one saves the most lives? Let us choose that one, no matter how hard it might be."

Arn shifted in his seat.

"Sure wish Thorda could answer that for us," he said. "I just want to hit things."

"The Vagrant is right, though," Dario chipped in. The looks sent his way were far from friendly, but he ignored them. "We can play it safe, and hope these cities can handle themselves, or we can take a gamble at victory where the populations will be most heavily concentrated. You people have made yourselves terrors here in Vallessau, but it's time you turn your attention to all of Thanet."

Cyrus scanned the room for everyone's opinion. The mood was dour, but they were fighters, and stubborn down to their bones. No one was willing to give up these lives to the God-Incarnate, no matter how dire their odds.

"So we split up," Keles said. "And we send who we can to where the need is greatest."

"If Pilus thinks he can stay the slaughter in Thiva and Syros, I say we trust him," Stasia offered. "And if he says the smaller force he can spare for Raklia isn't enough, I say we trust him there, too. Let me join it. I'll easily make up the difference."

"And Red Glade?" Clarissa asked. She leaned closer over the map and tapped a finger. "Some cities have resistances built up and ready, but Red Glade's is meager compared to its size. Worse, our reports place an army of at least two thousand soldiers holding the occupation."

"Arn and I will go," Dario offered.

"Will we, now?" Arn asked, glancing over at his brother.

"The two of you against an entire army?" Mari asked, and she sank deeper into the cushions. "Is there even a point?"

Dario strode over to the map, lifted one of the little markers Thorda had always used, and set it down on Red Glade.

"We Bastell brothers are a stubborn lot," he said. "We can handle an army, can't we, Arn?"

Arn squeezed Mari's knee, but Cyrus noted how he refused to meet Mari's gaze.

"Of course we can," the giant man said. "We can take on the whole world and win if we must."

Clarissa looked at the map while pinching her lower lip between two fingers.

"There are still so many places that will have to fend for themselves," she said. "We'll have to hope our warnings are enough, and that people flee to the wilds when the soldiers come calling. Though our map still lacks pieces for the Vagrant and the Returned Queen."

Cyrus's eyes locked on the drawing of the capital.

"We know of at least nine sacrificial locations here in Vallessau," he said. "I can cycle through them, hitting them as hard as I can."

"You will do no such thing, Vagrant," said the Nameless woman, her voice cutting through their gathering like a knife. They all turned to the door, through which She had entered with nary a sound. That She could avoid even Cyrus's senses unnerved him, as did the way her face seemed to blur in his vision. Was it because he knew what She was? Or was that faint cloud of gray hovering over her head an aspect of divinity his own eyes were now better at perceiving?

"Have you come to give orders?" he asked her.

Instead of answering, She positioned herself in their center, her hands clasped, her head high, and her spine as rigid as steel. Despite the plainness of her garb, She walked like royalty among their number.

"I come to give hope to a night most dreadful," she said. "With my aid, I would have you slay the God-Incarnate."

Another round of shocked silence, followed by Arn's boisterous laugh.

"It took Keles and Cyrus all they had just to beat Lucavi's son," he said. "How will you help them kill the damn father?"

Cyrus met Nameless She's gaze. From what little time he had spent with her, he knew She would not make this offer lightly. If She believed it possible...

"There will be nowhere more heavily guarded than Vallessau's castle on the day of the sacrifice," he said. "And what strength I possess is not enough to break the faith of millions. I desire your hope more than anything, I do, but what aid could you offer to make it possible?"

She showed not the slightest upset at his rejection. Instead She offered her hand to Keles, who reluctantly took it.

"I would put the Returned Queen upon her throne," She said. "During the ceremony, there will be a moment when Lucavi shall be rendered vulnerable. I can get you inside the castle. I can bring the two of you, Queen and Vagrant, to where your swords can do their work. You shall take your throne, while all others ensure there is a nation left to rule."

Her certainty was infectious. She spoke without doubt. She clutched Keles's hand with the strength of centuries of suffered oppression.

"Can you truly?" Keles asked. "No false promises. No gambles. Can you lead me and Cyrus to the God-Incarnate's doom?"

The Nameless woman knelt before Keles. The gray cloud over her face parted, and to Cyrus's eyes he suddenly saw a thousand faces, ever changing, and each and every one of them smiled.

"Am I not the great betrayer? Trust in me, and I shall see not only this island set free, but all the world."

CHAPTER 41

MARI

Mari walked the cliffs, free of the suffocating city. The waves crashed below her. It was a pleasant sound, one she could imagine growing to love if she had been born here. Instead, the trees had been her childhood, the rustle of leaves her lullaby. She'd come to the cliff overlooking the Solemn Sands, to a place most holy to Lycaena and her people.

"Except the waves and sands were not yours, were they, Lycaena?" Mari wondered aloud. She looked out upon the sea, infinite and majestic in its blue wonder. "They belonged to the Serpent. Why, then, did you choose this place?"

It was dangerous to walk Vallessau's streets now their family's subterfuge was revealed, but Mari refused to hide in their new home. She had covered her face with a shawl and avoided the soldiers when traveling to the cliffs. Their attention was on the docks and the city gates, anyway, not the isolated stretches where only the most persistent of smugglers might try to sneak in by climbing the sheer rock.

Mari knelt beside the broken butterfly that had once overlooked the sands below. Nearby were pulleys and cut ropes of the platform down, destroyed at the start of the battle when Cyrus had led an ambush on the paragon ritual performed upon Gordian Goldleaf.

"This was your chosen place for rebirth," Mari said, imagining the goddess beside her, listening. "But the twice-born fell from their cocoons to the sea, from your arms and into Dagon's. A mutual blessing. Yet you kept the act despite his banishment. Did you still love him, goddess? Have you always regretted your role in the War of Tides?"

Mari expected no answers, not yet. No matter the nature of the divine being, Mari had found them loath to explain themselves to humans, let alone apologize. Even her father, small god that he had been by the end, acted the same.

The remembrance of her lost father stung Mari's eyes with tears. She wiped them away. Stasia had inherited that power, and all the unknowns that came with it. They'd talked some about the change, in the rare quiet moments when they sat about the fire. Stasia tended that fire now. She said it comforted her in a way she couldn't understand. The prayers offered to the Ahlai name were faint, but she heard them, too. Stasia was clueless as how to answer them.

"How does one learn to become a god?" Stasia had asked in the aftermath of the prison break, when the pair finally had a chance to sit down and talk. Mari had laughed and tried to play it off.

"Go ask Cyrus," had been her answer.

"I'm asking you. You may not remain a god, and they may not pray to you, but I know you understand this feeling. This power. Help me, Mari. I have always walked my path without fear or doubt, but this is beyond me."

Mari stared at the base of the statue and tried to imagine what it had looked like when it was whole. It would have towered over her, twice her height at the least. When the sun set, its shadow would have been cast far across both sand and sea. She felt a pull on her chest, and the stone beneath her fingers sparked with electricity.

"Yet another marvel lost," she whispered. "Another sin to lay at the feet of the God-Incarnate."

Mari smoothed out her skirt, pulled away her shawl, and pressed her face to the feet of the broken statue. Eyes closed, she began to whisper.

Lycaena, hear my prayer. Hear it, and answer. I would speak, if you are willing.

With Endarius, Mari had demanded an audience with the stubborn god over many long weeks. With Lycaena, the simple, humbly spoken request was enough. The overwhelming presence of the divine struck

Mari, powerful even with its familiarity. Darkness followed, sweeping away sea and cliff and sky and sand. This place between the physical reality of the living world and the unknown eternity hereafter would forever inspire fear in her. It was a dangerous place, not meant for mortals.

But Mari bore the blessing of her father. There was a shard of divine light within her, and it had guided and protected her. As a child, she had been bathed by her father's tears. She had been washed with his prayers. Had she known? Not in the waking life, but here, in these moments communing with slain gods? How else had she stood before the raging Lion, the tundra wolf Fenwul, or Kasthan the Falcon Reaper and demanded they share a body and submit to her control?

"At last, you come to me," said Lycaena.

Mari gazed upon the Butterfly in all her splendor. Her body was as dark as the endless space surrounding them. Her eyes were brilliant rainbows of ever-changing color. Her wings and dress began as orange before shifting to yellow, green, and then blue, and they seamlessly wrapped her body so that it was hard to tell where wings ended and dress began. Her hair was long and braided, multiple gold and crimson strands swirled together that subtly shifted to blue by the bottom. In her left hand she held a ruby-tipped scepter, and in her right a golden harp.

She was beautiful, so beautiful. Mari had seen her only once in life, and it had been after her capture. The Anointed One had spent days humiliating her, carving into her flesh, shredding her wings, and cutting off her hair. Even before her execution, she had remained beautiful, but the efforts to despoil and defile her had been undeniable.

"I pray you take no insult from my wait," Mari said. "Endarius granted me strength when I needed it most, and with it, we nearly saved you. I would not abandon him in the hopes you would be stronger."

Lycaena hovered closer. There was always a ground in this endless space, thin and cold, and it rippled like water at any touch. Her toes brushed across its surface, leaving little waves like a passing boat. The waves continued on and on, far beyond Mari's sight. Perhaps they would travel forever, an eternal remembrance of this meeting.

"But you yourself were abandoned," Lycaena said. "The Lion has left you."

Mari pretended the wounds from that departure were fully healed. No weakness, not here.

"His followers were few, and the love of the people weaker than I anticipated," she said.

"And so he goes to his children in the beyond." Lycaena glanced over her shoulder, seeing something visible only to her. Longing overwhelmed her every word. "I feel it, too, little one. They pray to me there, rejoicing with reunited loves. They sing and dance amid the blooms. My children, my precious children, so eager to hear the song of my harp..."

The goddess turned away. Her voice hardened, and the world about them likewise shifted. The emptiness they stood upon became charred earth. The starless night above rippled with smoke. Untold miles and miles away, the darkness caught fire, forming crimson walls that swallowed the horizon.

"But my living children yet weep. They cry out for deliverance, and I will not abandon them. Eternity may forever wait, for that is its nature, but the suffering and the dying need me now."

Relief swelled within Mari. The goddess was still willing to fight. It might not be for vengeance like Endarius, but the desire to protect her faithful was equally strong, if not stronger. Mari would gladly welcome that protective need into her body.

"With Endarius gone, I cannot help my loved ones," Mari said. "Please, grant me your strength, Lycaena. Dwell within me, and together, we can protect your children. Your music, and your fire, shall return."

Lycaena's wings fluttered, and she lifted toward the sky of smoke.

"No."

The ground cracked with the answer. Mari cracked with it.

"No?" she asked, too tired and heartbroken to panic. "But why?"

"I have seen the Lion you presented to the people. You deny not his death, but embrace it. He was bone and teeth, pale fur and endless rage. I would not see myself so humbled. I am life, little one. I am beauty."

"But to Rayan, you were more than that," she said. "To him, you were the moth. You can be that again. The change does not deny your life, but reminds people of that which was lost, and must be reclaimed!"

"So many of my faithful have fallen to the sword. Others, through fear, desperation, or pragmatism, have turned their hearts to the god of Everlorn. What strength I have dwindles, but there are those who cling to me with such fervor it fills me with hope. It is for them I reserve what power I yet possess. Let Keles Orani and thrice-born Eshiel command my fire. If Thanet is to be saved, let us save it ourselves, and not through the borrowed strength of the daughter of a foreign god."

Mari's fingers dragged across the cracked, gray earth.

"But I'm not a god," she said. "I wouldn't need to beg and plead if I was. The sacrificial hour approaches, Lycaena. I need you. Without you, when the fight comes, when the poisoned wine flows, I'll only be able to watch. Please, I beg, I *beg*, do not render me so helpless. Do not make me suffer that torment."

Lycaena lowered herself until her feet finally touched ground. The charred earth sprouted flowers, and green swathes of grass shot out in random directions like veins. Her hand rested upon Mari's shoulder.

"But you are Thorda's daughter, even if not by blood. I will not trust you, Mari Ahlai. I will trust those who have held their faith in me all their lives. I will give myself to those who suffered in my name, who prayed to me when they were frightened and called out to me when they were broken."

She smiled.

"You have a kind heart, and a noble cause. You will find your path, Mari. But it will not be at my side."

The fire faded. The smoke dissipated. Earth and grass crumbled away. The loving touch of the goddess shimmered into nothing, her form dissipating until all that remained was the shattered remnants of the statue. Of all rejections Mari had suffered, none stung more cruelly than this, and she wept upon the cliff.

"No," she whispered. "Please, no, don't do this. Don't leave me alone."

There was no answer but the wind and the rolling waves of the sea.

CHAPTER 42

LUCAVI

Lucavi spent the entire day preparing to receive faith from the coming ceremony. He bathed in lavender-scented water and oil. He was scrubbed clean by servants; they brushed and braided his hair. His armor was polished to an immaculate sheen. In the main greeting hall, a choir sang his praises nonstop, with new singers brought in every four hours to allow others to rest their throats. Their voices reached his ears even in his bedroom, undeterred by stone or wall, for their song was a prayer.

None of it improved his mood.

"How fare you?" he asked his daughter. Sinshei knelt before him, quiet and subservient. Ever since her capture, her pride seemed properly subdued. He'd called for her, a strange sentimentality coming over him. He felt like he should say some words to her, but they were awkward on his tongue. Rarely had he shown Sinshei affection, for rarely had she deserved it.

"I am well, after your rescue," she said. "If I am unwell, it is because I seethe at the vengeance stolen from me."

She spoke of the prison break orchestrated by the Ax of Lahareed, Stasia Ahlai. Lucavi shared her frustration. For such an audacious attack on his own castle to succeed was humiliating, and the voices in his mind had freely shared that opinion.

"Do not let it trouble you," he said. "No matter how strong they believe themselves to be, or how cunning they delude themselves into thinking they are, it will not avail them. This island will drown in blood. Not a single Thanese shall walk this earth. That is my promise to you, a promise of what shall be my legacy."

"Your legacy," she said, and looked up to him. Though she guarded her heart closely, he sensed a strange hunger within her, a desire that he instinctively wished to snuff out.

"Yes, *my* legacy," he said. "Now, go, and leave me be so I may meditate."

When she left, he looked about the empty room.

"Everything is ready," he said to no one.

Not everything, Ashraleon whispered. *You know what must be done. All weaknesses must be purged if you are to endure beyond your allotted time.*

Lucavi looked to his grand balcony. Tomorrow would be the last time he watched the city come to life as the sun rose. It was beautiful: the stirring of people, the scurrying of the boats, and the light reflecting off the sand. One day, faithful people of Everlorn would repopulate this place, and they would perform their own traditions, but he would not be here to see it.

Sentimental to a fault, Aristava said. *Though we all grew sentimental in our waning hours.*

Sentiment is the cage of those who no longer bear ambition, Ululath argued. *We need no better proof than Lucavi's failures to name a suitable heir.*

Three firm knocks on his door. Lucavi turned, knowing who waited outside. He'd have known even without having requested the audience. Bassar's love radiated off him in visible golden waves. No magistrate, not even his own daughter, possessed such vibrant faith.

"Come in."

Bassar entered and shut the door behind him. The sight tightened Lucavi's throat.

"I trust you are ready for tomorrow?" the divine bodyguard asked. He crossed the room, his boots thudding heavily despite the thick carpet. "The entire city is abuzz. I fear the rumors spread by the Vagrant and his accomplices have seeded much doubt among the populace."

"A little doubt will not be enough," he said.

Indeed, said Drasden. *When the people of Numae died for me, many had known for days, yet they still drank. They always do.*

When death is their only fate, the common and meager will take the quickest path to the grave, Ashraleon agreed.

"I pray you are correct," Bassar said. He stopped before Lucavi and bowed low to show his respect. "Even so, we faithful are ready to carry out our duty. No Vagrant, no assassin, and no rebel shall prevent this great honor from being carried out in your name."

The words were meant to ease his burdens, but they only increased the tightness around Lucavi's throat. He stared down at the handsome man, his head bowed, perfectly shaved, oiled, and perfumed. So loyal. So true.

"I know," he said. "I trust you above all."

Bassar remained in his bow, his voice suddenly tense.

"My lord, would you allow me one question?"

Multiple voices called out in Lucavi's mind as he spun about. Warning him. Telling him to deny it. On the oak desk beside his bed was a letter written with his own hand and the reason for Bassar's summons. *Give it to him and be done,* insisted the echoes of the former God-Incarnates. He refused them all.

"What is it?" he asked.

Bassar looked up from his bow.

"The ceremony tomorrow. With Petrus and Kalath slain, I confess I know not why we continue. Have you chosen a new Heir-Incarnate, and if so, why have you not proclaimed it to your people?"

Lucavi closed his eyes. He rarely spoke with the voices in his mind, even though they so eagerly addressed him in kind. They were companions he never wanted, and a font of knowledge he seldom needed. But in this, he knew there must be cooperation. There must be acceptance, or the end result would be catastrophic.

The tightness around his throat constricted him so thoroughly he could barely force out the words, but he did. He must. The faintest whisper, strangled, so that even Bassar would not hear.

"Must the heir be linked by blood?"

He never anticipated the rage that followed. Multiple voices cried out, but none matched Ashraleon's. His was a thunderclap amid the patter of rain. Every syllable rattled Lucavi's skull. The power of it left him gasping. He fell to his knees and clutched his ears as the fury overwhelmed his thoughts.

Is your heart so impure that you would cast aside everything we have built? Every law, every tradition? Three thousand years of history is not to be broken by lustful, wretched deviance.

"I seek only an heir," Lucavi whispered in his defense.

You seek to elevate that which should only serve. You are broken. You are vile.

Lucavi beat his fists against the floor.

"I am not," he said, then louder, screaming. "I AM NOT!"

Then do what must be done, said Ashraleon.

Prove you are who you must be, said Drasden.

Deny the chains of your own creation, said Gaius.

Excise the rot you have allowed to fester for far too many years, said Ululath.

All of them, demanding compliance. Tradition must be obeyed. History must be given its due weight. Lucavi scraped his perfectly manicured nails across the carpet, gathering himself. This...unsightly failure of his must be undone. He looked up. Bassar remained kneeling, his eyes wide. Did he understand what he had witnessed? Did it even matter? His ever-loyal paragon would never speak a word of it to others.

Enough, Ashraleon thundered. *His loyalty is no greater than any other paragon's, as are his skill and faith. You see what you desire, not what is real.*

Lucavi slowly rose to his feet. It felt like his every limb was weighted down with stone.

"I have a task for you," he said, and pointed to the letter on the desk. Even saying that much was a burden.

"Whatever you ask, I will perform," Bassar said, and retrieved the letter. He unrolled it, his eyes skimming over the trio of sentences. A simple order. Bassar was to leave Vallessau and travel to Red Glade, where he would take charge of the ceremony there.

Bassar folded the letter once, then twice. His golden eyes gazed into Lucavi's. For the first time, Lucavi saw doubt within them.

"You would have me leave you?" Bassar asked.

"I suspect the Vagrant's allies will strike all across the island, and our defenses in Red Glade could use a skilled paragon." Not a lie, but a stretch of the truth. Red Glade was well guarded. Bassar would be safe there. "You will ensure the sacrifice proceeds uninterrupted."

"What of the Vagrant and his allies? Who will protect you?"

A bit of Lucavi's wounded pride stirred, and he clung to it for strength. His armor rattled as he pulled back his shoulders and drew his sword.

"I am afraid of no villain," he said. "I am the God-Incarnate of Everlorn. I am the eternal, the mighty, the blade that shall sever Gadir from its slavery to the heathen gods. Do you fear for my life, paragon? Has such blasphemy taken root in your soul?"

Bassar rose from his bow. His hands trembled at his sides.

"Blasphemy," he said. "To love my god with all my heart?"

The pain, the pain in his eyes, damn it all, Lucavi rammed his sword through the carpet and into the stone. He was the God-Incarnate of millions. No single soul, no matter whose it might be, should make him tremble so.

"Blasphemy, to question my orders and doubt my wisdom," he said. "Will you go to Red Glade, paragon?"

Bassar's handsome face lost all its luster. The shimmering gold aura swirling around him paled.

"If my lord orders it, I shall obey. May I be dismissed? My journey will be long, and I have little time to prepare for it."

Lucavi only nodded. The paragon exited, the door slamming shut behind him.

All was quiet, but for a moment.

You have done as you must, Ashraleon said.

Lucavi beat his chest once, twice, and then smashed his fists into his extravagant bed posts. He ripped and tore the Lion decorations to pieces and flung them out the balcony to the courtyard below. All the while, he snarled like a savage beast.

"Get out," he said. "Get out, get out, all of you, every last one of you, out, out. Give me silence, damn you, silence!"

Rarely did he dwell on it, for his sanity might not endure if he did, but now he felt suffocated by all the cruel contradiction that was his life.

Since Valshei's death, he had little company beyond the occasional concubine. His sons were lost to him, but even when alive, they had shown him little trust, and even less love. His entire existence was one of isolation and loneliness, and yet he was never alone.

The prayers of nations hammered his mind. The voices of the previous God-Incarnates never ceased their watching, their listening. There was no room private nor field empty enough for him to be himself. From the moment he accepted his role as Ululath's Heir-Incarnate, he had been shaped by the expectations and beliefs of others. When the people of Isul drank their wine six hundred years ago, and Ululath cut his throat, Lucavi had believed the power worth every price as it swirled into him.

He believed it still.

But the price. Oh, the price was so high. And there was no god for him to pray to, no divinity to ease his suffering. It must be carried on his shoulders, and his alone.

Lucavi ripped his sword free and stared at his reflection in its surface. Twenty years to marry anew and produce an heir. Twenty years until he became yet one more voice in the mind of another.

"None of you see the burden," he whispered, imagining the defiant people of the nations he conquered during his reign. "None of you know the cost. Savages, offering lives to beings alien to us, who could never understand our true suffering. But I do. *We* do. The line of Ashraleon. The blessing of the God-Incarnate, the true blessing, is this unmentionable burden. Every temptation. Every failure. Every sin. We know it. We walk it."

Tears rolled down his face, and when he wiped one away, he saw it was a droplet of liquid gold hovering atop his finger.

"I will do my duty," he told the audience in his mind. "I will do my duty. I will. I will. I promise."

And for once, finally, they gave him his silence.

CHAPTER 43

ARN

Arn found her atop the balcony, gazing up at Thanet's beautiful starlit sky.

"Hey, Mari," he said, lurking at the door. Her back was to him, and when she glanced over her shoulder, her long hair hid much of her face.

"Are you leaving?" she asked.

Arn joined her and leaned his elbows on the balcony railing so he would be at her height. Nerves had him look out upon the city instead of facing her. He feared the hurt he might see in her eyes.

"Yeah," he said. "Dario's waiting for me outside the western wall. Should be easier to sneak out at night, and sadly we don't have any time to spare if we want to reach Red Glade before Lucavi's sick plan unfolds."

He was justifying himself, he realized. Mari knew these things, but he laid them out before her, one after another, as if pleading for her understanding. He didn't want to do this. He needed to do this. Both were true.

"Just the two of you," she said quietly, still not looking his way.

"And whatever resistance they've built up in the realm of Scylla."

"Stop it. We're sending two paragons because such resistance is meager compared to the forces stationed there. I am not a fool."

Arn put his hand atop hers, his meaty fingers dwarfing her slender ones.

"No, you're not. Which is why you know I have to go. Too many lives are at stake."

"And what of your own? It's a suicide mission, Arn. It's not the first time I've seen my father send men and women out to die. And this time, he isn't even... He..." Mari bit her lip. Her free hand clutched the railing with a white-knuckle grip. "It's so easy to forget. My whole life, he was larger than the world. For him to be gone? Impossible, isn't it? I keep waiting for him to emerge from his forge, smelling of smoke and cinder, and bark out another order. But no orders are coming. It's just us, floundering, and now you're off to some city hopelessly outnumbered. I hate it. I *hate* it."

Her fingers trembled underneath Arn's hand. He wished to comfort her, but what was there to say?

"I'm sorry," he said. It seemed safe enough, even if a paltry balm against such a deep wound.

Mari sighed. A shudder ran through her, and when it ended, she seemed stronger, more in control. He'd seen such reactions before, usually in men on the battlefield steeling themselves for the coming carnage.

"I've decided I'll be sailing with Stasia to Raklia," she said. "I refuse to wait around for everyone else to save the day. Even if I'm useless, I'll be there to watch. It would be so much worse to hide here, not knowing what's happening."

Arn would have preferred she stay somewhere safe, but he understood her decision. He cursed Endarius's name, and it was hardly the first time. To abandon Mari now, when Thanet needed him most, was a cowardly act for a Lion supposedly embodying bravery and defiance. Then again, much of Endarius's history was steeped in cowardice, wasn't it? If he were truly brave, he'd have fought against Everlorn when they marched on his homeland instead of fleeing to Thanet.

"It'll work out," he said, brushing the thoughts aside. "Cyrus is a tough kid, and what he's capable of lately is something else. If anyone can bring down the God-Incarnate, it's him and Keles."

Mari nodded, but he could tell she was hardly listening. She was too wrapped up in her own thoughts.

"Do you regret it?" she blurted out.

"Regret what?"

She shrugged.

"Listening to my father. Coming here. Joining us."

Meeting you, he thought, silently voicing the real question she wished to ask. He brushed his fingers across her face to gently gather loose strands of her brown hair and tuck them behind her ear. So often Mari comforted others, but for once, he wanted to be the one to comfort her.

"Here on Thanet, I heard the voice of Velgyn, who I thought would show me only hatred. Instead I found forgiveness. Here with your family, I found friends, and companionship I never knew as a paragon. Even my brother has seen it, my brother, who I thought forever lost. I regret nothing of my life since setting foot on this island, not one part of it." He took her hands from the railing and held them against his chest, forcing her to meet his gaze, to hear the honesty in his every syllable. "And you are the best of it, Mari. Meeting you has been a gift, one I must convince myself every morning that I am worthy of. I would sacrifice all the world to see you smile. You are everything. No. I do not regret it. From now to my grave, I never will."

No more words. Mari pressed herself against him, her face burrowing into his shirt and her fingers digging into the fabric. Arn held her in his embrace. He wished this moment—this peace—could last forever.

But it had to end, and Mari ended it, pulling free of him.

"I won't say goodbye," she said. "I've done it too many times, Arn. Every nation, every city, every war, it's always been the same. Anyone I meet, or befriend, or fall in love with, they leave one day. Sometimes by choice. Sometimes by the sword. I'm not doing it again. I can't."

Mari struck his chest with her fist.

"I am tired of people leaving me," she said. "You come back. Do you hear me? You come back. You promise me that."

"Mari..."

"Promise me!"

She might be the Lioness no more, but he saw stubbornness and rage in her eyes that rivaled the slain god's. To make such a promise was foolish. Battle was never kind, nor fair. Even in his short stint in Everlorn's army, he'd lost friends to the most random of circumstances. A rock or twig underfoot to rob balance in battle. The shift of an arrow on a sudden wind. All these reasons withered before her stare. Mari Ahlai bore a strength to defy fate itself, and so he trusted her above all else.

"All right," he said. "I promise."

The woman extricated herself from him, and she wiped at her face while sniffling.

"Good," she said. "I'll hold you to that."

Arn looked to the moon. His insides shuddered.

"I should go," he said. "Dario's been waiting too long already."

"Of course," she said, all emotion draining from her voice. She stood there, her hands squirming against one another. Arn hesitated at the door. He could tell Mari was struggling with something, a final word or act.

"Mari?" he asked.

She looked like a dam filled with cracks preparing to crumble, but somehow she remained strong.

"It's nothing," she said. "Go to your brother."

He nodded. He did not offer her a goodbye, either, but instead another promise.

"I'll see you again," he said, and went inside.

This home, a new one of Clarissa's picking, was emptier than any before. Where once Rayan and Thorda would be chatting and drinking by the fireplace, there were only cold coals. Clarissa traveled to the village where her mother hid, and Stasia was busy seeing her off. Even Cyrus was gone, to where he could only guess. The kid liked solitude when he was nervous, and who wouldn't be nervous given the enormity of his task?

An empty, quiet home. That was what Arn was leaving Mari in, and he hated every second of it.

Outside, he patted his coat once more to ensure he'd packed his gauntlets and then started for the western gate. At least, he meant to start. His feet would not move. This was it. If he kept going, there would be no turning back. He'd leave Vallessau and not return until the vicious sacrifice was done. No one was making him leave. He could stay and help Cyrus in his fight against the God-Incarnate. But then his brother would be alone. His brother, who had only abandoned Everlorn at Arn's insistence.

Just go. You're making this harder than it needs to be.

The door opened behind him. He turned to see Mari sprinting toward him. He stood there, confused and unsure, but then her arms were around his neck, pulling him lower.

Mari's lips pressed against his, the kiss full of frantic energy. After his initial shock, he leaned into her, his arms wrapping about her waist to hold her against him. He let the kiss last as long as Mari needed, until she withdrew, silent tears sliding down her cheeks. Arn wiped those tears away with his thumb, and then he grinned at her, remembering a moment that felt a lifetime away.

"Next time," he said, "you ask first."

"I will," she said, and she laughed despite her tears. "I promise."

She leaned against him, her face against his chest. He held her, a thousand promises rattling off in his mind. To return. To protect her. To cherish her.

"I love you, Mari," he said, the only words capable of leaving his lips.

And then Arn walked away, and he dared not look back, because he knew this time, if she asked, he would stay.

The streets were unnaturally quiet, even compared to the uneasy silence that had befallen them since Lucavi's purge. Between the torches the patrols carried and the rattle of their armor, it was easy enough to avoid them on his way to the western exit.

Arn did not bother with the gate. There was zero chance he could pass any inspection. Instead he found a quiet stretch of wall a quarter mile south of it and then slipped on his gauntlets. They made it easy to climb the wall, his armored fingers crunching little handholds in the aged stone. Once up top, he vaulted to the other side and dropped down to a stretch of land heavily overrun with brush and thorn.

"You're late," Dario said. His brother waited for him, two packed rucksacks at his feet. Dario tossed him one. Arn caught it and slung it over his shoulder.

"Sorry," he said. "I had to say goodbye."

His brother gave him a knowing look and then grabbed his own pack of supplies.

"Fair enough. We'll need to travel most of the night to make up for it."

"Then we travel most of the night."

They walked side by side through the rough brush, avoiding the main road while still so close to Vallessau. Minutes passed, Arn hardly aware of his surroundings beyond placing one foot in front of the other.

"I get it, you know," Dario said, suddenly breaking the silence. "I've only met her a few times, but she's clearly special. I wouldn't blame you if you went back to her."

"I want to," Arn said. "But we've got a job to do, don't we?"

Dario did not look at him, but he extended a fist as they walked.

"Just like old times, then," he said. "The Bastell brothers against the world."

It was a remark they had shared enough to become a ritual, a brotherly bond that had kept Arn's love for him alive through the judgments and disappointments.

"And the world's gonna lose," he said, and struck his fist against his brother's.

The faintest hint of frost shimmered along his knuckles before they touched, but this time, there were no broken bones, no shrieking of metal. Just Dario's easy laugh, the soft dance of the wind, and the faintest rustle of movement through the nearby brush. That of nocturnal creatures, a possum, maybe, or a coyote.

Perhaps even a fox.

CHAPTER 44

KELES

Traveling anywhere in Vallessau was dangerous, but a runner from the Shed had come to request a meeting with Keles, and so she walked the bustling streets without any armor or weaponry, just a green cloth wrapped around her hair to disguise her face. It wasn't much, but she ducked and weaved through the streets to avoid any potential close encounters with the patrolling guards. Seeing so many people out and about after the slow quieting of Vallessau the past few years should have made her happy, but not when she knew the reason. Soldiers were gathering people for tomorrow's enforced attendance at the six-hundred-year ceremony. This was not life returning to a dormant city. This was a pen being crammed full of beasts for the coming slaughter.

Why did you not run? she thought. *Why did you not hide?*

Many had, of course, and in staggering numbers. People were flooding the outer villages. Some hid from patrols. Others sought weapons and guidance to fight back. But to Keles's heartbreak, so many remained behind. Some scoffed at the idea of the empire being so cruel. Others fully embraced the lie of Everlorn's kindness, and the salvation offered to those who accepted the God-Incarnate into their hearts. No one was ignorant; of that Keles was certain. They just did not believe the rumors, or trusted too strongly in the lies of the Uplifted Church.

They would willingly drink, and so, for their own sake, the resistance did all they could to interrupt the ceremonies or destroy the wine caches where they were stashed.

"Well met, paladin," the woman guarding the door said when Keles arrived. She had a hard look to her and a fresh set of scars across the left half of her face. "I pray your journey here was uneventful?"

"As could be hoped," she said.

The woman paused.

"Eshiel is resting," she said at last. "Come in. Maybe it will do him good to meet with you."

Together they entered the Shed. Keles's time at the Heaven's Wing had been cut drastically short when Everlorn invaded, limiting her training to hardly more than a year. So it wasn't quite nostalgia that filled her when she gazed upon the reworked storage facility beside the academy, but something akin to it. A stolen potential. She *should* have developed familiarity with this place. Generations upon generations before her had lived, trained, graduated, and returned as teachers. Now the academy was burned to the ground, and the Shed repurposed for war.

Keles followed the scarred woman with her hands clenched into fists. It wasn't just lives the empire took when it invaded. It went beyond even their gods. It was the childhoods of those who must grow up too fast. It was the innocence scraped away by the Dead Flags. Even those who lived must pay their price. Keles could see it on the faces of the few men and women who looked her way as she headed toward the back of the building. Sunken eyes. Guarded frowns. Joy would not return easily to Thanet, even if they should achieve the miraculous.

"Eshiel?" her escort asked, knocking on a door to a small room. "You have a visitor. Miss Keles Orani."

Keles barely caught herself from flinching. She shouldn't react so harshly to her newly adopted family name. It was a mantle she needed to bear proudly.

"Come in."

Her guide shut the door behind Keles, leaving her alone with the wounded priest.

"Forgive me for any indecency," Eshiel said with a tired smile. "This is no way to greet a queen."

Eshiel lay on a pile of pillows stacked together to form a bed. A thin blanket covered most of his body, with a second, heavier quilt stacked across his legs. When he sat up, the blanket fell to his waist, exposing the vicious scar across his abdomen. Though it did not bleed or weep pus, it bore burn marks and the surrounding skin was an ugly shade of purple she heavily disliked.

"How are you feeling?" she asked.

"If you want the truth, Keles, I ache all over, even down to my legs despite scoring no wounds there. It's like the pain is so much it floods outward to fool the mind into making it bearable."

Keles hid her frown. When Stasia told the story of their escape, she'd mentioned Eshiel's wound, and how she'd prayed over him to seal it. Keles had incorrectly assumed that meant the wound had been healed. A false assumption, given how unwell Eshiel appeared. The skin had only been cauterized, and whatever damage had been done to his innards was forced to heal on its own.

"Would you like me to pray over your wound?" she asked him.

"I already have, and if..." He stopped himself. "No. Excuse my pride. I gladly accept."

He lay fully on his back and shifted slightly to better expose the scar. Keles knelt beside him. When she laid her hands on the wound, the raw, burnt skin was hot to her fingers.

"You should have sent for me immediately," she said.

"And admit to my faithful here that I am incapable of healing myself?" Eshiel closed his eyes. "I can summon Lycaena's fire and unleash it upon the empire with such wrath even paragons now fear my name. Yet when I pray for healing, my words are as mighty as a snowflake. What does that speak of my faith?"

Keles gently pressed her hands upon the gash. Even that mild pressure caused him pain. Eshiel hissed air through his clenched teeth, and it was several seconds before his breathing slowed and the tension in his neck and arms eased.

"We are all uniquely blessed by our goddess," Keles said. "Do not condemn yourself because you cannot do what others can. Take pride in the gifts you do possess."

Eshiel laughed, briefly, before the motion caused him further pain and he had to cut it short.

"Do not recite platitudes to me," he said. "I've taught that exact one to so many students. The repetition robs it of impact, even if I know in my head it's still true."

"Then rely on your head, and be silent," she said. "Let me offer my prayer."

Keles bowed and closed her eyes. The heat of Eshiel's wounds pulsed beneath her fingertips. The damn fool, he suffered for his pride in more ways than one.

"Amid our sorrows you comfort us. Grant us healing, Lycaena, we pray. May your brilliance and light chase away sorrows, precious goddess above all."

Keles felt a new warmth in her hands, this time flowing out of her instead of coming from Eshiel. Calmness overtook her mind. Gratitude filled her.

Thank you, she thought, and opened her eyes.

The anger had left the wounds, red veins and puffy skin now pale and clean. The purple color was already fading from the skin. The burns were still there, but far less angry.

"You should still bandage them for a few more days, just to be safe," she said, leaning back. When she looked up, she was shocked by the intensity of his stare.

"The sacrifice tomorrow," he said. "What role are you to play?"

Keles withdrew her hands. For some reason those light brown eyes of his made her feel guilty. For what? Helping others? Fighting for her people? She couldn't shake the feeling as she retrieved one of the towels she'd displaced from the stool and slowly cleaned her hands.

"We've split our team into groups, to best help the largest number of people," she said. "Arn and Dario are headed for Red Glade, while Stasia will travel to Raklia. If all goes well, they'll stop the poisonings there. As for myself, I will accompany Cyrus sneaking into the castle. We will ambush the God-Incarnate during the sacrifice. Nameless She assures us there will be a time he is vulnerable, and together, we will bring that monster down."

Eshiel stared at the ceiling. His voice lowered.

"Ever since I fell off that cliff, and the false Lycaena I summoned perished at the Vagrant's hands, I have been having dreams." His eyes closed. "Dreams, or perhaps visions. Moments in the past, usually. My own life. My rebirth. Moments dear to Lycaena, festivals and celebrations throughout Thanet's history."

He gently tested the newly healed wound by tracing it with his fingertips.

"They are not always so kind. In one, I witnessed your uncle's death at the hands of the Heir-Incarnate. In another, I watched the sacrifice that led to the Vagrant's creation. But lately, I am tormented with one dream, one single nightmare, and I fear it is a fate yet to come."

Keles sat beside him again. It was not unheard of for their goddess to impart hints of the future. Lycaenean scholars had often debated if they were predictions, or merely possibilities, for sometimes those dreams came to pass, and other times the warnings were avoided entirely by those who acted upon their dreams.

"Eshiel," she said, wishing she knew how to better comfort him. "Do not fear for us. Tomorrow..."

"Don't go." His hand snatched her wrist. His eyes held her prisoner, and she swore she saw fire within his irises.

"What?"

"The attack against the God-Incarnate, don't go. Let someone else take your place. Please, I beg of you, do not set foot inside that castle until Everlorn is banished from our shores."

Keles yanked her arm free. Worry set her heart to pounding.

"Why would you ask this of me?"

"Because I watch you die."

The words shocked her silent. There was no questioning his sincerity. It wasn't anger she saw in his eyes; she realized that now. It was dread.

"Why would Lycaena show you such a vision?" she asked quietly.

"I don't know," Eshiel said. He shifted the pillows underneath him so he could better sit upright. "Trust me, Keles, I have asked myself that question over and over. But the dream never changes. You die, Keles. You die, and I watch it happen. Night after night, the same nightmare.

I open my mouth to scream, but I never hear the words. I wake, and my only solace is to reassure myself it is just a dream."

He lifted his head. To her shock, tears had begun to trickle down his face.

"Do not go. Do not die for Thanet. Do not make me witness it in a world where there will be no salvation upon waking."

Keles knew she should feel something, anything, but the knowledge of his vision washed over her and left her feeling numb. Was it a test? A warning? Or perhaps never meant for her at all, but to guide Eshiel in the coming days?

She might not know what her goddess wanted, but it was obvious what Eshiel craved to hear. She refused to give it to him.

"No," she said. "Ask anything else of me, but not that. I am going. My sword and shield belong to Thanet."

"Even if it means your death? Please, do not do this, Keles. Not to me. Not to yourself!"

To him? Her death, spoken as if it were a wound inflicted only upon him? Her insides hardened. She stood, and she wished she had her weapons with her. Her fingers twitched at her sides, seeking the comfort of her sword.

"Bear whatever burdens you must," she said. "Walk whatever path you are capable of walking. As for myself, I will not cower while my friends, and my people, die to save Thanet."

She shook her head, her conviction growing.

"What if we succeed, Eshiel? What if Cyrus kills the God-Incarnate, and we chase their paragons from our shores? What kind of queen would I be if I hid like a coward while others fought? To know that, with my help, many who died might have lived? And should we fail, what then? So what if I survive, only to be hunted down and murdered along with the rest of the people who hid from the ceremonies? Better I fight. Better I be worthy of the crown I would seek to put upon my head."

"The dead do not wear crowns."

"Then I was never meant to wear one." She tried to ease the tension with a smile. "You and your faithful are welcome to join us in the city's defense. We need every bit of help to stop the coming madness."

"Most have already gone to protect their families, or aid the other cities and towns of Thanet," he said. "As for my closest and most trusted, they shall stay at my side. I believe Lycaena has one last task left for me, if I have the strength to do it."

"And what is that?"

Eshiel grinned at her, feverish and grim and unbelievably handsome.

"Have I not already explained? When the time comes, I must be there. I must watch you die."

The certainty of it should have frightened her, but Keles stood tall.

"Farewell, Eshiel Dymling. May we see each other again, in this life or in Lycaena's glistening fields beyond."

CHAPTER 45

SOMA

Stripped of armor, weaponry, and human flesh, Soma swam along the shore of Thanet, enjoying the crisp cold against his scales. A hint of nervousness spoiled the pleasure. This was no journey to meet with his growing cult of followers. Amid his dreams he had sensed a call, one weak and confused. His presence was known but disguised, and the caller herself slain and fading.

Lycaena wished to meet.

Soma had responded with a single image of a sandy stretch several miles north of Vallessau, slipped out of the castle, and then began his swim. Curiosity urged him onward. Would the Butterfly repent of her crimes now the Lion had failed to protect Thanet? Or would she cling to her betrayal to the last?

His webbed feet touched sand. Beneath the calming light of the moon, Soma waited until torchlight flickered in the caves that wound through the nearby Emberfall Mountains. Already he felt Lycaena's presence, so familiar to him despite their centuries apart. Yet it was different, muted. Perhaps it was how his aura felt to her when he clothed himself in human flesh.

A man and woman emerged from the cave. The man he knew well: Eshiel Dymling, who by all rights Soma should have executed after their tumble off the cliff during the battle against the reborn Lycaena. Recent events must have been unkind, for Eshiel leaned heavily on the woman accompanying him. Fresh bandages covered his waist, and he held a staff in his free hand, its polished wood thudding deep into the sand.

As for the woman, she was a stranger to Soma, but the pair were both dressed in faded red robes, and he suspected her one of Eshiel's new converts.

"I was promised a meeting with the goddess," Soma said.

"And you shall have it," Eshiel said. They halted a respectful distance away, and he turned to the woman. "Return to the cave, Colette. This, I must do alone."

Colette's concern was writ plain as day on her face, but she obeyed without hesitation. Without her support, Eshiel was forced to lean on the staff, and he clutched it with shaking hands. This pitiful man was Lycaena's representative?

"You seem unwell," Soma said. "Are you truly the same man who unleashed such tremendous destruction upon Galvanis's fleet? Or did that display consume the Butterfly's waning power?"

"Her power does not wane," Eshiel said. "I am her voice, as is Keles Orani, her Returned Queen. Soon she will fly Thanet's skies, as we, too, awaken from the cocoon we wrap about ourselves."

Soma waved dismissively. If this was what he swam out here for, then he was sorely disappointed.

"I have not come here to banter with you, Eshiel. My dreams promised words with the slain goddess, and misguided or foolish as it may be, I have come to hear them. If she gave you a message to deliver, then deliver it, so I may be on my way."

"A message?" A smirk tugged at the priest's face. "No message, not from me, Serpent. Did I not tell you I am her voice? It is through me she shall speak, if you would have patience."

Eshiel bowed and closed his eyes. The staff shook in his grasp. Wind blew in from the west, carrying red petals. The scent of flowers conjured images of green fields in spring. Fire licked Eshiel's fingers, and when the priest lifted his head, wisps of flame leaked out from underneath his closed eyelids. Eshiel's voice changed to something more powerful, feminine, and all too familiar.

"Dagon. You lived. I am glad."

Soma had thought himself prepared for this moment. He had envisioned it a thousand times before, the fantasy giving him strength as the decades dragged and his time on Gadir slowly scratched at his mind.

"Glad, Lycaena?" he said. "You who witnessed my execution and did nothing would now claim yourself glad at my survival?"

"I gave you to the water, and within you found life. If only you had come to me afterward, dear Serpent. I thought that, once humbled, you might bargain for peace. The conflicts between you and Endarius could be resolved, and our island shared among a newborn triad."

"Humbled." Repulsion struck Soma with frightening strength. "Oh, I saw many humbled gods throughout my time on Gadir, dear Lycaena. Wretched, broken things surviving on scraps of prayer, their worshipers caged and hidden away like dangerous animals. Is that the fate you would have granted me? To slither around my own homeland, beaten and broken, fearful to lift my gaze to the Lion lest he smite me upon the sand?"

Eshiel lowered his head.

"I wronged you," the Butterfly said through him. "When Endarius brought his violence, I wanted only peace. To wage war, in protest of war? To spill blood, in protest of bloodletting? I could not conceive it, and so I blamed your pride. I accepted the Lion's demands."

"And yet the violence never left us," Soma said. He tried, and failed, to keep the bitterness from his voice. "But it wasn't enough to kill me, was it? You turned my name into a curse. You let tales of my supposed vile nature spread, and turned my paradise into a torturous prison beneath the sea."

"Forgive me, Dagon. The people birthed those stories on their own, and I saw them as a useful guide to keep them on a better path."

No. That wasn't good enough. He pointed at her with his teeth bared.

"Do you think I did not *feel* it? That even thousands of miles away, I did not hear those curses? They clawed at my chest. They screamed in my ears louder than my own thoughts. *Trickster. Deceiver.* I had to rage against it, Lycaena! I had to seethe, and moan, and swear to the stars that I was better than they would have me become. I had to cling to what faint prayers my believers offered me, their words my lone guide through the maelstrom. You may have let my body live, but you nearly destroyed my soul. How dare you ask for my forgiveness now?"

Eshiel dropped to one knee and bowed his face all the way to the sand.

"My eyes are open, even if it comes much too late. You are my greatest failure, Dagon. My one true sin to stain my divine soul. Long did I believe myself justified, but not anymore. My heart aches for reconciliation, if only so I may enter my paradisiacal fields knowing I have done that much to make amends."

Dagon's entire body quivered. Could…could she still be an ally, even after all her betrayals? Her followers were few, her faith dwindling, but it might mean not walking this long, arduous path alone.

"Amends," he said, feeling the sting of four centuries of anger and pride. "I do not want amends, Lycaena, not from you, not from anyone."

"What do you want, then, my wayward Serpent?"

"I want to crush the Everlorn Empire in my fist," Soma shouted. "I want to rip its rotten heart out of Eldrid and watch it bleed. The God-Incarnate chased the Lion to our shores, and though Endarius repaid in blood, Lucavi yet lives. Part of me seeks to claim a righteous cause, but I have none, nor need one. I want vengeance, Lycaena. I want retribution. I want the culmination of humanity's fear, greed, and prejudice to meet the fate it deserves. But it can't stop there, can it?"

He felt the spear pierce his spine for the thousandth time.

"My people deserve better. *I* deserve better. With the God-Incarnate dead, all of Gadir will crave a new leader, lest they shatter into a thousand petty kingdoms, their united tongue splinter, and their singular faith succumb to the whims of little gods growing fat off their fear and confusion."

He reached a hand out to the kneeling priest. It had to end. It had to *end*. Four centuries of healing, planning, waiting, and yes, even killing had brought him to this moment. Everything was in place. He needed only the strength to see it done.

"I will rule that which rises from Everlorn's ashes, and I need not rule it alone. I care not for the gods of Gadir, but you and I, born of Thanet?

We can show them the paradise we once had, before the Lion. Before the empire."

Eshiel opened his eyes. They were fire and smoke.

"I would suffer a thousand deaths at the hands of Everlorn rather than rule as you desire. I am my children's goddess. I am their beloved. I am not their *jailer.*"

It was the answer Dagon expected, even if it disappointed him. Soma tried to remember when he had walked with the goddess along the beach, the waves washing against their ankles, his scales shining a brilliant sapphire, her wings vibrant and golden despite the moonlight. She was kind, he knew that, kind and caring, but she saw life only in cycles.

She could not conceive what it meant to break one.

"I'm sorry, Lycaena," he said. "The birth of this new age will be bloody, but things of worth often are."

Eshiel stood tall, with no need of his staff. His red robes billowed in the wind. His shadow cast by the moonlight sprouted great wings.

"And how many lives will you take, how many gods will you destroy, to achieve your paradise?"

Soma crossed the sand between them. His scaly hands pressed the sides of Eshiel's face. At last, his rage passed. He knew only determination.

"As we are, we are nothing," he whispered. It would be his last message before retreating to the sea. "Fade away, Lycaena. Go to whatever eternal land was prepared for you. I shall make right this world so that its sins, its sorrows, and its blasphemies forever cease. That is my dream. When Everlorn crumbles to dust, and a sapphire kingdom takes its place, the people will know but one god, and it shall be *me.*"

CHAPTER 46

THE NIGHT BEFORE

Mari huddled under a blanket behind the home she and her sister had been graciously given to use upon arriving in Raklia. It was on the far outskirts of the city, and behind it was a trio of trees. She leaned against one and gazed at the stars not blocked by the thick, leafy branches. Was Arn staring at those same stars?

"Care for some company?" Stasia asked.

Mari didn't look behind her.

"I'm not sure, honestly."

Stasia plopped down beside her and, after a moment's hesitation, wrapped her left arm around Mari's shoulders. She held a tall bottle of Thanese wine, half full, in her right. A grin tugged at her lips.

"Yeah, well, I'm a goddess of Miquo, so I should get used to comforting my Miquoan people, don't you agree?"

Mari laughed, her somber mood cracking. She leaned against her sister, her head resting comfortably on Stasia's broad shoulder. The light of the stars settled over her, and though she sought their comfort, it did not come.

"Are you afraid about Clarissa?" she asked softly.

"She's with her mom in hiding," Stasia said, and took a gulp from the bottle. "She'll be fine. There's plenty of places to hide in the countryside for a single night."

Mari shook her head. "I don't mean that. I mean that you might not see her again."

"Ah. That." Another swig. "I don't think I need divine intuition to see what you're getting at here, Mari. Does Arn really mean that much to you?"

Mari focused on the stars and hoped her blush would not be too noticeable in the dark.

"Maybe. I don't know. I think that's what scares me most. That I might never find out. Tomorrow's going to be brutal, Stasia, and I can't...I won't even be able to..."

Stasia pulled her closer, her thick arms closing around her like a protective mother bear.

"Arn and his brother are the strongest, most stubborn paragons you will ever meet. If anyone can find victory, it's those two. Have a little faith in them. As for me, well." Another squeeze. "When have I ever needed your help? You sit back and enjoy the show I put on. After tomorrow, I won't be the Ax of Lahareed. I'll be the Ax of Thanet, and whatever remains of Everlorn back on Gadir will be gods-damned terrified at the thought of me coming after them."

What Mari would give to have her sister's confidence, real or fake. They'd met the leaders of Raklia's resistance and plotted where and how they would make their ambush of the sacrificial wine. Their numbers were few, but thankfully imperial presence here was less than in most places. So much of it would rest upon Stasia's broad shoulders.

"I pray you are right," Mari said, earning herself a poke from Stasia's thumb.

"Hey, now, let's set something straight," she said, her tone draining of levity. "Under no circumstances are you to *ever* pray to me, you hear? You're my little sister, and I'm your big sister. That never changes. Besides, prayer is just asking for things from gods, right? Well, you needn't pray, and you needn't even ask. I'm here for you, Mari, and always will be. That's a promise."

Mari felt her throat constricting. She fought back a sniffle.

"I love you, Stasia," she said. "Don't you dare die on me tomorrow."

Stasia laughed and drank the last of the bottle.

"So moody," she said, and turned. Her grin was ear to ear. So beautiful, so wonderful, her big sister. Only the faint fire burning in her eyes, like a reflection within the pit of her irises, gave away her divinity.

"Let the world burn, Mari, but I'm coming through alive, and you with me, whether you like it or not."

Arn leaned against the railing of their skiff. Given Red Glade's proximity to the Shivering River, the leader of the local resistance had deemed it wise to keep most of the fighters sequestered on boats instead of risking inspections within the city proper. Patchy clouds covered half the sky, but the stars shone clear through the other half, and Arn stared at them as his mind drifted. Was Mari looking upon those same stars?

"Why are you not in bed?" Dario asked as he emerged from belowdecks. Arn chuckled.

"Am I a young man again, and you come to check if I've wandered off with my mates?"

Dario joined him at the railing. They both wore simple clothes, their armor stashed in the cargo hold. Arn wished they could have a fire for warmth. But light could attract attention, and right now they couldn't afford the slightest misstep. The odds were already stacked heavily against them.

"You have no idea how much I resented that task." Dario elbowed Arn in the side. "Checking in on you meant I couldn't have my own fun. Mother and Father would have too many questions."

"Did you ever consider that was their plan in the first place?"

His older brother laughed, his smile lighting up the night.

"Of course I did, but it was a lot easier to blame you instead. If you'd just take matters seriously, then I could take matters less seriously. A fair trade, wouldn't you think? But it never happened, at least, not until I enrolled in paragon training. I thought you'd go to your grave a gambler and a whore. I never did tell you my surprise when you followed me to the Bloodstone, let alone when you succeeded in becoming a paragon."

Arn's turn to smirk.

"Is this your way of admitting you were proud of me?"

"Try not to go that far. I still thought you were trying to escape your responsibilities as future regent-king of Vashlee. I also thought you'd fail out within weeks. It seems my judgment has often been...inaccurate, when it comes to you."

Arn clapped him on the shoulder and then pointed. The city of Red Glade was visible through the trees, a shining swathe of yellow lanterns and squat wood buildings clustered around the winding river. Only one building reached above the trees, a well-guarded rectangle known as the Bastion. According to Kel, the leader of the resistance here, river bandits had been a constant concern until the Bastion's construction. Any trader could stash their goods there for an extended stay, nice and safe from any thieves. In preparation for tomorrow, the Bastion had been cleared out, its halls emptied to allow people within for the God-Incarnate's unfathomable sacrifice.

"You know what?" Arn said. "Your judgment *is* terrible, and do you know *how* I know it's terrible? Because you're coming with me into the Bastion to kill paragons and soldiers. It's madness, the odds are hopelessly stacked against us, and most importantly of all, it's the right thing to do. So piss on your judgment, good or bad. Just know that I am proud of you for once."

Dario waved his hands in surrender.

"I'm used to you being the one who messes things up, not the one who sets the example."

"Yeah, well, it's a nice change of pace, isn't it?"

"Indeed, it is."

They grinned, fell silent, and looked upon the city, comfortable together. How Arn missed it so, if it had ever been like this in the first place.

"You going to be all right?" Dario asked after a time. Arn needed no clarification. Mari's face seemed to hover everywhere he looked.

"I will be," he said, and departed for belowdecks. It would be a long day tomorrow, and he needed to rest even if he'd spend much of the time in his bunk tossing and turning. "Our story doesn't end here."

Dario remained, melancholy painting over his words as he looked to Red Glade.

"War doesn't let us write our own stories."

The house was very quiet. Keles heard the groan of every board and the rustle of every soft gust of wind. Cyrus was gone, more comfortable at night than in the day. The Nameless woman promised to return for them in early morning. Keles was alone in that house.

She sat on her bed, her knees pulled to her chest. Sleep would not come.

Because I watch you die.

"Is this what you want?" she asked, her voice muffled by her arms. The room might be empty, but she knew Lycaena lingered. The goddess never left her side.

Silence was her only answer. It was the answer given to her once before, in her deepest hour of need, and compassion had been its source. Was this compassion now?

"If giving my life saves my people, then I give it gladly," she told the darkness. "I don't need secrets. I don't need to be coddled. My life is yours, Lycaena. I can carry every burden, so long as I do not carry it alone."

Another gust of wind, rattling the rooftop. It felt like the inhalation of an entire city. A held breath.

And then nothing.

"So be it," Keles whispered. "My resolve remains unbroken, even if my heart must weigh all the heavier."

She slumped into her bed and curled onto her left side. Difficult as it might be, she had to try to sleep. Her arm hooked underneath her pillow for a more comfortable position. The touch of metal against her fingers startled her, and she withdrew them into the pale light.

Beneath her pillow, a silver ring. She need not read the side to know whose name was carved into it, and she clutched it tightly within her fist as she wept until sleep finally, mercifully, came to her.

Nameless She lurked at the bottom of the capital hill, watching the castle in the distance. Even now, in the deep of night, servants hurried to and fro, preparing. They were invisible to many, the lifeblood hidden in veins underneath the skin. She wondered if those servants believed there was poison in the wine they would distribute, or if they dismissed it as desperate Thanese lies.

One man certainly knew the truth. He stood on a balcony of the castle overlooking the city. He was a glowing golden ember to her mind's eye, a sickly sight.

Do the deaths mean anything to you, Ashraleon? She wondered. *Or does the pleasure of the dying bury any sense of guilt that might remain?*

She had debated making her presence known many times over the centuries. There was power in the stories given to her, and even more from those who heard and disbelieved, knowing in their hearts that Everlorn twisted the truth to fit their ambitions. But anytime She thought to approach whatever new name and body Ashraleon occupied, fear paralyzed her.

To Everlorn, She was the Whore, tormentor of the sinful.

To Ashraleon, She was dead, and the Whore merely a story he'd crafted.

Three thousand years later, he still sulked over her rejection. He still sought to disgrace her for turning from his madness. If he learned She walked in a divine body, he would hunt her relentlessly.

She shivered. No. She had always cowered at the end, walking in secret among conquered lands and helping those She could. With every war, She had hoped Everlorn would be crushed. With every war, Everlorn swallowed more of Gadir, until She stopped believing there would be an end. Everlorn would unite the world, and somehow, She would find her place within it. A sad, cruel fate, but there were no promises that humanity would be given anything better.

But here on Thanet, the impossible seemed within reach. The weight of three thousand years of sin had followed Lucavi. It burned black within her breast to counter the God-Incarnate's sickly yellow. And so

She would end her exile. She would dare hope the world could yet be saved.

"I give you my faith, Vagrant," She said, and turned from the castle. "I pray you are deserving of it."

Cyrus paid solemn vigil in the charred wreckage that had once been a home but was now Thorda's pyre. He knelt in the ashes, his head bowed and his hands clenched in prayer. But to whom could he pray, when he was the one others prayed to?

He heard them so clearly now. Word of tomorrow's sacrifice had spread throughout all of Thanet. Thousands upon thousands were afraid, and they sought comfort. No doubt many prayed to Lycaena, Endarius, perhaps even Dagon. They begged for gods to save them from the savagery other gods inflicted.

They begged for the Vagrant's swords.

Their prayers, some whispers, some loud, heartbroken cries, flooded his head. Cyrus trembled within the cacophony. Death. Murder. Retribution. They begged for violence, and he felt that need deep in his bones.

Cyrus answered them once, only once.

"Tomorrow," he vowed. "We will be free."

Soma cradled the spear that had almost murdered him, clutching it to his chest as he hovered deep beneath the waves, surrounded by darkness, and given respectful solitude by the creatures of the abyss.

Tomorrow, he vowed. *We dream anew.*

CHAPTER 47

SINSHEI

The air felt strange on Sinshei's neck.

She walked with quivering hands through the castle, ignoring the stares of what few soldiers and servants remained. The rest were gathering in their assigned areas throughout the city. Nine different ceremonies were to be held in Vallessau. The largest would be within the castle grounds, in the grand courtyard. Already barrels of poisoned wine waited in stacks. The thousands gathered there would be the last sacrificed, the final gift in the name of the new God-Incarnate.

A gift done in my name, she told herself. Her hands trembled, as did the gift she held.

Two paragons stood guard at the door to the chamber where her father would remain during the ceremony. It was strange, seeing neither of them was Bassar. The younger of them smirked at her. The other remained passive.

"Let me through," she said. "I would speak to my father."

"We are to deny all guests," the younger paragon said.

Sinshei stepped closer.

"I am Anointed One Sinshei *vin Lucavi*, paragon. Make way. This matter does not concern you, nor do you possess authority to deny me."

The younger man reached for his sword, but the older grabbed his wrist. He stared at her, contemplating.

"As you wish," he said.

Inside was Lucavi's grand bedroom, now fully prepared for the ceremony. Servants had stripped out the bed and wardrobe, along with all the dressers. In their place were five stone statues atop pedestals, each one depicting a former God-Incarnate. Sinshei had personally overseen their construction. It pleased her to see the finer details come through. Thankfully her father had brought Eldrid craftsmen with him across the sea. She doubted any stone carver of Thanet would have given the sculptures such loving attention. The statues were situated in the center of the room, all facing a single point between them where Lucavi would kneel, pray, and accept the blessing of the sacrificed.

The God-Incarnate was not there, not yet. He stood on the balcony overlooking the city. He wore his finest white tunic, his fingers covered with rings and his neck wrapped in gold and silver chains. His hair was carefully brushed so not a strand lay out of place. His ornate sword was buckled to his waist, and a hand rested casually upon its hilt.

"I did not wish to be disturbed," he said without turning around.

"I know, but this matter cannot wait," she said. She walked with soft, quiet steps across the carpet, purposefully striding through the center of the ring of five statues. They felt strangely alive, as if their eyes followed her. She paused, imagining the moment when the faithful and faithless alike gave up their lives in the name of Everlorn. The power would flow to the statues. It would flow to *her,* here in this exact spot.

Unease filled her belly, and she could not shake the feeling that the statues glared at her.

"What is so important?" Lucavi asked.

Sinshei knelt just shy of the balcony, where the carpet ended and the tile began. Head bowed, she lifted her arms.

"I bring a gift," she said in answer.

At last, her father turned.

Held in her arms was the entire length of her hair, fully cut from below her ears. She had spent hours that morning looping and braiding its nine separate strands, then lacing it with silver and gold thread. A crimson ribbon tied both ends together, forming a circle.

"All that I am, all that I will be, I give," she said. She bowed her head and closed her eyes. This must be honest. The words must be true. Nothing less would sway the heart of a god. "For my faults, and my failures, I beg forgiveness. My accomplishments, and my deeds, I present as offerings. I am mortal, and in my mortality, I cannot deny my fallibility. But I am your child, loyal and true, and I lift you up above all. I beg of you, accept my faith, not only in you, but in what all of Everlorn represents."

Heat flushed her neck. Her hands trembled holding the braid.

"No other sees the perfection you would build clearer than I. No other cherishes your name with such devotion. No other loves you as I love you. Take my gift, grown in a lifetime of servitude, and know that I am true."

"No other," her father said, his voice barely above a whisper.

"No other," she repeated. "I am here. I am ready. Bestow your gift. Name me Heir-Incarnate, as you did Galvanis before me, and I shall lead our people to a golden age of unification."

Silence followed, several long seconds, until at long last…

"Sinshei, look at me."

Sinshei opened her eyes and saw the face of her father. There was no love there, but she had not expected it. Neither was there rage, which she had feared. He was not insulted or furious that she would suggest such a fate. Somehow, what she saw was infinitely worse: disappointment.

"You truly believe yourself worthy of becoming God-Incarnate?" he asked.

Hold strong. She must not succumb to doubt now, not when her godhood rested on the edge of a knife.

"I am your last surviving child," she said. "I am the blood of your blood, and an Anointed of the Uplifted Church. I have studied our history, learned our creeds, and memorized our scriptures. I am ready to walk the difficult path. Look upon my accomplishments. I am ready to lead the Everlorn Empire forward. Grant me your blessing. Grant me your divinity."

She stared into those blue eyes, never flinching, never doubting. She thrust the braided circle for him to take.

"Yes, Father, I am worthy."

Lucavi's boots thudded upon the balcony stone. He wordlessly crossed the space between them. His face was as still and emotionless as the carved statues. He touched the braid with his fingertips. A look came over him, one she recognized. It meant he was falling into the past, seeing and hearing things long before her birth.

"You are Valshei's daughter, of which I am certain," he said. The strands of hair curled at his touch. Glowing. *Burning.* "But though you possess my blood, you are no worthy heir, Sinshei, and you could never be."

The braided circle caught fire. She refused to let it go, even as the flames licked closer to her hands. The stench of the burning hair filled her nostrils and clogged her throat. Her entire body locked still, and she felt ten years old again, watching her mother burn upon a pyre, only this time it wasn't Galvanis who lit it.

The last of the braid burned away. All that remained was pale ash falling to the floor, and a scar burned across her palms.

"If you are a student of history, then you know of God-Incarnate Drasden," said Lucavi, clapping his hands together to scatter the last of the ash. "With a powerful enough sacrifice, we may extend my reign another two decades. It is enough time for me to take many wives, and through them, bear a proper heir."

"A proper heir," Sinshei said. Timelines rambled through her mind. Her tongue burned as if she swallowed acid, yet she could not stop the words from pouring from her lips. "You would trust the fate of our empire to a son not yet born. You would hand over godhood to a child. Unknown. Unmet."

She stood, her rage and sorrow uncontrollable.

"I am here," she said. "I am before you, tested, blooded, and proven. Here. Right *here*. No other nation or island needs to die. No other sacrifice must commence. Give me godhood, Father. Let go of history, let go of your fear, and—"

His hand struck her across the mouth.

"We are nothing *but* history," he seethed. "Three thousand years of it, the God-Incarnate of an empire. We are Everlorn's divinity. Its beliefs are shaped by our wisdom, but so too must we obey that belief. I am not afraid, Sinshei. Not of you."

He grabbed her throat and lifted her. Sinshei felt so small compared to him, her neck a child's toy between those meaty fingers. She clawed at his hands but could not scratch his marble skin. His eyes glazed over. Her life hung in his hands, and yet it felt like he was not even there. The words he whispered next were not for her. Did he even know she heard them?

"History. Precedent. If I could not choose Bassar, why would I ever choose you?"

Bassar?

His bodyguard. Not of his blood. Not of his loins. That was preferable? Her fingers dug in tighter, her fingernails cracking. Blood poured down her hands as they twisted and tore. Her vision darkened, and she almost welcomed it.

Lucavi dropped her to the ground. She landed in a sprawl, hacking and coughing as her lungs frantically fought for air.

"Let us look upon your accomplishments as you desire," he said. "A nation whose faith is rotten despite years to spread word of my divinity. A people rallying around a supposed queen returned. An insurrection so powerful I lost an imperator, two regents, and three sons. You are a fool if you think your role as Thanet's Anointed came from your skill and not your blood, Sinshei. You are a fool if you think your accomplishments can compare to the nations Galvanis conquered or the armies Petrus commanded."

He knelt and jammed two fingers underneath her chin to lift her gaze to meet his.

"Did I not promise whoever brings me the Vagrant's head shall become heir? Yet the Vagrant still lives. You are *arrogant*, daughter of mine. You seethe that a child yet unborn will be named heir, but listen well. I do not yet know if whoever I sire will be worthy, but I do know, with all my heart, that you are *not* worthy, and that truth is echoed five-fold by the God-Incarnates of old."

What broken scraps remained of Sinshei's resolve kept her stone-faced before such humiliation. She bit her tongue hard, harder, until she tasted blood. She would not weep. She would not.

"Am I understood?" her father asked.

"You are," she whispered.

"Good." He stood, ran his hands through his hair to straighten out a few errant strands, and strode to the center of the statues. "I have much to pray on, and you have your own tasks. The ritual in the courtyard is yours to oversee. Have everyone prepare, but do not instigate until I give the word. They are to be the last, and I wish to savor it, and address them beforehand."

"As you wish," she said, and the words tasted like the bitter copper of blood.

Sinshei left her father's private chambers in a daze. She hardly acknowledged the two paragons standing guard outside.

"I pray your meeting was fruitful," one of them said.

She would not lash out. She would not scream.

"As always," she said, and strode toward her room. No running. No hysterics. Not until she reached her room and could shut the door behind her.

Only then did her mouth twist into a silent scream. Her hands struck wood. She writhed, silently shrieking, rage and sorrow mixing together to form tears that smeared the careful cosmetics she had applied. The scream turned to snarls and bared teeth. The cruelty of it, the unfairness, clawed at her and she clawed the wood in return, clawed until she bled.

Yet the door was an unsatisfying substitute. She turned away and saw her reflection in the mirror above her dresser. The nakedness of her neck. A thousand curses came to mind, but she choked them all down as she grabbed a nearby brush and smashed the glass.

Broken pieces scattered across the dresser and carpet, and in their every reflection, she saw a failure. Her failure.

A knock on the door had her spinning on her heels, glaring.

"Sinshei?" Soma asked. He entered without asking, that damn, disrespectful habit of his. He glanced to the mirror, then the scratched door. When he spoke, his voice betrayed nothing, but the coldness in his eyes showed he already knew the answer. "What word from your father? Shall he name you Heir-Incarnate?"

Sinshei stood tall, and she swallowed down a thin layer of bile scratching at her throat.

"I have been rejected," she said. "He will instead perform the same ritual Drasden used to extend his life for two decades. There will be no Heir-Incarnate for Thanet. Instead Lucavi shall return home, take an abundance of wives, and birth himself a new heir for a new sacrificial people."

Soma struck the butt of his spear on the floor, cracking the stone beneath the carpet. His teeth bared as he glared at the floor, lost in his own thoughts.

"So much time and hope put into you," he said. "Wasted."

Desperation pushed Sinshei forward. There had to be a way to salvage this. Her father's refusal did not mean the end of her chance at godhood.

"You are a famed slayer of gods," she said, approaching him. "This need not be the end of our plans. Could you do it? Could you execute my father before the deed is done, so I may take his place?"

Soma looked up at her, and she took a shocked step backward. Never before had she seen such an expression on the paragon's face. His eyes shone bluer than the ocean, and infinitely colder. His bared teeth were polished pearls. Shadows elongated behind him as he stalked toward her, taller somehow, more powerful, more dangerous.

"If I could kill Lucavi, what need have I of you, Sinshei?" he asked. "I was to be at your side the moment you ascended. Instead you will be elsewhere, and I, forbidden. As always, Sinshei, you are a *failure*."

"How dare you?" she asked, as if her rank and her bloodline would mean anything in that quiet room. "Get out, paragon. I command it."

Instead he stepped closer. She was intensely aware of the sharpness of his spear, and his tightening grip upon it. The man towered over her, and she could not have anticipated the rage that overtook his face. It twisted his handsome features into something horrifying and ugly, and when he spoke, his voice came out like the hiss of a serpent.

"Command?" he asked.

He would murder her. Right here. Right now. Instinct filled her to call upon the name of her father for her holy blades, followed immediately by shame and disgust. She would not call upon Lucavi, not even to save her life. Damn him. Damn him to the hell he built for others. And so she tilted her neck, met those eyes as rancorous as an ocean amid a storm, and awaited her fate unblinking.

The grip on his spear suddenly loosened.

"Farewell, Sinshei," he said. "I have met so very many during my long life, and you truly are the most piteous."

It was only when the door closed behind him that she released her held breath. Her body trembled. She should never have trusted the damned paragon. Whatever he wanted of her, he did not get, and she was lucky the wretch did not murder her in her own bedroom. Her mind groped and searched for a sliver of light amid the darkness.

"It's not over yet," she said. "Not until I set foot in my grave."

Sinshei wiped at her eyes, found them wet, and grabbed a handkerchief from her dresser. She had her duty to perform, and so she would, her sorrow and frustration hidden from the public. It was not the first time, nor would it be the last.

"Twenty years," she said as she began to clean her face. "Empires do not change in a day. You have twenty years. Twenty years to plan. Twenty years to prepare."

Foul, jagged lies to swallow, but what else had she to live for? She set down the dirty cloth and stared at the broken mirror. What other hope was there? She could not kill the God-Incarnate with a blade of his own faith.

Could she?

Sinshei lifted her right hand, surprised by how calm she felt. It did not shake or tremble. A numbing mist settled over her thoughts. The lessons of Thanet came to her, one after another. The nature of faith, and the purpose of gods. How even gods themselves could change, and become what they must be. Their purpose. Their role.

"I hold no faith in you, Father," she whispered. "But I don't need to."

Whatever his origins, the God-Incarnate was now the embodiment of the empire's beliefs. He was their shining pinnacle, a face and a name for the masses to worship. But it needn't be that way. A prayer built in Sinshei's mind, wordless, one only of emotions and images.

Sinshei hated her father, but Everlorn? The might of its armies, the scope of its power, and the goal of its grand unification? No. She did not hate it. Even as she saw its failures, the whole was too beautiful. Ashraleon was flawed. Aristava was flawed. All of them, flawed, but with every God-Incarnate came new wisdom to prepare the empire for the future. Forever growing in knowledge, forever strengthening it.

Everlorn was unity and clarity of the divine. It was freedom from heathen gods and their tangled mass of contradictory beliefs and religions. It was the sprawling city of Eldrid, its golden spires, and its clasped red hands. It was the cathedrals of the Uplifted Church built in every corner of the land. A million people, breathing as one.

Sinshei loved the promise of Everlorn, and it was to that she prayed. For Everlorn, Sinshei could be strong. She could take, to achieve what she must. She had faith in might. Faith in the one who held the blade.

Sinshei opened her eyes from her prayer, and within her lifted hand formed a gleaming sword of light.

"No," she whispered. "Not in twenty years. Change comes today, Lucavi, and not even you will stop this tide."

CHAPTER 48

KELES

The three waited near the walls of the castle, hidden within a bakery now closed and emptied for the sacrifice. The day crawled at an agonizing pace, and despite Keles's insistence, Nameless She demanded they wait until the very last moment to sneak into the castle grounds.

"I have witnessed this ceremony multiple times," She said. "There will be a chamber constructed for this purpose, high up in the castle overlooking the courtyard below." She closed her eyes. "I can sense him there, even now. The energies will gather to him as he kneels in a circle of statues resembling the God-Incarnates of old. He will be alone. None would dare intrude in such a holy place. It is there we go. It is there he will die."

"It is there we go," as if breaching the keep would be so easy. Keles could see the patrols in the distance, and they were numerous. Getting inside unnoticed was a laughable prospect, yet the Nameless woman seemed so very sure.

"Cyrus may be practiced at stealth, but I am not," she said. "How will we reach Lucavi without bringing an entire army down on our heads?"

"By becoming invisible," Nameless She said, and grinned at them. She pulled the covering off her basket and withdrew two servant outfits "Put these on. Do not worry for the fit, or your armor. Hold faith in me, if you please."

Keles exchanged a glance with Cyrus, who shrugged.

"I have no better plan," he said, and that was that. Keles took the dress and pulled it over her head. The fit was extremely awkward, given her platemail, and her sword poked out one side. Cyrus fared little better.

"I don't think we will be fooling anyone with this disguise," he said.

"That's putting it generously," Keles added. "Tell me you have something better than this?"

Nameless She approached Keles. Her hands settled onto Keles's shoulders, and her violet eyes burned.

"You still do not understand the truth of what I am," She said. "I am misery, I am suffering, and above all, I am *unseen*."

Keles felt the magic flow across her before she saw the change. Her armor faded away. Her hands and feet became bare skin. Her dress lowered, her sword no longer poking out and the shield on her back no longer pulling at the neck and bunching the waist. She still felt the weight of it, but its presence was hidden somehow, disguised.

"A neat trick," Cyrus said. Nameless She turned to him. A faint smile crossed her face.

"Do not compliment me yet," She said. "You have not seen my best one."

Her hands pressed to either side of Cyrus's face. Her eyes closed, and She whispered the faintest murmur of a prayer. Keles crossed her arms and watched, curious.

"You will meet no one's gaze," She said. "You will stare at the floor, preferring it to the faces of others. Your head is bowed, your shoulders hunched. The world has not broken you, but neither would you challenge it. Unnoticed. Unbothered. Invisible to your betters. Harmless to those who think themselves your rulers. Swallow down your pride, and become the least among us."

Her hands pulled away. Cyrus's hood, cloak, and swords were gone. His face, so young and handsome, changed. His hair grew twice its former length. The bump in his throat smoothed away. His nose sharpened slightly, and there was even a faint hint of powder on his cheeks. The change extended downward, growing his chest and narrowing his waist.

"I present you as beauty, as Thanet sees it," She said, stepping away. Keles stared at Cyrus with wide eyes and a growing smile. The prince examined himself, then glanced up at her, his neck already blushing red.

"Aye, beautiful," Keles said, igniting that blush to full bloom. "Very beautiful. Must you change him back afterward?"

"My illusions are not forever," She said, and paused to gather herself. Enacting the change must have taken significant power from her, for She swayed on weak legs. A heartbeat later, She steadied and winked at Cyrus. "If she would become this forever, then let her pray to Lycaena. With Lucavi dead, the Solemn Sands might yet resume their purpose."

Nameless She needed no dress for herself. A wave of her arm, and her clothing changed to match theirs. Her feet were bare and heavily callused. The intricate braids of her hair grew more subdued, a simple knot Keles's own mother had tied for her when she was a young girl. The memory hit her harder than she anticipated.

Cyrus, meanwhile, still looked at a loss for words. Keles stepped beside him and ran her fingers through his brown hair.

"The illusion is...very convincing," Cyrus said at last.

"Then let us not waste it," Keles said, and patted his shoulder. "So we have our disguises. How do we get past the wall?"

In answer, Nameless She pointed to a small window along the outer wall.

"In there. I sense no life within, and it is plenty dark. Can you work your magic, Vagrant?"

Cyrus took Keles's hand. She felt no glove, just soft, delicate fingers.

"I can," he said, and together they walked through the shadows. Her stomach twisted, and suddenly she was falling, falling...nowhere. Her feet stood on solid ground, even as the world momentarily spun. Suddenly they were in a little storage room built within the wall, cramped and smelling of damp stone.

"You could have given me warning," she said, separating from him.

"I could have." He vanished back into the shadows, then returned a moment later holding Nameless She in his arms. He resumed speaking as if he had never left. "But you were enjoying yourself far too much."

"Enough childishness, both of you," the Nameless woman said. Her tone was mild, but Keles felt the admonishment crack over her like a whip. "Our time is short. The God-Incarnate awaits."

Nameless She led the way. Keles remembered the orders She had given Cyrus and did her best to mimic them herself. Eyes low. Shoulders hunched. Move with a purpose. Even now, there were others like her hurrying about, preparing for the imminent ceremony. As they made their way toward the keep, they kept off the main path and skirted a side walkway marked with pebbles. The last thing they wanted was to pass through the crowd.

"Those here are meant to be the last sacrifice," Nameless She said, gesturing to the distant people. "A final boon, ordered by the newborn God-Incarnate, to help strengthen him."

"Or her," Cyrus said. "So far as we know, Sinshei is the only possible Heir-Incarnate left."

Nameless shook her head.

"No. It shall never be. If Sinshei believed so, she believed a lie she told herself. I suspect, when this night ends, Lucavi hopes to remain God-Incarnate for two more decades so he might repeat this entire travesty with a better heir."

Keles turned away from the gathered crowd. Hundreds of people there, milling about with anxious energy. No doubt they'd heard rumors of what was supposed to happen. Everyone in Vallessau had. The church insisted that it was nonsensical fearmongering. How many believed it? Worse, how many had no choice but to believe it, for they were brought into the castle at sword point?

"Hurry," Nameless She said. "We do not want to be out here when the order is given to begin the ceremony."

"Why did we not come sooner?" Keles asked. "Why cut things so close?"

"Because the door to Lucavi will not be sealed until the ceremony begins."

"Begins?" Cyrus stepped in front of She, not caring that they were still within view of the throng. "We won't stop it?"

"Did you think we would?" Nameless She gestured wide around her. "All across Thanet, the ceremony will happen, and not just here. Beyond the Crystal Sea, the people of Everlorn rejoice as well. They feast upon banquets, tell stories, pray their prayers, and yes, sacrifice unbelievers held in jails and camps for this purpose. People will die. Here. There. Even if we kill Lucavi, those deaths will happen. The power and faith that flow will be immense, Vagrant. It is our duty to ensure it finds no waiting vessel."

Cyrus stepped away. His hands shook at his sides.

"If what you say is true, then he shall be stronger than ever before, and we were already hard-pressed to kill the Heir-Incarnate. How can we kill one such as him?"

Nameless She closed the space between them. A loving hand pressed to his cheek.

"Because I am with you." She looked to the sky. "Do you see it, Vagrant? The rivers of blood and gold?"

Cyrus paused, and Keles wished she could see what they saw.

"I do," he said. "And it is vile."

Nameless She put her hand on his shoulder.

"But do you see the storm about it? The darkness, growing?"

He hesitated a moment.

"Faint, like a veil."

She withdrew from him.

"That is your destiny, Vagrant. That is how the deathless shall die. Now let us hurry."

The trio reached the keep's main entrance, which was guarded by a line of soldiers. Keles crossed her arms and stared at her feet. She itched to draw her sword and ready her shield, but they were still in the open. A battle out here would be noticed, and alert Lucavi long before they reached his chamber.

Nameless She led the three, and she tried to slip past the line only to be stopped by a visibly agitated soldier. He caught her by the arm and held her.

"Where are you three going?" he asked in the Eldrid tongue.

"We need more cups," Nameless She said in Thanese. She paused, then repeated it again, this time in the imperial language. Keles could not understand her, but She clipped her words and pantomimed taking a drink.

It was a fine act. The soldier released her arm.

"Get on, then," he said in Thanese before switching tongues. Whatever he said after had the other soldiers laughing. Keles fought down another desire to draw her sword. They were mocking them, surely. Their eyes leered, and the blackness within them seemed beyond belief.

How deep is your rot? Keles wondered. *Are we not even human to you?*

Once past the soldiers and inside, Nameless She took the lead. They left the main hall immediately, traveling through little back ways crowded with shelves. A haggard woman with graying hair and a dress matching theirs rushed from the opposite direction.

"What are you three doing here?" she asked.

Nameless She grabbed the older woman's wrist. Their gazes met. No words passed between them, just a look, but Keles could imagine it. She had felt it herself, when meeting "Nora" earlier in the forest. The older woman's countenance eased. She glanced to Keles and Cyrus.

"Never mind," she said. "Get on about your business."

Nameless She watched the woman leave, and then flinched as if struck. Keles reached for her, but she beckoned her away. Her body swayed on uneven feet.

"Do you not feel it?" She asked. Her violet eyes widened, and her voice hardened to stone. "It has begun."

CHAPTER 49

SINSHEI

Sinshei knelt in the heart of the castle library with tears in her eyes.

"My will be done," she prayed. "My will be done."

Shivers coursed through her as she felt the air ripple with power. She blinked her eyes open and saw the faintest wisps of golden light. The sacrifices. All across Thanet, they had finally begun. Guilt clawed at her throat, and she gritted her teeth against it.

"A worthy sacrifice," she whispered. "Your lives are not cast aside in vain. In me, they will accomplish the impossible."

She stood and brushed her hands across her dress. Lucavi was close, so very close to the library. Within his room, he would be standing between the statues of the former God-Incarnates, absorbing the gold and crimson rivers of faith and sacrifice flowing through the skies. She need only strike him down and take the inheritance that should have always been hers.

And yet her feet would not move.

Millions of lives across Gadir, to be made better through compassion and equal through reformation, and yet her feet would not move.

Sinshei clenched her fists and offered yet another prayer to Everlorn. She would seek no comfort or guidance from the God-Incarnates who ruled in its stead, but the purest essence of the grand empire. The collective will of her people would be what gave Sinshei strength.

Cast aside my fear, I beg, so I may walk the final path.

The sound of the library door opening interrupted her prayer. Sinshei turned, for the briefest moment afraid Lucavi had somehow sensed her prayer and come to punish her, but instead three women stepped inside, all dressed in servants' garb. Two were strangers to her, but the third? She would recognize that face anywhere.

"Keles?" she asked, baffled.

The former penitent pulled off her robe, and an illusion broke around her. Suddenly she stood tall within the library in her black armor, her sword strapped to her thigh and her shield held firm across her back.

"Shouldn't you be with your father?" she asked.

Sinshei's fingers trembled, and she fought against the desire to summon her weapons of faith. Not yet. With the fate of Thanet balanced so precariously, there still might be a chance the woman saw reason.

"That sacrifice is not yet in my name," she said. "But it can be, if you lend me your aid."

Keles glanced at the other two strangers with her, then paused.

"Your hair," she said. Her expression softened, became one far too close to pity for Sinshei's liking. "He rejected you. You offered him everything to become his Heir-Incarnate, and he cast you aside."

Sinshei drew a long breath to gather herself.

"Yes," she said. "He did. And so I have come to kill him. For us to meet now must be providence."

"You would have us help you, even after your betrayal?" one of the other women asked. Her skin was pale, her dark hair wispy and covering much of her face.

"The killing cannot be stopped," Sinshei said, hoping they would see reason. "The power will be gathered, no matter what we do here. Help me kill my father. Let the collective memory and worship of Everlorn flow into me, so I might build a better future for us all."

"A better future," Keles said. "While leaving me a queen of bones. You lied once. How am I to trust you again?"

Sinshei stood to her full height, and with a silent prayer, her four gleaming weapons of faith appeared to swirl about her, two swords and two axes.

"Because you need my help. You need a ruler of Everlorn capable of compassion."

"But would you be any better?" the third woman asked, stepping between the others. Upon seeing her face, a powerful sensation of vertigo swept over Sinshei. The woman's face . . . it was a perfect re-creation of her mother's. "Would you renounce the promise of Everlorn? Would you allow the return of the slain gods and grant reprieve to the worship of others beyond your own holy name?"

The golden weapons ceased their flow. Sinshei slowly shook her head. No lies, not here. The truth must suffice for these heathens, for they could be coddled no longer.

"The sins of my fathers are many," she said. "Their methods questionable, their freedoms unequally granted . . . but their dream has ever been true. I will guide us to its perfected form. Peace shall come to us at last, and I shall be the one to usher it to its eternal place. No old gods. No forgotten faiths. No warring kingdoms. Just Everlorn, and I upon its golden throne."

Keles drew her sword and shield. Her expression turned to ice.

"Go," she told the others. "Sinshei is mine."

The pale woman started to argue, but the imitation of her mother cut her off.

"Too many sacrifices have begun already. Come, Vagrant, before we lose our chance."

Vagrant?

So it seemed more illusions were at play. Could the Vagrant slay her father? She didn't know. Perhaps it would be better to let him try, to let Thanet's hero weaken Lucavi before Sinshei made her own attempt. But first, she had to convince Keles to see the light. Of all the blood and bodies that must pave the way toward Sinshei's throne, that was one she wished to spare.

The other two women hurried out the way they came, to take another path toward the sacrificial chamber. Keles paced the room, slowly, carefully. Sinshei's fingers twitched, and one of her shimmering swords flew toward Keles, a quick swipe easily parried.

"I had such high hopes for you," Sinshei said. A flick of her wrist, and down came both axes. Keles raised her shield and absorbed the blow. She kept her weapon ready, anticipating that the two swords would seek an opening, but Sinshei had no desire for blood, not yet.

"A heathen princess, once a hero, now broken. You confessed your heart to Everlorn while I watched. You could do so again."

Keles shoved the two axes away.

"You want my worship now, Sinshei? Never. My heart belongs to Lycaena."

Sinshei slowly approached, and her four weapons beat against Keles's sword and shield to keep her locked in place. Little jolts of energy sparked across the other woman's weaponry as she suffered the stings of divinity.

Sinshei tried to keep the desperation from her voice when she spoke, but it leaked through anyway.

"Let go of the traditions and gods you cling to, Keles, and see the greatness of what I offer. The Butterfly goddess is dead, but I am here, alive, and eager to embrace you. Do not die with the old. Live with the new."

"Your offer is poison," Keles said. She blocked a hit from an ax, dropped to one knee, and then lunged back to her feet to push away two more hits striking simultaneously. The way momentarily open, she lunged forward with her sword leading. It almost pierced Sinshei's breast, but one of her holy swords swooped down at the last moment to parry it aside. Her momentum continued, Keles pivoting so her shield led the way, aiming to crush Sinshei's body against the stone wall.

All four divine weapons faded as Sinshei crossed her arms. A shimmering shield of golden light appeared before her. Keles rammed into it, and though it cracked, she could not push through.

"Look past the blood to the future beyond," Sinshei insisted. Her eyes widened with exertion. Her hands pushed out, extending the shield, knocking Keles away. "I will be Goddess-Incarnate. A reformation. A new guide to reach a new age."

Keles retreated as the spherical shield broke and the four gleaming weapons returned. They battered her, overwhelming in their power. She dodged what she could and blocked what she could not. With each hit, Sinshei felt her faith growing stronger. The prayers of the dying created an aura of divinity visible like a gold-and-crimson mist permeating the air. Gadir celebrated, Thanet died, and Everlorn swelled with power. She need only tap into it and demand it be hers.

All four weapons swung for Keles, much too fast for her to dodge. The woman cowered behind her shield, and the jarring hits dragged a scream of pain out of her. She finally rolled aside, and a gleaming sword cut a groove through the carpet and into the stone below. Two axes chunked further, chasing her. She came up, blocked a hit, and then screamed as divine energy crackled through them and into her.

"Abandon your false vision of the past," Sinshei said, pressing the attack. "Thanet is no better, her history no cleaner, than all of Gadir. The lives that die tonight die for a glorious purpose. Millions upon millions, for centuries, shall reap the benefits of their sacrifice."

Keles retreated a step, then spotted the ax coming down for her shoulder. She tried to parry it, but it was too strong. The ax knocked her sword from her hand, sending it clattering across the carpet. She reached for it, only for Sinshei to flip the ax around and smack her in the forehead with its handle. With a thought, she shifted her divine weapons into clubs, and smashed them across Keles's body. That armor might be strong, but it could do only so much to absorb the impact. Blood splashed across the carpet from Keles's split lip. She gasped in pain as twin hits blasted her stomach. When she staggered, a hit to her spine turned her rigid. Another hit to her legs, and she dropped to her knees, unable to stand.

A little curl of Sinshei's fingers, and the four weapons faded. The other woman was beaten, her body overwhelmed with pain. Into that pain, Sinshei would offer mercy.

She reached down and gently stroked the woman's feverish cheek.

"Your goddess is weak, Keles Orani. Give your heart to another. To me. Bow, offer your love, and I shall make you a true queen. Not of this little forgotten island, but of a grand nation upon Gadir. My right hand. My most cherished and faithful servant. It can still be, if you would open your heart to me."

Keles dropped her shield. Disarmed, she bowed and slowly removed her gauntlets. Sinshei held her breath. Had her words finally pierced the woman's stubbornness and pride? Ever since the penitent ceremony, Sinshei had seen the beauty and power the young woman possessed. If only it could serve its proper goddess...

"My goddess is not weak," Keles said. She pulled a silver ring off her forefinger and lifted it in offering. Their eyes met. Within them, Sinshei saw fire.

"She is *furious*."

The ring burst apart in flame and shadow. Brilliant wings spread wide as if emerging from within a cocoon. They blazed, roaring, and their span stretched from wall to wall. Twice they beat. Twice their fire flashed over Sinshei, mocking any protection she might summon. The books burst into flame. The carpet was scorched. Sinshei screamed and screamed as she burned.

"Why?" Sinshei asked, collapsing to the floor. Tears wept from eyes she could not close, for she had no eyelids to close over them. Her fingers clawed the floor. What she saw of her skin was blackened and charred.

"Why must...everything..."

Before her stood Keles, unharmed by the fire. She knelt over Sinshei, her beautiful face looking down at her. Not with love. Not with hate. With pity. Sinshei dragged herself toward her inch by painful inch.

"Be beyond...my grasp?"

Sinshei reached out a shaking hand, and Keles accepted it into her own. For the briefest moment the pain that overwhelmed her mind eased away.

"I pray it is to the Nameless woman you go," Keles whispered. "To a place where She reigns without equal. A place you can live the life you should have lived, and see the dream of Everlorn false, and the beauty we worship, true and comforting."

Keles stroked Sinshei's burnt cheek.

"A place where your devotion might have meant something."

Sinshei lacked the strength to speak. Her hand slipped to the floor. The pain resumed, but it was dull; it was distant. Keles's face became a shadow, became darkness.

Became nothing at all.

CHAPTER 50

STASIA

Five men and one woman were waiting for Stasia at the cottage they were using as their base. They were dressed in patchwork leather armor, and all carried matching swords. They looked tired and nervous and barely spoke a word at Stasia's arrival.

"Are you six it?" Stasia asked.

"They are," Mari said, emerging from her bedroom. She'd tied her hair back and swapped a dress for some trousers and a loose shirt.

"A damn good many have fled Raklia," the oldest of the six said. His face was tanned from the sun, his dark beard flecked with gray hairs. "What remain have been gathered up over the past two hours and forced to sing songs at their assigned places."

Stasia nodded, conjuring a map of the city in her mind. There were five spots in total, all of them in the open. To keep things under control, the priests had ordered wood walls constructed to block off roads and seal in the areas so there would only be a single entrance. Then within they had brought dozens of tables and chairs, as if to hold a great feast. Only there would be no food, just poisoned drink.

The entire resistance in Raklia barely numbered two hundred, and so they'd divided up into squads of roughly fifty to assault four locations, with the fifth left for Stasia to break. She had practically demanded the resistance leaders give her the fewest number of soldiers. The last thing she wanted was for other ceremonies to proceed unimpeded because she could not carry the necessary burden.

"Are the other groups ready?" she asked.

"As best we know," the woman said, gruff-sounding, broad shouldered and with her hair cut closer to the scalp than some of the men. Stasia liked her instantly. "But they aren't our problem. The innermost celebration is. Are you ready to live up to your reputation one more time, Ax of Lahareed?"

Of the ceremony locations, Stasia's group would assault the one closest to the city center, which was expected to hold the most people. From what they'd told her, it was actually four little walled divisions linked together, with each segment expected to hold two to three hundred people. The plan was to assault one segment and then push on through to the next, until all within were freed. Stasia stood tall and rested her hands on the hilts of her weapons. Six fighters, and herself, tasked with taking down dozens of soldiers, the accompanying priests, and any guardian paragons.

No, she couldn't think like that. Six fighters, and a goddess. It would be enough. It had to be.

"Leave the fighting to me," she said, and offered her cockiest grin. "You six can play cleanup and kill any too stubborn to die."

At her dismissal, the six filed out of the house. Only Mari remained behind.

"You can stay here," Stasia offered one last time. "You don't have to torment yourself."

"Staying here alone is the torment," Mari said. "Don't worry about me. I'll keep hidden in your wake. If it helps, know that I'll be praying for you the whole while."

"As long as it's *for* me, and not *to* me," Stasia said. She winked and then left to lead her little squad toward its impossible task.

The city was eerily empty as their group traversed its gently curving dirt roads toward the city center. Anyone not rounded up by soldiers for the ceremony was in hiding, which left unnerving silence to fill the streets but for the occasional stray cat bounding atop street stalls to take advantage of the quiet.

"We're here," the older soldier guiding Stasia said. "And there's guards at the entrance."

Hardly a surprise. Instead of peering around the home, Stasia easily scurried up to the rooftop, climbed to its highest peak, and surveyed the area. The boarded-up roads formed four linked areas for the six-hundred-year ceremony. It vaguely resembled a honeycomb, with hastily built walls of wood planks carved from the nearby orchards of the Mane. They were unpainted and unvarnished, and the paleness of the wood made it look disturbingly similar to flesh.

People sat at rows of tables, and they showed no signs of panic or upset. Stasia felt a bit of relief. The ceremony was yet to start. She couldn't see how many soldiers were positioned within, but she hoped the number was smaller than anticipated.

She hopped back down and addressed her little squad.

"You stay behind me and focus on preventing anyone from stabbing me in the back," she told them. "Even if you think I'm in danger, trust that I know what I'm doing. If you can, focus on taking down anyone who ignores me to attack civilians instead." She glared. "And under no circumstances are any of you to engage a paragon. Is that clear?"

Nods all around.

"Good," she said, and pulled her ax from her belt. She stared at its edge, remembering the moment of her rebirth. Her rage had burned so hot that day. Could she summon it again?

She readied her hammer and then struck the ax's side. To her surprise, it relit with ease. Fire burned across the steel, and a momentary hypnotic sensation overcame her as she looked into the ax's flame. It swelled across her vision, and all the rest of the world darkened. She saw shapes within the flame, heard the prayers of her fledgling faithful.

And then it passed. She snapped alert and grinned at the six soldiers, plus her sister lurking a few feet behind.

"Ready to save some lives?" she asked, and then without waiting for an answer, she brought her ax to the nearby home. The fire leaped eagerly, spreading across the dry wood and then to the curtains. The smoke would be a signal to the other five groups to begin their assault. There would be no chance of any one place sending reinforcements to another. The resistance's goals were simple and clear: stop the ceremony, save the people, and then get out.

Stasia rounded another corner, coming into view of the four guards positioned before the entrance. They'd already drawn their weapons, having seen the smoke, but they startled at the sight of her. She wore no mask, for she had no reason to hide her face. Let them see the white of her teeth as she grinned at them, savagery pulsing in her heart and filling her with bloodlust. No more plans. No more plotting.

The strength of her arms would decide who lived and died.

She flung herself into them, her hammer colliding with a shield, her ax cleaving a man's head off at the neck. Their might felt so meager compared to hers. When one of them tried to run her over with his shield, she dug in a heel and met him with her shoulder. He screamed as the bones of his arm snapped. She silenced that scream with her hammer, clobbering the side of his face.

"With me," she shouted to the others.

Nearly two hundred people filled the tables, the hum of their conversation turning frantic at the sound of battle and the arrival of a bloodstained Stasia. A nearby acolyte in loose red robes wailed at her approach and held up his wine pitcher before him like a shield. Stasia took great pleasure in smashing through it to bash the young man aside.

"Out!" she screamed at the tables. "Out, to your homes, your fields, your forests, get out if you want to live."

With violence erupting around them, most were all too happy to oblige. They fled over the protestations of the presiding priest, and even those who stayed found their cups yanked from their hands by Stasia's group. The six ran alongside the tables, knocking over pitchers and spilling every cup they could find. Wine flowed across tables to the dirt, gathering in crimson puddles. So much better than the pools of blood that would follow if the ceremony proceeded unimpeded.

Stasia cut soldiers down without a care as she made her way toward the presiding priest. Upon seeing Stasia, he glared, clenched his hands, and began a new prayer.

Two golden swords shimmered into being beside him. Her eyes narrowed. A priest, not a magistrate, and yet able to command two faith weapons? Unusual, but tonight was far from the norm. She rushed him, clenching her teeth in fury as those weapons began slicing through the nearest Thanese who fled instead of drinking their poisoned wine.

"Your lives are meant for Everlorn," he shouted as the blood spilled. "You cannot escape your fate."

Stasia flung her hammer at him to show how little she believed in his fate. The two golden swords crossed before him, and they shimmered at the impact but held strong. Surprising. She followed it up with a leaping attack, her spine curling, her arm up to stretch her every muscle taut. Down came the ax, burning with fire and fury. The priest's two swords met the attack. Sparks showered the ground, and lightning crackled along all three weapons, but they held. Not just surprising. Actually worrisome now.

The priest grimaced and strained every muscle in his body. The veins in his neck visibly pulsed. His hand pushed forward, and he snarled at her, his spittle landing on her face.

"You will burn with the Whore."

"I'm not the one burning."

Like embers of a forge. Like the surface of an anvil. Like molten steel. She was all of them and more.

The fire upon her ax blazed with such heat the metal itself turned liquid, and it flowed at her command to spray across the priest's face. He howled as it sizzled into his cheeks and charred his eyes. His concentration broke, and the twin golden blades fizzled away.

The steel of Stasia's ax hardened. A swing, and she split the priest's head down the middle like a melon.

The priests are stronger, she thought, then chastised herself for being surprised. Of course they were. This was the night they'd dreamed about for hundreds of years. All across Gadir, tens of thousands of similar celebrations were being held, the poisoned wine replaced with songs of praise and faith. And here on Thanet, some of the ceremonies might have already begun. Lives lost, all to keep the line of Ashraleon continuing into eternity.

Stasia retrieved her hammer, paused for the briefest moment to catch her breath, and then turned toward the gate sealing the entrance between this first segment and the second. As best she could tell, it was boarded shut from the opposite side. Five of her six fighters remained, the youngest having fallen in the opening moments of the fight. They stood near that entrance, waiting for her. She nodded wordlessly at them, sprinted, and then used all her divine might to blast open the gate with her shoulder, making a mockery of the thin wood board meant to keep it sealed.

The second segment had finished doling out the drinks. The priest leading this portion of the ceremony climbed atop a chair, lifted his arms, and shouted to the people.

"Drink!"

"That drink is death!" Stasia screamed, and she leaped upon the table. Damn whatever stubbornness, fear, or faith led the people here. She would not give them a choice. She ran across the table, kicking over cups and slapping them out of hands. It didn't matter if she cut them or broke their bones. They could live without hands, so long as they lived.

"The way out is free," she shouted upon reaching the end of the table. A baffled soldier waited, his sword up, and she lunged at him. Her ax easily parried his defense, and her hammer smashed his rib cage with little care for his chainmail. "Run, all of you, run, cast aside this damn poison and *run*!"

Of the two hundred or so, only twenty drank despite her insistence. They were the faithful, the ardent converts, and she steeled her heart against what followed. The heavy silence, lasting a few seconds at most, and then the coughing. The gagging. The bloody vomit. All around, people saw and screamed. It took seeing it with their own eyes, but at last they believed.

"You interfere with this sacred act," the priest shouted. "Soldiers, stop her!"

The soldiers were scattered among the tables, escorting the acolytes carrying the pitchers of wine. Some tried to prevent the masses from fleeing, but at the priest's orders, most rushed Stasia from all sides. Only a few chose to attack the remainder of Stasia's squad, who positioned themselves before the exit to protect those who fled.

"Sacred?" she shouted and slammed her weapons together. Fire sparked off her ax. Yes, let them focus on her, and not the exit. She could endure their hate. She must. "There's nothing sacred about this butchery."

The first of the soldiers neared, and he thrust a sword for her belly. Stasia swept it aside with her ax, collided against him with her shoulder, and then pushed away. During the moment of separation, she swung her hammer with all her might against the top of his helmet. The metal dented inward, and she watched his eyes turn vacant and his body go limp. She kicked him as he fell, toppling him into two more that charged at the priest's insistence. As one stumbled, she assaulted the other, cutting him down with two hits of her ax that opened up awful gashes in his stomach and chest.

"More!" she screamed at the soldiers pushing through the crowd toward her, steadily growing in number. "Show me all your hate so I may break it!"

They mobbed her, no lines, no order, just attacks born of panic and desperation. Stasia bounded among them like a trapped animal, and she prayed her brutality would impress even the Lioness. Her burning ax hacked and chopped at limbs. Her hammer smashed bones and made a mockery of her opponents' chainmail. With no armor to protect her, she could only rely on her savagery. She parried what she could, sidestepped what she could not, and kept forever on the move. Break a man's arm, elbow his face, and then push away to avoid a spear to her back. Punish the bastard with a cut across his throat. Her left arm shot up, blocking a strike for her neck. Though the man pressed with both hands, she easily shoved him aside with just one. Another took advantage of her momentary hesitation to slash at her side. She dodged, not quick enough. Pain. Blood, down her arm.

Stasia leaped straight at him, her weight crashing into him, her knees landing atop his chest. Down came her hammer, turning his face into jelly. With barely a thought, she swung her ax to the right, severing a man's leg at the knee. He collapsed, howling. Stasia rolled toward him, avoiding another spear, and came back up to her knees with both weapons swinging. Her ax tore open his abdomen. Her hammer smashed his remaining knee.

Another thrust scored an impact, for she was too slow to stand, too awkwardly positioned to turn. She felt its edge slice along her thigh. Blood spilled down her leg in a worrisome burst. Stasia pivoted on the other leg, her ax shattering the spear when he brought it up to defend. The burning edge continued on, embedding several inches into his chest to puncture his heart. She ripped the weapon free, and she dropped her hammer with her left hand.

I am goddess, she thought as she shoved the free hand against the bleeding wound. *I am forge fire.*

When she withdrew her fingers, the wound was burnt and sealed. It hurt like blazes, but she could deal with pain. Pain would not stop her from fighting; it would only add to her rage. She grinned at the soldiers as she lifted her hammer. And oh, how her rage had grown. Let them cut her skin and bruise her flesh. In this little corner of Thanet, she would save these people from their fate. She would deny Lucavi his promised sacrifice.

Her foes attacked. Her foes fell. It was the priest who lived, and when Stasia saw her escorting fighters rush toward him, she shouted for them to halt. They ignored her orders, thinking the man vulnerable. An enormous golden glaive shimmered into being in the air above him. When the blood flowed, her companions realized their error. Stasia slaughtered the last of the soldiers and then raced to their aid.

"To Lucavi I give this offering!" the priest called, his glaive lifting to spear Stasia as she ran toward him. But he was still just a priest, and unused to battle. He didn't know her speed. He didn't know how fast one could move when powered with rage and blessed with divine strength. She sidestepped it in a single stride, teeth clenched, legs pumping, blood pounding in her ears. Another stride, and she was flying through the air. The glaive retreated, flipped horizontal, and tried to block.

Her hammer and ax shattered through it, dissolving it into light and mist. The same could not be said for the priest's body. It broke in a crumple of blood, gore, and robes. Stasia stood over it and screamed.

Battle lust was threatening to overtake her completely, and she let it drain out of her, just enough to remain in control, for the night was young, and the battle not yet won.

Wails from the next segment over. The cries of parents, of children.

Stasia closed her eyes and prayed to the gods of Miquo.

Be with me now, to the very end, she asked them, fearful of what she would yet find and knowing she must face it all the same.

CHAPTER 51

DARIO

Dario and Arn waited at Red Glade's edge with the leader of the Thanese resistance. She was an intense woman named Kel, weary in tone and yet excitable in movement when she described the final portions of their plan. Like many of the local fighters, she'd donned the Vagrant's skull, though hers was exquisitely drawn on her face with white paint instead of chalk.

"We've confirmed three gatherings outside the Bastion, and another ceremony held within," she said, tapping her foot. "What soldiers I have are ready. No paragons guard those outer three, just some priests I believe we can handle. I have been told, however, there's at least one paragon inside the Bastion."

"We could help take out those three gatherings, and save the Bastion for last," Dario said as he glanced around the corner. Imperial soldiers had swept through the entire city, forcing people to one of the four locations. Anyone out and about would be marked for trouble. Kel's people were safely hidden and would make their way to their ambush points once the sacrifice was closer and the signal given.

"There's more people out here than in there, yes," Kel agreed, "but there's one catch." She glared at the Bastion, which loomed over the rest of Red Glade near the Shivering River. "That's where they brought all the families with children."

Arn and Dario exchanged a look.

"Then the Bastion is ours," Arn said.

"The two of you, alone?" Kel crossed her arms. "I was told you were strong, but that's...a lot. I have only estimates, but there's a hundred soldiers in there, if not more."

"So fifty for each of us," Dario said, and winked at his younger brother. "Or I suppose sixty for me, forty for you. Unless you've stopped slacking off over these past few years?"

"Fuck you." Arn clacked his gauntlets together. "Leave the Bastion to us, Kel. Take care of the people out here. Once you have things in order, you can come join us."

"Order?" The wiry woman laughed. "We've archers on the rooftops and torches ready to set half this city on fire. We'll be causing chaos, and once you see the smoke, you'll know we're on our way to join you. My only question now is, When do we hit? It's been hard getting information out of anyone as to when this abominable sacrifice begins. Some say it begins at sunset, others when the first of the stars is visible."

Dario eyed the Bastion, imagining the people within, parents and their children seated at tables or standing in groups, awaiting the poisoned wine. Why hadn't they fled, as nearly half of Red Glade had over the past few days? Did they refuse to believe the rumors? Were their hearts committed to the Uplifted Church? Or perhaps they remained behind for their children, fearful to commit to unknown days in the wilds.

Whatever the reason, Dario would not surrender them to their fate.

"Start the moment your people are ready," he said. "Show them no mercy."

"After what those monsters are planning?" Kel's grin was made wider by the painted skull. "Mercy has no place this night."

She gave a Thanese salute and then dashed away. Dario watched her go, while behind him, Arn leaned against a wall and fiddled with his gauntlets.

"The numbers really aren't that terrible," he said. "Maybe we'll get lucky."

"Maybe." Dario turned once Kel was out of sight. "Or maybe all the damage your group has done over the past few years has finally added up. Supposedly a thousand soldiers were stationed to Red Glade, but I'd guess it's actually half that number. They're spread too thin, and word of the sacrifice spread much too wide. Every town we came across had people readying to flee, or fled already. And of those who stayed, many did so with an aim to cause chaos."

"My kind of people," Arn said.

Dario chuckled.

"We go when we see the first smoke. Do you want to lead, or shall I?"

"Eldest first. I'd hate to be disrespectful."

"Now you wise up. If only you'd matured years sooner."

"Then we wouldn't be here, would we?"

Dario's mood turned somber. He looked to the distant Bastion and imagined a world where Arn had never left. Where the pair arrived on Thanet together as conquerors. Where they would be overseeing the ceremony and administering the wine.

Perhaps a little childhood rebellion was necessary after all.

"There's smoke," Arn said, nudging Dario.

Sure enough, it wafted into the sky, signaling the start of the assault.

"Bastell brothers against the world," Dario said.

Arn smirked back and punched his knuckles together.

"Lead on, then, brother. Let's make havoc."

The pair ran through the tall grass alongside the Shivering River. The Bastion was built beside its waters, flanked by docks for trade boats to load and unload their cargo. Though the building was broad and tall, Kel had insisted the bulk of it was hollow, most of its rooms dedicated to storage but for a gigantic hall most often used for local ceremonies and weddings. It was there the people would be gathered.

The building's dark paint made it look like a black thumb rising from the river, attempting to blot out the sun setting behind it. The doors were shut and guarded by six soldiers with spears. Dario shifted slightly to his right, trusting Arn to step left. The soldiers shouted and raised their weapons, but they were unprepared for the speed with which the brothers closed the distance.

They leaped into the air, one after the other, and crashed into the soldiers with fists leading. Punches shattered their armor and blasted their bodies into the closed doors. Within seconds, the fight was already over.

"I've got here," Dario said, pointing at the main entrance. "Take the second entrance at the docks. No one escapes. No one sends for aid."

Arn saluted with two fingers.

"Remember, save at least fifty for me."

His brother sprinted toward the back, and Dario wished him well. Both were likely to be guarded, but his hope was that the entrance near the river, where supplies were loaded and unloaded by the docks, would have fewer guards. Having Arn attack there also meant no soldiers could flee that way when Dario made his entrance.

He clanged his gauntlets together. Enough stalling. He looped a quick circle before the door, gathering his momentum, and then leaped right at it with his shoulder leading.

Whatever held the doors shut, be it a lock or wood bolt, broke before his might. He smashed on through and into a hallway that appeared to lead straight to the grand hall Kel had mentioned. Side doors led immediately left and right, and when Dario raced past, he saw living quarters, presumably for the soldiers stationed here.

Up ahead, blocking the hall, were more than a dozen soldiers with swords and spears at the ready. They startled and lifted their shields at Dario's arrival. Alerted to the possibility of an attack, he suspected, but not prepared for a paragon. In the dim light, he saw another pair of closed doors. From within he heard the murmurs of a crowd.

Fighting them in such tight quarters, two abreast, would be difficult. The wood planks rattled from his weight as he charged. Difficult, but not impossible. Against normal foes, the soldiers would benefit from being stacked together so readily. Against a paragon, it made for easier targets. The front two thrust their spears at his approach, but he shifted to one side to avoid the first, and he grabbed the second in hand and shattered its shaft. Momentum unslowed, he barreled his full weight into the front pair. They screamed as his fists pounded their chests, shattering bones, but that was only the beginning. Legs churning, he pushed them back, slamming them into those behind. Chaos followed, the soldiers stumbling and screaming as limbs intertwined and joints broke from the pressure. On and on, Dario pushed, the slain bodies of the first a battering ram used against the others.

Line broken, space closed, their deaths were inevitable. At best, they scored a scrape or two as Dario's gauntlets did their work. When all twelve lay dead, he cracked his knuckles, stretched his neck, and carried on into the heart of the Bastion. Its doors were closed but not locked, and a swipe of his arm knocked them aside so he could enter.

The grand room was divided by three long tables with benches on either side. All the benches were completely filled with frightened residents of the town. Lit torches hung from braziers, casting long shadows across the tables. There were three pitchers for three tables, each held by a priest. Soldiers distributed the cups, and so many were already full. Other men lined the walls, guarding side rooms closed off with thin wooden doors. Dario crossed through the center as soldiers rushed behind him to block his potential escape. They did not attack, for they waited for a signal from the all-too-familiar paragon lording over the ceremony: the divine bodyguard, Bassar.

What are you doing here, so far from Vallessau? Dario wondered, but there was no time for that. He analyzed his surroundings, fear nagging at him when what he saw did not match what Kel had told him. There were children at the tables, yes, but not many, certainly not enough for a city of Red Glade's size.

Dario's horror grew. The side rooms. He could hear them in there, crying. The children without parents were forced into the six little side rooms, soldiers put to guard each one. Separated. Waiting. They couldn't see the deaths of those outside, but they would certainly hear them.

"Halt this at once," he shouted despite knowing they would not listen. He was no paragon, not anymore. It did stall them, if only for a moment, as they looked to Bassar. The paragon readied his sword, casually slicing it through the air as he approached down the aisle.

"Faithful of Thanet," Bassar said. "Offer your love to your God-Incarnate, and drink."

Between the fear, the confusion, and the priests with pitchers having filled the cups of only half in attendance, only a third obeyed.

"Don't!" Dario screamed to them, but they would not listen, not to him. His legs froze. A cold, alien feeling sealed over his mind, protecting him from what followed. He couldn't feel this, not all of it, not at once. These people. These children. It started with coughs, followed by vomit and blood. Their limbs shook. Their skin paled.

The priests sang and poured more cups.

"Leave him to me," Bassar told the soldiers who administered the tables. "Consider this duel the people's final entertainment."

Dario's stomach, already sick and tight, pained further. How could one look about this travesty and think it justified? Or worse, claim it holy? The soldiers holding the wine pitchers continued moving from person to person, administering scarlet death. Some took it willingly. Others sobbed, accepting it only at sword point. An older man refused entirely, and when a soldier speared him through the back, the others at his table cried out. Overwhelming it all like a cursed veil were the constant sobs of the frightened children locked in the side rooms.

"You would jest in the face of this madness?" Dario shook his head. "This rot of Everlorn?"

"I feared for your devotion, yet never did I think you would sink so low." Bassar pointed his sword. "Is your faith shriveled and dead? What lies could you have swallowed to join your brother as a heretic?"

"*My* faith?" Dario settled into a fighting stance, lightly bouncing on his toes while lifting his gauntlets. "Look around, paragon, and see the fruits of *your* faith among the dead."

He denied Bassar the first move. The space between them vanished with a single dash. His fists struck air, missing by the most minute of distances as Bassar weaved in retreat. Dario chased, refusing to give him space. He had to end this quickly. The wine was still flowing. The sacrifice would continue. The God-Incarnate must have his due.

Dues Dario himself had paid plenty using the blood of the conquered. He felt the guilt weigh on him with his every failed punch. Perhaps that was why he could not land a blow. Bassar was faster, his dodges perfectly executed so that his feet never landed unsteadily. Dario pressed further, taking a cue from his brother's fighting style. He smashed the nearby tables. He batted away a soldier carrying wine foolish enough to come within reach. The screams grew, but so too did the number of bodies, so many bodies...

Finally Bassar surprised him with a sudden attack. Dario's fist missed, plunging far past Bassar's head. A knee and elbow struck him in tandem, knocking the air from his lungs and hitting his throat hard enough that he coughed blood. Dario scored a quick hit as he retreated, a punch on the arm that meant little, and then endured a slash of Bassar's sword along his leg.

Bassar lifted his sword, showcasing the blood.

"Just a shallow cut," Dario said, his voice rough from the blow to his throat. "I've suffered worse."

"Have you?"

Bassar thrust, a deceptive angle that had Dario angling his body incorrectly. The tip easily punched through his armor to slice across his chest. Dario dug in his heels to halt his momentum, slipped on a smear of blood, and crashed through a table.

Dario bounced back to his feet, his thoughts hardening, his panic lessening. This nightmare was beyond what he could comprehend, and so he pushed it aside. All that mattered was his opponent. Let the bodies be counted in the light of day. This night, he must slaughter.

Bassar had hesitated during the roll, and when Dario finally came to his feet, he thrust his long sword to greet him. Dario batted it aside with his gauntlets, feinted a punch to get the paragon dodging sideways, and then chased the dodge. He finally scored a solid hit, his shoulder digging into Bassar's chest and then flinging him halfway across the room. He landed atop one of the tables, smashing it in half. The last man sitting at it screamed and panicked, only to die when racing for the door from a spear in his back.

Dario moved to chase, but a trio of soldiers blocked the way by nervously forming a wall.

"Stay back," Bassar ordered as he stood. "See to the children."

"I think you have bigger worries than that," Dario said.

Despite his exhaustion, he felt a little thrill in watching his brother's sudden and explosive arrival. Arn blasted through the main doors, knocking them from their hinges with a screech of metal. He was already carrying the body of a slain soldier, and he flung it like a missile at his nearest opponent. The remaining soldiers rushed the entrance in an attempt to overwhelm him, a hopeless endeavor.

"The side rooms!" Dario shouted. "There's children in there!"

Arn dashed for nearest, and to the panicked soldiers guarding the entrance. Bassar moved to intercept, but Dario blocked the way, his gauntlets up and ready.

"I thought you wanted your duel," he said, his macabre amusement the only thing holding off the horrors of the night. Corpses lined the tables. Blood and vomit covered the floor. Few adults survived. No matter what happened with the God-Incarnate in Vallessau, Red Glade would take years to recover, if ever. He could only pray that the ritual locations Kel attacked were less guarded, and the survivors far more plentiful.

"And yet you are distracted. Let me fix that." Bassar raised his voice to a shout. "Soldiers! Offer the children to our beloved God-Incarnate." He grinned at Dario with a perverse pleasure. "And do not bother with the wine. A blade will suffice."

Dario lunged at him, no hesitation, no delay. The panicked soldiers guarding the side doors were already opening them with swords and spears at the ready. Arn shouted in protest, and Dario wanted nothing more than to join him, but could not. He'd have to trust his brother to deal with the soldiers and to stop the murders. Bassar would be his to distract. His to kill.

He punched and kicked, and Bassar used his sword to parry the gauntlets in turn. The weapon's steel, while thin, was absurdly strong, and most certainly Ahlai-made. Each time they made contact, the reverberation numbed his fingers and made his wrists ache. They traded blows, a weak cut to his forehead matched with two vicious punches to the paragon's kidneys. Blood flowed, but it wasn't enough. If only he were faster. If only he could match that long, savage blade.

The frightened screams of the children slowly, steadily quieted.

"Arn, stop them, you have to stop them!" Dario shouted. There were too many places in need, and neither Dario nor Bassar could allow the other to stop the duel. He glanced one way, saw side rooms filled with corpses. The other, Arn battling a dozen soldiers trying to hold him at bay. He flung himself into the center, and the impact of his charge shattered a thin door, revealing five children within who retreated deeper into the alcove.

"Run!" Arn shouted at them as he cleared the way. Bassar attempted to interfere, and Dario punished him with a sweeping kick that struck his knee and sent him tumbling. The paragon rolled, bounced up to a stand, and slashed twice to keep Dario from following up the attack.

"Such stubbornness," Bassar said. "Do you think your rebellion here matters? Whether tonight, or in the coming months, every heathen and believer both will perish upon this island."

The world was a nightmare, and within it, Bassar stood so regal, so proud. Behind him, the five children Arn rescued rushed the broken main doors. Two soldiers guarded it. Two soldiers, still determined to see this nightmare through. Arn was trying to clear their way, but he was surrounded by soldiers who forced him to earn every step he took. Blood dripped from a thousand cuts across his little brother's body, and his coat was in tatters. It was too much. Dario looked to the exit, and to Bassar, and knew his choice was already made.

"The least among us," he said, remembering Arn's words, his plea to a broken older brother. He lunged aside for a piece of a broken table. It was too heavy for one hand, so he grabbed it with two, pivoted his hips, and flung the enormous chunk of wood through the air. It sailed over the children to slam into both soldiers with momentum so great it carried their bodies through the open door and to the hallway beyond.

Bassar's sword pierced Dario's ribs.

Dario gasped at the pain but was not surprised. To turn his concentration away from someone so skilled as the divine bodyguard? He stepped into the thrust, letting it pierce deeper as he stared into Bassar's golden eyes. If he could get one good swing...

Bassar denied him the chance. He pirouetted away while ripping the sword out in a bloody display. Ribs cracked with it. One of his lungs tore. Dario hitched, fighting for each and every weak breath. His legs went limp, and he dropped to his knees.

Arn screamed. Bassar scoffed.

"To think that this is how your proud legacy ends," he said, and slashed across Dario's chest. Muscle ripped. Blood flowed like a river. Dario turned to Arn, saw the pain on his brother's face, the growing panic as Arn killed the last of the soldiers. Silently, Bassar lifted his sword for one last swing.

"It's all right," Dario said as the world dimmed. "It's all right. Wherever I go, it won't be to him. It won't be—"

The sword struck. The pain was but a moment before the darkness came to cleanse it away.

And then.

Light.

CHAPTER 52

STASIA

Of Stasia's six fighters, only one still breathed. It was the lone woman who'd accompanied them, whose name Stasia had not learned. A habit from a lifetime of war. Learning names only made it hurt more when they died, and oh so very many people died when resisting the empire's brutality.

"I think this arm's done for," the woman said, holding the injured limb against her stomach. She lay with her weight stacked against the priest's platform. Stasia took one look at the exposed bone near the joint and the gash across the muscle and had to agree.

"Get that bandaged, and then get out of here," she told her.

"I have my other..."

"That's an order. Get. Out."

And then Mari was at her side, dropping to her knees with a torn piece of cloth already in hand. Stasia could only guess where she got it from.

"Go," Mari said as she began wrapping the wound. There was no doubting the resolve in her sister's voice. "The people need you."

"I know," Stasia said. The grip on her weapons tightened. "Trust me. I know."

Two segments cleared, and several hundred innocent people spared the poison, but she was not yet done. She approached the third wood gate, gaining speed with each step. Sweat poured down her face and neck. Every limb ached. Her ribs flared with pain from her every breath. Stasia ignored it all. Exhaustion would have to wait until the morrow. Move faster, faster, prepare for the next fight. But when she flung open the next gate, no soldiers guarded it. Perhaps they thought the slain paragon would keep them safe.

Then she registered what she was seeing. Her legs froze in place. Her mind went blank. She had witnessed wars. She had walked conquered lands whose fields burned and whose waters ran red with blood. She thought herself bitterly accustomed to all the horrors of the empire, beyond shock or surprise.

Nothing compared to this.

The children had been the first to drink, but not all of them. Some still wailed at the top of their lungs, frightened and confused by the vomiting, screaming, and collapsing bodies. Parents held cups to their lips, forcing them to drink. One parent refused, and so a soldier grabbed the cup from them, held the child's head, and forced the liquid down their throat. Close to Stasia, a woman lay in the dirt, and she wept even as she vomited. The body of a child was curled into her arms, so pale, so still. Not even a year old.

Through the rows walked the soldiers, their faces stone, their eyes dull. No compassion. No sympathy. They forced cups into shaking hands. They barked orders at those who stared at the dying around them and hesitated. Any who refused were run through with their weapons. All the while, a red-robed magistrate of the Uplifted Church stood at the forefront of the tables, his hands raised to the heavens and a song of praise on his lips. He alone sang, and the hymn of the God-Incarnate's love was so at odds with the surrounding nightmare Stasia found herself laughing.

Laughing, lest she sob. Laughing, lest she lose her mind. She had arrived in time to stop much of the death, but not here. Here, in the third of the segments, she came too late. She looked to the distant fourth gate, and her sinking stomach told her she would find a similar scene.

"Castor!" she screamed, for she recognized the bastard magistrate from when she'd rescued her sister from the castle prison. The man lowered his hands and turned her way. Tears ran down his face. Crying. He was crying tears of joy.

"Welcome to our glorious celebration, Miquoan," he said.

Stasia stalked him even as soldiers rushed to block her way. Nothing would stop her. Not pain. Not even death.

"My sister asked for your head," she said, pointing her ax. "Tonight, I'll give it to her."

"Is she here, too?" he asked. "Or must I hunt for her after I offer your life to glorious Lucavi?"

Weariness pulled at her limbs, but Stasia pushed on. Break her foes, before she herself was broken. With each swing of her hammer, she shattered bone. With each hit of her ax, limbs fell bleeding and severed. But these soldiers were far from the true threat. Castor raised his hands, and above him, three identical swords of golden light shimmered into existence. Their blades were impossibly sharp, their hilts crackling with energy akin to lightning strikes in a dark storm.

"You can see it, can't you?" Castor asked. "You, with your burning eyes, of course you can. You're divine-touched, one of their fledgling, heathen gods."

Stasia ignored his taunts and charged straight at him. He was bloated with power, and she would need to bring him low quickly. With a thought, he sent his trio of weapons to meet her halfway. With each parry, each block, she felt their energy travel through her weapons to sting her hands.

"Do you see the faith lighting the air?" Castor asked. He lifted his arms to the night sky. His smile stretched ear to ear. "Do you see the power of sacrifice? We, mere humans, command the forces of the heavens."

As much as she wished otherwise, Stasia could see it, too. It flowed like rivers into the night sky. It was as if the corpses strewn about burned in an invisible fire, only instead of releasing gray smoke, what flowed forth was sickly and golden. Most flowed like tributaries into larger rivers on their way toward Vallessau and the waiting God-Incarnate. Most, but not all. Some floated and were pulled into the body of the rejoicing magistrate.

It was making him stronger, terrifyingly so. The power of his swords was undeniable, and his faith unbreakable.

Stasia grit her teeth and tensed her legs for another assault. The fourth segment. The people there. She had to kill Castor and move on if they were to have any hope. But his weapons, they held against her, when steel and muscle could not. Worse, they were growing stronger, and faster. The night belonged to Everlorn, unless she could end this now.

Desperation pushed her to recklessness. The three weapons circled her, each slicing independent of the others. With her every step, she positioned her weapons to defend, closing the distance between her and the priest. Most times, she blocked or parried the hits, but not always. The divine weapons cut across her flesh. Worse than the blood loss was the pain that followed. Crackling golden light swirled into her body, and by all the gods and goddesses, did it hurt. Her vision would darken, and a sensation of *wrongness* would flood into her, force her to grit her teeth and choke down a most agonizing scream.

When she was almost close enough to attack, he brought his three swords before him, their blades crossed together to make a shield. Stasia forced her legs to leap, and she lifted her hammer high above her. She had broken these weapons already this night. She could do so again. Be strong enough. Give in to her rage. Show the damn magistrate her might.

The hammer met all three weapons at once, and for the briefest moment, she thought they would crack. Castor cried out in pain, and he braced his arms and legs. And then the hovering light, the aura of sacrifice and worship that blanketed Thanet, poured into him, renewing him. The swords held. The hammer remained at bay, unable to continue onward and break the man's bones.

"Praise be your glory," Castor said, weeping anew. He flung Stasia backward with a wave of his hand. "Praise be your might."

All three swords cascaded down, striking one after the other. The first two, she blocked with her hammer. The third knocked it from her grasp. Her ax was all she had left, and she weaved it side to side, the sound of ringing metal mixing with her own screams. Castor's swords cut into her arms and legs with heartless precision. Nothing stopped the barrage. Twice she tried blindly rushing the magistrate through the pain, and twice she was rewarded with slices across her legs that sent her tumbling.

"Praise the one true god of Everlorn," Castor prayed as his swords sliced along her forearm. The pain was too much, igniting her every muscle so her arm shook and quivered. Her ax fell to the ground.

"Praise the one true god of all the world."

An attempt to grab the ax resulted in a kick to her stomach. Not the swords, no, Castor wanted to inflict pain with his own physical body. She wished to repay him for the foolishness but was denied the opportunity. Two swords pressed to either side of her neck. Their golden power burned her skin, igniting horrid pain that locked the muscles of her throat. Stasia clenched her jaw and fought with all her willpower to force air through her nostrils and down into her lungs.

Get up, her mind screamed. *He's toying with you.*

The knowledge galled her, but exhaustion had taken its toll. The cuts, the blood, the broken bones, all combined with the pain inflicted with those divine weapons. It left her mind ragged and her body sluggish. She reached for her hammer, failed to find it. Deeper. More pain. She gasped, raged, bled.

"You are so little," Castor said. A wave of his finger, and the swords lifted, dragging Stasia up with them. "I am but a child before my god, and yet you, a heathen god, shall fall to my faith. You are a relic of a shameful past, and all the world is better without you."

The swords dug deeper, crackling with energy born of thousands of deaths and a hundred thousand prayers. Her limbs shook against her will. Her legs squirmed, barely able to hold her weight. The third sword hovered between the two of them, its tip aimed straight for her forehead. She stared at its golden shimmer, hating the priest, hating her helplessness.

Clarissa, she thought, seeing her wife's face, seeing her smile, just before the blade thrust.

CHAPTER 53

ARN

The world was silent and empty. The screams, the battle, the dying and bleeding, and the clash of steel were like still air to Arn's ears. Nothing pierced the veil about his mind.

His brother, dead.

Murdered by Bassar.

The paragon kicked away the corpse and flicked a bit of blood to the floor. He looked to Arn, and his beautiful face was a perfect portrait of disgust.

"A valiant life thrown away," Bassar said. "Did you convince him to do this, Arn? Did you use his love to stab heresy into his veins like venom?"

A battle raged outside, Kel's soldiers guiding the remaining survivors toward the Bastion. Arn prayed they could endure on their own, for he would not leave. One more corpse must join the blood-soaked floor beside his brother's.

Arn raised his fists and tensed his legs.

Him or Bassar. One of them was going to die.

He exploded into motion, his feet catapulting him across the room. The paragon lifted his sword, and he did not flinch. At the last second, just before Arn could smash his skull to mush, he rolled aside and swung. But Arn had already leaped to dodge, and he retaliated with a flurry of punches immediately after landing to keep the offensive.

"If only Dario had been stronger," Bassar said. He spun, two quick steps to gain distance, and then countered with a powerful overhead chop. Arn dove to his right and tumbled backward. "If only his heart had endured your lies."

Arn punched a fist into the ground, straight through the floorboards, to halt his momentum, and then used it as leverage to fling himself right back at Bassar. A one-two punch followed, Arn hoping to shatter the bastard's ribs. He barely even saw the paragon. His mind warped and rewound, showing him again and again the sword piercing his brother's chest.

"My blade is my faith in Everlorn," Bassar said as the flat edge of his sword blocked Arn's attack. "You cannot break it."

"Like hell I can't."

He uppercut for Bassar's chin but had to pull it back. Bassar's speed was unreal, and he'd already retreated out of harm's way. Worse, his sword looped up and around for a snap thrust at Arn's throat. He stumbled a step, narrowly avoiding being pierced, and then had to flail with his left arm to parry a second thrust.

Feet finally firm underneath him, he studied the paragon's movements and the delicate, graceful flow of his annoyingly long blade. The moment he saw Bassar swing wide he leaped forward. The sword cut across his coat, Arn mistiming the paragon's speed, but it was shallow, and deflected against the chainmail hidden underneath the leather. Arn endured it to punch for the man's chest. Bassar twisted his body, his spine arcing so that the hit only grazed, but at last they were back in close quarters. He swung again with his other fist, this one curling from the other direction to clobber the man's skull.

But just because Bassar could not use the blade of his sword did not make him harmless. Bassar ducked underneath the punch, smashed the hilt of his sword into Arn's gut, then attacked three times with his other fist, movements so fast they were but a blur. Two struck Arn's throat, a third square in his mouth. Arn kicked out of instinct, and for once, he made contact. Bassar flew halfway across the room before landing with feline grace.

Arn had no reprieve. Bassar was back on him in an instant, slashing and kicking. Multiple cuts ripped apart the leather of his armor to expose the chainmail, and though the armor held, the impact of the blows still carried through, and it felt like he was being beaten with a sledgehammer.

Arn twisted and danced as best he could on clumsy feet, now fully on the defensive. Twice he parried a slash only to be kicked in the stomach as punishment. Another time a swing that should have been lethal only cut a groove across his cheek. When Arn tried to retaliate, he punched air, and the hilt of Bassar's sword smashed his face like a brutal kiss. Arn staggered, and this time, his foe did not chase. He knew why, too, as much as it stung his pride. Bassar had tested him and found him wanting. He no longer saw Arn as a threat, only a nuisance to be ended.

"Do you not understand your folly?" Bassar asked as Arn spat blood. "I am Lucavi's most beloved. I am the one he trusts when fear worms its way into his heart. His trust, and his love, give me strength you cannot hope to best."

"And yet you're here," Arn said, lifting his hands into fighting position. It didn't matter his opponent's speed, nor how outclassed he might feel. His brother would be avenged. "Some trust. I bet Vagrant's killed him already. He'll die, without you there to help him, without you to protect him. Fuck you, Bassar, you won't even get to mourn him. Not after I'm done with you."

Bassar's knees bent as he lowered into a fighting stance, both his hands clutching the hilt of his sword. His eyes narrowed, and his hate was so strong it rolled off him in waves.

"Nothing will separate us," he said. "I am loved, Heretic. My place will forever be at his side. You won't stop me. No one will. No one can."

Arn gasped in a few greedy breaths and pretended not to notice how exhausted he felt.

"Join him in hell, then, Bassar, because that's where you're both going tonight."

Bassar's body was a blur when he lunged, the tip of his sword aimed perfectly for Arn's heart.

This time, Arn didn't dodge or block. He lifted his left hand and let it pierce his open palm. The tip easily parted leather, flesh, and bone. But the Ahlai steel on the other side? The sword hit it and halted. Bassar immediately tried to withdraw, but Arn would not let him. He screamed and shoved the sword deeper into his arm so that it caught even more in the gauntlet. And then Arn twisted his wrist, locking the blade in place.

Bassar pulled, every muscle in his body straining, but Arn knew it could not rip free. Those gauntlets were the last creation of Thorda Ahlai, a gift made at the request of his beloved daughter. They would not break.

Still Bassar refused to release the hilt. His arms flexed. His teeth clenched. All his strength, his power, his belief in the God-Incarnate, came together in an attempt to cut through heathen-made steel.

Arn leaned forward with all his weight.

The blade snapped.

Bassar stumbled and swiped with the remaining length of his sword. Arn felt it slide across his stomach, but there was no stopping him. His gauntlet struck Bassar across the temple with enough force to shatter the paragon's face. Bassar's body collapsed, the entire upper half of his head demolished. His broken sword fell from a limp hand. Arn gasped at the pain radiating outward from his stomach. He clutched his left arm against it, trying to seal the wound, and then grabbed the remnant of the blade still embedded in his palm.

There was no easy way to do this, so he just did it. The blade sliced through the interior leather of his gauntlets, but he managed a firm enough grip to yank the shard of steel out.

Arn spat on Bassar's corpse.

"Damned fool," he muttered. He turned, felt his body go rigid. Felt his mind belong to someone else.

"Dario," he whispered, and took two small steps toward the corpse. He wanted to kneel, but the pain in his stomach denied him. He reached a hand, saw it trembling, and pulled it back. What to say? What to do?

"You deserved a better brother than me," he said, and turned away. Each step required great effort to maintain his composure. He stumbled through hallways littered with dead soldiers, both Thanese and Everlorn. He passed rooms with little groups of men, women, and children gathered together for their last drink of wine. The numbness about his mind protected him from the horror. It was too much. They'd saved many, and failed so many more.

"Heretic!" Kel said, meeting Arn at the door to the Bastion. The city burned behind her. "We did it! We actually did it!"

Arn glanced over his shoulder, to a building filled with the sacrificed. Truth died on his tongue. They'd known from the start there would be no clean ending to this brutality.

"Yeah," he said. "We did."

Kel's smile faded.

"Are you all right, Heretic?"

"I'm fine," Arn said, pushing past her. While Bassar and the rest of the paragons might be slain, there was still so much chaos and fear all around. He did not wish to add to it. "Just fine."

Out. That's all he could think of. Get out. Out of the building. Out of sight of Thanet's people. The attention grated, and the fading light from the corners of his vision was growing worrisome. He labored forward, out the door, one leg after the other through sheer instinct and raw stubbornness.

Cool air blew against him, and he sighed with relief. At last, he'd stumbled out of the fort. Smoke lifted from various parts of the city. He watched it and choked back a cry. At least their mad plan had worked, and the people in the city would survive, so long as Cyrus accomplished the impossible and ended the life of the God-Incarnate.

Arn hurried into the grass, wanting solitude, wanting peace, and more than anything, wanting that damn tower far behind him. He made it halfway to the river before he collapsed to his knees in the grass. He gasped, and blood spilled across his tongue. Far worse was the gush that rolled over his trousers and down his coat.

"Too slow, Arn," he said, daring to open the coat to check the wound. "If you were faster..."

There was no point finishing that sentence. The possibilities tormented him. If he were faster, might his brother have lived? Might more innocents have been spared the poisoned wine?

He let out another half sob.

"Damn it," he said. "Gods damn it."

Back to his feet. His breathing had grown strained, and he felt cold sweat trickle down his neck and back, a stark contrast to the warmth of the blood that coated his waist and legs. If he could reach the river, maybe he could wash it all away and better see the damage. Maybe, once clean, things wouldn't look so bad.

His leg gave out. He dropped to one knee, and his right arm slipped. More blood. Not only blood. Arn was holding his intestines in with the pressure of his arm. His teeth clenched so hard he feared they would shatter, but it was the only way he could contain the scream. Let these people have their moment. Let them weep and celebrate in equal cursed measure. They need not shed tears for him and his brother.

"Get up," Arn said, even as his vision darkened. "Get up, you bastard. At least reach the water."

It was a goal. Stupid, perhaps. Pointless. But it was a reason to move, to lift his feet and fight for another step. And another step. Every breath was a nightmarish wave of pain, no matter how hard he tried to keep it shallow. The ground was growing soggier, the grass taller.

There. Not far, the flowing waters of the Shivering River.

This time, his legs gave no warning. He simply went from walking to falling. Arn caught himself with his left hand and then rolled to the side, doing his best to soften the blow on his wound. White-hot light washed over his sight, and this time nothing prevented his cry of pain. The white faded, replaced with vision much too dark. He saw stars. Blades of grass.

"Please," Arn whispered. "No. Not after all this."

But there was so much blood, and he dared not look. He could cry for a battlefield surgeon, if one were even among the haphazard collection of Thanese fighters Kel had brought with her, but Arn was no stranger to war wounds. His only hope was the trace of divinity within him, granted by those sacrificed in the name of the God-Incarnate.

Only those traces felt so very weak now. Had Cyrus succeeded? Was the head finally cut off the monster named Everlorn? Arn laughed. What a joke. What a crime. How appropriate. He laughed even as he cried, laughed until the emotions were so intertwined neither was decipherable from the other. Fingers into the dirt, he dragged himself toward the river. Even if he must crawl, he would reach it.

He heard the rush of the water over the stones, a pleasant little warble that reminded him of the springs near his hometown. He and his brother used to jump from stone to stone that peaked out above their rapids, daring each other to go that much farther.

His brother. Damn it. Tears trickled down his face as he rolled onto his back and stared at the stars.

"Will you go to him?" he asked. "Surely not. Surely his hell won't be yours. What, then, Dario? What god will take you?"

A sudden spike of pain had him hitching for breath. He fought through it, needing to speak, needing to remain himself until the darkness took him.

"I'm sorry, Mari," he whispered.

Arn closed his eyes and prayed. He didn't know to whom. He didn't even particularly care. All that mattered was that someone was listening.

"I won't ask for miracles," he said, to all the gods, each and every one, should the laws of the world allow it. "I don't know what awaits me. I ask…I beg. Please. Whoever hears this. Whoever cares."

His voice cracked.

"Please, take me to wherever she will go. When Mari first steps into eternity, I want to be there, smiling. I want to see her again, and hold her, and laugh, and do, and do all the things we never could, that we never…"

He was sobbing now. No more words. The gods could surely feel his heartache. This wish was all that mattered, and to whoever granted it, he would give his love and worship forever more.

The softest brush of fur against his hand stole his attention, and he looked down. A tiny little fox cub sat beside him, her body curling up against his waist. Her fur was orange like somber embers, her chest and stomach as white as snow-capped mountain peaks. Her head brushed against his hand a second time. Perhaps it was the tears, perhaps it was his fading vision, but he saw three tails on that little fox, not one.

"Thank you," Arn said, and he closed his eyes. He released the hand staunching the wound. Enough was enough. With acceptance came calm. He lay there and listened to the flow of the water. The night was peaceful. An urge to sleep came to him, and he did not fight it. Perhaps he might even dream.

At his side, the fox began to lick the edges of his wound.

CHAPTER 54

MARI

Mari followed in the wake of her sister, stepping over corpses and trying not to slip on the blood.

Why do you torture yourself? she had asked herself as the battle raged. But what else was there to do? Cower and hide? Spend this awful night in ignorance, wondering if her sister lived? They passed through walled-off segment after segment, and at first Mari walked the battlefield with a sense of hope. They could do this. Stasia was an unstoppable juggernaut, her ax and hammer obliterating every challenger. Not even paragons could stand against her, for she had spent years training to fight them before being granted the strength of a goddess.

But the night was long, and their enemies so cruel. The air itself changed with the start of the sacrifices. Mari was well attuned to the nature of the divine, and the entire island reeked of it. Thousands upon thousands giving up their lives, some willing, most not. It painted the sky red and gold, faith and murder inseparable. It sent shivers crawling up and down her spine. This sickly, consuming belief curled like tendrils as they lifted, stretched, and floated their way toward the wretched God-Incarnate in Vallessau.

And then Stasia battled the magistrate Castor Bouras.

Upon recognizing the man from his visit in her cell, she had hoped Stasia would immediately strike him down, granting him a well-deserved death, but his divine weapons had held strong. Too strong.

"No," she whispered, watching the fight unfold. "No, no, you can do this, Stasia, you have this."

Holy blades met Ahlai-made steel, and neither broke. Castor made Stasia work for every step, and punished her for it. Mari's dread grew as cuts opened across her sister's arms and legs. She knew what was happening, even if her sister did not.

The faith. The sickness. The atrocity. It fed these priests, strengthening their weapons and their bodies. This was the culmination of a lifetime of work, and Castor was positively drunk off it.

"No," she whispered. "No, it can't end like this!"

Yet there was no way for her to deny the horror. His swords would not be broken. Her sister's blood splashed across the ground. Castor was winning. Stasia was dying.

And Mari could do nothing.

Powerless.

Helpless.

She dropped to her knees and called upon the lands of the divine with enough savagery to shock even the Lion.

"Lycaena!" she bellowed to the heavens. "Will you deny me still?"

Silence.

"Endarius!" she cried next. "Will you remain a coward?"

Silence.

Castor battered the hammer away from her sister's grip. Twin swords curled around her neck, looping but not cutting. A third sword hovered before her forehead. Taunting her. Mocking her.

Damn the Lion. Damn the Butterfly.

"Anyone!" Mari screamed. Tears swelled in her eyes, but they were as much of fury as of fear and sorrow. "I don't care who, I don't care why, I will be heard, *I will be heard!*"

The golden sickness dimmed from the air. The world around her darkened. Time itself slowed, Stasia and Castor swallowed in darkness.

We are weak, and our power meager, a deep voice rumbled within the emptiness.

But we will aid you, said a second voice, lighter and feminine. *If you would have us.*

Mari stood, and though she could not see them, she knew their names.

"I will," she said. "Give me the power of Antiev."

The unnatural darkness peeled away, and amid this wretched night, her body changed. Fur sprouted across her skin, but unlike Endarius's gray, this was as pitch black as the night itself. Her teeth hardened into fangs. Claws stretched from her fingers. Her muscles grew, and her senses sharpened. This cohabitation was new to her, and yet it felt natural all the same. Her hair shifted, becoming vines blossoming with flowers and decorated with leaves and twigs. Her eyes turned green. Her hands and feet hardened into bark, as did portions across her body to protect her like armor. She let loose a savage howl to the moon, proclaiming to all the world what she had become.

The might of Rihim, God of the Hunt.

The grace of Amees, Goddess of the Forest.

Mari vaulted through the air with a flex of her legs. Castor raised his third sword, its shimmering edge aimed for her sister's forehead, but before it could descend she battered it away and landed a vicious swipe across Castor's chest. His robe tore, and blood splashed across them both. He gasped, his mouth hanging open with bafflement. Mari used his confusion to her advantage, ripping away the golden swords that imprisoned Stasia and then leaping them both to safety.

"Mari?" Stasia asked. She clutched her bleeding arm to her waist and tilted her head to one side. "Is that you?"

Mari set her sister down at the gate separating the third and fourth walled segments.

"Rest. Recover." She turned to the magistrate. "He is my prey."

No leaping this time. She approached steadily so Castor could get a good look at the beast come for his head.

"Do you remember me?" she asked with two voices. "The god you humbled?"

Castor crossed his three swords before him, turning them into a gleaming shield that meant nothing to her divine claws. She ripped into it, showering the ground with sparks. Sweat built across his brow, and she saw how tightly his muscles were clenched to hold her back. She could smell his fear, see it like little threads rising from his body.

"I broke you once before," Castor said, finally pushing back with his swords. "I can break you again!"

Mari smashed her hands into the three twirling weapons, trusting the bark to hold strong.

"There are no manacles to bind my wrists," she said, enjoying the savage thrill that surged through her. "No voices to scream in my ear. Just us, Castor."

She closed the distance, ramming him with her shoulder. He flew, landed hard, and then rolled. She followed with a leap, her body deftly twisting to avoid blind thrusts with the divine weapons.

"Where is your barbed whip?" she asked upon landing. Her claws sank into his chest, hooking through his ribs, and then lifted him up before her.

"Where are your prayers?"

He screamed as she cracked him open. The vines of her hair sprouted thorns and then slithered across his face. They crawled through his nostrils, his mouth, his eyes. His scream ended.

"Where is your god?"

Her teeth closed about his throat, clenched tight, and then ripped free in a spray of warm blood. She released his corpse, and it landed before her in a gruesome display.

"Gone," she said, and spat meat. "All gone, to burn and die upon the island of Thanet."

Her bloodlust was not yet sated. The way was clear. Beyond was the fourth and final segment of the sacrificial ceremony. Within were the remainder of those responsible for the sacrifice and death of hundreds of innocent men, women, and children. Mari destroyed the barricade easily and tore through the soldiers with claws dripping blood and vines blossoming with thorns. She was outnumbered, but she was a daughter of Miquo. She was the rage of Antiev. Betrayer and betrayed, united against conqueror. Nothing could stop her now.

Their weapons bounced off the bark Amees granted her. Her claws made a mockery of their armor. Blood and gore painted the ground, and to this savagery Mari finally gave her all. She bore teeth and claw, but she knew who the true monsters were.

The monsters bled. The monsters died.

Scattered silence followed, broken occasionally by screams and clattering of metal from fights elsewhere in the city. Mari walked among the bodies. Two hundred in number, perhaps more. They'd been fenced in and then seated along the tables. Wood cups lay scattered about, their interiors still red from the poisoned wine. Nearby, set up on blocks, was the cask that had brought death to Raklia. Mari wondered how many had drunk willingly, and how many had their mouths pried open and the liquid forced down their throats. Worst, though, were the children. So many children. What had their parents whispered to them, before the end? Comfort? Lies?

Her heart ached for them, and it was not alone. These dead belonged to Thanet, and yet within her the god and goddess of Antiev still wept. They understood too well the loss of the conquered. Mari lowered to a crawl, and her claws scraped along the ground, opening little grooves like veins.

Yellow shoots sprouted instantly in her wake. They thickened and darkened as they drank in the blood, becoming vines that stretched out farther, farther, until they swarmed the tables and benches with strength enough to break them. Once the bodies were free, the vines took hold of them, pulling them down to the dirt and wrapping them tightly in green shrouds.

Mari continued, circling the area, carving the earth. Roots dug deeper, softening the dirt, making way for the bodies. One by one the sacrificed sank down into the welcoming soil. Flowers sprouted to mark their place. When Mari finally stopped, she stood in the heart of a swirling path of flowers. Nothing remained of the bodies. No faces twisted in pain, no vacant eyes staring into nothing. Just white blooms to mark the grave.

"It is done," she whispered, and surrendered the power granted to her by the Antiev gods. Her skin reverted, and her bones reshaped. Painful, but welcome. Once more the world darkened as she stepped into the divine lands between the living and the dead. Two gods hovered before her, their forms faint. Belief in them was meager, and they had given much of themselves so Mari might save her sister. Amees curled within her husband's embrace, held as if he would never let go.

Mari smiled at them. She wanted to give her thanks but could not. Melancholy mixed with happiness, a bitter mixture on this most awful night, and it leadened her tongue.

"You found her," she said at last.

Rihim bowed his head and closed his golden eyes. When he spoke, she heard the echo of her own words.

"In an everlasting land, where the trees reach the heavens, the rivers flow unceasing, and time flows not at all."

Together, they faded away. The world returned, color flooding in to become the face of her sister, who had joined her in the center of the flowers. Her red eyes were wide with worry. Her shaking hands clutched Mari's shoulders.

"Mari?" Stasia asked. "Mari, what happened?"

Instead of answering, Mari flung her arms around her sister and held her, shedding quiet tears as the sky flickered gold, the flowers turned crimson, and the island writhed amid Everlorn's dying gasp.

CHAPTER 55

SHE

How many years have I waited for this? She thought. *How many nights have I bled and burned, imagining such a day?*

They'd reached the ceremonial chamber at last. Only a few soldiers had noticed their progress, and they had died quickly. Higher and higher into the castle they ran, the seething divine energy of the God-Incarnate growing ever closer, until at last they arrived at the bedroom turned sacrificial chamber. She peered around the corner, caught a brief glimpse of the entrance.

"Two paragons guard the door," She said. "Are they within your capabilities?"

The Vagrant smirked. Within a blink, his flesh was gone, replaced by the grinning skull.

"If they are not," he said, "then I stand little chance to slay the God-Incarnate."

"Then do your work."

She watched with cold disinterest as he turned the corner and assaulted the paragons in a flash of steel and swirling darkness. He would succeed. Nothing would deny her this moment. The Vagrant's swords spun, parrying frightened, unsteady strikes. His savagery was intense, and growing. Good. He would need it.

When the paragons lay dead on the floor, Cyrus reached for the door, but She rushed to his side and grabbed his wrist. His brown eyes peered at her from behind the skull. Shadows curled around him, little smoky tendrils that writhed with sentience. He was preparing for battle, but She had one last gambit to play.

"Lurk outside his vision," She said. "I know what must be done. You will need to be strong. You will need to be greater than you have ever been. Hold faith in me, Vagrant, as I hold faith in you."

Cyrus dipped his head in acknowledgment.

"I shall trust you, Nameless one. Repay him for the torment he has given you, and should you fail, I will be there to repay him for mine."

She closed her eyes and smiled. It was good to be trusted by a god, even if he was a young, fledgling one. Most other divinities shunned her. The stink of Everlorn repelled them. She touched her breast, felt the eager, squirming, infantile faith within. She was the empire's creation, through and through, but let tonight be a conclusion. Her hands pressed against the doors, just above a splash of blood from one of the dead paragons.

The Vagrant has the strength and the will, She told herself. *You need only prepare the way.*

Eyes closed, She shook, and forced down a shiver. Let it all end. On this day, good or ill, let it all end for her.

She opened the doors.

The room had once been the king and queen's bedchamber, lavish and grand. All of it had been stripped away. In its place, forming a circle around the center of the room, were five naked statues of the previous God-Incarnates. She knew from experience he would have brought sculptors with him from Eldrid, along with references so all might be precisely wrought. They were carved of the local granite, a uniform light gray smoothed to perfection.

She saw the statue of Ashraleon and knew it resembled him not at all. The lies and delusions had permeated deep. He had never been so handsome, his long hair so perfectly straight. He was taller in this statue, his chest exaggerated and his smile widened. His charisma, though, was captured perfectly. Remarkable work, all of it through the intensity of the eyes. The eyes of a man who could command a nation to die.

In the center knelt God-Incarnate Lucavi. His head was bowed, and his hands raised to the ceiling. He wore his splendid armor, for this was no true transference. Galvanis was meant to be the one in that circle of statues, to receive the blood when his father cut open his own throat. Galvanis, or Petrus, or Kalath. Sinshei had dreamed of kneeling there, the poor fool. The gazes of those five statues would never allow such a blasphemy.

Chills swept through her. The realms of faith and magic were familiar to her eyes, and a great river of crimson and gold light poured into Lucavi from the ceiling, forking at the last moment to swirl into his upraised hands. The flow was tremendous, the power nearly blinding, far worse than if She stared into the sun. Human sacrifice. It was power. It was horror.

But there was a third divine power building in the sky above. She could see it through the ceiling as if the stone and brick were invisible. A storm cloud raging, thick black in contrast to the crimson and gold. It swirled, a tornado aching to form.

Not yet, she thought, and turned her attention to the kneeling monster that was Lucavi.

"Hello, husband," She said.

Lucavi stood, his right hand reaching for the sword strapped to his hip. His fingers froze, barely touching the hilt. His eyes widened as he stared. His mouth opened but he did not speak, whatever words he intended instantly dying the moment he saw her. She stood tall and proud as She approached. No weakness here, not at the end. What form did She take? She wondered. What color her hair? What slope to her cheeks, what curve to her nose? Did she have freckles? Moles? Scars? She smiled and wondered if even her teeth adjusted to meet his gaze.

At last, he mustered words.

"You cannot be."

"But I am," She said. "A million sermons have declared me real. I am the tormentor, the betrayer, the cruel temptress, am I not?"

His sword flashed free of its sheath, and he pointed the blade at her throat.

"Not a step closer."

She halted, the steel an inch away. It hovered in the air, perfectly still, perfectly controlled. A lie. Within those blue eyes She saw the true maelstrom. Aristava and Drasden, Ululath and Gaius, each lurking like captives in a cage. They rattled the bars and shrieked, but so far Lucavi remained in control. Only one essence remained silent, but that was the one whose audience she desired most.

"I will speak to him," She said. Not a request. A demand.

"Thousands give up their lives to bless me this night," Lucavi said. "You speak to *me*, Nameless Whore, and me alone."

She ignored his drivel.

"I would speak to the first," She said, calling upon his seniority.

"Enough."

"I would speak to the strongest," She said, now drawing on his pride.

"Enough!"

Lucavi swung for her neck, with more than enough strength to decapitate her. She did not move, nor did She break eye contact. There was one individual in all of creation She understood better than even herself, and it was Ashraleon.

The sword halted just shy. Lucavi's eyes widened with surprise. She smiled, but it was one of pity.

"You truly think you are in control," She said. "You damned fool. You are five slaves in service to one master. *Now, come forth*, Ashraleon, so we may have words."

The strength of her divine power paled in comparison to the prayers of millions, but those millions feared, hated, and loved her in equal measure. What power She possessed, She gave to that command. It rolled off her like a silver wave, and at last Lucavi's demeanor shifted. His sword lowered. His lips curled into a cocky grin She recognized so very well, even if on a foreign face.

"I should have murdered you the moment I learned of your betrayal," the God-Incarnate spoke, now with Ashraleon fully in command.

She stepped closer, refusing to look away. The Vagrant should have slipped inside by now. If he was true to his word, he would be watching, and waiting. Would he be strong enough to do what must be done? She trusted he would. But first, She must render the impossible possible. Far,

far too many believed the God-Incarnate eternal. It was armor upon his flesh. It was balm to any wound.

But already there was a crease in the armor. The scar on his face, inflicted years ago by some unknown assassin. It should have healed, but it hadn't. And seeing it gave her the courage to continue.

"My name," She said, stepping closer. "Give me my name. I would have it before you see the grave."

The God-Incarnate spat at her feet.

"I would give you nothing," he said. "Your betrayal deserves only murder."

"And yet I still stand." She stepped closer, ignoring the blob of spit. "Your love for me was true, Ashraleon. I remember it well. My name, in exchange for a gift."

"You fled the hour I needed you most," he said. "You went running to my most hated enemy and told them all our secrets. We could have outlasted their siege, if not for you! You lacked faith in me, and in my cause."

They were lies, all lies. There had been no grand plans, no miraculous victories in store. Ashraleon wanted to die, and take as many people with him as he could, because when it all came crumbling down, he was a vain coward furious the world would not give him everything he desired.

Desire. It ruled him then. It ruled him now. She passed two of the statues. He was unafraid. He thought himself invulnerable. How could She, small and womanly, possess the strength to harm him?

"And now I return," She said. "Let us make amends for all we did those thousands of years ago."

Within her hands appeared her knife. This knife, which had cut into her flesh every single night for the past thousand years. This knife, which spared her the cruel duty of tormenting others. This knife, which She had awoken clutching on the first day of her return, when She had been birthed wholly formed by the curses of Everlorn and the wails of the conquered.

"Do you remember our parting?" She asked. "Do you remember our final moments?"

She was many things to many people, but to Ashraleon, She was a singular reminder of his human days. A reminder of when he had lived as a mere mortal. But She need not just give him a reminder. With her free hand she stroked his face. He tensed at her touch. Yes, he had loved her. There were times he had thought the world of her and would have moved the heavens to make her smile.

He had truly believed her dying with him was the ultimate culmination of that love. She had not.

"I dwell not on your betrayal," he said. "It is why I have banished your memory from the land."

"But not from your own memory. You never could, could you? There was too much happiness there to let go."

Yes, he loved her, for that love was also why he hated her so deeply, hated her so much he made her the enemy of his entire faith. It was desire rebuked. It was need unfulfilled. This reunion was one She had dreaded for centuries, and one he had forever dreamed of. And he hated himself for it.

She kissed his lips, remembering each and every one of those halcyon days. The tournaments held in breezy summers, preparing their soldiers for war. The feasts that marked the start of spring. The laughter of their retinues, the suitors, the foreign dignitaries, shared luxury as Eldrid prospered under Ashraleon's rule. How blind She had been to the struggles of her own kingdom, but her eyes were open now.

The kiss continued, longer, deeper. More memories. Their nights together. Their lovemaking, almost frantic after a year of trying for an heir she never gave him. Her hand stroked his cheek. Her true hand, no longer that of another. She saw a faint scar above her knuckle from when She'd startled a stray cat as a child. A smattering of freckles along her forearm. Her face, shifting. Her skin, darkening slightly. The strands of her hair, shoulder-length, braided, red.

She thrust her tongue into his mouth. Remember it all. Remember a life before godhood and sacrifices and the sprawl of an empire. Remember good days and bad, their first night together, when he'd been so nervous he finished in her mouth mere seconds after they started. Remember the dull days sitting by the fire as they watched rain pour outside their window. Remember cuddling in their bed, eating off trays brought by their servants, as they laughed and discussed potential names for the many children She was sure to have. Remember it all, as She prepared her knife.

On the day She fled Eldrid Castle, he had come to her alone to try to stop her. They had struggled, and in the struggle, She had cut a knife across his brow. Ashraleon, shocked that his kind, docile, obedient wife would do such a thing, had raged like a wild animal. That brief moment had been enough for her to slam the door of their room shut and bolt it with the same lock he'd used to keep her contained for the past week, when he first feared something was amiss with his precious wife.

Their kiss ended. Lucavi's body had changed with hers, his jawline softening, his nose widening, and his hair growing and shifting in color. This was the Ashraleon She remembered, the Ashraleon without exaggeration or divine blessing. All was true, but for one single detail. She leaned in closer, feeling the desire radiating off him like a desert sun. Oh, how he had hated her, and he might hate her still, but to have her back? He would surrender it all. Thousands of years spent with hundreds of wives, and all had been pale imitations of her, the one he forever chased. Her eyes held him captive. Her smile widened, and She spoke the words all the world wished for the God-Incarnate to hear.

"You. Are. Mortal."

And then She cut him across the brow, at the exact same place and depth She had all those thousands of years ago. Blood splashed across them both, and then he howled, he *howled*. The rage, the betrayal, they surged forth with unstoppable power. His sword rammed through her, burying all the way up to the hilt. Her blood spilled upon his hands as he snarled at her with bared teeth, his divine beauty now feral and ugly.

"I have always hated you, Calista," he seethed, and viciously, savagely twisted the blade, not yet knowing he had lost.

CHAPTER 56

CALISTA

Calista gasped, but not from the pain. Tears swelled in her eyes.

"Calista," she whispered. Her dagger fell from her limp hand, and with her other, she stroked Ashraleon's face. "You were always a damned fool."

Within those blue eyes she saw the specters of his children writhing in fury, for they knew. They knew, even when Ashraleon did not, for he was still lost in his fury and twisting his sword. He ripped it from her chest, but the wound meant nothing. She looked down and saw her own self, her own skin, and even amid the blood and carnage it was beautiful, so beautiful.

Her legs slumped. She lacked the strength to stand. The bones of her knees shattered upon hitting the carpet, as did her left wrist when she caught herself. The pain came from afar. She was breaking. As a creation, she could no longer exist. The god who had birthed her, who had decreed from the very beginning She be Nameless, had returned her name.

Ashraleon glared down at her. Blood from his cut brow trickled into the hollows of his left eye. There was no hint of Lucavi there. He was lost completely, wholly consumed by the first and true god of Everlorn.

"You lived in hiding for so long, and now you come to me just to die?" Ashraleon asked.

"I am free from you," Calista said. Her every word was a struggle, but she summoned the strength to say them. Her skin had begun to peel. Her legs were sinking into the carpet. "From your fate. From your hell. Let existence end, if it saves me from you."

He pointed his trembling sword at her, struggling to regain control. Over her. Over himself.

"You are not free," he said. "If the prayers of my church brought you forth once, then they can do so again. I will give name to the Nameless Whore. You will no longer be the temptress, but the tortured one. All of Gadir shall cry out your name, and know that you are alive and suffering at my hands. I will have my due, Calista, do you hear me?"

Calista felt like flower petals scattering upon the breeze. His words were air. She shook her head and looked aside, to the deep shadows of the curtains in the corner where the Vagrant hid. As her own power faded, she felt the stirring of the entity she had taken into her breast. It writhed in panic, so close to becoming whole, but the birthing was not yet complete. With one hand, she put her fingers to her throat. With her other, she reached to the sky and the swirling cloud of hate, fear, and loathing coalescing like a storm, visible only to eyes blessed by the divine.

"Yes, dear husband," she whispered. "You shall have your due, all three thousand years of it."

Calista pulled the storm into her, the divine power sundering a hole in the ceiling and raining stones upon the statues. She gasped, feeling the temptation to keep it all for herself. The seed within her bloomed, the entity feeding, but she could not be its host. She had walked this world for far too long. Let the Nameless Whore die, and Calista with her.

She withdrew the entity from within her, the roar of wind and hatred blistering in her ears, and gave it to the Vagrant. The entity, and all its power, flew across the room to strike the young man's forehead. He convulsed in place, his back arched and his eyes bulging behind the skull face that was no longer a mask.

"Become what you must," she whispered, her final words.

Her shell broke completely, and she shattered like stardust.

CHAPTER 57

VAGRANT

Lucavi was thoroughly enraptured by his former wife's arrival. Cyrus had to resist the impulse to ambush him with a blade to the back, but he trusted Nameless She to hold to her word and prepare the way. He slipped inside the room, the shadows curled about him keeping him safely hidden.

Calista, he thought, upon hearing the ancient woman's name. A good name, a beautiful name, and he clung to it as the God-Incarnate's sword tore through her. Rage would have him attack, but again he held faith in her. Even as her body broke, she radiated victory. Then came the surge of dark power, shattering the ceiling and whipping the curtains about as if Calista were the heart of a maelstrom. From within her breast she withdrew an orb of black so pure, so colorless, Cyrus thought his eyes were playing tricks on him.

And then she cast it his way.

Cyrus's body rocked backward, his jaw locked open in a silent scream, as it pierced his forehead and sank into his mind.

Who are you?

The voice echoed as all the world sank away to purest darkness. The storm cloud poured into him, and he learned its source.

For three thousand years, the Everlorn Empire had spread across Gadir. It had slain gods and subjugated millions. So very many were left adrift and hopeless. They were bitter and broken. Heads down and mouths shut, they lived amid the humiliation. They swallowed the shame. But they never stopped praying, even if they knew not to whom they prayed.

It was a wish. A hope. A desire.

Someone, anyone, must slay the God-Incarnate.

Those prayers flooded into Cyrus, and they were a thunderstorm compared to the gentle patter of rain that was his own prayers. Cyrus felt lost among them, his body tumbling in the center of a black tornado. A million words assaulted him simultaneously, indecipherable when presented in such a flood. His mind, still too human, threatened to crack. His heart could not endure such vicious hate and pain. He was falling. He was flying. The world was breaking.

Cyrus screamed and clutched at his head. Let the world break, but no, damn it all, no, he would not break with it. This burden, he would bear it, he would. Amid this maelstrom, there had to be an order, a reason, a way to…

Mari's voice pierced the veil.

I don't care who it is, I just want him dead.

Cyrus clung to the words and followed them like a moth toward a flame. The shadows lifted, and he saw the Ahlai sisters crossing a bronze desert, both looking much younger than they had when they arrived on Thanet. The sun beat down on them from high above. They were tired and broken. Lahareed. They fled their failure in Lahareed.

Do you think it's even possible? Stasia asked. Her face was covered with a thin scarf to protect against the light and heat, but it also hid the tears she shed. *It's hard enough to kill a paragon. Are we just wasting our time with this… this stupid war of ours?*

We've seen gods can die, Mari argued back. *So yes, even him. I only pray it happens in our lifetime, and that when it does, I get to see it.*

It was a thin prayer, a little droplet of faith placed into an entity with no form and no name, but there were a million such droplets forming together into an ocean. Cyrus swam among them, starting to grow comfortable with the flow. Names. Times. He could reach for them like threads.

Thorda knelt at the edge of a bed. Stasia and Mari were underneath the covers, fast asleep. They were younger now, so very young, yet Thorda himself looked unchanged. He bowed in prayer.

Fellow gods of Miquo, hear me, he said. *If our disparate strength is not enough, then grant me your power alone.*

As we did to Rhodes, and it was not enough, answered one.

Let it not be enough, I will still try! Someone must bring justice to the beastly god's head. We are infinite. We are majestic. There must be a god who can do what must be done, and if you all reject me, then let my prayers go to that god instead.

A prayer born of pain and rejection in the wake of Miquo's burning, and one he often repeated. It joined the flood. It added to the waves. Time had no meaning here amid prayer and memory. The darkness receded.

His passage through the tornado resumed anew, but this time it was slower, more controlled. Wisps of it lashed his eyes, granting him sight. Pieces of it flowed through his ears, granting voice to the prayers. They were many, so many.

A young girl at the grave of her parents, pounding the dirt with her fists.

A man staring at corpses swaying from the Dead Flags, his jaw locked tightly shut in fear of the nearby guards.

A soldier atop the walls of an unknown city, watching the armies of Everlorn approach with red banners held high.

Hope. Desperation. Hate. It merged and swayed, nameless, shapeless, seeking only an outcome. The death of the God-Incarnate. An end to the life that could not end.

A new image washed away the rest, guided by unseen hands. The walls were golden, the windows stained-glass amber and crimson. Lucavi knelt in the center of a grand cathedral, deep in prayer. That prayer ended with a sudden turn toward the ceiling. A cloaked and hooded assassin descended from above with sword in hand. That sword struck the left side of Lucavi's face, and though it scratched the faintest line of blood, it could drive no deeper.

The sword broke. The attacker fled. As Cyrus watched, the furious god howled for his paragons.

"Assassin! There is an assassin!"

Reality shifted, hardened. Cyrus felt more real, the swirling tornado calmer. Lucavi had gifted the presence a name, and a semblance of form, even though the deed had been committed by another. Rumors spread. Stories of an unknown assassin who had drawn blood from the immortal. To some, it was a far-fetched tale, and to others an unforgivable heresy. But to the rest? A dream almost fulfilled. Across an entire empire, thousands upon thousands heard and whispered the same shared prayer.

Whoever you were, they wished deep in their hearts, *please try again. Try, and succeed.*

Cyrus floated among those collected prayers, fully carried now. He was guided to another memory, one that shone so visibly it was a golden thread for Cyrus to reach out and touch.

He saw himself in the mud amid a thunderstorm, collapsed just shy of the gate to Thorda's countryside mansion. He knelt and beat his fists, his heart aching, his mind torn with fear and hate as he shouted, *I can't, I can't, I can't.*

Cyrus, wanting nothing more than vengeance. Cyrus, wanting nothing more than for someone else to take that burden.

"I am ready for it now," Cyrus said. The storm calmed. The shadows were all-encompassing. "I can bear this burden, if you will grant me your aid."

Within the emptiness the entity appeared, hovering before him, its own essence so much darker than the surrounding maelstrom. Its white eyes shone like stars. Its body was cloaked and limbless. It bore no mouth, but it spoke nonetheless.

End him.

Cyrus screamed as the power overwhelmed him completely. Divine essence blasted away the last of his mortal form. Bone and flesh? Unnecessary. He was no longer human. He wasn't even a meager god. He was a purpose. A concept. He was the Assassin, come for one who thought himself safe from every blade and arrow. Cyrus screamed and screamed, but oh how glorious that power felt despite the pain.

The darkness peeled away like a withdrawn curtain. Cyrus knelt in the royal chamber with his head bowed. Only a single heartbeat had passed within that ceremonial chamber. The God-Incarnate stood over Calista's body, blood dripping from his sword and the wound across his brow. He shouted out his protest, yet Cyrus realized his face looked not at all like Lucavi's, but another's.

"What are you?" asked Ashraleon.

Cyrus slowly stood. His cloak darkened to the deepest shade of black as it enveloped his body. His swords shimmered with pale light. He grinned, and the shifting of his jaw clacked bone against bone from the moving teeth.

"I am your death, come for you at last."

CHAPTER 58

ASSASSIN

God-Incarnate. Lucavi. Ashraleon. Whatever he was, he would not survive the night.

"Many have tried," Ashraleon said while lifting his sword. "Even gods stronger than you. They break beneath my blade. They cower before the might of my armies. You are nothing, Vagrant. Just another god to be forgotten as the epic of Everlorn marches on."

"It doesn't matter how many have tried," Cyrus said. "It doesn't matter how many have failed. We need to succeed only once."

He sprang forward with the slightest flex of his legs. The world felt light to him, time slow, gravity meaningless. Ashraleon's sword shifted, blocking one of the thrusts. The other thrust scraped across the God-Incarnate's cheek, bouncing off without drawing blood. It left an indent, though, faint but there. Cyrus pirouetted away with a flourish of his cloak.

"Just once," he said, and laughed.

Ashraleon dashed into him, aiming to overwhelm with speed and strength. Cyrus met him, fearlessly weaving side to side to avoid chops that smashed enormous cracks in the floor. His swords carved grooves into the God-Incarnate's platemail, each one proof of his slowness.

Cyrus ducked underneath a wide swing, twisted on his heels, and came up swinging with both his swords. They slashed across Ashraleon's arm, cutting the pauldron free. Ashraleon curled his weapon about, trying to punish Cyrus, but he danced away far too quickly for the counter.

"Too slow," Cyrus mocked. "Who is that sword meant to kill? A lumbering ox?"

"You think this my only blade?" Ashraleon asked. He spun his sword and then jammed it straight into the stone, lodging it in place. Swords, axes, and spears manifested around him in a surge of golden light. Twelve of them, their surfaces sparkling and translucent. Ashraleon ripped his physical sword free and held it at the ready as the twelve divine weapons took orbit about him, protecting the empire's ultimate manifestation of faith.

Despite the increased danger, Cyrus felt excitement pulse through him. There. There was the strength of Everlorn unleashed, and Cyrus was eager to match it. The world itself felt malleable to his desires. Ashraleon would die. He knew it like he knew the sun would rise in the east. Certainty guided his movements. He was shadow. He was murder. He was death.

"End it, the entity demands," he whispered. "So let us end it."

Ashraleon's legs braced. The thirteen weapons trembled. Cyrus grinned.

"No more words."

Half the divine weapons shot for him, faster than any arrow. Cyrus leaped into the air before they were halfway, his body contorting into a shape he more sensed than saw. An ax swung beneath him, a spear thrust above, but they hit only air. His feet touched ground but an instant before he was vaulting again, his entire body horizontal as he rolled over a tremendous wave of three golden swords.

His swords raked the God-Incarnate's chestplate, cutting the steel as if it were butter, yet still the edges bounced off the flesh underneath. The armor collapsed to the floor, exposing muscle of such definition Ashraleon looked like he'd been carved from stone. His physical sword cut upward, trying to slice Cyrus in half at the groin, but Cyrus's movements never slowed. He could never stop moving. He held speed over Ashraleon, and he would torment him with it until his last breath.

Cyrus vaulted overhead and smacked Ashraleon across the cheek with the flat edge of the Endarius sword for good measure, the divine weapons already racing for him. They came from every angle, trying to trap him, to overwhelm him. Let them. One after another, he parried and dodged the strikes, and as the darkness grew beneath him, he danced among the shadows. All the while, he heard voices in his mind, growing louder in their chorus.

Stasia, smashing through walled-off segments in distant Raklia.

Arn, his gauntlets painted with blood, fighting through the tight corridors of a wooden fort.

Commander Pilus, leading a portion of his army in a desperate bid to overtake a distant city.

Ashraleon's weapons fully surrounded Cyrus, and they struck as one to deny him a chance to parry. Those divine weapons might gleam with light, but Cyrus laughed as he dropped to his knees. Nothing, no torch, no sun, not even the sickly energy rolling off Ashraleon in waves, would stop his shadows. Darkness pooled beneath him, and he sank within it. The divine weapons struck empty stone. Cyrus fell from the ceiling, his body twisting, multiple slashes already in motion.

His swords cut twin grooves across the God-Incarnate's back. They did not bleed, but neither did the skin close over them to heal. More damaging were the faint shadows that peeled off Cyrus's blades and sank into Ashraleon. They were the counter to his divine light. They were the prayers of thousands, whispered in pain, in sorrow, in agony. They were the hope of death, and they seeped into the God-Incarnate like venom from a snake. Ashraleon howled, and the castle shook with his fury.

Cyrus shifted away, taking stance after stance taught to him in the summer heat by a shouting Thorda. Up and around, the sword of each hand moving of its own accord, its own independent thought, as the divine weapons beat down upon him. His off hand weaved left, right, deflected thrusts of two spears, while his right blocked an overhead chop of an ax. The strength of the hit should have broken the bones of his arm.

Nothing. He felt nothing.

Up and over he continued, and when the divine weapons tried to retaliate, he sank right down into Ashraleon's own shadow. In the darkness, he saw Thanese soldiers battling Everlorn troops in some distant village, one of a thousand contests this cursed night. A cask of wine lay overturned beside them. Their foreheads were marked with red paint, and their masks bore the Vagrant's grinning skull.

Cyrus emerged directly above, and he descended like a hawk. The moment Ashraleon blocked, Cyrus's entire body dissipated, bursting into shadow that coalesced into another dark corner. From the east wall, he attacked, his swords leading. Again, the moment their weapons connected, he reappeared, this time from the floor near the balcony. His Endarius blade chopped into exposed calves as more armor crumpled and littered the sacrificial chamber. Ashraleon pulled his weapons in tighter about him, trying to deny an opening.

Cyrus found them anyway. He ran along the wall, the pull of the world meaningless to him. Two spears broke from the defense, stabbing for him, missing every time. Momentum increasing, Cyrus vaulted with such power he crossed the entire room side to side even as his body twisted. Deception. Assassination. Every concept. Every trick. They were his to command.

One leap, from one side of the room to the other. One leap, yet afterimages of himself remained, nine hovering in the air with their swords ready. They descended upon Ashraleon, a hunting pack. The God-Incarnate's swords cleaved through them, scattering the illusions like ash, but he could not stop them all. They struck his exposed body, carving into him, breaking him. Cyrus felt himself in each one, a piece taken and then returned when Ashraleon's weapons scattered their essence.

Prayers empowered him further. Not just Thanet. All across Gadir, the hope of freedom still lived. Men burning temples and destroying prisons. Women whispering codes to smuggle wanted criminals beyond the reach of inquisitors. Worship in deep woods and distant pastures, attendees weeping and holding carved idols of slain gods. Even the smallest resistances kept the hope kindled. Those who refused to attend the six-hundred-year ceremonies. Those who closed their eyes and mouthed only emptiness during their forced attendance at the Uplifted churches.

Glass vials appeared in Cyrus's hand the moment he desired them, and he threw them by the dozens. Ashraleon crossed his arms, and they shattered upon his flesh, hissing with acid. A snap of Cyrus's fingers, and holes appeared in the walls, firing off dozens of poison-tipped darts. They broke against the God-Incarnate's skin, failing to puncture. The God-Incarnate howled his frustration, but Cyrus was already sinking into the floor. He reappeared at the entrance of the room with a burst of smoke. It billowed toward Ashraleon, black and sudden.

The God-Incarnate withdrew his divine blades, and with a whisper, they burst with sudden light. Ashraleon was trying to deny Cyrus his darkness. He was trying to banish the smoke and overwhelm it with the power of his divinity. Cyrus could see the prayers wafting into Ashraleon so clearly now. The power of millions, intermixed with the sacrifice of Thanet, twin streams of red and gold light pulsing from the skies above. But they were faith forced into a mortal shell. All gods could die.

All gods, no matter how loudly they denied their mortality.

Cyrus waved his arms, sending forth more smoke to hide his charge. Deft twists of his body and shifts of his legs avoided the panicked, blind assault of the divine weapons. Only twice did he have to block, and then he was close enough. Another leap, and he soared into the air. Not one of him. A dozen. Two dozen. They formed a full circle, weapons raised, blades hungry, and then hovered there for the briefest moment so Ashraleon might see his doom.

Down they fell. The divine weapons vanished, Ashraleon drawing all of his power into his flesh. It shimmered gold as he lifted his physical sword. Cyrus struck all at once, with all his pieces, his illusions, battering a weapon he knew down in his bones was Ahlai-made. He could see the faintest hint of divine power within the steel, power that now belonged to Stasia. It was nothing compared to his. Not when the desperation of the conquered united in one single prayer. Past and present, time meaningless to these prayers that had waited so long for a god to hear them. How many had died, sacrificed not to Everlorn, but to a hope of something greater?

Cyrus saw his friend, his mentor, Rayan Vayisa, standing strong before the Heir-Incarnate, even as a sword pierced his chest. He heard his words, defying the wound inflicted upon him. Cyrus heard, and felt rage fill him, felt a gathering not just of prayers and devotion of humans but of the gods themselves. Lycaena and Endarius, Rihim and Amees, Lorka and Puthora and Velgyn and Anyx and so many others, names unknown to him, but their fury real, their loss a bleeding wound on a continent stripped of beauty and grace.

Against that power, against the strike of a thousand shadows, the God-Incarnate's sword broke.

We will remember, swore a dying Rayan, his voice echoing through the realms of the divine.

Light surged from Ashraleon's skin as he screamed the name of his empire. It burned, and it was blinding. Cyrus rolled away, tried to sink into shadows, failed. Too much light. Anger filled Cyrus. To be denied, here and now? No, oh no. There was no denying this. He skidded to a halt and spun to face Ashraleon. Darkness crawled along the walls and ceiling. It squirmed and writhed, growing tentacles and claws. He was its master, and he gave it one pure demand: slay.

Feet like a bird of prey descended from the ceiling. Bladed tentacles lunged from the walls. Six-fingered hands clawed up from the ground. The golden light pulsed off Ashraleon in great waves, blasting into the shadows, threatening to unmake them, but it was not enough. They cut into his impossible flesh. They raked his body, relentless, showing no mercy.

They drew blood.

We will rise up.

Cyrus bid the shadows depart. He sheathed his shorter Lycaena blade and lifted the Endarius sword in both hands. Ashraleon stood tall, his face shifting, changing, becoming new faces, new men from ages past, before returning to Ashraleon's. Blood trickled in the thinnest of streams along his pale body. They stared; eyes met. Words passed unspoken between them. Promises. Challenges. Just as there were those who wished for Ashraleon's death, there were those who praised the guidance of Everlorn. They lived in opulence, cherishing the words of the Uplifted Church and the simplicity it brought. Those who knew only the comfort of victory and saw only value in superiority.

Year after year. However long it takes.

Ashraleon lifted his bare hands. A sword appeared within them, made of solid light. Cyrus readied his own, and within his mind, he felt the Assassin entity tremble with excitement. They charged each other, the exact same movements, the exact same swing. Their weapons crashed overhead. The world about Cyrus shifted, becoming surreal. Every image, every prayer, flooded him until the present world faded away.

I will walk that path, and I will not walk it alone.

Cyrus was in a forest. He was in a city. He stood upon a cliff. He was half submerged beneath a river. Unseen. Listening. Hearing the screams of the furious as they buried loved ones, hid treasured relics of gods, and lamented the coming age of Everlorn. A thousand faces. Ten thousand dead. A hundred thousand prayers. Year after year, pooling, collecting, denied answer, denied vengeance.

Ashraleon wielded divine golden light, yet when it hit that shimmering black blade, it shattered. Cyrus struck the God-Incarnate in the chest. The tip touched flesh, pushed, pierced, sliding in deeper, deeper, its surface lacking all color and texture. It was purest darkness, and Cyrus channeled every shred of the power flowing through him into that blade. The God-Incarnate was believed invincible by hundreds of thousands, and to deny them, Cyrus offered broken, desperate prayers for death. He gave Ashraleon the weeping, the pain, the loss of nations, gods, and identities. Let the golden light meet a shadow so furious, so angry, nothing could hold it back.

The rage of millions, stretching on for thousands of years, come together into one single blow.

The sword pierced flesh that knew no weakness.

The sword tore into a heart that beat everlasting.

The sword ended the life that could not end.

Power exploded out of the God-Incarnate as his mortal shell broke. Though Cyrus had seen similar when Endarius and Lycaena died, this went far beyond that. This was a golden aura rolling outward, smashing furniture, cracking walls, and shattering the statues meant to honor his lineage. It washed over Cyrus like lava. He felt its heat seep into him, felt its power turning his bones to mush.

I have done all I was meant to do, whispered the entity within him. *Let go, and live.*

And so Cyrus relented. Shadows burned across the surface of his body, meeting the golden light. They crackled and burst with sparks, counteracting one another, defusing the power that should have obliterated Cyrus no matter his godly state. The otherworldly strength that had guided him faded away. His perception of time quickened. The roar of Ashraleon's death rattle faded, as did his power, leaving Cyrus alone in shocking silence.

Cyrus gasped in a ragged breath. He was, while not human, at least back to what he had been as the Vagrant. It hurt, adjusting to the change, but let it hurt. Let it take years, if it must. A smile spread across his face. Ashraleon was dead. The God-Incarnate of Everlorn, slain at last.

"We won," he whispered, hardly able to believe it. Again, louder, and laughing. "We won!"

He saw the spear before he felt the pain. It pierced through his chest to emerge soaked in crimson, embedded halfway up the hilt in his rib cage. His jaw locked, and his knees buckled, unable to support his weight. When he landed, Soma stood over him, a beautiful smile upon his face.

"Well done, Cyrus. You played your role to perfection."

CHAPTER 59

VAGRANT

Cyrus gasped as he lay on his side, the spear sticking out of his chest, its tip resting against the floor to keep him propped up. He clutched its blood-slick shaft and struggled for breath.

"Why?" he asked. "Your god... he's dead."

Soma stood over him, resplendent in his blue armor. His smile was false. The disgust in his eyes, though, burned true.

"He was never my god. But all this divine energy?"

Soma stepped into the storm of golden light that remained even after the God-Incarnate's death. The paragon lifted his arms, tilted his head, and then breathed it in as if it were smoke. He laughed. The man sounded giddy.

"The faith of millions," he said. "Stolen. Caged in an unworthy host. Can you not feel it, Vagrant? If you had been willing, if you had understood, you could have taken it for yourself."

But Cyrus couldn't have. They had been polar opposites in all things, a desire to live meeting a desire to kill, the skulking dark and the gleaming light counteracting each other. It had burned through so much of Cyrus's strength and left him exhausted and hollow.

And into that hollowness, that bastard had thrust a spear.

The golden light paled as it settled into Soma. He stood taller, his skin seeming to glow with new strength. He laughed again and clapped, the sound grating in Cyrus's ears. If only he had been more aware. With the God-Incarnate slain, he'd thought...he'd thought the war over. The battle was won.

Soma exhaled slowly, the last of the divine essence either absorbed or dissipated.

"What a feeling," he said. "It won't last, but it will be enough for now. Enough to reclaim what is rightfully mine."

His every action hurt, but Cyrus had to know, and he forced out the words. "I don't...understand."

Soma turned Cyrus's way, and his face stretched into a horrifying grin.

"I suppose it would be cruel to let you die in ignorance."

The paragon walked toward one of the paintings gracing the walls. It was of King Tolbert fighting during the War of Tides. Soldiers lined the sands at the shores of Gallos Bay to do battle with Dagon. The serpentine god writhed on the sand, impaled by a spear. This was the war's final battle, and Endarius's great victory.

"To have you lie before me, dying from a spear?" he said, touching the scaly, monstrous depiction of Dagon. "I must admit, the invisible laws of fate have a penchant for irony."

Soma turned, and the flesh of his face peeled away. Cyrus looked to the gleaming sapphire scales underneath, then the spear piercing his body, and knew. He knew, and could not hide his horror.

Every part of him throbbed with agony, but he could not remain silent.

"The disguise," he said. "Sinshei. The empire. Why?"

Soma's hair crystallized as he crossed the room. His armor fell from him, the clasps coming undone as if of their own accord. Beneath lay shining scales of deep blue. The ugly image upon that painting could not be further from the truth. Soma was majestic in his beauty, graceful in his movements, and stunning in the glow of his divinity. He knelt before Cyrus and pressed a casual finger on the tip of the spear, grinding it against Cyrus's innards.

"I failed in my first attempt to kill the God-Incarnate. My hope for a second was to strike after Lucavi had slit his own throat but before the divine strength fully took hold in Sinshei. My own plan faltered, but thankfully you performed beautifully. That the bloodline of the Lythan invaders would give up their life to restore me to my proper place? Well. It has a poetic justice to it, wouldn't you agree?"

Cyrus dug shaking fingers into the stone. There was no need for this betrayal. He'd have knelt before Dagon and pleaded for forgiveness for all his family's crimes. It felt so cruel, so unnecessary.

"We . . . we could have . . . worked . . . together," he gasped. Blood pooled underneath him, sticky and foul.

"No," Soma said. "I warned you, did I not? You cannot be Thanet's savior. Besides, you would never agree, not while this controlled you."

Soma reached toward one of his discarded armor parts, grabbing a small brown pouch attached to its side. From within, he retrieved Cyrus's discarded mask, the one first carved for Rhodes. It seemed the sea had not claimed it after all.

"I must thank you for all your work in building the Vagrant legend," Soma said. He held the mask up to his face. "A legend I may now use for myself. Whispers say the slain prince is the returned warrior, but what if that was only a disguise? What if the real hero was not a prince, but a god?"

The theft burned Cyrus's insides almost as badly as the spear.

"You would . . . take . . . all I . . ."

"All you've done?" Soma asked. "Yes. Just as your family took everything from me, I will take everything from you. I will take faith in the Vagrant and mix it with the lingering faith of my followers. The forgotten, betrayed god shall return as a savior. I will rebuild faith on Thanet, but I will not stop here. Not after I have walked the lands of Gadir. Not after I have seen what I have seen."

Soma knelt closer. His hands cupped Cyrus's head to force their gazes to meet. The scales of his fingers and palms were as soft as feathers.

"In the chaos that follows, I will arrive upon Gadir with my faithful and declare myself the slayer of the God-Incarnate. I will be the savior, not just to Thanet, but to millions of people in conquered nations across that enormous expanse. I will build a new faith in the shadow of the old and take Everlorn as my own."

So much blood lost. So much pain.

"You. Monster."

Soma stroked his cheek. His eyes, bluer than any ocean, widened.

"I learned so much on Gadir as I lived hidden among humans and slew their gods. The wisdom of Eldrid is not wrong. Humanity does need to serve under one throne, speak one tongue, and worship one god. The crime of Everlorn was not their goal, but that their worship was tainted and impure. They elevated a mere human. I will unite all of Gadir underneath a true god. That is my dream, Cyrus, my sapphire dream that has carried me through four centuries of exile."

He slid the mask over his face, then removed Cyrus's cloak and slid it over his shoulders, hiding his scales until it was time for the reveal. Last, he took up Cyrus's discarded swords.

"For all you have done, consider your sins against me forgiven, Cyrus Lythan. When the tale of my ascension is retold, it will be my hand that slew Lucavi. You will be forgotten by the world and remembered by me alone. Consider it an honor."

Thanet's god of the sea approached the balcony, and with one foot on the banister, he turned.

"I leave you to die impaled, just as your forefathers left me. If you can, listen to how easily the crowd turns from you, and know how fickle your race truly is."

Soma clanged the stolen swords together, pulled his cloak tight, and then leaped out of the balcony to the crowd below. Cyrus watched him, furious, impotent, his blood pooling beneath him. All he had ever done was about to be stolen, and by a mad god, no less. If only... if only...

"Well, this is certainly a mess."

Keles knelt beside him, her hands on the spear. Hearing her voice, Cyrus felt ready to cry, it was so beautiful.

"Soma," he gasped. "Soma is... Dagon."

"Interesting," she said, and shoved the rest of the spear through his body without warning. He howled at the pain and then collapsed onto his back. Darkness clawed at his sight, but Keles's face hovered within the center of his remaining vision.

"Hold fast, Vagrant," she said. "You're strong enough, I know it, so don't prove me wrong now."

Her hands settled over his gaping wound. Her eyes closed. Prayer flowed off her lips.

"Lycaena, grant me succor. Grant me healing. Mend the body. Make new this torn flesh and broken bone."

Healing warmth flowed through Cyrus. The agony within his chest abated. The bleeding ceased. The crowd beyond was a muted roar, and Keles's prayer all that mattered. He wished to thank her, to explain how he had both succeeded and failed, and how it all meant nothing if Soma stole that victory.

"Can you stand?" she asked when she finished.

"More than stand," Cyrus said. He lurched to his feet and tested the wound. Sealed, scarred flesh. It still hurt, but he could handle hurt. There was no time. He would have to trust the divine nature of what he had become. "I can kill."

"But your swords..."

Cyrus staggered to where Calista had been slain. Nothing remained of her body, but the same could not be said for her knife. He lifted it, found its grip comfortable. Next was the spear, still soaked in blood and lying where Cyrus had nearly died. He picked it up and tested its weight.

"I have all I need," he said.

He found Keles leaning on the banister, watching the display below.

"What is happening here?" she asked.

"He's claiming to be the Vagrant," Cyrus said, joining her. Sure enough, Soma was in the center of the crowd, and he'd already cast aside his cloak to reveal his scales and removed the skull mask to hold it in one hand. Whispers and shouts accompanied him, Dagon and Vagrant becoming one in the people's minds. They were so few, but already Cyrus felt a draining within his chest, like a boat that had sprung the tiniest leak.

"But why?" Keles asked.

"He wants to replace the God-Incarnate and rule humanity in his stead," Cyrus said. He lifted the spear. "I won't allow it. Time to repeat history."

With one clean motion, he reared back, rooted his feet, and flung the spear straight through Soma's back. The tip ripped out his chest and struck the cobbles of the tiled pathway below. Screams sounded throughout the crowd, but this was only the start of the violence.

"Down we go," he said as he held out a hand for Keles. No need to retreat for shadows. The shadows came to him, enveloping them. Within the blink of an eye they reemerged in the heart of the crowd, not far from where Soma bled. Gasps accompanied their arrival.

Cyrus glared at the crowd, at the people already willing to throw their faith off from Thanet's prince to the forgotten god of old.

"The Vagrant is among you," he shouted to them. "And it is no scaled monster."

Soma snapped the spear in half and pulled it from his body. His wounds immediately closed with a flash of golden light horribly reminiscent of Lucavi's power.

"Ignore this impostor," the god bellowed. "I am the one who saved you from the empire."

Soma had Cyrus's swords, cloak, and painted mask. So much evidence, but he lacked one crucial thing. Soma might have Cyrus's mask, but he did not have his face.

Cyrus spun, letting all look upon him, as he lifted Calista's knife. Already he felt his forehead hardening, the skin there bulging. The dark voice whispered eagerly in his mind.

If you would seek victory, give me everything, Cyrus. No more hesitation. No more fear.

"You would seek your Vagrant?" he asked them. He pressed the knife to his jaw and slashed, carving a line toward his forehead.

The last of your humanity.

A second slice along the opposite side, loosening the folds of his skin. The knife cut easily, its edge sharper than even an Ahlai-made blade.

Cast it aside.

One last cut across his forehead, but the knife was hardly needed. The jagged edges of his crown were already pressing through the flesh.

Reveal your true face.

Cyrus ripped free his mortal flesh. His lips, his cheeks, his nostrils and eyebrows: They all peeled like a scab from a wound. Blood flowed with them, coating the grinning skull underneath and dripping from the five-pointed crown of silver that rested across his forehead.

The teeth parted. There was no tongue behind them that Cyrus could feel, but he spoke nonetheless.

"I am Thanet's Vagrant," he said, and pointed at Soma. "And I shall have my crown."

Soma readied the two blades Thorda had gifted Cyrus so very long ago. Though divine strength radiated off the god in golden waves, his bluster was false and the fear in his eyes far too real.

"With what weapons, impostor?" he bluffed.

Everything, the dark voice screamed within Cyrus's mind. *Give me everything. Accept what you are, accept* me, *and know.*

Beyond all limits. Beyond humanity. Cyrus gave it, gave everything. Thanet's god of death needed no steel. He cared not for weapons crafted by a foreign blacksmith.

Cyrus opened his hands, and he screamed as bones tore through his palms. They stretched and grew, ripping flesh and spilling blood. With his own body, he would slaughter any and all invaders. The last of the swords pushed through, and Cyrus clutched them tightly within his fingers, these blades of bone, curved and filed to match those he once wielded.

"My face, and my blades," Vagrant told Soma. "Who here can deny me now?"

He didn't need Keles's help. He didn't need anything but the prayers and adoration of the crowd. The God-Incarnate of Everlorn had bled out before him. What was Dagon but a vulture feasting on the carcasses of others? Weak faith. Scattered followers. Those who fought across Thanet wore bloody crowns, not sapphire scales.

"You boast moments before the slaughter," Soma said, crossing his stolen swords before him. Stolen, like all else he had taken these past centuries. "My dream cannot die."

Vagrant grinned a skull's grin. The pain in his chest felt far, far away.

"All may die," he said. "Dreams. Nations. Even gods."

The people fled as he crossed the space between them. Their weapons collided, bone meeting Ahlai-made steel.

Soma's swords bent inward, and his feet staggered unevenly.

"I am Thanet's true god," Soma insisted, even as Vagrant tore into him. Their swords looped and crashed. Twice Soma's entire body flared with light, the god crying out as he drew upon his divine power. Both times, Vagrant weathered the assault with ease, and after the second, he parried a dual thrust and then countered with his left-hand sword. The cut opened a thin line along Soma's arm, and from it dripped blue blood intermixed with golden light. The god hissed and withdrew.

"You feel it, don't you?" Vagrant asked as he maintained the offensive. "Their faith isn't in you. It seeks a future you cannot give. The power of Eldrid rejects you, Soma. The prayers loathe you. The golden light would see you burned and slaughtered like all other heathen gods."

"No," Soma shouted. He lunged at Vagrant and was batted aside with ease. Vagrant needed no tricks here. The damned fool had poisoned himself without ever realizing it. What faith he had was weak, and it could do nothing to counter the hate of Eldrid.

Pitiable, if Vagrant were in the mood to offer mercy.

Again their weapons crossed, and again it was Soma who faltered. Vagrant pushed on, batting away parry after parry. Nothing would stop him. Nothing *could* stop him. One sword tore through Soma's thigh; the other sliced across his rib cage, cracking bone. Golden light leaked out of him in torrents. Perhaps Soma had denied it throughout his exile, but upon his return, he was everything Thanet believed him to be. He was a trickster come bearing a false face. He was a coward who stabbed his enemies through the back. He was a thief, wielding Vagrant's swords and clinging to the broken essence of Everlorn's slain god. Over the bodies of the Lion and the Butterfly, the Serpent would try to claim a throne.

He was not mighty. He was not majestic.

Vagrant beat down Soma's uplifted swords, hammering into him, cowing him, breaking him. Striking, striking, until the Ahlai steel shattered in half. Soma screamed as the shards flew, digging into his body. Vagrant's swords continued, puncturing his chest to pierce his lungs. Harder. Deeper. Deny him breath, deny him voice. Thanet needed no final words from the deceitful god that had abandoned it.

"I uphold the legacy of my forefathers," he told this wretched creation once known as Dagon. "Begone from my island."

Vagrant tore his swords free to either side, opening Soma in half at the chest. The god died without a sound. The stolen power of Everlorn flowed out of him, and Vagrant closed his eyes and breathed it in. At last, Thanet was free. Free from distant empires. Free from the chains of the past and the gods of old.

But the scar of what had happened here tonight would forever run deep.

Vagrant retrieved his stolen cloak, a savage need striking him in the chest as it settled over his shoulders. His people were suffering. They must be attended. Healed, with guidance of the strong. United, to protect the weak. This tragedy must never be repeated.

Vagrant glanced about the crowd. Faith rolled off them in thick waves. Adoration and fear, mixed together with their relief. He gave them a smile of bone. Slowly, carefully, while they all watched, he cut a bloody crown upon Dagon's corpse.

"It is done," he told them. "At long last, Everlorn is excised, and your king returned."

Some wept. Others bowed. Vagrant crossed his swords of bone above his head, and he wondered why he ever felt satisfied with mere blades of steel. Ahlai-made they may have been, but they did not convey the gravity of his presence, nor the power he wielded. If only he had been stronger, and slain Thanet's foes when they first arrived upon his island.

He'd been weak. He'd been human. And for such failures, thousands died. He heard their death rattles in his mind, little needles incessantly stabbing. Raklia. North Cape. The wide plaza of Red Glade. The rivers of Thiva, now choked with corpses. It must not be repeated. It must not.

Weariness swept over him, and he let his shoulders sag. His hood fell low over his grinning skull. So much done, yet so much left to do, and all in the shadow of horror committed in Everlorn's name. But such was the path before him, and he would walk it.

The doors were open into the castle, and beyond, he saw his throne. It called to him, and he allowed himself to fully, truly smile.

"Mother, Father," he whispered. "I've avenged you at last."

He approached the grand doors, but a small seed of doubt wormed its way into his heart. No, this tragedy could not be repeated, but was the might of Thanet enough? Even with the God-Incarnate slain, the vast infrastructure of empire remained. Magistrates still had their churches. Regents still lorded over their territories. The hundreds of thousands of soldiers within the Legion would not suddenly lay down their arms. Wars would follow. The future was so uncertain.

The bone blades shook in Vagrant's hands. What terror might emerge from the chaos? What if... what if the God-Incarnate returned, just as Eshiel had summoned forth a darker version of Lycaena?

No. It could not be allowed. It had to be stopped.

Vagrant looked upon his throne and knew it was not enough. To let Everlorn rot was far too kind a fate. It had to be broken, its magistrates beheaded, its paragons slain. He felt the call of Soma's sapphire dream, of boats full of missionaries come to spread the word of the God-Incarnate's fate and give name to the one who slew him.

Another step toward the castle, the burden on his shoulders so heavy, so very heavy. His killing was not at its end. Far from it. Faith in him needed to remain, perhaps grow even stronger. He would sail across the Crystal Sea. He would arrive in Gadir and proclaim to the world he was the death of Everlorn. Anyone who cherished its memory would be put to the sword. Anyone who sought the God-Incarnate's return would face his grinning skull and know their doom. He would shatter it, all of it, shatter and smash and break until the world was put into its proper place.

Another step, but then a woman blocked his way.

"The war is over," Keles said. He noted she held her sword and shield at the ready. "We have no need of your mask."

"It is no mask."

He stepped closer, but she refused to move.

"You relinquished your throne," she said, as if she could read his mind. "You promised that the blood of the Orani would reign again, did you not?"

Vagrant stared at the paladin, remembered his promises, and realized what a fool he had been. Keles was skilled, yes, but could she protect Thanet from Everlorn reborn? What happened if the empire endured until a new God-Incarnate emerged? That deity would surely return to Thanet, and he would avenge his death with a slaughter that left not a soul on the island alive.

"You're not strong enough," Vagrant said. "There is still so much to be done. Make way."

She lifted her sword. Her deep brown eyes bored into his.

"A god on a throne," Keles said. "We know where this leads."

Did she? Perhaps she thought she did. But Keles's mind was ever on her own faith, and the fragile love of the Butterfly. The Vagrant knew the truth. When the fate of Thanet lay on the line, it was the sword that had protected them.

"Step aside," Vagrant ordered. "Do not make me do this, Keles. Step aside, and make way for your king."

The paladin lowered her weapons. She tilted her chin, and she stood before him in all her regal beauty.

"I will not move," she said. "Not for you. Not for all the world."

Vagrant cut her throat open. He felt the resistance of her flesh against his bone blade, and it was meager. For the briefest moment, he saw the shock in her eyes, the disbelief. For the briefest moment, he dared let himself feel it, too, but then the call of the throne buried it down deep. This was it. This was the final step to become who he must. Of course it hurt. Of course it ached. The righteous path often did.

"I am sorry, Keles," he said as her body crumpled before him. "But if I must choose between your life and the life of my people, then it is no choice at all."

He was the Vagrant. He was death to all who would threaten Thanet, and if Keles were to challenge him? To deny his blood and crown? Then she, too, was a threat. She would let Thanet become weak and complacent, let her people think peace could be had when the work of tyrants continued afar.

Vagrant stepped over her body on the way to his throne, but it seemed peace would not yet be his.

"Vagrant!" screamed a familiar voice. "Is this how you would begin your reign?"

Vagrant turned, and he narrowed his eyes. Eshiel Dymling stood on a parapet overlooking the crowd. He wielded a staff in hand, his weight braced against it. He was bare-chested, his shirt cast aside to reveal his many scars and tattoos. Where ink should have been was instead fire, yet it paled compared to the rage in his voice.

"Long did I witness your betrayal in my nightmares," he shouted. "Long did I pray it was false. Yet there is no greater truth than the blood you have spilled. It cannot stand!"

First the God-Incarnate, then Soma, and now Eshiel? Vagrant felt deeply tired. Was the world determined to burden him so?

"Must I slay you also if I am to have peace?" he asked.

Eshiel stood to his full height and raised his staff.

"Those faithful to the true god of Thanet, lift your voices," he cried. "Let her hear your fury!"

A dozen men and women within the crowd cast off their robes and cloaks to reveal the colors of Lycaena. They raised their palms to the sky, and they sang out a wordless chant. Tattoos covered their skin, and they glowed like embers. Wind swept through the courtyard, and it carried the aura of the divine.

"Goddess of our land, heed our prayer!" Eshiel screamed. He slammed his staff to the stone. The castle shook from the impact. "Give us back our queen!"

Fire burst out around Keles's corpse. Her body lifted into the air, righting itself as blinding white light seared across her throat. The blood on her armor charred away, as did the blackened plate, until it returned to the pure white of a Lycaenean paladin. Her cloak split in half, becoming wings that curled around her, sparkling a rainbow of color that shifted and changed with her every movement. The fire grew higher, swirling into her flesh, her hands, her hair, flowing down into her drawn blade. There it seethed, frightening in its power.

Her feet touched the stone. Her eyes shimmered crimson and gold. The crowd gasped and wept.

Eshiel collapsed upon the parapet. His whisper was a thunderclap in the shocked silence.

"Save us, Lycaena, from our own vengeance."

Vagrant lowered his stance and readied his bone swords. Keles pointed her own blade, meeting his challenge.

"Vagrant," she said, her voice thunderous and deep. "I come to claim my due."

CHAPTER 60

LYCAENA

The air shimmered gold in intangible waves fused with crimson and sapphire threads. The world of faith and divinity was fully opened to Keles's eyes, and she saw the ghostly remnants of the fallen God-Incarnate as well as the slain Dagon. Within this color, burning an impenetrable black, lurked the fully realized Vagrant. Her throat itched, and she knew she should be furious.

Instead, she felt only sorrow.

"You have done so much good," she said. "And you could do so much more. Yet you covet a throne. You seek conquest. Is your power not enough, Vagrant? Will godhood not suffice?"

The crowd within the courtyard had fled to the farthest reaches within the walls. The twelve who had prayed for her were the only ones to remain kneeling. High above, she sensed more than saw Eshiel atop the parapet, having collapsed from the exertion of changing her.

Resurrecting her, from a death most wretched.

"I seek to protect Thanet," Vagrant said. His deep voice rolled over her, meant to sound like death itself, but not to her. Death was a kind place, full of emerald fields and the songs of loved ones. His voice was suffering and pain.

"And will you protect it from me?" she asked.

Vagrant crouched low, his bone swords pulling back for attack.

"Who speaks? The paladin, or the goddess?"

Keles lifted her shield. She knew the answer, even if she would not give it. Never had she felt so close to Lycaena, not even when the goddess had comforted her after her uncle's death. An aura of fire washed over her, and whether it was real flame or a divine illusion she did not know. When she spoke, it felt as if another whispered in her mind, giving words for her tongue to speak.

"She who loves our people most."

"Love." Vagrant tensed, and Keles tensed in return. "You would speak of love?"

He lashed out with incredible speed, his body twirling end over end to add power to his slashes. The bone blades came together right before impact, striking Keles's raised shield. She felt the impact travel through her, but her feet held firm. Lycaena was with her. Lycaena had become her.

"I would," she said, shoving him away. "It is always what has guided me."

"Then, where were you when our people suffered?" Vagrant raged at her. He dashed into another attack, hammering away at her with his swords. "Where were you when they hung your beloved from the Dead Flags? You were weak. You were absent. You failed, and yet you would condemn *me*? I gave them hope, when your death bred despair."

Keles absorbed the first two hits on her shield, leaped over a sweeping kick meant to knock her off-balance, and then slashed to force him to block.

"And what hope would you give the people now? A hope of vengeance? A hope for cruelty returned? You took your throne over my corpse!"

At the mention of her murder, he hesitated, and Keles gave him no reprieve. She tore into him, her burning blade slicing through the air with speed to rival his own. Showers of sparks rained down upon the cobbles with every meeting of their weapons.

"Even as my body was slain, I offered my love," Keles said, the words flowing so easily from her tongue. "Even as Everlorn washed away our symbols and denied our prayers, I gave comfort to those who sought it. I was a promise for something better, a remembrance of a beautiful time. I wiped away tears with the gentlest touch of my wings. But you?"

Keles slammed her sword down upon him. His bone swords crossed and met it, trying to deny her strength. His legs quivered, and his feet slipped backward.

"You offer our people nothing for their faith," she shouted at him. "It is built only on vengeance. You give no peace. You know no love. You plant no gardens, sow no beauty, and what hearts you lift up are tainted with poison. You are a hunger, Vagrant, and you will never be sated if your sole desire is the conquest of your enemies."

"I am what our people need!" he howled. "I am the fury desired. I am the bloodshed craved. Everlorn must suffer. Its people, its conquerors, its soldiers and priests and followers must die, and let my hand wield the killing blade if all else lack the strength!"

Keles kicked off her braced legs, surprising him with the reversal. Her shield bashed into his body, and he screamed as its light arced across him like lightning. He rolled, flipped backward, and landed in a splay of shadow.

"Our people needed a protector," she said. "They needed a defender. But what you are now? They need not at all."

Vagrant sank into the shadow up to his waist. Circles of darkness burst around Keles, and from within emerged four tentacles that sharpened into jagged blades, slashing for her legs and waist. Keles cut one, then lifted her shield and cried out the name of her goddess. Light flared from its surface, banishing the darkness.

"They needed to be saved, and I saved them!" Vagrant shouted. He dropped fully into the dark. Little holes of shadow opened around her, along the ground, the castle wall, even atop the parapet. Two dozen Vagrants reemerged, their movements perfectly synchronized. He readied for a leap, his weapons hungry.

"I'm sorry, Vagrant," Keles said. "I have failed my people too many times before. I will not fail them now. Thanet cannot be yours. The killing blade must serve or be cast aside. Never reign."

"Then take it," the multitude of Vagrants whispered. "If you possess the strength."

Vagrant leaped at her from all sides, all heights. Were they real? Were they illusions, with only one true enemy? She didn't know, and to gamble was to lose. Keles let them come. She let them dive at her, their bone blades thrusting and slashing. Let the Vagrant trust his tricks and his speed.

She would trust her goddess.

Keles dropped to her knees, bowed her head, and crossed her sword and shield. Her cloak curled around her, hardening into colored crystal. In less than the blink of an eye she was wrapped fully in a crystalline cocoon, and it was so bright, so beautiful. Light sparkled through its surface, and she felt it on her skin like a loving touch.

Then came the shadow. Vagrant relentlessly assaulted the cocoon. Bone blades snapped against its surface. Keles felt the cocoon shudder, the attack instant and vicious, but not enough.

"No more shadows," she whispered. The cocoon shattered, its shards exploding outward in a violent display. The many Vagrants shattered with it, their forms melting into shadow as the pieces ripped through their bodies. Only one withstood the barrage. Keles charged into him, blinding him with the light of her shield. He howled even as he weaved his swords into a defensive pattern. His control was gone. His bloodlust was supreme. Perhaps it had always been this way, except Cyrus had held its worst impulses at bay.

Keles pushed him back with her every swing, her every blow. Vagrant retreated, out from the courtyard and into the castle. Keles followed him into the throne room, the light of her wings flaring bright and his shadow withering against it. When he tried to force her away, she punished him with a strike of her burning blade, slicing open the shadow that was his chest. More blood spilled, dark and oily. She trusted her armor to hold fast against his frantic counter, the bone striking off her pauldron instead of cutting down into her collarbone. In payment, she smashed her shield into his face, pivoted, and cut across his shoulder.

More blood. Another scream of pain. Vagrant leaped at her, nothing more than a savage animal. Keles held firm, letting the motions of her sword and shield flow. All the while, Vagrant screamed his impotent rage.

"I am our protector! I am our savior! It won't happen, never again, do you hear me? We won't watch it all again. *I* won't watch it again. The beheadings. The flags. The boats, burning, no more burning, no more burning..."

I'm sorry, Cyrus, Keles thought as her opponent's movements slowed. *But it must be done.*

He thrust at her waist, and in response, Keles lifted her shield. Lycaena sensed her prayer, her desire, and made it real. Her goddess was beauty. Her goddess was fire. Both billowed off her shield, becoming whole. A single creation flowed into being, a phantom caravel composed of purest flame. It sailed out from her shield as if it were a portal from a nightmare world, rapidly growing in size.

Vagrant saw this image and froze. His white eyes widened, and she could see the fear in them, could feel the scar on his psyche just moments before the ship washed over him. Vagrant screamed as fire burned across his entire essence. It torched his cloak. It licked away at what should have been flesh. It blackened his skull and blades. The pain must have been tremendous, for he stood rigid, his weapons at his sides and his head tilted back. Just screaming. Screaming.

Keles withdrew her shield, flipped her stance, and then plunged her sword directly into Vagrant's chest. The shadow retreated at its presence. More blood like oil. The bone weapons fell from limp hands. Vagrant's knees buckled. He collapsed onto his back, gasping and wheezing mere feet away from the throne he so desperately desired.

Keles stood over the beaten, broken shadow that had once been Cyrus Lythan. The skull no longer grinned at her. It seethed. It coughed blood. The tip of her sword tucked underneath his chin, lifting his head to meet her gaze. He did so without flinching.

"Do it," he said. "I am not afraid to die."

"No," she said. "I think you are afraid of something more."

She knelt down, careful to keep her sword in place. He was a wounded animal, and even weaponless, he was exceedingly dangerous. She had to trust the strength of her gaze and the pull of her will. She had to trust Cyrus was in there somewhere, listening.

Keles's voice softened, and she felt the acceptance of the Butterfly for what she was about to do. This hope might be futile, but she must try, if only so this horrid, blood-soaked night might have a less wretched end.

"There was once a kind young man who spent his nights reading in the library," she said. "One who was scared of crowds, and who barely knew how to dance. Sleep came to him rarely, and when it did, he dreamed of his parents, and their loss. This man cherished his friends above all else. This man wanted nothing of the power you now possess, and sought only to help those he loved."

She knelt closer, able to see the way the skull mask was bathed in shadow so no skin was visible anywhere else upon his face. His eyes vibrated, with no flesh or pupils to widen, and no tears able to be shed.

"That man is still in there," she said. "I trust in him. I believe in him. He is wounded, broken, and afraid, but he is alive."

Vagrant's teeth rattled. His arms trembled. He spoke no words. Perhaps he couldn't, given his obvious struggle. So close, Keles sensed, so very close. She lowered her sword and shield. Though he flinched, she put her fingers to his face and ignored the sickening feeling of bone against her skin.

"You offered me hope when I would have accepted death. You vowed to protect those you loved, no matter the cost. You knelt and called me your queen, because you knew who you are, and who you are becoming, was ever within your control."

She lifted her neck so that he could see the fresh scar across her throat.

"Remember who you were, and look upon what you are now. See, Cyrus Lythan. See, and then *choose*."

It built slowly within Vagrant. At first, it was but the faintest buzz, like the passing of an insect, but then it grew, and grew, until the thunderous power shook the walls of the castle.

Vagrant, screaming.

He thrashed away from Keles's touch. He curled onto his knees, his stomach hitching as if he were about to vomit. On and on, this scream continued, deep and furious. The people in the crowd beyond shouted in fright and confusion. Only Keles remained still, watching, judging, her sword within reach if it must come to that.

The thrashing ceased. Vagrant knelt before Keles, his hands pawing at the sides of his skull mask. His fingers curled underneath the bone, digging deep, spilling blood, and then they pulled. The shadows clung to the bone like tearing flesh. The scream heightened, composed of not just fury but excruciating pain. The fingers slipped in deeper. Keles shuddered. She could *hear* the tearing of skin and cracking of bone.

Vagrant doubled over again, but despite the torment, he did not succumb. The shadows refused to relent as he pulled away the skull, and they stretched out several feet like loosed veins. Dark blood flowed down his neck. His eyes were impossible to see. Amid the scream, Keles heard new voices, new sounds.

The castle was gone. All around her, boats burned. Men and women burned with them. At the helm of the nearest stood Cleon and Berniss Lythan, their faces charred black from the flame. They wept as Vagrant screamed at them.

"I am mortal!"

Shadows pooled underneath him, mixing with the blood. His fingers cracked at the joints, the skin turning purple.

"I am human!"

The boats faded one by one, becoming ash and dust.

"I am no god!"

The skull tore free, and the shadows flowed with it. Cyrus flung it across the room, where it rolled twice before settling. Keles watched with a mixture of fascination and horror as the skull lifted up, now firmly attached to a body of purest shadow whose features were hidden underneath a cloak darker than any night. Gleaming white eyes glared from behind his grinning skull. The tips of bone swords peeked out from below the edge of his cloak. There was no silver crown across his forehead, just a single line of dried blood.

A naked Cyrus coughed and sputtered on his hands and knees. His skin was slick all over with blood. His cheeks and forehead were a mess of bruises, and his fingers were bent wrong. A long, angry red scar marked his chest. Despite his obvious exhaustion, he glared at Vagrant.

"Whom do you serve?" he asked, tired and trembling.

When Vagrant answered, his voice was the depth of stone and the chill of the deep ocean.

"I serve the people of Thanet, and whom they put upon a throne."

Cyrus pointed a crooked finger toward Keles. "And twice now I have renounced my throne. There is Thanet's true queen. Do your duty, Vagrant."

Vagrant turned her way. He lifted his swords from underneath his dark cloak, crossed the bone blades over his head, and then bowed. Keles nodded, silently accepting his obedience.

"Good," Cyrus said. His arms shook. "That's good."

Keles slid to her knees so she could catch him as he collapsed. His tired, battered form crumpled against her. He lay there, faintly smiling. Groggy eyes peered up at her as she stroked strands of hair away from his face. His real face. After a moment, his eyes focused, and he seemed to grow in awareness.

"I would kneel," he told her, "but I fear I am too tired."

Keles held him close, shocked by how thin and frail he felt in her arms. The power of the Butterfly faded from her, all her flame and fire spent, and she wondered if she looked as hollow as Cyrus felt.

"It's enough," she said, embracing him as the distant crowd looked on. "You've given everything, Cyrus. I need nothing more."

"As you say, my queen."

Behind them, the Vagrant circled the walls, took up a perch near the ceiling, and began his watch.

CHAPTER 61

THE NIGHT AFTER

The shore was quiet, its sands empty.

Here on this southernmost tip of Thanet, gentle waves washed across pale sand glistening in the moonlight. What wind blew was tame and mild, for the world held its breath.

The first butterfly landed upon the sand. Another settled beside it, and then another, and another. They came from the distant fields beyond. They came from the spires of Lycaena's Cocoon, the orchards of the Mane, even all the way from the fields east of the Broadleaf Forest. They swirled down from the skies, growing in number until they were a torrent. Thousands upon thousands, their wings each and every color of the rainbow. The shoreline became a carpet of fluttering wings above black bodies, its beauty dazzling and yet unseen by mortal eyes.

There they waited.

The serpent arrived without fanfare. It was a small thing, hardly longer than a man's forearm. Its scales were blue like sapphires, its eyes solid black orbs. Slow and careful undulations took it from the water, and some few dozen butterflies took flight to give it room as it twisted and tumbled to drier ground.

Its bloodred tongue flicked in and out of its mouth. Scales closed across its eyes. Perhaps it could speak, perhaps not, but no words were needed. The serpent bowed its head, its nose burrowing into the sand, and waited.

Gusts blew across the shore, unnatural in their source. The butterflies took to the skies by the dozens, flooding the air like a pulsating cloud. They soared higher, higher, becoming a swirling funnel, and then from deep within came the first spark. Fire burst across the multitude of wings. Embers fell like rain to twinkle out upon the sand. Hotter, brighter, the fire spreading as the rage of the butterflies reached its zenith.

The serpent lay still, head bowed, accepting judgment.

The fire faded. The blinding brightness dimmed, and instead of flame only beautiful color remained. The tornado dispersed, and the butterflies scattered to the four corners of Thanet. Thousands of men, women, and children lay dead across the island, most still waiting to be buried. For each and every one of those thousands flew a single butterfly. They landed on stiff hands. They settled over closed eyes. They flattened themselves atop blood-soaked chests, refusing to move even when shovels came and dirt fell over them to fill the graves.

Only one butterfly stayed behind. There was nothing special about it. If anything, its color was paler, its wingspan shorter. It landed before the serpent, opened and closed its wings once, and then remained still.

The serpent rose up, its lower half curling to grant itself height. It peered at the butterfly, shook its head once, and then turned away. The water greeted it, and when a wave offered its foamy embrace, it did not resist. The great deep awaited. Moonlight would fall upon those sapphire scales no more.

Wind blew, a held breath exhaled.

Another wave reached its fingers across the sands. The butterfly accepted the grasp of its cold hands. A visitation for every life taken, to mourn over what was lost and to guide the soul to the hereafter. That was the gift offered, the promise made.

Deep down in the depths, one last death must be mourned. The butterfly sank, its fragile body crushed by the weight of the sea.

The shore was quiet, its sands empty.

CHAPTER 62

CYRUS

"We couldn't ask for finer weather," Mari said. Cyrus leaned against the ship's taffrail and gazed out upon Vallessau. The city upon the cliffs sparkled in the midday sun. Mari stood beside him, looking beautiful in a blue dress cinched tightly at her waist with a red sash.

"I've never sailed for longer than a few hours at a time," Cyrus said. "What's it like, to be on the waves for months?"

"A nightmare, if you don't get your sea legs quickly. Everyone being cramped into one space doesn't help, either. We'll all be nipping at each other's heels before long. Try not to take any of it personally."

Cyrus laughed.

"I'll keep it in mind."

The passage of sailors was a steady occurrence up and down the gangplank of the *Windward*, loading supplies for the journey ahead. Travel between Gadir and Thanet was uncommon, but the captain had done the trip once before. They were bound for the port city of Garlea along the southwestern tip of the mainland continent. Today was the day, and Cyrus was wound up with a heady mixture of nervousness and anticipation.

Mari waved at the city. Her breezy smile lessened.

"Now's your last chance to change your mind. Do you think they'll be all right without you?"

Cyrus propped his chin on his fists. His vision blurred as he stared into nothing.

"With or without me, we will heal," he said. "It is only a matter of time. Vallessau won't burn to the ground just because I left."

"True, true. It's just...the past weeks have been rough. So much killing, and so many burials. It makes it hard to hold hope for a better fate."

Cyrus chuckled.

"I thought you were meant to be the cheerful one."

Mari rolled her eyes.

"I don't know. Let me be dour at least once, if you please. You can be the chipper, cheerful member of the group in turn. All the gods and goddesses know you have far too much practice as the gloomy, dour man in the corner, and far too little as anything else."

Cyrus laughed, and it felt so good how easily the joy came.

"Fine. Fine. For this boat trip, I shall be the heart of our party. Will that make you happy?"

"Maybe." She winked at him. "I'll be watching you. No breaking your word."

"I'd never."

They fell silent, comfortable together as they watched two burly men in Thanese fisher trousers and waistcoats carry burlap sacks of food up the gangplank.

Cyrus turned his attention back to the city. Mari had tried to be gentle, but "rough" failed to describe the days following Lucavi's death. There wasn't a family alive on Thanet that had not lost someone that night. Many coastal cities had suffered worse, for when Everlorn's forces learned of their god's death, they looted what they could, burned what they couldn't, and sailed back for Gadir. The pettiness of it only infuriated the island's survivors. Soldiers trapped deeper inland received no quarter. They died to a man, hunted down by Pilus's army...and the vengeful Vagrant.

Vallessau had been spared that looting, but smoke still hovered in her sky. No looting; there had been fires, joyous ones. Nothing remained of Everlorn's schools and language centers. All literature brought by the Uplifted Church was now ash. There had been weeping, too, now allowed free and in the open, for the loss of loved ones, the cost of the invasion. Thanet was free, the crowds shouted, but only of the empire's immediate grasp. The past was irrevocably scarred. The future was forever defined by what had been taken. Those were grim thoughts, ones Cyrus wished he could banish from his mind.

He had to be the heart of the group, after all. It was his turn to smile.

Granted, the company on the *Windward* would make that easier. The next pair up the gangplank stirred him from his thoughts, and he beamed at them both. Stasia and Clarissa walked hand in hand, with Stasia carrying two enormous leather packs stuffed to bursting with belongings. Stasia's dark trousers and sleeveless shirt matched those of the sailors. Clarissa looked to have attempted similar practical attire, but her white shirt was much too bright and loose and her short skirt of far too thin a fabric to endure the hard work of the sea.

"I hope you weren't thinking of leaving without us," Stasia said. She lifted Clarissa's arm and shook it. "This one was particularly panicky about what to pack."

"I didn't know what to bring," Clarissa said, elbowing Stasia in the side. "How could I? You were supposed to *help* me know."

Stasia kissed her cheek.

"Yeah, well, I was busy hunting down Everlorn soldiers too stupid to flee to their boats."

Cyrus turned and put his back to the railing as the other pair joined them. Yes, it would be so much easier to smile with the Ahlai family around. Clarissa looked like she could hardly stand still, she was flush with so much excitement. As for Stasia, she was as cocky and sure as ever, and easily the one most eager to return to Gadir.

"It's going to be fun watching you puke your guts out the first week," Stasia said to him. She plopped her two leather sacks to the deck. "It'll be nostalgic. Your first week of training, all over again."

"Don't remind me of those horrid times," Cyrus said, grinning. "Only sixteen years old, and you had me running every morning on an empty stomach. Never before has the world seen such a cruel taskmaster."

"Just following orders to make you into something useful," Stasia said, but her smile suddenly wasn't quite so easy. Cyrus sensed the specter of her father hovering over her. They'd grieved for the man a few days after the ceremony. It had been the first time since Thorda's death that they'd had a chance to simply...be together. To tell stories of the god in disguise. Even amid the hard life he had pressed upon his daughters, there were times his stony demeanor had cracked and his love for his children revealed itself.

They had no body to burn, but they lit a fire for the slain God of the Forge nonetheless. More smoke to join the skies above Vallessau. Cyrus had breathed it in, let it coat his throat. When he exhaled, he vowed to forgive the man for all he had done, even if Thorda himself might not have desired that forgiveness. Cyrus would carry no hate for him, nor bear any grudge. Desperation had driven Thorda to extremes, but Cyrus was no more innocent. The scar on Keles's throat was proof of that.

"I guess I should ask you two the same thing I asked Cyrus," Mari told the pair. "Nothing is making you leave Thanet. I bet you two could settle down and make a happy life for yourselves somewhere on this beautiful island."

"Indeed we could," Clarissa said. She leaned against Stasia, her easy smile fading into contentment. "I'll miss home, I'm sure, but Stasia's home is not here on Thanet."

"I almost wish it could be," Stasia said. She lifted their belongings again and flung them over her shoulder. "But whether I wanted to be one or not, I'm somehow a god of Miquo. It's time I return home and learn what that even means."

"Which means *I* get to see this home you've told me so much about," Clarissa added. "I cannot wait! It's one thing to imagine these trees so high they blot out the sky, but another to see them."

"It is indeed," Stasia said. She leaned down, quickly kissed her wife, and then appeared to have second thoughts. She kissed her again, longer, more insistently, until Mari turned away in exaggerated disgust.

"Your little cabin is belowdecks, you know," she said.

"I know," Stasia said. She winked, took Clarissa's hand, and then the two descended the stairs heading deeper into the ship.

"I hope their room isn't next to mine," Mari said the second they vanished. Cyrus glanced her way and lifted an eyebrow. Her neck reddened slightly. "They try to be quiet, but they're . . . not."

Cyrus laughed again. Oh yes, he would very much enjoy his time around the Ahlai family. Perhaps by the end of three months of sailing, they would hate one another, but surely the first few weeks would be ones of joy and relaxation. For the first time since Cyrus had met any of them, they were at peace. No war. No battles.

He prayed, despite knowing it impossible, that it stayed that way when they arrived on Gadir.

"I see the girls have arrived," a deep voice boomed from behind them.

Cyrus glanced over his shoulder.

"Giggling like little children, even," he said, grinning at Arn coming up the stairs. The former paragon wore a loose shirt, unbuttoned no doubt to ease the irritation on the huge swathe of bandages wrapped about his waist. Riding upon his shoulder was a three-tailed fox, the creature so small, and Arn so broad, that she was able to curl up and sleep despite his movement.

"I've unpacked everything wise to unpack," Arn said, joining Mari's side. His arm slipped about her waist. "Some things are best kept carefully stowed away, in case the waves get rough."

"You do know I sailed here the same as you did?" Mari asked.

"Yeah, but I assumed you did so on some fancy boat owned by your father where you had your own wardrobe and a dozen servants catering to your every whim. We won't be afforded any sort of luxuries on the *Windward*. It's going to be cramped, smelly, and loud."

"You're not aiding my nervousness about my first real voyage," Cyrus said.

Arn smacked him across the chest with his free hand.

"Then be nervous, you twit. I'm done looking out for you."

Cyrus tilted his head toward Mari, whose face was slowly growing redder. She appeared at a loss for words. Perhaps it was because Cyrus had noticed the hand around her waist, or how Arn held her against him so casually.

"Are you certain I must be the nice one for this voyage?" he asked her.

"Yes," she said. She reached up to pet the fox on Arn's shoulder. The little creature stirred, tilted her head, and accepted the touch with eyes closed. "Even to this giant tree trunk of a man."

Arn smiled at the fox and then let out an exaggerated sigh.

"I suppose I should set up a comfy bed for Velgyn that isn't my shoulder. Besides, I've already had three men ask me to aid them in moving and stacking supplies. Time to make myself useful, injuries be damned."

He leaned down, kissed Mari, and then strode for the stairs.

"Don't hurt yourself," she called after him.

"Yeah, yeah," he said, waving, before vanishing belowdecks.

Silence followed his departure as Mari stared at the city. Her jaw locked tighter than a castle gate.

Cyrus leaned against the railing beside her and cleared his throat.

"So," he said. "Should I hope my room isn't next to yours?"

Mari's face blushed beet red, and she punched him square in the chest.

"How dare you?" she said, and stomped for the stairs.

"That's not a no!" he called after her, earning himself a very emphatic rude gesture made with her fingers. Cyrus laughed (oh, how good it felt to laugh) and gazed upon Vallessau once more.

This city had been home for so much of his life. The only time he'd been away for long was when training with Thorda, but even then, a return to Vallessau had ever been the goal. Not so anymore. This was goodbye. He could not stay, and when he saw the reason approaching surrounded by four soldiers, Cyrus's blood cooled.

Queen Keles climbed the gangplank, her face passive, revealing nothing. She looked splendid in her silver armor, which shone brilliantly beneath the midday sun. Gold threads looped through her braided hair, coming together to attach to her silver crown. Perhaps future descendants would wear different garb, but Keles would be a warrior queen for the island in the wake of Everlorn's defeat.

Keles was not alone with her escort, either. Eshiel greeted Cyrus with a surprisingly emotional embrace.

"I have seen so much of you, both good and ill," the priest said. "Know that you are not condemned for where you failed, nor forsaken by your deeds. You are beloved by Lycaena even now, and are ever welcome to return home."

"Thank you," Cyrus said stiffly.

The priest backed away, whispered something in Keles's ear, and then shouted an order to the soldiers. They marched down to the dock, leaving Keles and Cyrus to converse alone. Silence built between them, awkward and unwelcome. Cyrus wished they could return to the ease with which they had sat together and watched the stars flicker over the docks from atop a tower.

His gaze flicked to the scar across her throat. No, that time would never return, no matter how much he might wish for it.

"How are your hands?" Keles asked, forcing an end to the silence.

"Better than they have any right to be," he answered. She had prayed over his injured hands twice daily over the past weeks. Despite the initial bruises, broken bones, and torn muscle, they were all but healed, so that he did not even require bandages.

"That's good," she said, and scanned the ship. "Where are the others?"

"Belowdecks, preparing."

Keles shook her head.

"The saviors of Thanet deserve a better farewell."

"We are being seen off by our island's Returned Queen," Cyrus said with a shrug. "How could we ask for more?"

She joined him at the railing, and together they gazed out upon the city they had fought, bled, and nearly died for.

"I've been working closely with Eshiel to prepare a proper history of our war," she said after a time. "Not just this one, either, but the War of Tides as well. The truth of Dagon, then and now, will be told. I will ensure your part is remembered, too, and as more than just a vessel for the Vagrant. We will not live in ignorance of our past."

"Some of that will cast the goddess in an unflattering light."

"As the goddess herself will admit. But if she is to reclaim the heart of our island, it must be done in truth."

Cyrus found the aspiration necessary, but he wondered how well it would go in practice. Perhaps with Lycaena's direct intervention, the lies of human history and memory would be prevented.

"Do you think she will once more grace our lands, in body as well as spirit?" he asked.

Keles waved at the shore.

"How could we even know? I suspect she will. The love for her is still strong, and stronger now with Everlorn's defeat. Maybe not in our lifetimes. Maybe not until everyone who witnessed her execution passes on, and a new generation venerating her replaces us. With gods, not much is ever known for certain, is there?"

That was putting it mildly. Still, he hoped she was right. The idea of Vagrant remaining the only god of Thanet did not sit well with him. As Keles had made so clear during his battle against her, the people needed more than vengeance to guide their lives. Destruction would be meaningless without something new built in its place.

Keles shifted her weight from foot to foot. Something was bothering her, and he waited in silence for her to finally give it voice.

"Please, do not feel like you are forced to leave," she said.

"But I am forced. As you consolidate your power, there will be those who would see the Lythan family returned to prominence. If I stay, I will feel compelled to stop them, and I am done fighting for a throne. Let it all end. I would be neither god nor king. You once told me the choice would always be mine, and this is what I have chosen. I wish to be Cyrus, just Cyrus. I ask that you honor that decision, my queen."

She pushed off from the railing, turned, and wrapped her arms around him. He felt the divine strength within her, lingering even after the deaths of Dagon and Lucavi. Eyes closed, he smiled and returned her embrace. Thanet would be well cared for with her in charge.

"I had to be certain you did not think yourself exiled," she said. "And I will honor your choice, Cyrus. It is the least I may do."

They pulled apart, and he bowed low in respect. That he was in such meager clothing, and she in her shining silver armor, amused him. Who would look upon the pair and think he was the one so recently meant to hold a throne? That was just fine with Cyrus. The part of him that had been Vagrant was linked to his identity as prince, perhaps irrevocably, and it was only in casting off both that he felt... free.

"I cannot imagine travel between Gadir and Thanet will be common, but I shall try to write you letters so you may follow my escapades," he said. "Difficult times await the entire mainland. I suspect members of the Uplifted Church already know of Lucavi's death. They'll have felt it, even all the way across the Crystal Sea. Wars will follow. This empire the God-Incarnate built will fracture once the strength and fear holding it in place are toppled. It's going to be awful, I hold no illusions to that."

"There is so much work to be done," Keles said in agreement. "I wish my own here were not so daunting. The coming winter will be harsh with famine, but Eshiel insists Lycaena will provide. The years after? That's what I fear the most. We must rebuild what was lost, appoint new lords of the four realms, and already I hear rumblings about marriage and heirs and..."

She stopped and laughed.

"Forgive me," she said. "I ramble, when I should be saying farewell."

"I will take your ramblings over any farewell, Keles. I've had enough of the latter already."

"Very well. Less of me, more of you. What are your immediate plans once you arrive on Gadir?" Her brown eyes sparkled. "Or do you plan on toppling every last remnant of Everlorn all at once?"

"Would that I could," Cyrus said, struggling to ignore the pain he felt in his chest knowing he would, barring a miracle, never see Keles again. "Mari wants to visit conquered nations and use her gifts to reignite the faith that was lost when Everlorn invaded. It is a task far beyond the work of one lifetime, but it is still worth doing. Where Mari goes, so, too, will I. So long as I possess breath in my lungs, I will bury the horrid faith of Everlorn."

"And so you go to another war. The regents, magistrates, and paragons won't give up their domains easily." A shadow passed over her face. "Some may even seek to bring the God-Incarnate back. I pray they do not succeed."

Cyrus slowly nodded.

"I still have my training. I still have my swords. Mari and Stasia gave so much to help us here. It's only right I give in return, and not just for Miquo. For Lahareed, Onleda, and Aethenwald." He lifted the black ring on his finger. "Maybe I'll even get to meet Anyx and thank her for her generosity."

Keles stepped close, and he thought she might embrace him again. Instead she took his hands in hers and slowly dipped her head.

"You will be missed," she said. "I shall pray to Lycaena for your safety, every night, I promise. And should you ever tire of war, you have a home waiting for you here. I swear it."

Cyrus smiled, touched by her offer.

"One day, when I lack the strength to wield these swords, perhaps I will take you up on that offer. I cannot wait to see the wondrous future you build in my absence."

The queen released his hands. The vulnerability she had shown vanished, her face cool and collected.

"Safe travels," she said, and exited down the gangplank. Cyrus kept still, his hands casually resting atop his hips. Deep in his chest, he felt an impulse to cast it all aside, his fears, his ideals, his ludicrous thoughts of somehow bettering the fates of nations in the chaos to come on Gadir. A part of him yearned to stay. To make a humble life. To remain comfortable.

Step aside, and make way for your king.

No, there would be none of that. The separation between him and Vagrant, from king and god, must be solidified. He would put an entire ocean between them if he must. If not for Lycaena's intervention, and Keles's brilliant faith, he would be on a path to become the next God-Incarnate. Never again, he swore. Let that cruel dream die with Soma and Lucavi.

As for what remained? Cyrus saw the Vagrant lurking only moments after Keles was gone. The god was a shadow atop a nearby dock house. His bone swords were drawn and held crossed before him as he huddled at the building's edge, watching his queen's return to the castle. His entire body was cloaked, and the lower half of his body appeared formless, like liquid darkness.

Vagrant and Cyrus locked eyes. The pale skull grinned wide. He no longer bore a silver crown, but instead a single stripe of blood across his forehead. The crown had broken when Cyrus ripped the skull from his face, and it would stay broken. Promises passed unspoken between them. Vagrant would ever be the island's protector. Cyrus need not fear any power struggles or attempts to usurp the Orani line. Keles bore the blessing of Lycaena and the guardianship of the Vagrant. No one in all of Thanet would be more protected.

"Do your duty," he whispered, trusting the fledgling god to hear him. "Seek no crown, not even one of blood, but abide no tyrants, either. You serve all the people, not just a throne."

Vagrant lifted both bone swords and crossed them to form an X over his forehead. Then, as quickly as he had appeared, he was gone, trailing Keles in his divine vigil.

With the queen's departure, the gangplank was clear, and the last of the preparations began apace. Cyrus observed the bustle and controlled chaos. He felt unnoticed, forgotten, with hardly anyone casting him a second glance as they did their work. It felt good. It felt like he was just one of many.

His friends returned from down below, eager and excited as the captain gave the order to cast off. They gathered as the island of Thanet slowly receded into the distance. Arn and Mari were to his left, Clarissa and Stasia to his right. They watched, and laughed, and chatted as if all were right with the world. Perhaps in that boat, at that very moment, things were.

The deck swayed beneath his feet. The sea breeze teased his hair. Slowly, carefully, when no one was looking, Cyrus pressed his hand to his face, touching it with the gentlest brush of his fingertips.

And smiled.

A NOTE FROM THE AUTHOR

And so here we are, at the end of another trilogy. Hopefully you've enjoyed the ride as much as I have. In terms of characters, this is probably my favorite little bunch that I've had the pleasure of writing about for a pretty long time. Mari, in particular, rapidly became a favorite of mine by the end of *The Bladed Faith*, and cemented herself as one of my best ever throughout *The Sapphire Altar.* Her relationship with Arn was also just so much fun to write. Who doesn't love a giant, muscle-bound hulk of a man acting like a complete fool for the woman he likes?

The most fun for this novel was getting to tell chapters from Soma's point of view. I'd been itching to write them since way back in *The Bladed Faith*, able to only give snippets of what was to come when he dropped his façade before a dying Magus. There's a certain archetype I tend to enjoy in all my various series. A character who is most certainly evil...but at the same time, one whose motivations are complicated enough that readers will insist maybe they aren't all that terrible. For you longtime readers, think Velixar from the Half-Orcs, or for slightly newer readers, Janus from the Keepers Trilogy. And I knew from the start I had another character like that with Soma. Showing that, though, was going to be a bit trickier given so much of his motivation was hidden from the other characters, as well as having taken place over hundreds of years. Hopefully I did okay, and you enjoyed delving into the mentality of the bitter, betrayed Sapphire Serpent.

Speaking of betrayal, Cyrus's final turn at the end has gone through so many different iterations in my mind as I led up to it. My outline left it pretty vague because I knew I'd have to rely on my gut to determine what path to take. Briefly, I considered having him die, thoroughly ruined, but that felt a bit too dour, as well as giving Cyrus too little credit to resist what he might be becoming. For a long time, I thought the Vagrant deity itself would be destroyed once Cyrus was free of it, but that felt like too clean an ending, and just not as interesting. Originally Keles wasn't to be "killed" and brought back by Eshiel, either. Instead Mari and Stasia would arrive to help Keles in a three-versus-one against a Cyrus fully consumed by the Vagrant (Amees was going to use some nature travel magic to get the pair to the capital, in case you were wondering how the heck I planned to circumvent that particular issue). But as I developed Lycaena into a more present character in the story, culminating in an incredibly fun chapter to write with her meeting Dagon, I knew I wanted the Vagrant to be confronted by the Butterfly. From there, things fell into place, and I knew exactly what role Eshiel himself would play.

Even then, I still was torn about whether to have Cyrus remain behind on Thanet or go with the rest of the gang to the mainland. I pitched the question to my editor, and she agreed with my own assessment: Cyrus had to leave if the ending was to feel satisfying. As tempting as it might be to have him and Keles marry and be king and queen and live happily ever after...I think that would never be enough for Cyrus, nor would he feel free of the Vagrant while there on the island. Helping others, even as a mere human, is what he'd still want to do. And there's something poetic about the novel starting with him watching boats arrive on his island, and by the end of the trilogy, he is departing his home on one such boat.

As for how all that goes down...I suppose I should directly answer the question I'm sure I will be asked plenty: No, I have no clue if there will be more books in the world of the Vagrant Gods. I have tried to deliver a satisfying ending while making it clear more story is there to be told, just by the sheer nature of the world and the size of the Everlorn Empire, but you don't need to know how all that ends to know how *this* story ends. Thanet is free, and the Vagrant now walks alongside the Butterfly. Perhaps Stasia and Mari will help revive the slain gods of Miquo. Maybe a fully human Cyrus will create a new persona for himself, one of his own making. One day I may write it, if I feel there is enough story to tell and interest from others in reading it.

Okay, time for some thanks. First off, thank you to all my longtime readers who have followed me from world to world, still eager to listen to what stories I have to tell. I hope you enjoyed the little Easter eggs around Haern the Watcher during the climactic battle against Ashraleon, as well as the homage to the ending of the Paladins during Arn's final chapter (and in case you were wondering, yes, Arn was always meant to survive—I've had that scene in my head since before I even started *The Sapphire Altar*). Thank you to any new readers who have stuck with me throughout this trilogy, holding faith that I might know what I am doing. Thanks, Rob, for enduring my lengthy phone calls to figure out Dagon's character and history. Thank you, Michael, for being the perfect agent for these past few uncertain years. Thank you to Lauren and the rest of the art team at Orbit who grace my novels with unbelievably good artwork and design. Thank you, Megan and Essa, for always being there for me to rant, joke, or question this entire writing process. Thank you, Brit, for shaping this entire trilogy into the best it could become, and for not being too upset as this novel ballooned in size. Thank you, Angelica, for coming in with a hacksaw to chop it back down after said ballooning in size.

Last, yet never least, thank you, dear reader. You allow me to tell stories for a living, to escape into a world of my own creation, of my own characters, and draw out from them something, I hope, of value and entertainment. You let me live a dream, and for that, you have my gratitude. I hope to see you again, in another note at the end of my books, be it in old stories already written, or whatever new stories I may choose to tell. From the bottom of my heart, thank you.

David Dalglish

September 13, 2022

extras

meet the author

North Myrtle Beach Photography

DAVID DALGLISH currently lives in Myrtle Beach with his wife, Samantha, and daughters, Morgan, Katherine, and Alyssa. He graduated from Missouri Southern State University in 2006 with a degree in mathematics and currently spends his free time tanking dungeons for his wife and daughter in *Final Fantasy XIV*.

Find out more about David Dalglish and other Orbit authors by registering for the free monthly newsletter at orbitbooks.net.

if you enjoyed
THE SLAIN DIVINE
look out for
A FLAME IN THE NORTH
Black Land's Bane: Book One
by
Lilith Saintcrow

The Black Land is spent myth. Centuries have passed since the Great Enemy was slain. Yet old fears linger, and on the longest night of the year, every village still lights a ritual fire to banish the dark.

That is Solveig's duty. Favored by the gods with powerful magic, Sol calls forth flame to keep her home safe. But when her brother accidentally kills a northern lord's son, she is sent away as weregild—part hostage, part guest—for a year and a day.

The farther north Sol travels, the clearer it becomes the Black Land is no myth. The forests teem with foul beasts. Her travel companions are not what they seem, and their plans for her and her magic are shrouded in secrecy.

With only her loyal shieldmaiden and her own wits to rely upon, Sol must master power beyond her imagination to wrest control of her fate. For the Black Land's army stirs, ready to cover the world in darkness—unless Sol can find the courage to stop it.

They thought the old ways were dead. But now, the Enemy awakens....

HASTILY DONE

For seidhr *is a tree, and some branches wider than others. Those gifted with its touch may bend one of the great forces of nature to their will, and those with any of the weirding may call a spark. The most blessed among them we call* elementalist, *and they perform not mere kindling but hold actual flame...*

—Navros, First Scholar of Naras in the days of King Edresil

By solstice day the great Althing at Dun Rithell was almost over. Our father took Astrid and Bjorn to the last day of the riverside fair but I did not accompany them; I was already thinking upon the fire.

Mother was abed with winter ague and Bjorn her firstborn useless when it came to organizing, both by temperament and upon account of maleness. If you wished something heavy lifted, something bulky heaved a great distance, stabbed, slashed, or thumped into submission, he was not only willing to oblige but also an expert of such endeavors, but should you wish for aught else disappointment was the result. Astrid had already done her part with the great feast upon the penultimate day; many a toast was drunk to her health and Ithrik the Stout had already gifted our hall with a great gem-crusted plate as a sign of earnest.

My sister liked the sheep-lord's middle son Edrik well enough; he was a fine fighter and careful with his father's great flocks. Astrid's marriage, while not final by any means, at least was assured in *some* direction. Come spring Bjorn might be married as well, if any of the visiting girls and their kin liked the look of him. Both prospects pleased me like they should any good sister, but did not mean I wished to go a-fairing that day.

Besides, crowds are always... difficult. Though the quality of my cloth and the marks upon my wrists grant me space and there is always Arneior, I did not cherish the thought of being called to render a summary judgment between drunken warriors *or* perform some small trick to please a wide-eyed child among a press of visitors and jostling neighbors. Arn might have wished to go upon her own account, but I did not think of that until Father had already left with my siblings and my shieldmaid gazed longingly down the road, her ruddy hair a beacon in the strengthening dawn. Twin hornbraids crested on either side of her head, their tails dangling behind her shoulders wrapped into clubs with leather thongs, and the stripe of blue woad down the left side of her face shouted *One of the Black-Wingéd's own, do not touch.*

If she had not the woad, her very carriage and steady glare would serve as warning enough. It is known the battlefield maidens of Odynn's elect choose those of quick tempers, not to mention swift spears.

"Oh, fishguts," I said, spreading my hands; the last band upon my left wrist—ink forced under skin with a sharp point—twitched. The scab was almost off, but I had to refrain from scratching or drawing the pain aside to heal it more quickly. One does not use *seidhr* upon such marks. "I did not think, small one."

One coppery eyebrow shot up, and Arn scowled at me. Which is usually a cheerful sign; I have called her *small one* since she was sworn to me at Fryja's great festival during my sixth springtime—and my shieldmaid's ninth, for she is older, though I am supposed to be the wiser of our partnership.

"I do not wish to go," my shieldmaid said, her generous mouth pulled tight. The scales and rings sewn onto her daily hauberk glittered fiercely as the sun's first limb reached above the horizon, frost and thin metal both gilding the roof of our home. *When sun rises, Eril's hall echoes it,* our men said, and one or two might even lift a drinking horn to the eldest daughter when they did.

One born with *seidhr* is considered lucky, even if 'tis best to be cautious of a *volva*'s temper. What is the sun but the largest bonfire of all, and if I could produce flame to hold back the night who knew what I could darken? It was a logical enough assumption, though the trepidation somewhat misplaced.

I did not think it wise to dispel such caution wholesale, though. Nor had my teacher Idra.

"You do not wish to attend the fair?" I mimicked astonishment, letting my eyes widen and the words lilt. There was a snapping, growling, baying explosion in the direction of the kennels; the houndmaster Yvin would be taking his shaggy, nose-drunk charges upon their traditional run through the South Moor soon. When they returned, there would be scraps for both dogs and pigs, and both groups might be exhausted into reasonable behavior for the rest of the day. "Not even after the bonfire is laid?"

"It will take all day to stack," Arneior replied stiffly, and I laughed, taking her left arm. The other, of course, was not to be touched even by her charge. Her longhead spear—well upon its way to earning a name in its own way—occupied her right hand, its butt resting easily upon swept cobbles.

Soon the tables would be brought out for the Fools' Feast before the great evening celebration to mark the Althing's ending—though not the end of legal cases and other matters to be decided—and I would be very busy indeed.

For the moment, though, I could tease my Arn. "Not if I hurry things along. *A* volva *is hard to please*." The proverb used to pain me; I watched as Father's golden head sank into the crowd passing down the road, just outside our courtyard's great timbered gates—ajar to show hospitality during the Althing, as was the custom. Astrid, as she only reached Bjorn's shoulder, was already lost to view; my brother, though he had his final growth upon him, would not quite match our father's height. Still, both of them were well-named, a big good-natured bear and a shimmering star.

I oft considered my own naming a great jest, for I am dark-haired as my mother and my father's mother. For all that, I have my mother's eyes; they said there was some of the Elder in Gwendelint of Dun Rithell's line, but I know not the truth or falsity of such a tale.

Despite a dark head my temper is much like Eril the Battle-Mad's, and those who see us together are unable to think me anything but his get. I have his nose, and my chin, while rather more pointed, is also shaped just as his, though my mouth and cheekbones belong to Gwendelint. More than that, Father and I share the same quality of gaze—the word is *piercing*, as an awl will go through even thick leather, and when applied to a pair of eyes it means we see much more than we wish to, though Father's are dark and mine clear pale blue.

A steady stream of freedmen, bondsmen, servants, and thralls carted wood from every household and camp to the great green across the ancient stone-paved trade-road; the large flat outcropping of greyish rock in the midst of vast grassy space was black-topped from other burnings and bore a stubby crown of stacked logs already. Hopfoot my mother's steward, his reedy tenor aquiver with age, had been fussily directing the laying of the base since the grey mist before a winter dawn. The wicker cages along one side of the Stone would be quiet at this hour, though—they were small and relatively few, holding only promised sacrifices of fowl and rabbits.

There had been no war or raiding to bring excess livestock lately. Perhaps that accounted for my unease. I could even say I sensed somewhat amiss, but it would be a lie. That morning the blessèd gods—Aesyr, Vanyr, foreign—nor any other passing spirit gave no indication of the future, not even to me.

I was merely nervous in anticipation of what I had to do that evening.

My skirts touched Arn's knee as we slipped back through the gate; the green-and-white winter festival dress was last year's, true, but I had grown no more and would not reach even Astrid's height. Small am I, *little Solveig like a paring knife*, Father had crowed more than once, lifting child-me in his brawny arms.

As I grew older he became uneasy with my strangeness, but that was only to be expected.

"Hastily done is ill done." Arneior rolled her shoulders precisely once, a sign she was ready for the day's labors, whatever they might be. "And where is your mantle, my weirdling? Your mother will scold."

I shrugged in return. Mother would not glimpse me from her bedroom window; I had mixed her morning medicine with a sedative so she could not fret overmuch at being unable to oversee the feasts. My great fur-hooded green mantle was warm, yes, but I had merely stepped into the courtyard to bid Astrid good hunting in the market and also bring Bjorn the blundering his new beard-pin, forgotten at table. The night's frost was already turning to steam, lifting from our greathall's gilded roof just as the weary sun hauled itself above the black-timbered breast of white-hooded Tarnarya for the last time that year.

Our great mother-mountain would be renewed with dawn, like the entire world.

Tonight was the Long Dark; the bonfire would burn throughout, holding vigil. I would not sleep much either, making certain the flame kept steady, but at least it was dry weather. I did not taste much snow or ice upon the wind. Our river kept much of winter's worst excesses away, and we thanked her each spring for the blessing.

Even if it did include cold mud to the knee, and more than one shoe lost in quagmire.

"My lady! My lady Solveig!" Albeig, holding her cheerful blue festival skirt high so the embroidered hem did not touch the ground, waved from the top of the great stairs. She did not like to leave the inner fastness; our housekeeper hated disorder and there would be naught else in every corner, begging to be set aright. "The tables? Shall we?"

And thus it begins. There was no use in sighing; Albeig knew I wished to order the household myself, if only to show Mother she need not worry. "Make it so, then," I called up the stairs. "But do not set out the meat just yet."

She knew that as well, but Albeig's fair round face eased at proof that *I* was thinking with more than one finger, as the saying goes. She bobbed gently, a tiny wooden boat upon a disturbed puddle, and hurried back inside through the big black carven doors.

"They have not brought the pillars yet." Arn did not move. No doubt she would prefer chivvying those building the bonfire to the thankless work of setting out board for fortunate beggars and any of my father's men who wished a mouthful outside before going to the fair's colorful, hurrying sprawl.

Each oiled wooden pillar upon the Stone in the green bore a great rune-carving and would sink into prepared holes in the Stone's back, ready to keep the lower mass of the bonfire from tipping. Come morning, having done their duty, whatever survived of their guard-watch would be given to the flames as well.

The old must be sacrificed before the new is brought in. So my people believed, and I have not found them wrong. "Then make certain they are placed properly for my first lighting, and return for the nooning." I rose upon my slippered tiptoes, pressing my lips to her cheek as if we were sisters; she gave an aggrieved sigh. "What? I promise not to stir a step past the gate without my Arn. Go."

Even a year before she would have refused, but the bands upon my left wrist were seven in number just as the ones upon my right were five, thin dark double-lines of ink and ash forced under the skin, angular runes dancing within their confines. Not only that, but my hair was braided in the complex fashion of a full *volva* by

Astrid just that morn, red coral beads at special junctures, and Father himself had gifted me his mother's silver torc, the bees of her house and lineage resting heavy and comforting below my collarbone.

In short, none would dare offer violence, jostling, or even a light word to a woman so attired inside a riverlord's walls. Why risk exile, or a curse taking the flavor from your mead as the old saying warns? There are stories of weirdlings running hot lead into a warrior's marrow to answer an insult, too.

Every child knows those tales, and is taught to keep a civil tongue when speaking to those with even the weakest *seidhr*.

Arn gave in after a few moments of token resistance, and glared at me afresh from her relatively imposing height. Even her freckles glowed in thin golden winterlight, and her breath was a fine silver plume. "Not a single step past the gate, Sol."

"Then don't be late. Or I might find myself walking alone, riverside-bound to find Astrid." It was an empty threat delivered only to make her bristle, since I would not willingly stir from the hall's safety until sunset. "And mind you don't make Hopfoot stammer; he is very afraid of you."

"As well he should be." She hefted her spear, its long bright blade winking conspiratorially. "I go, then. Put your mantle on, daughter of Gwendelint."

I dropped her arm and stuck my tongue out, making a battle-face; she laughed and set off with springing steps. I climbed my father's great wide stairs, their grain worn to satin smoothness by many visiting feet, and plunged into the dimness of the entryway, an explosion of hurry and babble enveloping me from slipper-toe to the top of my braided head. The tables were to be dragged out into the courtyard and hung with roughcloth; the feeding of fortunate fools should always begin at midmorn.

Questions leapt for me from every side—where should this be settled, how many dishes should be taken forth, where were the extra trenchers, Father's huntsman Yngold was drunk among the pigs and who should drag him forth—oh, I did not mind even *that* occurrence, for I could set his friends Tar and Jittl upon his track and they would take him to the fair for a sobering fight or summat else. There was Mother's noontide medicine to mix in the stillroom while I was interrupted every few moments for another decision, and the kitchen's smoky clangor to brave for shouted conference with Nisman and Ilveig, the latter furiously calm while the former wielded knife, ladle, or whisk with a warrior's grim determination. There were the great casks to order tapped or set aside, yet more tankards and trenchers to be found, children to be collared and sent to their duties with a tug upon their ear to remind them a *volva*'s request is not a negotiable matter.

Of such things were the last festival I spent with my family made. I would like to think I remember everything about that busy day.

But if I am to be honest, I do not.

if you enjoyed
THE SLAIN DIVINE
look out for
THE COMBAT CODES
The Combat Codes: Book One
by
Alexander Darwin

In a world long ago ravaged by war, the nations have sworn an armistice never to use weapons of mass destruction again. Instead, highly skilled warriors known as Grievar Knights represent their nations' interests in brutal hand-to-hand combat.

Murray Pearson was once a famed Knight, until he suffered a loss that wounded his homeland—but now he's on the hunt to discover the next champion.

In ruthless underground combat rings, Cego is making a name for himself. Murray believes Cego has what it takes to thrive in the world's most prestigious combat academy—but first, Cego must prove himself in the vicious arenas of the underworld. And survival isn't guaranteed.

CHAPTER 1

Into the Deep

We fight neither to inflict pain nor to prolong suffering. We fight neither to mollify anger nor to satisfy vendetta. We fight neither to accumulate wealth nor to promote social standing. We fight so the rest shall not have to.

First Precept of the Combat Codes

Murray wasn't fond of the crowd at Thaloo's. Mostly scum with no respect for combat who liked to think themselves experts in the craft.

His boots clung to the sticky floor as he shouldered his way to the bar. Patrons lined the counter, drinking, smoking, and shouting at the overhead lightboards broadcasting SystemView feeds.

Murray grabbed a head-sized draught of ale before making his way toward the center of the den, where the crowd grew thicker. Beams of light cut through clouds of pipe smoke and penetrated the gaps between clustered, sweaty bodies.

His heart fluttered and the hairs on the back of his neck bristled as he approached. He wiped a trickle of sweat from his brow. Even after all these years, even in a pitiful place like this, the light still got to him.

He pushed past the inner throng of spectators and emerged at the edge of the action.

Thaloo's Circle was eight meters in diameter, made of auralite-compound steel fused into the dirt. Standard Underground dimensions. On the Surface, Circles tended to be wider, usually ten meters in diameter, which Murray preferred. More room to maneuver.

Glowing blue streaks veined the steel Circle, and a central cluster of lights pulsed above the ring like a heartbeat, shining down on two boys grappling in the dirt.

"Aha! The big Scout's back. You runnin' out of kids already?" A man at the edge of the Circle clapped Murray on the shoulder. "Name's Calsans."

Murray ignored the greeting and focused on the two boys fighting. One of them looked to be barely ten years old and had the gaunt build of a lacklight street urchin. His rib cage heaved in and out from beneath the bulk of a boy who outweighed him by at least sixty pounds.

Many of the onlookers flicked their eyes between the action and a large lightboard that hung from the ceiling. Biometric readings for each boy in the Circle flashed across the screen: heart rate, brain wave speed, oxygen saturation, blood pressure, hydration levels. The bottom of the board displayed an image of each boy's skeletal and muscular frame, down to their chipped teeth.

As the large boy lifted his elbow and drove it into the smaller boy's chin, a red fracture lit up on the board. The little boy's heart rate shot up.

The large boy threw knees into his opponent's rib cage as he continued to hold him down in the dirt. The little boy writhed, turning his back to his opponent and curling into a ball.

"Shouldn't give your back like that," Murray muttered, as if trying to communicate with the battered boy.

The large boy dropped another vicious elbow on his downed prey. Murray winced as he heard the sharp crack of bone on skull. Two more elbows found their target before the little one stiffened, his eyes rolling into his head as he fell limp.

The ball of light floating above the Circle flickered before it dissipated into a swarm of smoldering wisps that fanned out into the crowd.

"They call the big one there N'jal; he's been cleaning up like that all week. One of Thaloo's newest in-housers," Calsans said as the boy raised his arms in victory.

Beyond a few clapping drunks, there was little fanfare. N'jal walked to the side of his Tasker at the sidelines, a bearded man who patted the boy on the head like a dog. The loser's crew entered the Circle and dragged the fallen fighter out by his feet.

"Thaloo's been buyin' up some hard Grievar this cycle," Calsans continued, trying to strike up conversation with Murray again. "Bet he's tryin' to work a bulk sale to the Citadel, y'know? Even though they won't all pan out with that level of competition, there's bound to be a gem in the lot of 'em."

Murray barely acknowledged the man, but Calsans kept speaking.

"It's not like it used to be, y'know? Everything kept under strict Citadel regulations. All the organized breeding, the training camps," Calsans said. "I mean, course you know all about that. But now that the Kirothians are breathin' down our necks, Deep Circles are hoppin' again, and folk like Thaloo and you are making the best of it."

"I'm nothing like Thaloo," Murray growled, his shoulders tensing.

Calsans shrank back, as if suddenly aware of how large Murray was beside him. "No, no, of course not, friend. You two are completely different. Thaloo's like every other Circle slaver trying to make a bit, and you're a… or used to be… a Grievar Knight…" His voice trailed off.

The glowing spectral wisps returned to the Circle like flies gathering on a fresh kill. They landed on the cold auralite steel ring and balled up again in a floating cluster above. As more of the wisps arrived, the light shining on the Circle grew brighter. Fresh biometrics flashed onto the feed.

It was time for the next fight, and Murray needed another ale.

* * *

Murray drew the cowl of his cloak over his head as he exited Thaloo's den, stepping directly into the clamor of Markspar Row.

Stores, bars, and inns lined the street, with smaller carts selling acrid-scented foods on the cobbles out front. Gaudily dressed hawkers peddled their wares, yapping like bayhounds in a variety of tongues. Buyers jostled past him as ragged, soot-faced children darted underfoot.

Much had changed since Murray had first returned to the Underground.

Two decades ago, he'd proudly walked Markspar Row with an entourage of trainers in tow. He'd been met with cheers, claps on the back, the awed eyes of Deep brood looking up at him. He'd been proud to represent the Grievar from below.

Now Murray made a habit of staying off the main thoroughfares. He came to the Deep alone and quietly. He doubted anyone would recognize him after all these years, with his overgrown beard and sagging stomach.

A man in a nearby stall shrieked at Murray, "Top-shelf protein! Tested for the Cimmerian Shade! Vat-grown in Ezo's central plant! Certified for real taste by the Growers Guild!" The small bald hawker held up a case with a mess of labels stamped across it.

Compared to the wiry hawker, Murray was large. Though his gut had expanded over the past decade and his ruffled beard was now grey-streaked, he posed a formidable presence. From beneath the cut-off sleeves of his cloak, his knotted forearms and callused hands hung like twin cudgels. Flux tattoos crisscrossed the length of Murray's arms from elbows to fingertips, shifting their pigmented curves as he clenched his fists. His sharp nose twisted at the center, many times broken, and his ears swelled like fat toads. His face was overcast, with two alarmingly bright yellow eyes penetrating from beneath his brow.

Murray turned in to a narrow stone passageway sheltered from the central clamor of the row. He passed another hawker, a white-haired lady hidden behind her stand of fruit.

"The best heartbeat grapes. Clerics say eat just a few per day and you'll outlive an archivist." She smiled at him and gestured to her selection of fruit, each swollen and pulsing with ripeness. Halfway down the alley, as the sounds of the market continued to fade, Murray stopped in front of a beat-up oaken door. A picture of a bat with its teeth bared was barely visible on the faded awning overhead.

The Bat always smelled of spilled ale and sweat. An assortment of Grievar and Grunt patrons crowded the floor. Mercs keeping an ear to the ground for contract jobs, harvesters taking a break from planting on the steppe, diggers dressed in dirt from a nearby excavation project.

SystemView was live and blaring from several old boards hanging from the far wall.

And now... broadcasting from Ezo's Capital, in magnificent Albright Stadium...

The one thing that brought together the different breeds was a good SystemView fight. Though most of the folk living in the Underground were Ezonian citizens, their allegiances often were more aligned with the wagers they placed in the Circles.

Most of the Bat's patrons were tuned in to the screens, some swaying and nearly falling out of their chairs, with empty bottles surrounding them. Two dirt-encrusted Grunts slurred their words as Murray pushed past them toward the bar.

"Fegar's got the darkin' reach! No way 'e'll be able to take my boy down!"

"You tappin' those neuros too hard, man? He took Samson down an' he's ten times the wrestler!"

Grunts weren't known for their smarts. They were bred for hard labor like mining, hauling, harvesting, or clearing, though Murray often wondered if drinking might be their real talent. He didn't mind the Grunts, though—they did their jobs and didn't bother anyone. They didn't meddle with Grievar lives. They didn't govern from the shadows. They weren't Daimyo.

The man behind the bar was tall and corded, with near-obsidian skin. The left side of his face drooped, and his bald head gleamed with sweat as he wiped down the counter.

Murray approached the bar and caught the man's good eye. "Your finest Deep ale."

The man poured a stein of the only ale on tap, then broke into a wide half grin. "Old Grievar, what brings you to my fine establishment on such a sunny day in the Deep?"

Murray took a swig of the ale, wiping the foam off his lips. "Same thing every year, Anderson. I'm here to lie back and sweat out my worries at the hot springs. Then I figure I'll stop by the Courtesan Houses for a week or so 'fore returning to my Adar Hills mansion back Upworld."

Anderson chuckled, giving Murray a firm wrist-to-wrist grasp from across the bar. "Good to see you, old friend. Though you're uglier than I remember."

"Same to you." Murray feigned a grimace. "That face of yours reminds me of how you always forgot to cover up the right high kick."

Anderson grinned as he wiped down the bar. Both men were quiet as they watched the SystemView broadcast on the lightboard above.

The feed panned across Albright Stadium, showing thousands of cheering spectators in the stands before swooping toward the gleaming Circle at the heart of the arena. Two Grievar squared off in the Circle—one standing for Ezo and the other for the empire of Kiroth.

Murray downed his ale and set the cup on the bar for Anderson to refill.

A list of grievances popped up in one corner of the screen to remind viewers of what was at stake in the bout: rubellium reserves in one of the long-disputed border regions between Ezo and Kiroth, worth millions of bits, thousands of jobs, and the servitude of the pastoral harvesters who lived out there.

The fate of nations held in the sway of our fists.

The fight began, and Murray watched quietly, respectfully, as a Grievar should. Not like crowds modernday—booing and clapping, hissing and spitting. No respect for combat.

Anderson sighed as Ezo's Grievar Knight attacked the Kirothian with a flurry of punches. "Do you remember it? Even taking those hits, those were good days."

"Prefer not to remember it." Murray took another gulp of his ale.

"I know you don't, friend. But I hold on to my memories. Blood, sweat, and broken bones. Locking on a choke or putting a guy down with a solid cross. That feeling after, lying awake and knowing you'd done something—made a difference."

"What's the darkin' difference? I don't see any. Same lofty bat shit going on up above." Murray sniffed the air. "Still got that same dank smell down here."

"You know what I mean," Anderson said. "Fighting for the good of the nation. Making sure Ezo stays on top."

"I know what you mean, and that's just what those Daimyo politiks up there say all the time. *For the good of the nation.* That's why I'm down here. Every year, the same thing for a decade now. Sent Deep to find fresh Grievar meat."

"You don't think the Scout program is working?" Anderson asked.

Murray took another long swig. "We'll discover the next Artemis Halberd. That's what that smug bastard Callen always says. The man doesn't know how to piss straight in a Circle, yet he's got command of an entire wing of Citadel."

"You never saw eye to eye with Commander Albright—"

"The man's a coward! How can he lead? The Daimyo might as well have installed one of their own to Command. Either way, doesn't make a difference. Scouts—the whole division is deepshit. Grievarkin are born to fight. Thousands of years of breeding says so. We're not made to creep around corners, dealing out bits like hawkers."

"Times are different, old friend," Anderson said. "Things are more complicated. Citadel has got to keep up; otherwise, Ezo falls behind. Kiroth's had a Scout program for two decades now. They say even the Desovians are on their way to developing one."

"They know it's just the scraps down here, Anderson," Murray said. "Kids that don't fare a chance. And even if one of them did make it? What have we got to show for it? Me and you. For all those years we put in together in service. The sacrifices—"

Their conversation was interrupted as the door to the bar swung open with a thud. Three men walked in. Grievar.

Anderson sighed and put his hand on Murray's shoulder. "Take it easy."

The first to enter had piercings running along his jawline, glinting beside a series of dark flux tattoos stamped on his cheekbones. The other two were as thick as Murray and looked to be twins, with matching grizzled faces and cauliflowered ears.

The fluxed man immediately caught Murray's stare from the bar. "Ah! If it isn't the mighty one himself!"

Murray left his seat with alarming speed and moved toward the man.

Anderson shouted a warning from behind the bar. The man threw a wide haymaker at Murray, who casually tucked his shoulder, deflecting the blow, before dropping levels and exploding from a crouch into the man's midline. Murray wrapped his arms around the man's knees, hoisted him into the air, then drove him straight through a nearby table, which splintered in every direction.

Murray blinked. He was still in his seat by the bar, the pierced Grievar hovering over him with a derisive smirk on his face.

"Nothing to say anymore, huh, old man? I can't imagine what it's like. Getting sent down here to do the dirty work. Digging through the trash every year."

Murray ignored the man and took another swig of his ale. "Think any of your trash will even make it through the Trials this year?" the man taunted. "Didn't one of your kids make it once? What ever happened to him? Oh, I remember now..."

Anderson pushed three ales across the bar. "Cydek, these are on the house. Why don't you and your boys find a place over in that corner there so we don't have any trouble?"

Cydek smirked as he took the drinks. He turned to Murray as

he was walking away. "I'm scouting Lampai tomorrow. Why don't you tail me and I can show you how it's done? You can see some real Grievar in action. Nice change of pace from watching kids fighting in the dirt."

Murray kept his eyes fixed on the lightboard above the bar. SystemView was now replaying the fight's finish in slow motion. The broadcaster's voice cut through the quieted Ezonian crowd at Albright Stadium.

What an upset! And with the simple justice of a swift knee, Kiroth takes the Adarian Reserves!

Anderson leaned against the bar in front of Murray and poured himself an ale as he watched the knockout on replay. "The way things are going, I hope the Scout program starts working... or anything, for that matter. Otherwise, we'll be drinking that Kirothian swill they call mead next time I see you."

Murray let a smile crease his face, though he felt the tension racking his muscles. He downed his ale.

* * *

Murray realized he'd had a few too many, even for a man of his size, as he stumbled down Markspar Row. The duskshift was at its end and the arrays that lined the cavern ceiling bathed the Underground in a dying red glow. Murray had stayed at the Bat chatting about old times with Anderson for the entire evening.

Though he often denied it, he did miss the light. He wished he were back in fighting form, as he had been during his service.

That's the thing with us Grievar. We rot.

He cracked his knuckles as he walked in no particular direction.

Murray felt his body decaying like the old foundations of this crumbling Underground city. His back always hurt. Nerve pain shot up his sides whether sitting, standing, sleeping—it didn't matter. His neck was always stiff as a board. His wrists, elbows, and ankles had been broken multiple times and seemed like they could give way at any moment. Even his face was numb, a leathery exterior that didn't feel like his own anymore. He remembered a time when his body was fluid. His arms and legs had moved as if there were a slick layer of oil between every joint, seamlessly connecting takedowns into punches into submissions.

He'd seen his fair share of trips to medwards to sew up gashes and mend broken bones, but he'd always felt smooth, hydraulic. Now Murray's joints and bones scraped together with dry friction as he walked.

It was his own fault, though. Murray had his chance to stay young and he'd missed it. The first generation of neurostimulants had debuted when he was at the top of his fight game. Most of his team had started popping the stims under the *recommendation* of then–Deputy Commander Memnon. "We need the edge over the enemy," Memnon had urged the team of Grievar Knights.

Coach hadn't agreed with Memnon—the two had been at each other's throats for those last few years. Coach believed taking stims was sacrilege, against the Combat Codes. The simplest precept of them all: *No tools, no tech.*

The man would often mutter to Murray, "Live and die like we're born—screaming, with two clenched, bloody fists."

It wasn't long after the stims started circulating that Coach left his post. The breach in Command had grown too wide. Memnon would do anything to give Ezo the edge, even if that meant harnessing Daimyo tech. Coach would rather die than forsake the Codes.

Even after Coach left, Murray kept to his master's teachings. He'd refused to take stims. A few of his teammates had stayed clean too—Anderson, Leyna, Hanrin, old Two-Tooth. At first, they'd kept up with the rest of the team. Murray had even held on to the captain's belt. It wasn't until a few years later that he'd felt it.

It had been barely perceptible: a takedown getting stuffed, a jab snapping in front of his face before he realized it was coming. Those moments started adding up, though. Murray aged. He got slower and weaker while the rest of Ezo's Grievar Knights maintained their strength under the neurostimulants.

And then came the end. That fight in Kiroth. His whole team, his whole nation, depending on Murray. Everything riding on his back. And he'd failed.

Wherever Coach was right now, he'd be spitting in the dirt if he could see what Murray had become. Skulking in the shadows, stuck with a lowly Grievar Scout job, to be forgotten. Another cog in the Daimyo machine.

Before Murray realized it, the light had nearly faded. The streets were quiet as most Deep folk returned to their homes for the blackshift.

Murray was walking on autopilot toward Lampai Stadium, now only a stone's throw away, looming above him like a hibernating beast. Shadows clung to him here, deep pockets of darkness filling the folds of his cloak as he made his way to the base of the stadium.

Murray stopped abruptly, standing in front of Lampai's entrance. He stared at the old concrete wall and the black wrought-iron gates. He craned his head at the stadium's rafters towering above him.

Murray placed his hand against a gold plaque on the gate.

It was cold to the touch. It read:

> Lampai Stadium, Construction Date: 121 P.A.
> Let this be the first of many arenas, to serve as a symbol of our sworn Armistice and a constant reminder of the destruction we are capable of. Here shall Grievar give their blood, in honor and privilege. They fight so the rest shall not have to.

"We fight so the rest shall not have to," Murray whispered. He had once believed those words. The first precept of the Codes. He would repeat the mantra over and over before his fights, shouting it as he made entrances into stadiums around the world.

The Mighty Murray Pearson. He'd been a force of nature, a terror in the Circle. Now he was just another shadow under these rafters.

Murray inhaled deeply, his chest filling with air. He pushed it all out again.

* * *

Murray returned to Thaloo's every day that week and saw more of the same. Just like it had been every year before. The well-nourished, stronger Grievar brood beating down the weaker lack-lights. There was little skill involved; the brutal process pitted the weak against the strong. The strong always won.

Eventually, the weaker brood wore down. Patrons didn't want to buy the broken ones, which meant that Thaloo's team of Taskers was wasting their time training them. Thaloo was wasting bits on their upkeep. So, like rotten fruit, the slave Circle owner would throw the kids back to the streets where he found them. Their chance of survival was slim.

Murray's head throbbed as he stepped back to the edge of the Circle. Spectral wisps gathered above as the light intensified on the dirt fighting floor.

The first Grievar emerged from the side entrance, stopping by his Tasker's corner. He looked to be about fifteen, tall for his age, with all the hallmarks of purelight Grievar blood—cauliflowered ears, a thick brow, bulging forearms, bright eyes.

The boy's head was shaved like all the brood at Thaloo's to show off the brand fluxed on his scalp. Like any other product in the Deep, patrons needed to see his bit-price. This kid looked to be of some value—several of the vultures were eyeing him like a slab of meat.

The Tasker slapped the boy in the face several times, gripping his shoulders and shaking him before prodding him into the Circle. The boy responded to the aggression with his own, gnashing his teeth and slamming his fist against his chest as he stalked the perimeter. The crowd clapped and hooted with anticipation.

The second boy did not look like he belonged in the Circle. He was younger than his opponent and gaunt, his thin arms dangling at his sides. A mop of black hair hung over the boy's brow. Murray shook his head. They'd just taken the kid off the streets, and hadn't even put in the effort to brand him yet.

The boy walked into the Circle without expression, avoiding eye contact with his opponent and the crowd around him. He found his designated start position and stood completely still as the glowing spectrals rose from the Circle's frame and began to cluster above.

"The taller, dark one—name's Marcus. Saw 'im yesterday." Calsans pulled up to Murray's side, just as he'd done every day this week. Murray expected the parasite to ask him for a favor any moment now. Or perhaps he was one of Callen's spies, sent to ensure Murray didn't go rogue.

"Nearly kicked right through some lacklight." Calsans smirked. "This little sod is gonna get thrashed."

The skinny boy stood motionless, his arms straight by his sides. At first, Murray thought the boy's eyes were cast at the dirt floor, but at second glance, Murray saw his eyes were closed. Clamped shut.

"Thaloo's putting blind kids in the Circle now..." Murray growled.

"Sometimes, he likes to give the patrons a show," Calsans said. "Bet he's workin' on building Marcus's bit-price. Fattening him up for sale."

The fight began as Marcus assumed a combat stance and bobbed forward, feinting jabs and bouncing on the balls of his feet.

"It's like one of them Ezonian eels about to eat a guppy," Calsans remarked.

Murray looked curiously at the blind boy as his opponent stalked toward him. The boy still wasn't moving. Though his posture wasn't aggressive, he didn't look afraid. He almost looked... relaxed.

"Wouldn't be so sure," Murray replied.

Marcus approached striking distance and feigned a punch at the blind boy before whipping a high round kick toward his head. A split second before the shin connected, the boy dropped below the kick and shot forward like a coiled spring, wrapping around one of the kicker's legs. The boy clung to the leg as his opponent tried to shake him off vigorously, but he stayed attached. He drove his shoulder into Marcus's knee, throwing him off-balance into the dirt.

The boy began to climb his opponent's body, immobilizing his legs and crawling onto his torso.

"Now this is getting good," Murray said as he watched the blind boy go to work.

Marcus heaved forward with his full strength, pushing the boy off him while reversing to top position. Hungry for a finish again, Marcus straddled the younger boy's torso, reared up, and hurled a punch downward. The boy slipped the punch, angling his chin at just the right moment, his opponent's fist glancing off his jaw.

Marcus howled in pain as his hand crunched against the hard dirt. Biometrics flashed red on the lightboard above.

Capitalizing on bottom position, the blind boy grasped Marcus's elbow and dragged the limp arm across his body, using the leverage to pull himself up and around onto his opponent's back.

Murray raised an eyebrow. "Well, look at that. Darkin' smooth back take."

The crowd suddenly was paying close attention to the turn of events. Several spectators hooted in approval of the upset while others jeered at a potential bit-loss on their bets.

Murray saw the shock in Marcus's eyes. This was supposed to be an easy win for the Grievar, a fight to pad his record. His Tasker probably told him to finish the blind boy in a brutal fashion. Instead, Marcus was the one fighting for survival, looking like he was treading water in a tank of razor sharks. Marcus grunted as he pushed himself off the ground. He stood and tried to shuck the boy off his back, bucking wildly, but the climber wrapped around him even tighter.

The blind boy began to snake his hands across Marcus's neck, shooting his forearm beneath the chin to apply a choke. Either as a last resort or out of pure helplessness, Marcus dropped backward like a felled tree, slamming the boy on his back into the dirt with a thud. A cloud of dust billowed into the air on impact. The crowd hushed as the little boy was crushed beneath his larger opponent's bulk.

Murray held his breath as the dust settled.

The blind boy was still clinging to his opponent, his two bony arms latched around his neck, constricting, ratcheting tighter. The boy squeezed until Marcus's eyes rolled back into his head and his arms went limp.

The light flared and died out, the spectrals breaking from their cluster and dissipating into the den.

The boy rolled out from beneath his unconscious opponent, his face covered in dirt and blood, his eyes clamped shut.